The Xanadu Talisman

Peter O'Donnell began writing at the age of sixteen, when he sold his first story. He has lost count since then but thinks the tally reaches over a thousand short stories and novels. He also writes television and film scripts.

Born in 1921, he spent two years working on juvenile periodicals and served in the Royal Corps Signals during World War II. He began writing strip cartoons – the best known are probably 'Garth' in the *Daily Mirror* and 'Tug Transom' in the *Daily Sketch*. 'Modesty Blaise' took him a year to create and in 1962 she was presented as a strip-cartoon character in the *Evening Standard*. The cartoon was an immediate success, soon syndicating in over forty countries, and the 'Modesty Blaise' series of novels followed.

Peter O'Donnell
The Xanadu Talisman

Pan Books London and Sydney

First published 1981 by Souvenir Press Ltd
This edition published 1982 by Pan Books Ltd,
Cavaye Place, London SW10 9PG
ISBN 0 330 26847 3
Printed and bound in Great Britain by
Hunt Barnard Printing, Ayelsbury, Bucks

for Peter, Michael and Paula

one

The Frenchman huddled beside her was unconscious again. She shifted her position on the rubble that bruised her body through the short towelling bathrobe. Reaching out a grimy hand, still encrusted with dried blood, she groped for his neck in the darkness and laid two fingers on the pulse there.

It was a little fast, a little weak, but steady. His breathing was ragged, but so was her own in the dust-laden air. Turning on her back in the narrow concrete pit, she flexed her hands. They still ached from the hours she had spent clutching the great gash in his thigh, holding the sides of the wound together against the pumping blood from within until at last it clotted.

The Frenchman stirred and muttered a word that sounded like 'aladdin'. He had spoken the same word several times throughout the long hours, amid fretful and barely coherent mumblings. After a moment he said distinctly, "*Le talisman? Le talisman . . .?* She knew now that he was speaking of the broad strap he had been wearing on his right wrist. During a period of feverish lucidity in the early hours he had insisted on her taking it off and strapping it on her own wrist. At the time, she felt something flat and hard between a double thickness of the leather, but had been too concerned about soothing him to wonder what lay within the strap.

"*Le talisman?*" he repeated on a rising note of agitation.

Modesty Blaise rested a hand on his forehead and said reassuringly, as if to a child, "*Ne t'inquiet pas. Je l'ai, je l'ai.*"

He mumbled for a few moments, then relapsed into silence. She looked up through the bars of the grating to check the tiny pencil of wan light that found its way through the mass of wreckage above. There had been no change since sunrise, the light had not moved or grown larger or smaller, so presumably the shattered building had settled no further in that time.

Carefully she eased over on to her side. Above and to the left of the shallow pit was the crushed Volkswagen, half its normal height, with a long steel girder slanting down from its crumpled roof, holding back the tons of masonry that had once been part of the Hotel Ayachi. By a freak of chance there had been light for the first eight hours of their entombment, for when the Volkswagen had burst open under the hammerblow from above, its interior lighting circuit had remained intact, and the automatic operation of the door switch had turned on the courtesy light.

There was more space above the pit than in it. She could still see in her mind's eye the cave of jumbled concrete as big as a double wardrobe laid on its back. Before the last tremor, that cave had been still larger, though it seemed desperately small when she had been fighting off the Arab with the knife. He had been dead for hours now, crushed when the last tremor shook the debris and caused it to settle. By then she had manoeuvred the Frenchman down into the inspection pit with her, and set the grating in place above them as a precaution. Bad luck on the Arab, but an inspection pit the size of a large coffin was no place to share with a man intent on pushing a knife into you.

She felt gently for the bandage she had bound round the Frenchman's wound when at last the bleeding stopped. It was still dry. Something to be thankful for, at least; that and the fact that there had been no more tremors since the one that dropped a ton or so of concrete and rubble on the bound Arab.

The first shuddering of the earth had come twelve hours before, just after she had emerged from beneath the shower in the new, rather small and rather ugly hotel a mile east of El Jadida on the Casablanca road. She was there in response to a cable which had arrived at her London home and been phoned through to her in St. Jean de Luz by her houseboy, Weng. It read: AM BETWEEN JOBS FOR A FEW WEEKS CAN YOU MEET ME EL JADIDA HOTEL AYACHI FRIDAY IF NO TROUBLE LOVE GILES. The cable had originated in Chad two days before. Since it came from Dr. Giles Pennyfeather, whose notions of making arrangements were endearingly nebulous, it gave no address for a reply, neither did it specify any particular Friday.

When it was phoned through to her by Weng at ten o'clock on Friday morning she had laughed, rung the Biarritz-Anglet airfield with a flight plan for take-off at noon, then gone out into the quiet grounds of the big house to make excuses to her hostess, Consuela, who was watching a hard-fought game between Willie Garvin and her husband, Etienne, in the shadow thrown by the towering wall of the pelota court.

The weather was fine throughout the flight, and she brought the Piper Comanche down at Casablanca-Anfa soon after five-thirty. This was her old stamping ground, for it was from Tangier that she had operated *The Network*, as it came to be called, the criminal organisation she had built from nothing when only in her middle teens. She still spent some time each year at her house on The Mountain, the hill to the west of Tangier looking out over the Straits.

A phone call before take-off to her steward, Moulay, had ensured that there would be a car waiting for her at the airport, and by seven she was at the Hotel Ayachi; cheap, clean, four storeys high, entirely without character, less than half full, and with a basement carpark. The manager knew nothing of Dr. Giles Pennyfeather, but assured her that he was most happy to receive Miss Modesty Blaise as a guest at Hotel Ayachi. His nervousness and the occasional knowing look told her that he knew her by reputation, probably because Moulay had been on the phone to him to ensure that she was well looked after.

Giles's non-arrival did not particularly surprise her. It would be almost impossible to get from Chad to Casablanca without some kind of hold-up en route, but Giles was an unshakeable optimist and would have made no allowance for delays. She took a room on the ground floor because it was the biggest room, and with Giles you needed plenty of space. Also he was the kind of man who had only to enter a lift for it to stick between floors.

The first tremor came as she was slipping into her bathrobe after a shower. For a few seconds she thought the vibration was caused by water-hammer in the plumbing, but the noise grew swiftly louder, battering at the ears, and the whole building began to tremble about her. For long moments she stood frozen with disbelief as her inmost being fought to reject the concept that the earth itself could split and crumble beneath her; then came acceptance, followed by swift anger that her reaction had been so slow.

The divan bed was joggling on its legs as if trying to walk, and moving gradually across the terrazzo floor towards her. Holding down the acid thrust of fear, she dropped her sponge bag, took

9

two strides, gripped the edge of the bed and overturned it with a single fierce heave. As she dropped to the floor to slide under the pathetic protection the inverted bed offered, the noise and vibration dwindled swiftly. Within ten seconds all was still. For a long moment there was an eerie silence, then came a distant wailing of human voices. She guessed that it was from the lifts. There had been no sound of collapse within the building, but the shaking could well have trapped one or both lifts between floors.

Still on one knee, head cocked to listen, she breathed deeply and steadily while she decided what to do. It might be all over. Or there could be more tremors to come, perhaps less violent, perhaps more violent. They might come within seconds or not come for hours, but this was a part of the world where it would be wise to expect the worst. Agadir lay only two hundred miles away to the south, where twenty thousand had died when the city was destroyed by two earthquakes. Fire and a monstrous tidal wave had contributed to the killing, but most had died under the rubble of fallen buildings. So the best move was to get out fast.

She stood up, moved to the dressing table, checked that her passport and traveller's cheques were in her handbag, and hung it round her neck by the strap. She had slipped her feet into sandals and was picking up the shirt and slacks she had discarded for the shower when the second shock came. This time it did not build gradually but seemed to strike like a falling bomb. A great roaring filled the air as million-ton plates of rock far below the earth's skin thrust and ground together. The Hotel Ayachi shook as if hit by a giant hammer, and she saw a three-inch crack appear in the wall by the door.

She jumped the bed to reach the window and dragged at the wooden shutters, but they would not budge, even when she smashed at them with a chair. The sweat on her face and body was like ice as she realised that the frame had twisted and the shutters were jammed. The roaring grew louder, the shaking more violent. She was half-way to the door when she saw that the lintel above it had cracked and dropped, jamming the frame down on the head of the door.

With a dreadful noise, something enormous fell very close to the room, and almost in the same moment the walls about her became a crazy jigsaw of cracks. Then one wall began to bow inwards, and she dived for the overturned bed, slithering along the floor, burrowing under the fallen mattress, chillingly aware that this and the flimsy wooden base of the cheap bed were her only protection against whatever mass of concrete and plaster might come down upon her.

For seconds only she lay hugging the cold terrazzo tiles as they shook and heaved, then they opened beneath her like a biscuit being broken, tilting her so that she slid down into the darkness below. She knew that this must be the last moment of her life, and heard herself cry out as she fell, a cry of protest that the end should be so pointless. Her body struck a smooth metallic surface only a few feet below, a surface which yielded a little. The mattress fell upon her and bounced off to fall again as she herself slid sideways. Again she fell, this time to a hard surface, but the mattress was beneath her now to save her from a bruising impact. Then, with a long and malevolent roar, the whole building collapsed above her.

Arms wrapped about her head, she waited numbly for the end. Dust choked her, and she dragged up her towelling robe to hold the bottom of it across her mouth and nose. The crashing and thudding, quite different from the grinding roar of the earthquake itself, seemed to grow more distant, as if the building had been destroyed at the base first and was toppling in upon itself, breaking up as it fell.

Slowly, slowly, the noise faded. The heaving of the ground dwindled to a throbbing vibration. There came a whispering stillness. Long minutes of small sinister sounds. Creaking. A slither of rubble. A groan of settlement. Screech of ragged stone on metal. And silence at last, but for a distant voice screaming thinly. She wiped a layer of dust from her face, opened her eyes, and was astonished to find a pale light shining into the hollow where she lay unharmed, scarcely bruised. When she turned her head she saw that the light came from the interior of a car half crushed by a steel beam that lay angled over her like a huge rafter, supporting an untold weight of tangled debris above.

Understanding came. This was the basement garage. She had fallen through the floor of her room and into the garage below only a fraction of a second before the building collapsed, bouncing from the roof of a car en route. Her nerves crawled as she smelt petrol that must have spilled when the tank was ripped open. It only needed a spark now . . .

A croaking voice from no more than a few feet away said, "*Mam'selle . . . je vous prie . . . ma jambe . . .*"

She rolled carefully on to her side, and looked down the length of her body. The hollow in which she lay was perhaps ten feet long and eight wide, irregular in shape and with only enough headroom to allow movement on hands and knees. Just beyond her feet she could see what was left of the base of her bed, some broken boards covered with dust and small rubble. From beneath the boards protruded the head and shoulders of a man, his head strained back to look towards her, face so coated with dust that the eyes and mouth were like holes in a mask. "My leg," he repeated in French. "It is badly cut . . . bleeding."

She snaked round on the mattress and edged towards him, fearful that part of his legs lay crushed beneath the wreckage, but when she slid the boards aside she saw that he lay curled in a ball just clear of the shattered shower-basin at the base of the debris. A broken piece of copper piping jutted from the jumble of concrete, blood dripping from it. The man was gripping at his left thigh with both hands, but even as she peered at the torn trouser-leg and the flesh showing between his clutching fingers he spoke again, feebly but on a rising note. "Mam'selle . . ." His eyes stared beyond her, and when she turned to look back she saw what seemed for a moment to be a headless body moving purposefully across the rubble on the far side of the mattress. Then a bowed head came up, and the dim light from the shattered car was reflected in the man's eyes. He was in working overalls, smothered in dust, and had a dark face with a down-curving moustache. There was no obvious sign of injury. She spoke in Arabic, calling him to help, and then saw the knife in his hand, a knife with a stiletto blade, a round and tapering blade without an edge. A knife made only for killing.

For a moment unbelief warred against her long experience in recognising danger, but as she looked at the eyes again all doubt vanished. The man was in shock, and he used drugs, she was sure of it. But he was here to kill, and whatever was driving him had not been obliterated by the earthquake. From the fixity of his gaze she sensed that shock had numbed him to such a degree that he was clinging to his original purpose as a way of shutting out the dreadful reality of his situation. She moved a little so that she was squatting on her heels between him and the Frenchman, the girder inches above her head, and said quietly, "Blessed be Allah the All-merciful for this deliverance—" stopping short as his empty hand swung forward to push her aside. She blocked it with a raised elbow to catch the inside of the wrist with numbing effect, and saw the stiletto in his right hand angle instantly towards her for the rising thrust that would slide under the ribs and up into the heart.

There was no room for manoeuvre, and from the breadth of his shoulders she knew the man was very strong. In a hands-and-knees grapple in this confined space he would be able to stab her to death in seconds. The chance that she could get any useful sort of grip on his knife-wrist was too small to be worth considering, and there would be nowhere to go with it. That part of her mind which was a fighting computer assessed a dozen permutations of possibilities in milliseconds, and as the blade leapt at her she took it two inches below her raised forearm, through the sleeve of her robe, rolling back from the squat position, swinging her arm wide to carry the trapped blade out and down so that it drove aslant into the mattress.

He had come forward with the thrust, kneeling up, leaning above her, but her left leg was drawn up tightly and turned so that her shin was a bar across his throat, the other leg over his shoulder. Her right hand was closed in the ninth fist-form of karate, the *ippon-ken*, with the single knuckle protruding, and she drove it forward with a fierce outward breath to smash into the man's upper lip where it joined the nose.

There came a grunting squeal as his head went back, and she knew he would be blind with pain. Her right leg was poised in readiness, and now she drew it back to slam the heel deep into his solar plexus. Breath exploded from his lungs with a high whinnying sound, and he slumped back against a tangle of broken concrete. The debris groaned, and somewhere something heavy slithered ominously. Her relaxing nerves snapped taut again. She turned to look at the Frenchman. He was staring up at the tangle

13

of wreckage above them, head cocked, listening, still gripping his leg.

She shut her mind against all but immediate necessity. There was a handkerchief in the pocket of her robe. She tore off the hem, twisted it into a string, and crawled towards the Arab. The ground under her hands and knees felt odd . . . there were long slits in the dusty concrete . . . no, this was metal, steel bars . . . a grating set in the floor of the carpark.

She drew the Arab's hands behind him and tied the thumbs firmly together with the strip of twisted linen, then turned to clear rubble from the grid. It covered a narrow pit about eight feet long, and though heavy was resting loosely in place. An inspection pit, she assumed, rather shallow, but good enough to allow a mechanic to get under a car. Working awkwardly in the cramped space, she managed to lift one end of the grating and drag it aside.

The Frenchman said dully, "Please, mam'selle . . . my leg . . ."

She crawled towards him, panting a little, pushing hair from her eyes as she crouched in front of him, and said in French, "I'll see to your leg in a minute, but first we'll get down into that pit before another tremor brings the whole place down on us. Understand?"

He nodded slowly. She realised that what she had thought was shadow was in fact a huge bruise across one side of his head, and guessed that he might be concussed. More gently she said, "Come on, then. Try to edge across, I'll help as much as I can. You keep a tight hold on that leg."

It took a full minute to get him positioned on the edge of the pit. She climbed in and lay on her back, supporting him with hands and feet as he came over the edge, then wriggling out from beneath after she had lowered him. There was ample room for them to lie side by side, and just room for her to crouch beside him with her head a few inches below floor level.

She dragged the grating into position above them, checked that by looking obliquely through the bars she could see the limp figure of the Arab lying on a heap of rubble, then turned to the man beside her. He lay on his back, the injured leg drawn up, hands tightly encircling the thigh, his face paper-white in the dim-light filtering through from the car.

She sat cross-legged, her back to one side of the pit, and made herself smile down at him. As she tried to think of something encouraging to say he whispered in a fading but urgent voice, "Mam'selle . . ." Then she saw blood spurt from between his fingers as his grip relaxed.

Her hands shot out, finding the four-inch gash in his thigh made by the broken piping, crushing the edges together as his head fell limply to one side. She said sharply, "M'sieu! M'sieu!", then contrived to double forward and butt his cheek gently with her brow in an attempt to rouse him. When there was no response she began warily to shift her grip on the wound so that she could contain the bleeding with one hand. With the other, and using her teeth, she managed after a long minute to tear a large enough piece from her robe to make a thick pad, quickly pressing it down over the wound before gripping with both hands again.

His trouser leg was soaked with blood, but when she pressed a thumb into the flesh of his inside thigh she found a good pulse and knew she had been in time. He would not bleed to death in the next few minutes, for what that was worth. If the building did not collapse further, breaching their small haven, and if no fire started, and if they were not flooded by a broken water-main, and if the Arab did not break loose, then with luck she might stop the bleeding in an hour or so, and manage to improvise a dressing for the wound. She would then be free to explore the hollow in which they were trapped, in the unlikely hope of finding a way out.

She looked down. Her tattered robe hung open, her body was covered with sweat and grit. There was dust in her hair, in her nose and mouth, and fresh blood on her hands. Looking back, she estimated that perhaps six minutes had passed since the first tremor. It was not a long time in which to encompass an earthquake, entombment, a fight with a killer, and an attempt to save a stranger from bleeding to death.

She seldom swore, but now she shook her head and said softly, wonderingly, "Bloody hell . . . why me?"

Standing well back from the forty-foot wall of the court, Willie Garvin watched the small hard ball flashing towards him, a ball of hand-woven virgin rubber finished with linen thread and covered with two layers of hardened goat-skin. On his right hand was a leather glove fastened to a curving wicker basket thirty inches long, made of Spanish chestnut over which had been woven a layer of Pyrenees Mountain reeds.

Quick-footed, he angled sideways and back, lifting the hand with the *cesta* attached, yet still having to jump high to catch the ball near the tip of the basket. As his feet touched the ground he spun round with his back to the wall and brought his arm down in a smooth accelerating sweep, the *cesta* just clearing the ground. With the backward swing of his arm, centrifugal force hurled the ball towards the wall a hundred and twenty feet away, on a rising trajectory and at a speed approaching one hundred and forty miles an hour.

It came back high and fast, angling towards the side of the court, but Etienne Aranda was there, leaping to trap the ball in his *cesta*, but holding it there with a little scooping movement. "We stop now," he said. "The light is begining to go."

Willie Garvin glanced at the sky. "It's not too bad," he protested.

Aranda said, "I do not wish to have my head cracked open. Or even your head. And we have put in six hours of play since this morning."

"I suppose so." Willie began to take off his *cesta*. "But it's a marvellous game, and I only get to play it when I come 'ere, so I like to make the most of it."

"You could be very good," said Aranda as they walked through the small grove of pines to the pool. "Very good indeed." He was not given to flattery, and had himself been a pelota champion ten years ago.

Willie said, "I always like a sport where you 'ave to throw something."

Aranda laughed. "You have a gift for it. I observed as much at the circus."

He was speaking of an occasion two nights before. Willie Garvin, a man with a wide spectrum of activities, owned half a small tenting circus. The other half was owned by his partner in the venture, a Hungarian, Georgi Gogol, who ran the whole operation and played ringmaster. Willie was virtually a sleeping partner, but over several years had found it absorbing to spend a few weeks with the circus from time to time, either touring or in winter quarters. It was another world, and one that Modesty had found equally absorbing when he introduced her to it.

This week it so happened that Gogol's Circus was in San Sebastian, just over the border, and Willie's host and hostess had greatly enjoyed being taken behind the scenes for an hour or so before a performance. To provide a special treat for Consuela, who was artless as a child in many ways, Willie had conspired with Georgi to put on an extra act that evening. As a result, Consuela and Etienne were puzzled when both Modesty and Willie vanished during the intermission; and later, between the trapezists and the big cats, they were astonished to see Modesty appear in spangles, fishnet tights and heavy make-up, to act as target for the knives, machetes and tomahawks hurled alarmingly close to her by a character Georgi announced as Pancho Caramba the World Famous Thrower of Knives. Wearing an enormous Mexican sombrero, a red shirt, black trousers with silver buttons down the legs, and a ten-inch drooping moustache Willie Garvin had hammed his way outrageously through a six-minute act to leave Consuela weak with laughter.

For her and for her husband it was a delightful in-joke, but it was also a performance of superlative skill. Remembering it now as he came with Willie from the pelota court, Aranda said soberly, "Consuela has told me of a time when she had cause to be thankful for your gift, Willie. When you got her out of Rodelle's hands."

"Did I?" Willie said vaguely. "It's all long past now."

When they had swum and changed, drinks were waiting for them on the patio where soft lights shone from the cork tree in the corner. Consuela was there, twenty-five years old but still looking eighteen, a small gossamer girl, smiling and beautiful. She had once worked for Modesty Blaise in the days of *The Network*, acting as a courier between Europe and North Africa for the industrial espionage section of the organisation.

When she fell utterly in love with Etienne Aranda, head of the Franco-Spanish ship-building consortium, and he fell equally in love with her, she had gone to Modesty Blaise and asked to be released. Her wish was accepted without argument, and since she had no parents or family it was Modesty who had provided the memorable wedding and reception.

Now, relaxing on the patio before dinner, crocheting a diminutive something for the baby she was to have in another five months, Consuela said, "Willie, is it all right to ask who is this doctor Modesty has gone to see? This Giles Pennyfeather?"

Willie's rough-hewn brown face split in a grin. "He's a walking disaster, love. Everything 'appens to Giles, but he just goes bumbling on, innocent as a baby, leaving a trail of chaos."

Aranda's eyebrows lifted. "Rather alarming for a doctor, surely?"

"You'd think so. He carries an enormous bag around, filled with all sorts of old-fashioned gear and medicines, and when he's operating he's all thumbs, but there's something special about 'im. His patients get well." Willie shook his head with a baffled air. "What 'appened was, Modesty bumped into 'im in the middle of Africa one day, in Tanzania, helping a couple of black missionaries to run some crummy little 'ospital. He'd got the job from a mission society, and he was doing everything from major ops to sore feet, working from a book with diagrams telling you what to do. Anyway, Modesty stayed on and helped for a bit."

Willie drank some sangria. Consuela said, "I think she is what you call a sucker for that sort of person, if they are nice."

"Lame dogs," Willie agreed, then laughed. "You must get 'er to give you an imitation of Giles doing an operation, next time she's 'ere. It's hilarious, with 'im chatting away, dropping swabs and scalpels, trying to figure out the diagrams. But then he'd sit up all night with a patient, just sort of thinking about them, so he said. And they got better, mostly."

"A man with healing?" said Aranda.

"I suppose so." Willie pondered. "There's nothing mystic about Giles. He's awkward and clumsy and a bit of an idiot sometimes, but there's not a malicious corpuscle in 'is body. And he wishes everyone well, not because it's the thing to do but because that's the way he is."

Consuela smiled. "I think you like him very much."

"You can't 'elp liking Giles."

"He and Modesty have been — you know. Close?"

Willie nodded. "He was with her at the penthouse for a while."

"It is strange to me," said Aranda. "I cannot image that she would find such a man to be of interest to her."

His wife said, "You know nothing, *querido*. This man is a baby."

"That is a reason for Modesty to take him as a lover? Modesty?"

"I mean that he is an innocent. To one who has had to fight the world at its worst, as Modesty did, innocence would have great appeal." She gestured. "You heard what Willie said. No malice. No unkindness. That is very rare."

"But not enough. A woman needs more."

"So he must have more, Etienne. Why should one who is innocent not also be a man, and a quite marvellous lover?" She turned to Willie. "Go on, please What happened after she met him in Africa?"

"I wasn't making a story of it, love. We all got involved in a bit of trouble around that time." He put down his glass and made a wry grimace. "A lot of trouble. At the end of it, Giles married this albino girl, Lisa. Lovely girl, but with 'er mind in a terrible mess because of what someone 'ad been doing to her over a good few years. I bet Giles got her straightened out, though. He joined the medical emergency section of the Red Cross, with Lisa acting as nurse for 'im, and they went off to Peru, then on to wherever there was any kind of trouble that called for a medical team. Just the sort of job for Giles."

Consuela said, "But if Modesty has gone to spend time with him now, then he and his wife can no longer be together."

"No. After a bit she met a bloke in Turkey, an American, and fell for 'im like a ton of bricks. He was an engineer. Giles wrote and told us about it, and he wasn't blaming Lisa. I suppose she needed Giles to get her better, but after that it wasn't quite the same. She'd never 'ad a chance to choose anyone before, and when this bloke came along it just 'appened."

"You have seen Giles since?" Aranda asked.

Willie shook his head. "Not me. Modesty went out to spend a couple of weeks' leave with 'im in New Guinea last year, then we 'ad a card from 'im in Chittagong around Christmas. Now he's turned up in Chad. I just 'ope he's managed to turn up in El Jadida today, but you can never be sure with Giles."

"Well, I am glad the cable did not come earlier," said Consuela. "You were leaving tomorrow anyway, so it has made little difference that Modesty went today. We enjoy having you here to stay for a while." She smiled, widening her already enormous dark eyes. "I used to be quite frightened of Willie Garvin in the old days, and of Modesty, too. But not any more." She got up, moved to her husband, kissed him on the cheek, then went on towards the open patio doors. "Now I will see what is happening in the kitchen."

Aranda refilled their glasses. Willie said, "You're off to the States the day after tomorrow?"

"Yes. I hope it will not be too much for Consuela."

"Ah, don't start the anxious father-to-be bit, Etienne. She looks as fit as a fiddle and she hardly shows yet."

Aranda laughed. "Wait till your turn comes."

"That'll be the day."

Consuela reappeared in the doorway and said anxiously. "Moulay is on the phone from Modesty's house in Tangier, and he says he must speak with you urgently, Willie."

He put down his glass quickly and stood up. When he had gone through into the house Aranda said quietly, "Do you know what it is about, *querida*?"

She shook her head and fidgeted with the gold bangle on her wrist, eyes troubled. "No. But Moulay was not quite calm. I never knew him to be not quite calm before."

He stood up and slipped an arm about her. "Let us hope it is not bad trouble."

They waited in uneasy silence. Two minutes later Willie Garvin appeared. As he stepped from the big living room on to the patio his face was completely without expression. He said almost absently, "I'm sorry, Consuela, I 'ave to leave at once. There's been a bad earthquake." He looked at Aranda. "Can I borrow one of your company aeroplanes?"

"Of course. There are two Cessnas at Anglet. But do you mean this earthquake has struck El Hadida?"

"Close to it. Moulay reckons the news'll be on the radio any time now. It's a big one." Willie's voice was flat, his blue eyes distant as if he was concentrating on one thing while speaking of another. "Moulay rang friends in Casablanca soon as he heard, told them to drive out and see if the Hotel Ayachi was all right. They've just rung back, and it's not there any more. Flattened."

Consuela gave a little cry and ran to him, taking his big hand in her own small ones. "Oh Willie, no. But perhaps she and her friend were not there when it happened, perhaps they had driven into Casablanca. Perhaps . . ."

She began to cry. Willie's eyes focused and he patted her shoulder gently. "Take it easy, love. You mustn't let yourself get upset." He looked at Aranda. "Moulay says the rescue work will be concentrated in El Jadida, so nobody's going to bother about an out-of-town 'otel for a while. I've told 'im to get 'old of a couple of breakdown trucks, cutting equipment, medical gear and digging tools, and to meet me at the Hotel Ayachi with some extra hands."

Aranda said, "He can do all that?"

"No problem. A lot of people around there owe 'er favours."

"I also," said Consuela. "I will arrange some food to take with us, and we will come with you."

"No," he said gently, and put his hands on her shoulders. "If things are bad, I'm not 'aving you around. And maybe they're not bad. For all we know she met Giles and they drove into Casablanca for dinner, and they're 'aving a very nice time thank you."

"No, Willie. She would have phoned you by now to stop you worrying. That is something you know as well as I do." She turned to her husband. "Etienne, we cannot leave for America without knowing."

"I agree, *mi nina*."

Willie said, "Look. Your flight's not till tomorrow evening. I'll phone you as soon as I know the score."

"There could be hours of delay on the telephones," Aranda said doubtfully.

"All right, I'll give you the name and number of a bloke in San Sebastian. He's an amateur radio operator and we 'ave regular chats. There's an FT101 radio in the plane Modesty flew to Casablanca, so I'll call 'im from that. You ask 'im from me to listen out on the hour from O-eight-hundred tomorrow, right?"

Ten minutes later he was away. When Aranda came off the phone after speaking to the man in San Sebastian, Consuela put her arms round him and pressed her cheek to his chest. "He was frightened," she whispered. "Willie Garvin was afraid. I have never seen that before."

He held her close, stroking her hair. "Modesty has survived many dangers, *querida*."

"Yes, but those were from people." She shivered in his arms. "This is not the same."

"I think", said the Frenchman slowly, "that we have little chance to escape."

She wiped the sweat from his forehead and said, "Stop worrying. We have more than a good chance, I promise you. Almost a certainty."

Six hours had gone by since the earthquake struck. Sometimes the Frenchman was awake and quite lucid, as he was now. Mostly he lay in a fretful sleep, which fell short of delirium but in which he mumbled, groaned, and occasionally cried out, as if in a nightmare. She had long since stopped the bleeding and contrived a makeshift dressing for his injured leg. There had been one more tremor, half an hour after the big one. It had been slight, but sufficient to bring down the roof of half the cavity, though only a single sixty-pound piece of masonry fell on the protecting grid. Immediately after this a curious muzziness in her head cleared abruptly, and she had a strong conviction that the earthquake had run its course.

Later, when she had bandaged the Frenchman's leg, she managed to lift the grid, tilting the piece of masonry aside, then crawled out into the small hollow that was left. There was still light from the car, filtering between a jumble of dangerously poised chunks of concrete and twisted reinforcing bars. Where the Arab had been there now lay several tons of debris. The mattress had been buried too, much to her regret. By bending a piece of copper piping she managed to coax a trickle of water from it, sufficient to moisten a small piece of her diminishing robe so that she could let the Frenchman suck a few drops from it. Then she returned to the pit and dragged the grating into place again.

There had been no exchange of names with the Frenchman, and it had not even occurred to her that there might be, for it would have seemed ludicrous. Here, in the strange intimacy of this womb of broken stone and twisted steel, where both might soon die, there was no doubt of identity and no need of it. They were 'you' to each other, for there was nobody else. He was a man in his middle thirties, she judged, with straight dark hair, a square face, and quietly watchful eyes. He was not a big man, but his body was well muscled and without fat. He might have been Moroccan or Algerian, but she identified him as French because her sharp ear had picked up inflexions she associated with southern France. Perhaps Corsica.

In the hours since the disaster he had spoken no word of complaint and given no sign of panic, either in troubled sleep or when fully awake. During his first lucid period he had thanked her, politely but without effusion, for saving his life. He had shown intelligent interest when she explored the confines of their tomb, but refrained from anxious warnings. When she told him that the new fall had killed the Arab he had simply shrugged.

He had been down in the basement garage, he told her, checking his radiator when the first tremor came. After it passed he had lingered to cap the radiator and close the bonnet, with the idea of driving his car out into the open. The risk had seemed small, but the swiftness of the main shock had trapped him. He had been running for the exit when he had actually glimpsed her falling with her mattress on to the Volkswagen just ahead of him, falling through the great gap which had suddenly opened in the roof above. Then the building had collapsed. He had felt something slice at his leg and had flinched away from it, dropping to his knees, protecting his head and expecting to die, then finding himself miraculously alive but with blood pumping from his thigh as he lay half smothered by dust and small rubble.

He knew nothing, he said, about the Arab with the knife, and had not been aware of the man's presence in the garage when the earthquake came, but thought he must have been an attendant or mechanic employed by the hotel, and that the shock had completely deranged him to the extent that he had tried to kill her. She knew this was wrong, knew that the Frenchman himself had been the intended victim, and suspected that he was well aware of this, but did not dispute his suggested explanation.

Later he fell into a comatose sleep, but now he was awake and lucid again. As she wiped his brow with the damp rag he gave a wry smile, the first she had seen on his impassive face, and said, "I much admire your confidence, mam'selle, but I think perhaps you exaggerate a little when you say our escape is almost certain."

She shook her head. "No. I mean it, truly."

"Truly? Then what is your truth, please?"

"Well . . . the news of the earthquake will have been broadcast within, say, two hours of the occurrence. So rescue operations will have begun by now, with help in men and equipment coming from all quarters."

"Yes, but it will be concentrated on the town of El Jadida."

"If the epicentre was there, yes. But perhaps it was here, or to the east, on open ground where it may have done little damage."

"I will play devil's advocate, mam'selle, because I wish to be convinced. Suppose the epicentre devastated El Jadida. Then who will come to rescue us here?"

"Someone will come."

"Truly?"

She smiled. "I am not simply trying to reassure you."

"Who will come?"

"I have a friend who will have heard the news on the radio by now. He is in St. Jean de Luz—or was. He will hire an aeroplane at once, and fly here. He will obtain whatever equipment he thinks may help. He knows I am at this hotel. He even knows my room, because I spoke on the telephone with him after I arrived."

"So your friend will come. One man."

"A man of much force and ability, I assure you. And one who has friends here who can be called on for help."

"But your friend cannot yet know whether or not the Hotel Ayachi has been demolished by the earthquake. For all he knows, you may be quite safe. Or dead."

"It makes no difference. Until he has proof one way or another he will act with urgency."

"A formidable friend, mam'selle."

"Yes."

"And you have much faith in him."

"Complete faith."

He smiled again. "Then I accept that our rescue is almost certain." His eyes closed and there was silence. She thought he had fallen asleep again, but two or three minutes later he said, "I am out of practice, but I am trying to say a prayer to help your friend in his task. Will you tell me his name?"

"It is an English name. Willie Garvin."

He opened his eyes and stared up at her without expression. "Ah. Yes. That is a name with . . . with a most reassuring sound, mam'selle."

two

"Aladdin," said the croaking voice. Then, in accented but very reasonable English: "Peacock . . . shadow." A pause. "By June . . . by anything." Another pause. "You have the talisman, mam'selle?"

For what seemed the hundredth time she said, "Yes, it's quite safe. Don't worry."

On the first few occasions she had thought he was awake, but then realised he was rambling. He had switched to English after she mentioned Willie Garvin's name, but she had wasted no energy wondering about it. She was wearing no watch, and the one the Frenchman wore had been smashed from the beginning, but her internal clock was as good as an animal's, and she knew it was almost noon.

They had been buried for twenty hours now, and if she had allowed herself to receive the complaints of her body she would have known that she was intolerably parched; but she had mentally withdrawn, leaving only a small part of her awareness on watch for the man beside her and for the sounds from above. The sounds had begun four hours ago, and had been very distant at first . . . a siren, a motor revving hard, the chink of steel on stone, and later, much later, faraway voices shouting. She had steeled herself not to start calling. She would not be heard until the rescuers were much nearer, and her arid throat and mouth would soon reduce her shouts to little more than a croaking whisper.

Then it came, the sound she had waited and hoped for, a long shrill whistle made with fingers and mouth, varying through four notes, like the command whistle of a shepherd controlling a sheep-dog at a distance. She roused, and allowed herself a small grin of relief in the darkness. Her greatest fear had been that over-hasty rescue work might start the wreckage moving and kill them both. It was good to know that Willie Garvin was there.

She thought of a lemon and imagined herself biting into the sharp pulp, feeling the reaction on her tongue. After a few seconds the effort produced a tiny flow of saliva. She slipped the little finger of each hand into the corners of her mouth and blew the same varying whistle. At once came the response, several quick and joyous repetitions of the signal.

The husky voice in the darkness said, "Villefranche . . . he is in Villefranche. Take the talisman to Georges Martel." Silence and ragged breathing.

She said, "Willie Garvin is here. They will have us out soon now."

"The oath . . . it must be honoured. Aladdin has it. *Pas la vie*. Peacock . . . shadow." A curious chuckle. "Enough for a thousand women. Shake . . . shake . . . Georges must bargain . . . by June."

"Yes. Don't worry now, just try to sleep." She found his pulse. It was uneven and too fast, but he was not dying yet. "Everything will be all right," she said, and held his hand. "Everything will be all right soon."

The sound of digging was restrained and wary, creeping closer very slowly. Once every fifteen minutes or so she whistled to guide the rescuers, but another two hours passed before there came the sound of careful probing above and a little to her left, followed by a trickle of falling rubble and the sudden dazzle of a powerful lamp being shone into the hollow. The beam dropped to the grating, and she had to shield her eyes, then it was turned to shine up and back on to a mask of sweat-soaked grey dust from which two very bright blue eyes looked down. She heaved the grating aside, knelt up in the pit, and said, "Hallo, Willie."

He let out a long sigh and shone the beam slowly round the hollow. "So now it's earthquakes, I don't know 'ow you do it, Princess."

She gave a croaking laugh. His face disappeared and his arm came through the hole holding a water-bottle. She took it thankfully and drank. Willie set down the lamp, shifted some more rubble with a trowel, and eased himself through the hole, crouching to stare down into the pit. As she handed back the bottle he said, "What about your friend?"

"Can't give him anything to drink yet, he's unconscious. It's not Giles, by the way."

"I know it's not. Giles is up top with his amazing supercolossal bag of 'erbs and simples, doing his doctor act. He got 'ere soon after midnight, about an hour before I arrived meself." He edged back a little and tested the sides of the hole. "Right, Princess. I've been shoring up any dodgy bits on the way, so we shouldn't 'ave much trouble."

"Good. But get me something to splint his leg with before we start, Willie. It's a hell of a gash, and if it busts open half-way he could bleed to death before we get him out."

"You come out first. I'll come back and see to 'im."

"Willie, love. Please."

Ten minutes later she said, "Right. Now you take his shoulders and we'll ease him through on his back. I'll crawl behind to take care of his leg."

With the splints and ties, Willie had brought strips of blanket to bind round her knees, and she was thankful for this as she edged her way gradually through the twisting hole. The tunnel grew lighter, hotter, the murmur of the outside world grew clearer, then at last the sun struck down upon her head and she had to close her eyes against its brightness. A pause, two or three voices, the sound of movement. Willie saying in Arabic, "Gently . . . gently with the stretcher."

She was rising painfully from all fours when she felt him pick her up, cradling her as he carried her over rough ground. She put her arms round his neck and opened her eyes. As they focused she saw a scattering of cars and vans, two breakdown trucks among them. Half a dozen figures lay on palliasses under a makeshift awning, a man and two nurses moving among them. A little way off was a line of some twenty still forms, each covered with a blanket. A small group of women and children were crying together, but apart from this the scene was strangely quiet.

Willie Garvin set her down and turned her to face him. He was begrimed from head to foot, shirt and trousers ripped, abrasions

27

on arms, legs and chest. She had no more than a glimpse of him before he put his arms round her and held her close, not saying anything, simply holding her.

She slipped her arms about him, surprised. It was not the first time Willie Garvin had seen her emerge from danger she had faced alone, but she had never known him show his relief so openly before. Then, over his shoulder, she saw the great pile of broken masonry that had been the Hotel Ayachi, a monstrous heap of rubble with not a wall or a floor remaining, and she knew that for most of the night and half the day he must have believed her to be dead, crushed beneath a hundred tons of steel and stone.

He let her go, held her at arm's length by the shoulders, and shook his head. "Don't ever do it again, Princess. Please?"

"Once is enough, Willie. I'm not hooked on it." She turned her head. "I want to keep track of the man who was with me. I think he'll be all right, but I'd like to know for sure." She looked at the strap on her wrist. "Oh, and he gave me something when he was rambling. I think it's important to him."

"You'd better get some clothes on."

She looked down at herself. The bathrobe, her only covering, hung about her in strips. A car came round the shattered building and pulled up beside her. Moulay got out with a suitcase and said, "Good afternoon, mam'selle. I am glad you are safe." He laid the suitcase on the bonnet, opened it, and produced a pair of her cotton trousers, a shirt, shoes, underwear, and a toilet case.

She nodded her approval and said, "You were always an optimist, Moulay. Thank you."

"Mam'selle." He hung a blanket over the open car door to provide a screen, and moved away. She said, "Is there any water handy, Willie?"

"Two four-gallon jerricans in the boot."

She stripped off her rags and opened the toilet case. "Pour one over me, will you?"

"Sure. You can do the same for me."

There were towels in the car, a change of clothes for Willie, food, a small stove, a comprehensive case of medical equipment, and such other items as Moulay had decided might possibly be called for. They had just finished dressing when she saw the gangling figure of Dr. Giles Pennyfeather makings towards them, large hands and feet flapping about at the end of loose-jointed arms and legs, spiky fair hair jutting like a halo above his guileless face, leaning sideways under the weight of his huge and ancient leather bag.

"Modesty! There you are, darling. Sorry, but I was busy doing an emergency job on a chap with half his ribs sticking into his poor old lungs, but he'll be all right I think."

She doubted that Giles Pennyfeather would know what to do in a properly equipped operating theatre under sterile conditions. On the other hand, and despite his admittedly sketchy medical knowledge, few doctors could have matched his success in keeping patients alive under the most primitive conditions. He was thinner in the face than when she had last seen him, and she was almost certain that he wore the same khaki drill suit and slacks, rumpled, clumsily repaired and now a patchy white from countless launderings.

As always with Giles, she had to suppress a quick stab of pity for him by reminding herself that he needed pity from nobody. Giles Pennyfeather would always be poor, always struggling to do a job with inadequate resources, always a figure of fun to the sophisticated. But he was quite incapable of feeling sorry for himself under any circumstances, and she had a deep and abiding respect for him. When he put down his bag she kissed him, hugged him, ruffled his hair, and said, "Let me pick the hotel next time, Giles."

"Eh? Oh lord, yes. Sorry about that, but this chap recommended the Ayachi, you see, because of it being awfully cheap. It was the same chap who gave me a lift back from Chad. He was flying cargo and had a spare seat, and I'd taken a tooth out for him. Now, what about you, Modesty?" He eyed her sternly. "I'd better check you over.

"I'm fine. You can make a leisurely check later." She looked beyond him to the figures under the awning. "Let's get on with whatever needs doing."

Willie said, "It's pretty well finished 'ere, Princess. Everyone's accounted for now, and you were the last out by a good few hours, you and the bloke with you."

"How bad is he, Giles?"

"Don't know, darling. The other doctor's having a look at him.

Local chap, and jolly good." Pennyfeather gestured vaguely towards the scene of operations. "There are still some bodies to be taken away, and a few injured to be got into hospital, but beds are a bit short, of course."

"The earthquake caught El Jadida?"

Willie said, "Just the eastern edge of it, but that was enough. Most of the rescue work's concentrated there."

She said to Pennyfeather, "I'd like you to go and have a look at my Frenchman. If he can be looked after at home, we'll take him with us. It'll mean one less bed for the hospitals to find."

Pennyfeather ran fingers through his spiky hair. "Home?" he said. "The penthouse?"

Willie gave a snort of laughter. Modesty said patiently, "No, Giles dear. My home here. You know I used to live in Morocco, I still have a house here."

"Ah, that's right, I remember now." His eyebrows shot up suddenly. "Good God, do you realise we could have met there instead of at the Hotel Ayachi? Then you wouldn't have been here when it fell down."

"Yes, I did realise that, Giles. You were the one who didn't. Now go and see about my Frenchman, there's a love."

"Right." Giles heaved up his bag and stalked off with his jerky stride.

Modesty watched him, and said quietly, "He does more good in a month than I've done in all my life."

Willie shrugged. "We can't all be nutty doctors, Princess."

"Don't worry. I'm just saying it, not feeling put down by it."

"That's all right then." He took her arm and they began to walk slowly towards the cluster of vehicles. "I've got a Cessna belonging to Etienne at the airport, Princess. We can fly to Tangier with your Frenchman if you want."

"Yes." She lifted her wrist and looked at the strap. "You know what this is, Willie? It's a talisman. At least, there's one inside it, I think."

"A talisman?"

"That's what my earthquake friend kept saying. And in case he didn't survive, and I did, it was very important for me to take the talisman to Georges Martel, whoever he may be, in Villefranche."

"Go on? And then what?"

She frowned. "Well, that part's a bit obscure. Aladdin comes into it. And Georges has got to . . . well, to shake something and bargain by June."

"And then a genie pops out from nowhere? Lucky old Georges."

She laughed, and pressed his arm. "It's weird, isn't it? But he was deadly serious. I must play back his ramblings to myself and jot them down." She turned her head to look at Willie, warmed to see him still aglow with the euphoria that her safety had brought him. Then his face changed and his eyes narrowed a little.

"Wait a minute, Princess," he said slowly, "Georges Martel?"

"Do we know him?"

"Well . . . not exactly. But when I was down in Antibes a couple of months back I 'ad a night out with our old sparring partner, Girard. He's an Inspector now, and I was asking if things 'ave changed much since the days when he was up against your Riviera Section of *The Network*. He said it's not the same. It's all got very nasty and uncivilised, with a lot of killings between rival gangs, and he mentioned a few names. One was Georges Martel. Might not be the same one as your earthquake friend spoke about."

"Or it might be. What about him, Willie?"

"He's the top killer for the Union Corse."

Pennyfeather came stalking towards them from the shade of the makeshift canopy, drying his hands on a paper towel. "Your French chap's all right, darling," he said cheerfully. "He's been concussed and he'll need looking after for a bit, but there's nothing serious. We've stitched up his leg and sedated him, so we can pop off whenever you like now."

The island was called Le Dauphin, because it rose from the sea in an elongated hump, the shape of a dolphin skipping along the surface. It lay less than half a mile from the coast, between Ceuta and Oued Laou, a small, lightly wooded piece of land with a number of small bays, occupied mainly by a yacht club. At the eastern end of the island, separated naturally from the rest by a land fault which left a low bluff running across the quarter-mile width, a sandy beach rose to a more heavily wooded area against which stood the house . . . gabled, roofed with ancient slates,

31

dark oak beams standing out against white walls, leaded windows catching the sun.

Take away the palm trees from the background, show a photograph to anyone who knew England, and he would guess the location to be one of the counties within a hundred miles of London, with Surrey or Kent as most likely.

The interior of the house maintained the same illusion. In the dining-room, the French windows were open to the morning sun and a view of calm blue sea. The woman who sat at the head of the oak refectory table wore a plain dark blue dress with a white lace collar. She was in her late thirties, brown hair drawn back in a bun, wide-set brown eyes in a broad face. Eyes, nose, chin, brow, each feature was good in itself but seemed not quite to match the others, so that the overall effect was odd and rather intriguing.

Jeremy and Dominic Silk sat one on either side of the table. They might have been twins, but in fact were brothers with only fifteen months between them. Jeremy, the elder, was twenty-four. Both had sunbleached straight fair hair, an aquiline nose, a fresh complexion, and freckles. They wore slacks and beach shirts, and having finished their porridge were eating a breakfast of eggs, bacon, sausages and kidneys.

Jeremy Silk looked across at his brother and said, "What about that girl at the casino, the one Mandrou reported for holding out?"

"Finished with. I attended to her last night."

"You mean you didn't delegate?"

"Why should I?" Dominic gave a dismissive shrug and went to the sideboard with his empty plate to serve himself with more bacon and kidneys from the silver chafing dishes there.

The woman in the blue dress with the white lace collar tapped a finger on the polished table and said with a touch of singsong cadence that hinted at Welsh origins, "I think we're forgetting our manners, aren't we, Master Dominic?"

He flushed behind his freckles, and looked down. "I beg your pardon, Nannie. I forgot to say, 'Excuse me' when I left the table."

"Manners makyth man."

32

"Yes, Nannie."

"Well, we must try to remember, mustn't we?" She smiled suddenly, fondly, and her unmatched features became harmonious and almost beautiful. "Come along, serve yourself and sit down, Master Dominic. We'll say no more about it."

Jeremy Silk suppressed a smug grin. It was nice to hear Dominic being told off, but it wouldn't do for Nannie Prendergast to catch him smirking, and she was looking at him now, sharp-eyed. "If your brother decided not to delegate but to do the job himself," she said firmly, "it was because I said he might."

"But you always tell us how important it is to delegate, Nannie."

"So I do, Master Jeremy. But before you can do that successfully, you boys must first become fully experienced yourselves. Experience is the father of wisdom, remember."

He smiled. "Yes, of course I remember. But we've really had a great deal of experience, Nannie. There's not an operation from Bizerta to Casablanca we don't either control or own a piece of now. We're the biggest thing since the old *Network*, thanks to you, and we couldn't hold all that together if we weren't very well trained and very experienced."

"I know, dear, I know. Oh, I've made sure you were schooled in every possible subject these ten years past now, and I'm proud of the way you've both become expert in the little white powder business and the protective insurance business and the girlie business, but you're never too old to learn. I think you and Dominic have done *especially* well when there's been a call for capital punishment to make an example of somebody, or because of aggravation from business rivals. But this was the first time there's been an opportunity for Dominic to make an example of a girl, you know."

She turned to the younger brother as he sat down with his replenished plate. "Did you have any problems?"

"No, it all went very smoothly, Nannie." He hesitated. "Though I did just wonder . . ."

"What did you wonder, Dominic?"

"I felt it might be a waste. I mean, we could have sold her to any one of a dozen clients from here to the Gulf."

"We don't sell loose women to our royal clients, do we, dear? And in any event it was necessary to make an example of her. How did you go about it?"

"Oh, I used a piece of green nylon cord. Made quite sure she was dead, of course, and left it tied round her neck. It's a well-established signature now, and you wanted this to be recognised as an El Mico killing."

"Any exemplary killing must be seen as the work of El Mico, naturally. Example is always better than precept, remember. Will you have another cup of tea, Jeremy?"

"Thank you, Nannie." He passed his cup and watched the play of her smooth bare forearms as she handled the milk-jug and teapot. Watching her arms had excited him even when he had first known Nannie Prendergast eighteen years ago, long before he reached puberty.

As she handed him the cup she said, "Now, there's quite a lot of paperwork for you boys to do this morning. We mustn't get behind with our daily prep, must we? It's often tedious, I know, reading reports, checking consignments, cross-checking to make sure we're not being cheated by our own people. Tedious, but necessary, so we just have to buckle down to it. More tea, Dominic?"

"Thank you, Nannie."

"Then pass your cup, dear. And this afternoon we'll devote to general training in the manly pursuits. I shall come down to the games room to watch you." The games room lay under the big boat-house and was fully equipped.

"Pistol practice?" asked Jeremy Silk.

"All weapons, please. Handgun, knife, garotte, and that curious thing Little Krell was demonstrating recently."

"The kongo."

"Kongo was it? Well yes, then. And of course you must do some hard practice in all those unarmed combat systems, so that one day you'll be as good as Little Krell himself."

Dominic smiled. That was an unattainable ambition. Little Krell was five feet fall and thirty inches across the shoulders, with no fat; yet he was not muscle-bound and that squat body could move with astonishing speed and grace. His normal day consisted of four hours swimming, four training, and four teaching combat.

Apart from this he had no other interests, except that he liked to be provided with a girl once a month.

Jeremy stirred his tea thoughtfully, wondering if he dared raise the subject which had been taboo for the last three days. He had no wish to get into trouble with Nannie Prendergast, but at the same time the matter was really very important. He decided to broach it obliquely, and looked at Dominic as he said, "I've been wondering if Little Krell is quite safe, you know."

"Safe?" Dominic stared in surprise.

"I mean, he knows about us. He can finger us, to put it crudely."

"Can he? I know he's not a deaf mute, but he might as well be. I can't even remember hearing him say anything much, other than *doucement, plus vite*, and *comme ça*. And he's been here for . . . how long is it? Five years?"

Nannie Prendergast said, "You need have no worry about Little Krell now, Master Jeremy. Oh, he knows our little secret, but he also knows I have evidence in pictures of his killing a man, so he'll always be very biddable. The only reason I've not suggested making use of him in the business is that he's so distinctive in appearance. But perhaps it would be quite a good idea to have him do odd jobs for us now and again, on occasions when he wouldn't be obtrusive. I'll think about it."

Gazing out absently at the sea, Jeremy Silk said, "I didn't know you had a control on him, and I probably wouldn't even have wondered about him except that we've been let down rather badly recently." There was a silence. Dominic held his breath for a moment and darted a furtive glance at Nannie Prendergast from under lowered eyebrows.

Face expressionless, she said, "What do you have in mind, Master Jeremy?"

"Well . . ." He stirred uncomfortably. "You know."

"I'll thank you to be more specific, young man."

"Well, I'm talking about that treacherous bastard Gautier," he said sullenly.

"I did *not* hear that."

"I beg your pardon, Nannie. About Gautier."

"Yes?"

"I realise that when Meloul was killed two years ago we needed

35

somebody urgently, somebody to act as a link between us and the various operations, so we picked Gautier because he'd done some marvellous jobs for us and we all thought he was absolutely trust-worthy." He risked a glance at Nannie, and relaxed a little when he saw that she was looking at him with polite attention.

"Go on, dear," she said.

"I know it upset you awfully, Nannie. It upset us all when he cheated us, and I don't like to talk about it, but I feel we can't just let it go."

Dominic said, "Yes, but finding Gautier and dealing with him isn't as important as making sure The Big One goes through smoothly. All right, I know he made off with a whole month's takings, but that's a bus fare compared with The Big One." He leaned forward, eyes sparkling, and put his hand over Nannie's as it lay on the table. "And it was all your idea, Nannie. You saw what was coming, you planned the whole job, and we spent eight months and a fortune setting it up. But it's the biggest ever. We can do what you've always wanted. We can retire, and buy an estate in England and live like gentry there, even today, because we'll have millions and millions." He looked across the table at his brother. "I'm all for killing Gautier if we can find him, but is it going to be worth the effort now?"

Nannie Prendergast said, "It's necessary, Master Dominic, in just the same way that it was necessary for you to make an example of that girlie last night. We must always do the day's work that is set before us. And besides, we haven't yet succeeded with The Big One because we've not yet taken delivery, have we? The best laid schemes of mice and men gang aft a-gley, remember."

The two brothers looked at each other across the table, then at Nannie Prendergast. Jeremy Silk said slowly, "You don't really believe anything could go wrong, do you, Nannie? The . . . the Object is safely aboard the *Kythira*, and we'll get a call from Baillie-Smythe in the next couple of days. Then we simply take the launch, rendezvous with the ship, and collect."

"I hope so, dear, but let's not count our chickens before they're hatched, shall we?" She smiled, and again for a moment was transformed from a *jolie-laide* to a beautiful woman. "But con-cerning the man Gautier, I have good news for you, since I can see that neither of you has read the morning's reports yet."

Jeremy put his hand on her arm. "What is it, Nannie?"

"One of our police contacts in Casablanca sent it through to the *poste restante* address. It seems Gautier was among those injured in the El Jadida earthquake. Our contact happened to be on the spot, and recognised him. He'd been trapped in the ruins of the Hotel Ayachi."

"The Ayachi?" Dominic echoed incredulously. "Oh, it must be a mistake, Nannie. Gautier's well out of the country by now."

"It's not a mistake, dear. The man who recognised him is our paymaster for the area, and he used to collect the money from Gautier every month. Gautier had a false passport on him in the name of Martel, but that's hardly surprising. He wouldn't dare to travel in El Mico territory under his own name."

"I can't imagine why he's still here," said Jeremy Silk wonderingly. "Is he in hospital now?"

"No. It appears he was trapped with a young womam who later had him taken to her own home in Tangier to recover, because the hospitals were already over-crowded. I telephoned our Tangier man, as El Mico's secretary of course, and he was able to confirm at once that an injured man from the El Jadida earthquake is still staying with the young lady."

Dominic said, "How could he know without having time to check it through?"

"Because she's a young lady well-known in Tangier, who unwittingly served us very well when she retired. As I'm sure you remember, she left some nice operations which ran down very quickly and became ripe for El Mico to take over."

Dominic leaned back in his chair and grinned. "Modesty Blaise?"

"Herself."

"Well I'll be damned."

"I beg your pardon?"

"Sorry, Nannie." He shook his head. "It's strange we never crossed swords with her when she was running *The Network*."

"We were very careful not to," said Nannie Prendergast.

"It's different now, though."

"Yes, it is, but we have no interest in her now. The important thing is that Gautier should be made an example of, and in no uncertain manner."

"And by El Mico himself," said Jeremy. "It's important for the image. Did you have anything particular in mind, Nannie?"

She stood up, and the two men rose with her, watching her as she moved towards the terrace, skirt swinging about long slender legs, body firm and trim as that of a woman ten years younger. She stood in the open French windows looking out over the sea, then turned and smiled, but this time the smile did not transform her mildly chaotic features. "Yes. Nannie has something in mind," she said.

Modesty Blaise sat at the dressing table in her bedroom, carefully filing her nails. They were in need of considerable attention after her efforts beneath the rubble of the hotel. The curtains were drawn back and the stars were very bright in the dark canopy of the sky. A long window faced across the sea to Spain, and the wings of the balcony ensured that it could not be overlooked. She had not put on a robe after her shower, for the night was warm. Her hair, black and shining, hung loosely to her shoulders. The soft glow from one of the lamps made her body golden, picking out highlights on the firm curves.

Dr. Giles Pennyfeather gave an audible sigh. He lay on the big bed under a single sheet, hands behind his head, watching the woman at the dressing table. Without looking up, she said, "That's two in three minutes."

"Eh? Two what, darling?"

"Gusty sighs. Are they signs of impatience?"

He chuckled. "No, of course not. Well, I mean, I *am* impatient, but I wasn't sighing because of it."

She looked up now, her midnight blue eyes warm and smiling. "Then why?"

"Um, let's see. Oh, the first one was sort of a despairing sigh. I wonder . . . which is the best way to cook eggs, do you think?"

She was used to Giles non-sequiturs, and simply asked, "Fried, boiled, poached or scrambled?"

"Boiled. You see, I've been doing my own meals while I was in Chad, and I don't seem to get the hang of cooking at all. Mostly I boil eggs. I don't mean that's all I eat, because I make up with bread, dates, fruit, raw vegetables and so on. But do you put an egg in boiling water for four minutes or do you put it in cold water and bring it to the boil and then do it for three minutes?"

"Either way is all right, darling."

"But they simply don't work, Modesty. I've tried heaps of times."

"I expect it's your watch." She glanced to where it lay beside him on the bedside cabinet, a large and battered wrist-watch with an almost opaque glass. "It's always wrong by anything up to half an hour, and the minute hand's loose anyway."

He lifted himself on his elbows to stare at her with open admiration. "My God, I think you've hit the nail on the head. I really do. That's marvellous. You get terribly fed up, either having to chew eggs or drink them."

"Giles, how do you manage when you're taking somebody's pulse against the watch?"

"Oh, I don't actually take any notice of the watch. I just look at it to reassure the patient."

"Then how do you know his pulse rate?"

"Ah, well, I don't really know the precise rate, Modesty. I just know if it feels a bit funny."

She nodded. That was undoubtedly the Pennyfeather style of medicine. "It's a pity it doesn't work with eggs," she said, and moved a little to examine a torn nail under the light. Watching her, Pennyfeather caught his breath, then sighed again.

"That's three," she said.

"The last two were sort of contented sighs, like when a cat purrs. I'm just lying here thinking how jolly lucky I am."

"In what way, darling?"

"Being here with you, of course. Beautiful house, everything laid on. Seeing old Willie again. He's very good company. But most of all, being with you. I often think how awfully lucky I was that we bumped into each other that time in Tanzania."

She put down the nail file, stood up, moved to the bed and slipped into it beside him, lying on her side, her head propped on one hand so that she looked down at him.

"Lucky?" she said quietly. "I'm the bird who got you involved with Brunel and his playmates. You ended up with a broken arm and half your toenails pulled out."

He frowned. "That wasn't your fault. And anyway, we all run into a difficult patch now and again."

She laughed, smoothed a hand across his brow, then rested it on his chest. "I like you, Giles."

"I like you, too. God, I was so scared all the time you were under that heap of wreckage. I pretended not to be, of course, because of Willie. And *he* pretended not to be, but he threw up three times. That chap Martel is a bit of a rum customer, isn't he?"

"In what way?"

"Well, I don't mean medically. His leg's healing all right and he'll be as good as new in a week or two, but he doesn't say anything about himself, and I fancy he's got the wind up about something."

"So do I. Willie and I had a word about it, but we decided it's nothing to do with us. He's no trouble as a house guest, and I think rather well of him. He didn't get the wind up when we were buried alive for over twenty hours, and that says quite a lot."

"Does he know who you are?"

"You mean does he know that Modesty Blaise used to have a formidable reputation in these parts two or three years ago? Yes, I'm sure he does. I think he knows a lot more than he tells, but I've stopped being curious. It gets me into all kinds of trouble."

She slid down on to her stomach, an arm and leg across him, head turned towards him, and after a little silence she said, "Do you still miss Lisa?"

He thought about it, brow furrowed, then said slowly, "I've missed being generally looked after, and I've missed having somebody to go to bed with, not just for sex, but as a friend." He smiled. "I'm a tactile chap. I like contact. But that's not really missing Lisa as Lisa, is it? We got along well and I'm still very fond of her, but I can't pretend I was shattered when she went."

"You married her to heal her, Giles. I believe you thought it was the only way, after what Brunel had done to her mind."

"Oh, I wouldn't say that." He eased a hand under her body.

"No, but it's true. So you gradually repaired her, and when you'd done it she didn't need you any more and she could start a new life. I'm not blaming her, because it was almost inevitable, but I'm glad you weren't hurt too much. Are you listening to me, Giles?"

"Not actually very closely. I was concentrating more on the nice sensation of holding your breast."

"Quite right, too. I was getting all serious, and that's no way for a lady to behave in bed. What are you doing now?"

He had got to his knees and thrown the sheet back, bending a little to study her closely, his big clumsy hands touching her surprisingly gently as they moved from her back down to her legs. "I'm checking your scars," he said. "You heal so well they barely show, but I remember what you used to have. Can't see anything new here. That cut on the buttock you got when you were fighting that chap Chance has vanished completely. Right, turn over."

She said meekly, "Yes, doctor."

"Now, then. We'll work our way up. H'mm . . . good. All clear. Here's that old one on the thigh. Yes. And that one on the arm, the rapier wound. Wait a minute, I nearly missed this." He peered closely at her stomach. "Hardly visible, but they're scars all right, very small, one each side of what we doctors call the belly-button. What have you been up to?"

"A man shot at me in a house in Guatemala. I was in a crouch, sideways on, and the bullet nipped in and out of the fold of flesh without doing any serious damage."

Pennyfeather glared indignantly. "Why on earth was he shooting at you?"

She reached up with both hands, took his face between them and drew him down upon her. "Giles, do you want to hear a long story or do you want to make love?"

"Make love, please."

"Good. But I'm not cheap, so you have to agree to do me a big favour."

"I'd love to do you a favour if you can think of one, Modesty."

She drew his head down, touched his ear with her lips and whispered. "Then let me buy you a really nice egg-timing watch."

"Oh, now wait a minute. You're already housing and feeding me, I can't have you buying me presents."

"Please, Giles. Don't be rotten to a girl just because she's stinking rich."

He lifted his head to look down at her, and with the pressure of his body upon her she felt the swift surge of longing that swept him. She laughed, still holding his face between her hands and said, "Come on. Give in?"

His answering chuckle was a little breathless. "This is . . . no time to refuse a lady. And thank you very much."

"A deal?"

"A deal."

"And we can concentrate on enjoying ourselves now?"

"Absolutely."

"Then have at you, sirrah."

three

Willie Garvin surfaced, shook the water from his hair, and perched himself beside Modesty Blaise on one of the underwater seats which formed part of the bar at the side of the pool. She wore a green one-piece swimsuit and was sipping a glass of fresh orange juice.

Willie picked up his own glass, and together they watched with interest as Giles Pennyfeather mounted the ladder of the three-metre board at the deep end. Oddly enough, he looked less spindly stripped than when dressed, probably because the clothes he wore were always so abysmally ill-fitting. He was still a far from handsome figure though, for his head and neck, hands and forearms were deeply tanned, while the rest of him was white, as if by some error in manufacture he had been put together with parts from two different designs.

Beyond the tiled surround of the twenty-metre pool lay flower-beds, and beyond the beds were dwarf pines set close together to form a screen. A high wall separated this part of the grounds from the drive which led up from the road. A wide patch of well-kept grass lay between one end of the pool and the patio. Here, in the shade thrown by the wall, the man with a passport in the name of Bernard Martel sat in a lounging chair wearing borrowed shorts and shirt. One leg, bandaged at the thigh, was supported on an extension to the chair. A crutch lay beside him, and there was a small table with cigarettes and a drink at his elbow. One his right wrist he wore what appeared to be a wide support strap. He too was watching the figure now on the diving board, but a little absently, as if his mind was elsewhere.

Pennyfeather hitched up his swim-trunks, which were shapeless, colourless, and appeared to have been improvised from a very large old tea cosy. He walked to the end of the board, lifted his arms in readiness for a dive, and lost his balance. For several seconds he teetered, arms waving wildly, then with an indignant cry he fell sideways into the pool with an enormous splash. He emerged grinning, entirely unembarrassed, and swam down to join Modesty and Willie with a slow breast stroke.

"I fell off," he panted.

Modesty nodded. "I thought that's what you'd done. Can I get you a drink, Giles?"

"No thanks, darling. I say, I do like you in that swimsuit. She looks like a million dollars, doesn't she, Willie?"

"Not a penny less, Giles. And that's a model pair of trunks you're wearing yourself, isn't it? I've never seen any others like 'em."

"Really? I think they're quite old. I got them out of an Oxfam delivery in Calcutta. I think I'll try my crawl stroke now." He moved slowly away amid a froth of churning water, achieving minimum results for maximum effort.

Willie said, "It's nice to 'ave Giles around for a while. How much leave 'as he got, Princess?"

She said, "It's not exactly leave, because he's not going back to Chad. He complained to some bigwig about medical supplies vanishing on to the black market, and promptly got the elbow. Then somebody told him about a job on offer from one of the oil sheikdoms, running a small specialised hospital. Giles applied, and was accepted."

"Great," Willie said with satisfaction. "He ought to manage more than a new pair of trunks out of what oil sheiks pay. I know Giles is always good for a laugh, but it sticks in my craw when I think of 'im flogging 'imself to death in all sorts of lousy back-of-beyond dumps, and never 'aving two ha'pennies to rub togeth-er." He took another drink of orange juice. "I know Giles doesn't care. But I do."

Modesty nodded. "I'd be glad to set him up in any way he wanted, but it's no use. I had to trick him into just letting me get him a new watch. And it isn't a matter of pride or even principle. It's just . . . Giles."

"Which sheikdom is it?" said Willie. "Anyone we know?"

"Ah well, Giles can't actually remember the name of it, or where it is. The application went through an agent in Cairo, and Giles has either lost or thrown away all the correspondence. He travels light, you know. So all he has is the name and address of the agent written down in the back of his notebook amid sundry amazing medical formulae, together with the date he's supposed to report to Cairo. Presumably the agent then provides transport to wherever it is. That's on the eighth of next month. I want to give him as good a time as possible till then."

"Sure." Willie put down his glass and glanced towards the Frenchman in the lounging chair. "If you want to push off somewhere else with Giles, I'll look after Bernard till he's fit to leave."

She put a hand on his. "No. This is fine." After a few moments, during which they watched Pennyfeather practising a remarkable backstroke, she said, "It's odd about his name."

"Bernard Martel? And when he was rambling he wanted you to take the talisman to Georges Martel, in Villefranche?"

"Yes. I somehow don't read this one for a villain. Not the kind you associate with a Union Corse hit man."

"Maybe it's a different Georges Martel he was speaking of."

"Maybe. But never mind. Sorry Willie, I said we wouldn't speculate on it, and here I am doing just that."

Moulay came out of the house through the big window leading on to the patio, crossed the patch of lawn and made his way to the pool bar. "A gentleman to see you, mam'selle."

"Do you know him, Moulay?"

A smile touched the calm dark face beneath the grey-flecked hair. "An old friend, mam'selle. Inspector Hassan Birot."

She smiled, drew herself out of the pool and took the wrap

Moulay handed her. "At this time of the morning he'll drink coffee, and he'll have come on business. I wonder what it can be?"

"He did not indicate to me, mam'selle."

Willie said, "Want me along, Princess?"

She shook her head. "No, it's all right. Should I slip a dress on? He's very westernised, but . . ."

"It'd be a courtesy."

"Just my thought." Then, to Moulay: "Say I'm delighted he's called and I'll be with him in three minutes, then fetch some coffee, please."

"Mam'selle."

As she went into the house Pennyfeather came thrashing across to Willie. "I've been meaning to ask," he panted. "Why's that major-domo chap called Moulay? I mean, it's really the title of a high-up official, isn't it?"

"Clever lad," Willie agreed. "Also used for a descendant of the Prophet."

"Is he really?"

"I doubt it. He used to run the catering side of one or two respectable *Network* establishments, years ago. Then when the Princess built this 'ouse she put him in as steward. I started calling 'im Moulay as a bit of a joke. Like the equivalent of 'squire'. And it stuck."

"Ah, I see. A sort of nickname." Pennyfeather gave a chuckle. "They used to call me Jack Ketch when I was a medical student."

"Ketch? The bloke who was the old public 'angman?"

"That's right. I got the name one day after I'd made a bit of a mess trying to put a chap in traction. I didn't actually strangle him, of course, but his face turned a bit blue. He used to joke about it with me later."

"It's nice to 'ave patients with a sense of humour."

"Oh lord, yes. How about a race, Willie?"

"A swimming race?"

"Yes. Up the length and back."

"Giles, do you swim as well as you dive?"

"Oh, I don't know. Almost as well, I suppose."

"Then you're on. But we'll 'ave a little bet on it." He tapped the bottle of white burgundy that stood in an ice bucket at the end of the bar. "If you win you buy me a bottle of plonk, and if I win I buy you a new pair of swim-trunks."

Five miles away, on the eastern outskirts of Tangier, a small grey van turned out of Place d'Europe and headed along Boulevard de Moulay Youssef. The driver had long greasy black hair hanging to his shoulders, and wore dark glasses, blue overalls and a single earphone. Another man sat a little way behind him, out of sight of pedestrians or other road users. He wore a dark suit, his hair was short and black, and he had a broad moustache, as long as his mouth and trimmed square.

The driver said in Spanish, "About twenty minutes now."

"The car is in position?"

"Yes, El Mico. I have checked personally."

"And the report from the light aircraft confirms that Gautier is in the garden, and in the same position as before?"

"Impossible to recognise Gautier from such a height, but it is a man with an injured leg."

"Good enough. There is only one of those in the house."

"They will confirm again when we are on the final approach." There was silence for a while, then the driver went on hesitantly, "With respect, El Mico, has it been considered how Modesty Blaise might react to the killing of one who is a guest in her house?"

The other said, "It has been considered. She can make no reaction of any importance. Her organisation no longer exists. She has no people, no eyes, no ears, no authority."

The driver thought, *But she is still Modesty Blaise.* He did not voice his thought, however, for he had learned from the experience of others that it was imprudent to irritate El Mico.

The man in the dark suit bent down, lifted the apparatus at his feet, then settled the container on his back and tightened the strap across his chest.

Inspector Hassan Birot sat deep in a leather armchair, sipping excellent coffee and well content that his present duty involved looking at the girl who sat facing him. She had obviously been in the pool when he called. Her damp hair had been pinned up, hastily by the look of it. She wore sandals and a corn-coloured summer dress. Inspector Birot suspected that she wore nothing else, but did not permit himself to dwell on that suspicion, for he was of a puritanical leaning.

He was half French, but also half Arab, and this latter half was dominant, so he was pleased that she fell in naturally with his delayed approach to the matter in hand and was prepared for the long and polite preliminaries. She had changed, he thought, since the old days. He could detect a warmth, a softness. That was to be understood. But he had come to realise that even though her manner had been cold and hard in the days of *The Network*, the other side of her had lain there beneath the surface, revealed only by actions which had seemed puzzling at the time.

He said, "I have sometimes wished you had remained in business here, Miss Blaise." He always used the English form of address in preference to "mam'selle", because Mam'selle was the title by which she had always been addressed or referred to by all members of *The Network*—with the exception of Willie Garvin.

"You spent a great deal of time trying to make sure I did not remain in business here, Inspector," she said with a solemn air of reproach.

"In the early years, yes. But then . . ." He waved a hand. "I came to the conclusion that you were doing more to fight drugs and vice than my own department."

"My hands weren't tied by regulations."

"Even so." He drew on the cigarette she had offered him, and exhaled. "You devoted much effort to destroying the worst organisation."

She smiled, "You musn't regard me as a crusader. I simply made better use of their assets."

"Whatever your reason, I know that such affairs have become worse since you retired from business, Miss Blaise. Crime becomes more savage, more vicious, more horrible now."

"Not just here, Inspector. Everywhere."

"Yes. So I observe, but I am concerned with weeding my own small garden, naturally. Do you know who controls all major crime in North Africa since you wound up *The Network*?"

She said, "I have old friends here, and they like to tell me things, even though I point out that I'm no longer interested. I've heard the name of El Mico."

"Yes. El Mico. The monkey. May I ask what you know of him, please?"

She was sitting upright but relaxed in her chair, her hands resting in her lap, knees together, turned a little sideways, her manner grave and courteous as she considered his question. Watching her, he felt a little sense of shock as for a moment it seemed to him that time had turned back and she was perhaps seventeen again. This was just as he remembered her in the beginning, the first time he had come to question her at the club in Rue d'Italie, soon after she had taken over the small-time Louche gang.

She said, "I understand El Mico exercises control by fear, and that he's now re-established drugs and vice as prime operations."

"This was to be expected," said Inspector Birot. "What is curious about El Mico, however, is that he has no location. In a sense one might say he does not exist."

Modesty shook her head. "I don't understand."

"He has no base. No residence. No location. No name, except El Mico. This is something not easy to deal with. El Mico is El Mico is El Mico."

She said, "Is there any particular significance in the name?"

He considered the question. "Apart from 'the monkey', it is used colloquially for . . . how do you say it in English? *Le marmot?*"

"Brat. Or kid. In English it can be a kind of endearment. A mother might call a mischievous child a little monkey. I'm not sure if that applies in Spanish."

He stared reflectively. "It had not occurred to me that the name might hold a clue. It seems unlikely, but I will give thought to the possibility."

"Has nobody ever seen El Mico?"

"Ah, yes. Certainly he has been seen. We have excellent photofit pictures. It is even said that he may be seen in two places at the same time. He appears, he acts, he disappears."

"When you say 'he acts'?"

"He gives order. Or he leads an operation. Or carries out an execution if it is important enough to warrant his personal attention."

"But he must have links with his various organisations, Inspector. There must be channels of command."

"Of course. We assume he has personal contact with an inner circle of lieutenants. Three, perhaps four. But we have questioned a dozen or more possibles, and nobody has talked." Inspector Hassan Birot paused, then added, "Not even your present guest, Gautier, who was and is our favourite suspect as first lieutenant to El Mico."

She did not show surprise, but sat looking absently past him at the open window and the distant sea beyond. "His name is not Bernard Martel?" she asked.

The Inspector shrugged. "It may be. But he is known here as Louis Gautier, and is certainly an important man in El Mico's organisation."

"Have you come to take him away?"

"No, no, Miss Blaise, not at all. We have no case to bring against him. But I should be most grateful if you found yourself able to learn anything about him which you think might be useful to me."

She looked at him and said quietly, "He is a guest in my house."

Hassan Birot gave a shrug. "He sells heroin. He sells women. Or is involved in doing so. I have known you to kill men for this."

"Yes." There was no softness in her now, and her eyes were dark with anger.

"Then?"

She made a small gesture. "He is still a guest in my house. He has eaten my bread."

Inspector Birot sighed. The French half of him was annoyed, but the Arab half was in sympathy with her. Long ago he had heard that she had spent her childhood wandering the Middle East and North Africa, and that for part of it she had lived with a tribe of nomad Arabs. Desert law laid down that the guest in your tent was sacrosanct; his welfare came before your own. It was a well-founded tradition, and one which the child Modesty Blaise had evidently absorbed.

The Inspector spread the fingers of one hand in a gesture of acceptance. "It was my duty to ask," he said.

"Of course, I wish I could help."

He stood up. "My journey is not wasted. It has been a pleasure to talk with you again, Miss Blaise."

Her smile warmed him. She said, "Will you have dinner with us one evening, after my guest has gone? Willie Garvin is here with me, and I seem to remember that you enjoy his company."

"Very much." Inspector Birot rubbed his chin. "I find it curious that Gautier has remained here with you. He usually lives in a small hotel suite in Melilla. One might almost think he did not wish his friends to know his whereabouts."

"Well . . . he hasn't attempted to contact anybody, as far as I know."

"Thank you."

There was silence, but for the muted sound of a single-engine aircraft passing nearby at a few hundred feet. Inspector Birot stood turning his hat round in his hands, then said slowly, "I think I would like to speak with him, Miss Blaise."

"Officially?"

"Yes. There is the question of identity. From the passport he carried, we have recorded that Bernard Martel was among the survivors of the earthquake, yet there are many who can identify the man in the photograph as Louis Gautier. I wish to check that he is in fact the man known to us by that name."

"Of course. I can't refuse to let you see him officially. Will you come through to the garden? It's easier than fetching him in here."

He went with her out on to the terrace. This ran the whole length of the north side of the house, then turned the corner to join the patio outside the big living-room. As they passed through a trefoil arch into the patio, Inspector Birot saw Willie Garvin standing by the pool some fifty paces away with the lanky and rather odd-looking English doctor who was said to be an old friend of Modesty's.

Gautier was in a lounging chair near the far edge of the grass, angled away from the house so that he had a view of the pool. Birot lifted a hand in greeting to Willie, then saw that he was not looking his way but was standing with head cocked as if listening, and with a vaguely inquiring air. Birot heard Modesty Blaise, beside him, murmur, "More visitors?" In the same moment he became aware of a sound from beyond the wall, the sound of an engine ticking over rapidly in the drive which lay on the other side.

He looked towards the high white wall, and was astonished to see a man step up on top of it from the far side, evidently from something almost on a level with the wall, for he stepped up easily enough, even though he carried an object in his hands and some kind of pack on his back. Then Birot's eyes focused on the short black hair, the brown face, the distinctive long rectangle of moustache. He caught his breath, and the adrenalin of alarm went flowing into his bloodstream. "El Mico!" he said, and it was as if the words triggered a nightmare.

From the nozzle of the hose El Mico held, something spurted through the air towards the man in the lounging chair sixty feet from the wall, a spreading jet that became a cloud, bursting into flame as it engulfed its prey. Two sounds, the soft explosion of ignition and the dreadful scream, came almost as one, but the scream continued. A blackened figure writhed on charred grass beside the seared chair and table, flames flickering from wood and canvas, clothing, hair and flesh.

The great ball of flame vanished almost at once, so that it was as if some monstrous frog had flicked out a tongue of fire at its victim. Then the figure on the wall was turning a little, bringing the flame-thrower to bear on Modesty and Inspector Birot, and Willie Garvin's voice was rising above the hideous screams, shouting "*Back Princess!*" He was running forward, in his hand the unopened bottle of wine from the ice-bucket, his arm swinging up and over to send it flying through the air in a long long throw.

Modesty had swung round, an arm across Birot's waist, lifting him, almost hurling him back into the cover of the patio's wing. As they fell together she twisted to see the flung bottle strike a glancing blow on the shoulder of the man in the dark suit. It could have done little serious damage, but was enough to throw him off balance. He teetered for a moment, then was compelled to turn and step down from the wall, the nozzle falling from his hands as he flung them wide for balance.

For a moment half his body showed above the wall. The tickover became a roar as a motor was revved. The strange face, split by the bar of black moustache, turned briefly towards them, then the man ducked down and was gone. The engine roared again, and there came the screech of tyres finding a grip.

The screams from the blackened and flickering thing that had been Louis Gautier or Bernard Martel continued. Modesty came to her feet and saw Pennyfeather running forward, calling, "The pool! The pool!" Then Willie was there, scooping up the obscene thing in his arms, lunging towards the pool, jumping into the shallow end with it. Pennyfeather leapt clumsily in beside him, calling, "Good! Good! Now just keep his head up so he can breathe, Willie."

She caught Inspector Birot by the arm and hauled him to his feet. Her face was chalk-white and there was sickness in her throat as she said, "Come *on!*" Then she was running through the house to the front door, calling to a bewildered Moulay to go and help Mr. Garvin. Birot was on her heels as they came out through the porch and on to the broad crescent where the drive ended. Her own cars were in the garage, but Birot's car was standing there and he had the keys ready in his hand as she flung open the door and slid across to the passenger seat. As the engine of the Simca came to life they saw a plain grey van two hundred yards away at the end of the drive, then it turned on to the road and disappeared behind a mass of tall oleander.

Birot said, "That was El Mico," and sent the car flashing down the drive. As he braked for the turn he slid a hand under his jacket and passed an automatic to her. She saw that it was a French M1950 pistol, a gun carrying nine rounds of 9mm Parabellum. Pulling back the slide, she checked the loaded-chamber indicator mounted in it and thumbed off the safety catch.

Birot was driving well, getting the best from the car, bringing it neatly round the frequent sharp bends without losing seconds by constantly over-correcting. As they dropped down towards the main road he said, "Which way at the fork?"

There were two ways down, one reaching the main road a mile nearer Tangier than the other. She said, "Right." It was no more than a guess, but that was the quickest way into town and therefore the most likely way for anyone wanting to shake off pursuit.

Birot said, "I agree," and the car heeled as he swung past the grove of olive trees where the road divided. Two minutes later

Birot said uneasily, "We should have sighted them by now. We are almost at the main road."

"Yes." A picture of the black thing in the ball of flame rose in her mind, and she thrust it away. "Better turn west on the main road, Inspector, and go back up the other leg of the fork. We might be lucky."

There was little traffic on the road to Cape Spartel, and no sign of the grey van. After a mile, Birot turned away from the coast, and as he did so Modesty said through her teeth, "God, I'm a fool!"

"What is it?"

She pointed ahead. Far up the hill, a column of smoke had risen high in the air. "They switched," she said. "That's the van burning, somewhere in that grove of olives near the fork, I think. We must have passed within fifty yards of them, but they won't have left much evidence for you to work on, Inspector. And they'll be in a car or some other vehicle, half-way back to Tangier by now."

Inspector Hassan Birot sighed. "*Insh' Allah*," he said. "Let us go and see."

Ten minutes later they were back at the house, walking through to the patio. Pennyfeather's great battered medical bag was on the table beside her own first aid box. Willie Garvin stood with an arm half lifted while Pennyfeather completed a bandage between elbow and shoulder. Willie's other forearm was already bandaged. Both men were still in their swim-trunks and both looked grey-faced and shivery as if with cold, though the day was hot.

To one side, something lay on the patio tiles under a sheet, surrounded by a damp patch.

Birot said, "He is dead?"

Pennyfeather, absorbed in his work, did not answer. Willie said, "About five minutes ago." He looked at Modesty. "Giles did what he could, but it was 'opeless. So we shot 'im full of morphia."

She came across to Willie, took his free hand and peered searchingly at his arms and body. "How bad, Giles?"

"Painful but not serious. The napalm didn't stick to Willie much, it was sticking to . . . that." He indicated the body under the sheet with a jerk of his head, then finished the bandage and

53

turned to look at her, his lean face working with anger. "Did you catch that bastard, Modesty?"

"No." She was still looking at Willie. "They switched cars, and we missed out."

Pennyfeather stared morosely. "Ah, sod it, I was hoping you'd killed him."

She said dully, "Doctors aren't supposed to hope that sort of thing."

"No? Take a good look at what's under that sheet, and then tell me what I'm supposed to think." He caught her arm as she turned towards the dreadul shape. "No, for Christ's sake don't. I'm sorry, darling, we're a bit on edge."

She remembered her glimpse of the screaming creature in the ball of flame, and said, "Don't apologise. What I said was stupid."

Birot had gone through into the garden. Now he returned, carrying in his hands a piece of green cord, twisted about itself and knotted in such a way as to form a tiny primitive doll. "The sign of El Mico," he said. "I found it at the foot of the wall, as I had expected. This was an execution." He looked at the shape beneath the sheet. "If I may use your telephone, Miss Blaise, I will have an ambulance and a police team sent here at once."

"Please carry on. Ask my steward for anything you need."

"Thank you." He pocketed the knotted green cord and went into the house. Pennyfeather shut his battered medical case. Modesty said, "Willie, go and get some clothes on right away. You've got goose pimples. Can you manage all right, or shall I come and help?"

"No, I'm in good working order, Princess. A bit sore in patches, but I 'ad me arms under the water for about ten minutes, and that stopped any bad blistering. I'll be fine in a couple of days."

"Yes." She looked up at the quiet sky, half closing her eyes against the sun. "I expect we'll all be a lot better when we've got a couple of days behind us."

At some time between two and three in the morning, when Giles Pennyfeather shook her gently by the shoulder, she woke at once and turned towards him.

"I think there's somebody downstairs," he said quietly. "I just heard a door closing."

She listened, but heard nothing. "It can only be Willie or Moulay. This is a well-protected house, Giles. Nobody could get in without setting off alarms."

"Oh, I didn't think about anyone breaking in. I'm just concerned about Willie."

"Willie?"

"Yes. I think he can't sleep. Or doesn't want to, because of nightmares."

She put on the bedside light and sat up. "Nightmares?" she echoed. "Giles, I know it was a rough day, especially for you two, but Willie's made of teak. And one way or another he's seen too many nasty casualties to be squeamish."

Pennyfeather lay looking up at her, and shook his head. "I thought I'd seen every kind of mess that could be made of the human body. Some of those earthquake victims had to be taken away in sacks. But what napalm did to that Frenchman really shook me, Modesty. I don't want to describe it to you, but there's something you don't know. While I ran to get my case, the man stopped breathing, so Willie started to give him mouth to mouth respiration, holding him there in the pool with just his face above water. Or the little that was left of his face. I don't care how tough Willie is, that was the stuff nightmares are made of. For anyone."

She rested her elbows on her drawn-up knees, and pressed the heels of her hands to her eyes. "Dear God," she said softly. "You'd better go down to him, Giles. Being alone can't help."

"No. But I think it's you he needs, darling. I mean, I'm a chap, you see, and what he needs is a girl."

She lowered her hands and stared down at him. "Giles, you're not saying I should go to bed with Willie—?

"No, no, no, that would be sacrilege for him, and it would change a relationship neither of you wants to change. But all men are really little boys in some ways, and when they're hurt or have bad dreams they need to be cuddled up. That's really what would help him most, Modesty. He'll feel nice and secure and cared for and all that sort of thing. I mean, it was the same for me. I didn't even think of making love tonight, but I wanted you close to me. It makes all the bogey men go away, you see."

She gave a half laugh, without amusement. "Yes. As a matter of fact I do see, Giles. I'll tell you something only one other person in the world knows, apart from Willie. And he's a doctor, too. Sometimes, after capers where things have been very bad, I have a little weep. I can't help it. And then Willie Garvin takes me in his arms and just cuddles me, and after a while I'm fine again." She shook her head. "I never realised it could happen the other way round one day."

She got out of bed, belted an ankle-length misty blue velvet dressing gown about her, and bent to kiss Pennyfeather on the tip of his long nose. "After all this heart-searching," she said, "it had just better be Willie Garvin down there, doctor."

He had put on a standard lamp and was sitting on the long settee, wearing slacks and a shirt, idly flicking through a National Geographic. As she came into the room he looked up in surprise, then gave her a cheerful smile and started to rise. " 'Allo, Princess, Did I wake you? Sorry."

"Sit down, Willie love. No, you didn't wake me. It just seems a poor night for sleeping." She closed the door. "I see you've given up and got dressed. Is it the burns?"

"No, they're pretty good." He had not sat down but was prowling about aimlessly, hands in pockets. "I thought I might go out and walk about a bit, so I put some clothes on."

"I'll come with you, if that's what you want to do."

He made a wry grimace. "Well, by the time I got down 'ere I didn't fancy it so much. Then I thought I'd make a cup of tea, but that didn't grab me either. So I was just sitting around 'oping for inspiration."

She sat down at one end of the settee, turning a little so that her back was in the corner, and drew her feet up beside her, careful to keep the dressing grown from falling open. Normally it would not have mattered, for they could go naked without being particularly aware of it; but tonight she wanted to be especially careful not to cause a moment's misunderstanding.

He said, "Anything I can get you, Princess? A drink? Or how about a game of backgammon?"

She shook her head. "It's nice just to be quiet for a while. Come and sit with me, Willie." She patted the cushion beside her. When he obeyed, she slipped a hand through his arm and said, "Giles told me how you tried to keep Martel alive with mouth to mouth. I'm sorry."

He gave a small laugh, looking down at his hands in his lap. "I always thought I 'ad a strong stomach, but I'll be glad when that little memory's a bit further off."

"I won't talk about it any more, but I wanted you to know I knew." She reached up, slid an arm round his shoulders and drew him down against her, settling his head in the soft warm cushion formed by shoulder and breast. "I know what. You tell me a story, Willie."

She felt him relax a little, and heard his long exhalation. "What sort of story, Princess?"

"Oh . . . about one of your girls. Wait a minute. Put your feet up and get comfortable. There, is that all right?"

Another barely audible sigh, "That's fine, Princess. Let's see. Did I ever tell about the first girl I ever 'ad?"

"Wasn't that the caretaker's daughter at the orphanage? The one called Annie the Bang, that you won in a game of conkers?"

"Ah, I must 'ave told you. What about the second girl, Grace?" His words were leisurely now, and she could feel the tension slowly draining from him.

She said, "No. Grace is a new one."

"Well . . . I met 'er when I was fifteen, and the orphanage put me out to learn a trade. There were two other lads in the workshop with me, and we used to call 'er Amazing Grace . . . she was about thirty, I suppose, married to a bloke much older who ran this radio and TV repair shop where we worked. She was plump and chirpy, with a pretty face and a two-track mind. No interest in anything except bed sports and watching television. Any television, from university stuff to kid's stuff."

He gave a sleepy chuckle. "No problem about the TV. She even 'ad one fixed on the wall in 'er bedroom. But the old chap, Arthur, he wasn't interested in sex. Spent most days with his 'ead stuck inside TV sets, and I don't think he cared what she did. Anyway, what she used to do twice a day was appear in the workshop and say that 'er television was acting up, and she wanted one of us to come and see to it. Soon as you got up there, she pounced, and then you were busy on the bed for the next 'alf hour, with 'er giggling and whispering and full of ideas. She could've opened a school for it, I reckon."

Modesty smoothed a hand over his forehead. "Twice a *day*, Willie?"

"Regular as clockwork. Ten-thirty and five. The old chap must 'ave realised it was a farce, pretending her set was going wrong twice a day, but maybe he was grateful. And it suited us lads all right. We loved it. The five o'clock shift was best, because you got a cup of tea. after, so we worked out a roster for the three of us, to make sure we took proper turns. The only thing that bothered us a bit was that she kept the TV set switched on all the time, and she kept an eye on it too, no matter which way up she was."

Modesty felt laughter threatening to shake her, and struggled against it. There was growing drowsiness in his voice now as he went on, ". . . so you'd be going at it 'ammer and tongs, and suddenly there'd be some crucial bit in *Crossroads*, or whatever she was watching. Then she'd stop and 'old still till the crucial bit was over . . ."

His voice trailed to silence, but after several seconds he said sleepily, "What was I saying, Princess?"

"About Amazing Grace combining sex with watching television."

"M'mm. Well . . . one day I 'ad an idea for a bit of a giggle. She was a good sport, see. Bit of a giggle. Nobby was on five o'clock shift. Next day, I mean. So we . . . Charlie Gravett and me . . . we ran a flex up to the speaker of the television set. The one on the wall of 'er bedroom. Ran a flex up . . . with a mike the other end . . . so we could . . ."

His voice became a mumble, then with a deep sigh he slept. She looked down at the head of rumpled hair pillowed upon her, listened to the deep steady breathing, and felt a glad satisfaction. She had settled herself comfortably to begin with, and would have no need to stir. With luck, Willie Garvin would sleep quitely till sunrise now.

She looked up at the ceiling and thought, "You're not a bit clever, Giles, but you have a lovely gift." Then, with a small inward smile, she wondered if she would ever know what had happened that day in the bedroom of Amazing Grace.

four

Jeremy Silk lay face down on his bed, wearing pyjama trousers, while Nannie Prendergast massaged his bruised shoulder with embrocation.

After his morning's task he had presided at business meetings in Tetouan, Fez and Melilla before returning with all the usual security precautions to Le Dauphin in the early hours.

"You've done very well indeed today, Master Jeremy," she said, "and Nannie's well pleased with you."

"I can't claim ten out of ten though," he said with a touch of chagrin. "The meetings were satisfactory, but I was a bit indecisive during the Gautier operation. After I burned him down I saw Modesty Blaise standing there with Birot, and it seemed a good chance to get her out of the way. But I wasn't sure what you wanted, so I hesitated, and then the bottle caught me."

Her palms kneaded gently. "Well, I'm glad you didn't use the flame-thrower on her, dear. It would have confused the issue. El Mico was making an example of Gautier, and we don't want the working people we employ to have any doubts about that. Besides, you must always remember our Golden Rule: We never indulge in *unnecessary* violence. If it became *necessary* to kill Modesty Blaise, that would be a different matter, of course. Is your shoulder a little easier now, Jeremy?"

"Yes, very much so, thank you, Nannie. It wasn't too bad, just a bit stiff, but you've made it all better now." He turned on his back to look up at her. She wore a plain grey dressing gown over a high-necked white nightdress with broderie anglaise edging the bodice. Her hair was tied back with a small ribbon. As she moved away to wash her hands he felt the thrust of excitement in his loins.

It was his turn tonight, and Nannie was always scrupulously fair. She might withhold herself as a punishment if she was cross with you, but if it was your turn she would not dream of going to Dominic just because you were out working half the night. She had waited for Jeremy to return, as he had known she would, and listened to his report as he took his bath, scrubbing his back with the loofah just as she had done throughout the years since she had first come to the Silk family, soon after his eighth birthday, when they lived in Cairo. Like so much else in the life he and Dominic shared with Nannie Prendergast, bathtime was a ritual, one of many. If they could have imagined being deprived of such rituals, the concept would have induced a sense of panic.

She had dried her hands and was coming back to the bed now, wide-set eyes smiling conspiratorially. He shivered with excitement. She switched off the bedside lamp, and he heard the spine-tingling sound of wool slithering across cotton as she took off her dressing gown, then the rustle of cotton on flesh as she drew the nightdress over head. He saw the white blur of it in the darkness. She whispered the ritual words she had first said on his fourteenth birthday, when the staggering, tremendous, exquisite thing had first happened: "*Nannie's just going to pop in with you for a little while, till you're nice and warm.*"

After that it was the way it had always been, the way he never wanted to change, with the lemony smell of perfumed soap, the first tentative touchings, then the holdings, the unbelievable sensation of her firm warm breasts against his chest, the little kisses, the whispers and gentle guidance, the murmurs of encouragement, the gasping delight that seized him as she received him lingeringly into her.

The glorious twinings and manoeuvrings went on longer now, much longer, for he had achieved more control of himself over the years, but the essence of their ritual proceedings never varied, and at last she was kneeling astride his loins, possessing him. In the darkness he could see her eyes as she leant forward above him, whispering endearments calling him her little monkey. His hands were on the moving hips and his body arched beneath her, lifting her with a last long and enduring thrust as the spasms shook him.

They lay quietly for a little while, and as always he relived the wonder of that first time, when he had been dazed with revelation and delight. Then she slid off his body and out of the bed. He heard the rustle of her nightdress and dressing gown. Seconds later he felt her breath on his cheek and her hand on his brow.

"Night-night, Master Jeremy," she whispered. "And sleep well."

"Night-night, Nannie."

A gleam from the dim light in the hall as she opened the door, a glimpse of her silhouette, then the door closed and he was alone.

Jeremy Silk sighed and stretched luxuriously. It had been a really splendid day. He started to wonder, not for the first time, if Dominic did exactly the same things with Nannie when it was his turn, then quickly closed his mind against this forbidden field of speculation. Nannie had always treated both her boys alike in every way, but they never dared to discuss her or compare notes. On Dominic's fourteenth birthday she had stopped coming to Jeremy every night and started to come to him every other night. When he had shown sulky displeasure at this she had punished him by not entering his bed for six weeks. Some time later she had administered a similar punishment to Dominic, and had contrived to convey obliquely to Jeremy that it was for the same offence. Nannie would not tolerate jealousy, and it was better not to wonder about what happened when she was with the other brother.

Half an hour later Jeremy woke with a hand shaking him. The light was on, and Dominic, in slacks and a thin roll-neck shirt, was bending over him. He sat up, blinking. "What's wrong, Dom?"

"Plenty." His brother's face was pale, the freckles standing out sharply. "Baillie-Smythe's here."

"Here? But he was supposed to call us from two miles off-shore in the *Kythira*. Then we go out and pick up the—" he broke off sharply. "The Object."

"That's right, but unfortunately Gautier did just that, *six days ago*! Get something on and come down right away. Nannie's waiting." He turned and went out, trembling with fury. For several seconds Jeremy could not absorb what had been said, then he went cold with shock and scrambled out of bed. Three minutes later, when he entered the study, Nannie Prendergast was sitting behind the big desk and Dominic at one end of it.

A tall man, wearing a pea-jacket, sat in an upright chair a little way from the desk, long legs stretched in front of him. He had thick auburn hair, an aristocratic face, and a languid manner. This was Edmund St. Clair Baillie-Smythe, one of only five men who could have put a name to El Mico. Nobody was speaking.

Jeremy took the empty chair opposite Dominic, and nodded to Baillie-Smythe, who responded without expression. Nannie Prendergast wore a dark green dress and had her hair in a single plait. She looked scrubbed, as usual, and at first sight appeared to be cool and unruffled, also as usual. But the curiously unmatched features were too rigid, the posture unnaturally still, and Jeremy knew that she was very angry indeed.

"Captain Baillie-Smythe arrived only fifteen minutes ago, Jeremy," she said in a strained voice. "He reports that our task force carried out Operation Peacock successfully. The Object was conveyed by light aircraft to Turkey, as arranged, and Captain Baillie-Smythe received it while at anchor off Mersin some four days ahead of the expected time of delivery. He sailed at once, maintaining radio silence as instructed, until he arrived by night at the rendezvous two miles north of here last week. Then he made radio contact. That was on the Wednesday evening, unfortunately."

Dominic looked across at his brother and said, "Nannie was dining with the Yacht Club secretary, I had to go and check the new *maison* in Rabat, and your plane was late arriving, so we brought in Gautier to man the radio for a few hours. Edmund's call must have come in during that time."

Baillie-Smythe nodded. "It was logged at twenty-one thirty hours," he said in a slow, cultured voice. "Ten minutes later I got an answer in standard code to say Number Four would come to collect The Object. That's Gautier. He came out in the launch and I handed it over to him. He gave me fresh instructions. I was to sail at once and rendezvous off Algiers with the ship from Libya for transfer of small arms for the I.R.A. We waited two days at the rendezvous, and the Libyans didn't come. My orders were to keep radio silence, so in the end I brought the *Kythira* back. I still don't know what's gone wrong."

Jeremy Silk opened his mouth to ask a question, but left it unspoken and looked at Nannie Prendergast. She sat thinking for a few moments, then said, "I am sorry to tell you that Gautier was disloyal to us, Captain Baillie-Smythe. He turned traitor and he is now dead."

Baillie-Smythe pursed his lips and stared at the toes of his boots.

"I can accept no blame, Miss Prendergast," he said. "You've sent me orders by Gautier before, and I had no reason to believe that the orders didn't come from you on this occasion."

She said, "He did not discuss The Object with you, Captain? Did not ask questions?"

Baillie-Smythe shook his head. "No questions. In any case, I had no answers. The Object is code for whatever was in that steel box with the special lock and seals. I've no idea what that was."

She rested her broad, capable hands on the desk and said, "No blame attaches to you, Captain. Please anchor at Melilla tomorrow, and report here on Saturday morning for instructions. There is a good cargo of parts from stolen cars to be picked up in Malta for Naples, a delivery of girls to our agent in Latakia, and a quantity of base morphine to be collected by transfer off Izmir. We shall wish to devise an economical itinerary."

Baillie-Smythe stood up. He was less languid than usual, his eyes a little wary. "Have you a preferred time on Saturday, Miss Prendergast?"

"Eleven hundred hours will be suitable. May I say that we feel you acted promptly and wisely when the Libya rendezvous failed and you began to have doubts about the situation. There will be a suitable bonus, Captain. Thank you, and good night."

Dominic went to see Baillie-Smythe out. When he returned he said, "It's always possible that he and Gautier were in this together."

Jeremy shook his head. "Edmund has plenty of nerve, but he'd never come back and try to pitch us a story like that if it wasn't true."

"He would have no need to come back at all," Nannie Prendergast said in a tight voice. "This was Gautier alone. He was always a good opportunist. But all the same, I think Captain Baillie-Smythe must now go. He knows that something very valuable indeed has gone missing, and we have lost some authority in his eyes, I could tell. He might well start making inquiries on his own account, and I don't intend to tolerate competition in a search for The Object. Prevention is better than cure." She picked up the telephone and pressed the button which would ring the bell in the room above the boat house, where Little Krell slept.

Dominic rubbed his chin and said doubtfully, "Edmund is a gentleman, though, isn't he? And reliable. I mean, he's always done a jolly good job for us—"

She lifted a peremptory hand to silence him, then spoke into the phone, in French, very carefully, to make sure there was no misunderstanding. Half a minute later she put the phone down and said: "Captain Baillie-Smythe was *born* a gentleman, Dominic, but he turned his back on family, position, and duty. He is a black sheep. It is quite in order for another gentleman to *employ* such a person, if need be, but you are in no way beholden to him." She pushed a stray lock of hair back from her temple. "Beside, this is a very good time to begin shortening our roots. We *will* recover The Object, and then of course the others who know El Mico's identity must also go."

Jeremy nodded. "We'll want a complete cut-off, and that would include Edmund anyway. But why get Little Krell to do the job, Nannie? Dom or I would have seen to it for you."

"I know that, Jeremy dear, but this was a good moment to start Little Krell on serious duty. It will bind him to us more closely, and that's a wise precaution, because we might use him right up to the end of the cut-off, leaving him as the last to go."

There was a short silence, then Dominic said, "What I don't understand it why Gautier decided to grab The Object. I mean, he didn't know what it was. Only we three knew that."

"Don't keep saying 'I mean' please, Master Dominic, it's rather common. As for Gautier, it was sufficient that he knew this operation was something very big. So big that we would be retiring when it was completed. He took a gamble, of course, because once he'd broken open the box there could be no going back, but it wasn't a huge gamble in the circumstances. He got Captain Baillie-Smythe out of the way, and he was clever enough to steal the month's takings when he ran for it. That stopped us suspecting anything worse. It meant we would assign three or four men to seek and kill him, which was much better than having every soul we could muster hunting him twenty-four hours a day."

"It was almost too clever," said Jeremy Silk. "One of the men we assigned was Sadeen, and they dug his body out of that hotel, so it looks as if he'd caught up with Gautier and was close to putting him down."

"What the hell does it matter?" Dominic said impatiently. "Maybe you're still half asleep, Jeremy, but you don't seem to grasp what's happened. Gautier made off with The Object. When he saw what it was, he knew he had to find a buyer for it, and meanwhile he'd have to hide it somewhere safe. He wasn't an idiot, so he must have hidden it well before he turned up at the Hotel Ayachi. I'll bet anything you like he didn't have it with him there, but I'll also bet he was the only man in the world who knew where it was hidden . . . *and you killed him yesterday morning*."

Jeremy said angrily, "Are you blaming me for that? Or Nannie?"

"Of course I'm not, stupid! I'm just saying what's happened—"

He broke off, and both men stared in dismay. Nannie Prendergast sat with hands clasped on the desk, and though her chin was lifted so that she stared across the study, tears were running down her face. They moved to her at once, taking a hand, patting a shoulder, almost in panic.

"It's all right, Nannie."

"Please don't cry."

"You mustn't—"

"We'll find it somehow."

"Everything will be all right."

"And anyway, we've got everything we want."

She drew in a long breath and stood up, angrily dabbing her eyes with a handkerchief. "I'm sorry, Master Jeremy, Master Dominic. Whatever will you think of me? It's just . . ." she moved out from behind the desk and crossed slowly to the window, drawing back the curtains a little to look out at the night sky. "It's just that I've tried so hard for so long."

Dominic said, "Never mind, Nannie—" and broke off again as his brother waved him irritably to silence.

Standing with one shoulder to the wall her oddly attractive face in profile to them as she looked up into the sky, she said musingly, "So many difficult years. Oh, I had nothing to worry about at first. I wasn't much more than a girl when I came to look after two little boys in that nice house in Cairo, where their Daddy was an English diplomat. But I'd been well trained as a nannie—not just at the school in Tunbridge Wells, but from childhood, you know, for it was old Grannie Prendergast who brought me up, and *she* had been a nannie with top-drawer gentry for forty years, going right back to the Boer War days."

The corner of Nannie Prendergast's mouth lifted briefly in a reminiscent smile. "She was very strict of course . . . iron hard when it came to teaching me proper values and the ways of the old gentry. Some of the modern misses at training school would have been sent away with a flea in the ear if Grannie had been in charge there, I can tell you. Oh dear, what was I saying? Yes . . . about those two little boys I came to look after in Cairo long ago, and how we were all so happy together . . . until that day two years later, when the aeroplane crashed, and their Mummy and Daddy were killed."

Jeremy sat quietly on the edge of the desk, Dominic leaned against the wall. Both were silent. They remembered well enough what had happened, but they had never before heard Nannie speak of it in this way, almost as if talking to herself.

"There were some relatives," she said in a faraway voice, "but none who wished to be troubled. And there was only a little money, for your parents were gentry who lived up to their position. But there was the small trust . . . and the old solicitor who asked if I would be willing to look after the little boys." She sighed. "I knew they just wished to be rid of the problem. I knew the master's pension and the trust income would never be enough, but I said I would manage, and that I'd take care of Master Jeremy and Master Dominic . . ."

Her voice faded. She stared sightlessly into the darkness, seeing the past.

Even at the time it had all seemed unsurprising to her, almost inevitable. Within weeks the jeweller in Qasr el Nil had sought to bring her to his bed, and instead she had procured for him the red-haired Irish girl who was a hairdresser at the Hotel Leroy but had no work permit. It had been easy to blackmail her into acquiescence.

Other men . . . other girls. And mostly she needed no lever to persuade them, for it seemed there was something within her that made them afraid. The money came in. The Foreign Office had paid rent on the house for six months, and when that expired she moved to a small neat house across the river in El Guiza. She would not consider putting the boys to boarding school in

England, but continued to send them to the privately run Ecole Anglaise, which was attended by many children of Cairo's expatriates.

The chance meeting with Mentash, through one of the girls, had opened new horizons. From him she had learned the complexities of the drug trade, the extent of the vice trade, the possibilities of the murder trade. After five years she had acquired enough money to lease part of Le Dauphin and build the English country house there. It was a good position, centrally placed for control of operations throughout North Africa and the Mediterranean. The last major thing she had done before leaving Cairo was to have Mentash killed. He had begun to have delusions of grandeur, and wanted to challenge *The Network*, which was madness. The key to success at this time was to remain unobtrusive and avoid falling foul of *The Network*. Master Jeremy was then sixteen, and Mentash was his first killing. She had been very proud to see how well he had done it.

Then . . . the years of quiet progress and consolidation, of training for the boys, of steadily increasing their experience in all areas of the business. Control over the widespread activities was not easy, but the creation of El Mico immediately following the end of *The Network* era had been a great help. El Mico inspired fear, and fear was a potent discipline.

Her brow pressing against the cool glass of the leaded window, she wondered where the years had flown. Throughout all that time she had sought to find the master-stroke which would complete her work in the only way that could satisfy her. She had waited, and she had found it—what the boys code-named The Big One. It had called for infinitely delicate planning, for negotiations with other groups, playing one against the other, and for betrayal, murder, and a series of cut-off operations.

She had foreseen events long before the so-called experts. She had spent months in the planning and briefing. At precisely the right moment, amid massive chaos, the Inside Group had seized The Object. They had conveyed it to the P.L.O. group, not knowing them to be enemies. The P.L.O. group had killed them and sealed The Object in the steel box. They in turn had been killed by the Kurds at the rendezvous south of Mosul, and the box had been delivered to Nico Razak in return for one thousand automatic rifles. Razak had flown it into Turkey and delivered it to Captain Baillie-Smythe, off Mersin. The four men of the P.L.O. group had been the last to know what The Object was.

And now . . . Gautier had ruined everything. She hoped he would burn in hell for ever.

With an effort she straightened her back and turned towards the two men watching her. "You were wrong, Master Jeremy," she said quietly. "Wrong when you said a few moments ago that it didn't matter about losing The Object since we already have everything we want."

"I just meant . . . well, we're very comfortably placed, Nannie."

"Yes." Her eyes and mouth grew hard. "But we are in *trade*, Jeremy. I have accepted it through all these years because there was no other choice, but I will not have you and Dominic go through your lives in trade. Oh, I know people today don't look down upon it, but a principle is a principle, and you cannot be a gentleman if you're in trade."

"Yes, Nannie, you've always said that, but—"

"It's not polite to interrupt, Master Dominic."

"I beg your pardon, Nannie."

"Very well. Now you know what I've said so many times. When our ship comes in, we shall go to England and buy a beautiful estate there. A manor house, with farmland and stables, outbuildings and cottages, and acres of woodland. That calls for an enormous sum of money today, not just for the purchase but for the upkeep. As young gentry it will be quite wrong for you to work, and quite wrong for you to live on capital, so several millions will be needed. As Jeremy says, we are comfortably placed, but that is in terms of going concerns, not in terms of assets we can realise." She looked from one to the other, and her face softened. "Now perhaps you understand why Nannie was so upset just now."

They muttered embarrassed assent. Then Jeremy said diffidently, "If it's a question of finding where Gautier hid The Object, perhaps he said something to Modesty Blaise when they were trapped in that earthquake together."

She smiled and gave a brisk nod. "I have that well in mind, Master Jeremy. We must explore any other lines that occur to us of course, and we must *all* put our thinking caps on. Two heads are better than one. But I'm quite certain that our main concern must be to keep a very close eye on Modesty Blaise."

Dominic said, "And if we think she may know something?"

"Then we shall have to question her about it with great determination. But first things first. I think, Dominic, that when Little Krell has put Captain Baillie-Smythe down, you must take the launch and go out to the *Kythira*."

"As El Mico?"

"Yes, of course, dear. Please think before you speak. Tell Mr. Jamieson that he is to be in command, as Captain Baillie-Smythe is taking some leave. He is to sail now and anchor at Melilla tomorrow, where he will receive further orders." She looked at the grandfather clock in the corner. "I expect Little Krell will report very soon, so you might as well start to get ready. Still time for the Sandman to return to *you*, Master Jeremy, so it's back to bed and off to sleep again now. Come and give Nannie a kiss, both of you, then away you go. We'll have a good chat about everything after breakfast."

Three hundred yards away, Edmund St. Clair Baillie-Smythe stood in the cover of the trees which fringed the moonlit beach of the little bay where he had left the small tender. He had come alone from the *Kythira*, as he always did. Nobody aboard could know exactly where he reported to El Mico or his representative.

At this moment he was less concerned with El Mico's security than with his own safety. He had an instinct for danger which had kept him alive for thirty-nine years so far, and it was sending out powerful warnings tonight. This was why he had not taken the natural path from the house to the bay, but had swung west to come down through the trees. Nobody had followed him from the house. He had waited in the shadows of the hedge after leaving, to make sure of that. But there was still Little Krell. She had never used him for executions before, but there was always a first time.

Baillie-Smythe usually thought of Nannie Prendergast as She. He could not think of her as Nannie, and though he addressed her as Miss Prendergast he found it difficult to associate her with the name. She attracted him enormously. He had lusted after her for several years now, but had long since abandoned any thought of being able to indulge his desires. Once, in the early days, he had begun very warily, by word and look, to test her response to him; and had almost instantly abandoned the project. She had said nothing but the shock-wave of anger and menace emanating from her had been almost tangible. Even the well-tried Baillie-Smythe nerves had jumped with fear, and the attempt had never been repeated.

He was used to the whole El Mico set-up now, but it was still weird, he reflected. Bloody weird, when you really thought about it. Nannie and her boys. They were still frozen in attitudes of fifteen years ago. Master Jeremy and Master Dominic, for God's sake . . . the nannie-like proverbs that peppered her conversation, even when She was laying on an execution. *Familiarity breeds contempt, remember. Well begun is half done. The early bird catches the worm.*

Then that crazy house. Ye olde English country house off the coast of Morocco. She was a throwback, and She had made the boys into throwbacks. The *boys?* He shook his head. She even had *him* thinking of them as boys now. Not surprising. They talked and acted like fifth-formers half the time. But the other half . . . by God they were dangerous when they took on the El Mico persona. He did not think there was any mental change on such occasions, simply that whatever they did was akin to a game for them, an exciting pretence, remote from reality. But it was real enough for the man or woman who died under either pair of El Mico's immensely capable hands.

Baillie-Smythe moved very slowly parallel to the small beach, keeping just within the trees and checking every shadow. Nobody lurked in wait for him. He returned to his original position, wondering if his instinct had played him false. In the moment when She had dismissed him with a word of approval, he had felt the warning bells ring in his head. It was as if She had read the thought that flashed into his mind only minutes before—the notion that it might be well worth initiating his own private search for whatever was in that damn steel box Gautier had stolen. The Object, whatever it might be, was up for grabs. So finders keepers, losers weepers, as She herself might say.

For the tenth time he very slowly scanned the crescent of sand. No movement, no hiding place, no shapeless rock which might prove to be a crouching man. The boat rocked gently in a couple of feet of water, where he had dropped the little anchor.

At last he shrugged. The warning bells must have been wrong for once. She couldn't read thoughts. He grinned inwardly. Just as well She couldn't, for if She'd known some of his fantasising about her She might have sent one of the boys with a cheese wire for his neck. Or some other little gimmick. As it was, he had nothing to worry about.

Yet when he stepped from the cover of the trees, he kept the Heckler and Koch P9 automatic in his hand with the safety off. Neither hurrying nor dawdling, he crossed the fifty yards to the sea's edge, watching the boat house. He could see only the top of it, the gabled upper floor where Little Krell lived, for the building lay on the far side of the bay's eastern arm, fronting on the next bay. There were no windows on this side, and no gleam of light from the boat house below.

He walked into the sea, checked that nobody lay huddled in the tender, pulled the anchor free and tossed it inboard, then gave a push and climbed in quickly over the stern. The outboard started at the first pull, and the boat responded smoothly. As he took her through the jaws of the bay he pushed the automatic back in his pocket and relaxed, a little surprised to find how taut his nerves and muscles had become. He grimaced ruefully in the darkness. Apologies to She for his suspicions. He must have let his imagination run away with him.

The engine stopped abruptly. When he tried to re-start there was resistance. He tilted the outboard, peering astern as the propeller came out of the water, and swore as he saw the tangle of netting that jammed it. The boat lurched abruptly, lifting at the stern. He looked quickly over his shoulder, and shock sent adrenalin pumping through him as he saw the monster coming out of the sea over the bow, black and brown, shapeless against the moon, then no longer shapeless. Short tree-trunk legs in footless black tights, immense arms, squat body filling a leotard-like top.

Edmund St. Clair Baillie-Smythe's brain was lit by a flash of terrible understanding. Little Krell, the tireless swimmer. Waiting. Under the bow of the moored tender. Clinging to one of the rope handles piercing the gunwale. Endlessly patient. Letting the boat carry him out. Trailing a strip of netting to jam the propeller, so that the man at the tiller, the man marked for death, would face astern to deal with it, and—

Captain Baillie-Smythe twisted violently, a hand diving for the gun in his pocket. Too slow. Like a great block of sorbo Little Krell bounced forward, a long arm flashing out, hand rigid as a spear-head driving in under the heart, cutting off breath, paralysing, bringing the handsome auburn head forward and down as the body doubled over in helpless reaction. Then the axe-hand to the exposed back of the neck, shattering the vertebrae.

Little Krell looked down at the body in the well of the boat and said apologetically, "Pardon, capitaine." He detached the small anchor, slid over the side with the end of the rope made fast round his waist, and began to swim back to the bay with the boat in tow, using a leisurely sidestroke.

A white-eared bulbul skimmed low over the sunlit waters of the pool. With a flick of the tail it banked across the bougainvillea hung walls, dipped towards the flower beds, then darted away over the dwarf pines and the great black patch on the grass where a man had died.

Willie Garvin and Dr. Giles Pennyfeather sat together on the swing seat. Modesty Blaise, in a cotton shirt and very short denim shorts, paced the matt tiles of the pool surround, arms across her middle, holding her elbows. Willie saw the dark blue eyes grow darker still with anger, and winced inwardly, wishing he had a newspaper or magazine he could pretend to be studying as a means of indicating that he had no part in the present dispute. As an alternative, he lowered his gaze to contemplate her long brown legs as she turned and paced away again. Without prejudice, they remained the best he had ever seen, and watching them was an occupation of which he never tired.

Unabashed or unaware, Dr. Giles Pennyfeather persisted. "I'm simply telling you that you're wrong, darling," he said firmly. "That's all."

She turned to pace back, a muscle tightening at her jaw. "Well, I'm glad that's all, Giles. I thought for a moment you might be telling me what to do."

"Oh, I suppose I'm telling you what I think you *ought* to do. Or rather, ought not to do."

"Oh, don't be such a smug prig, I've decided to go after whoever killed Martel, and Willie's with me. That means we have to get you right out of the firing line until it's time for you to take up your new job." She stood still for a moment. "Wait a minute. You're not a prig and not smug, so I'm sorry I said that, but the rest stands."

"All right, darling. Now what I'm saying is simply that I wish you wouldn't go after whoever murdered poor old Martel, because it's the wrong thing to do."

"For God's sake, Giles, you were the one who hoped I *had* killed El Mico! Remember?"

"Oh, yes. The sooner a frightful bugger like that gets knocked off, the better for everyone. He was here, he did that ghastly thing, and you went hurtling after him. Naturally I hoped you'd get the bastard. You were on the spot and you sort of represented all the ordinary decent people who hate such things—"

"I'm not ordinary and decent."

"That's irrelevant. Anyway, once you failed to catch him, that changed the situation. Because of the time factor, you see. If you go after him now, it's for the wrong reason."

She stared, then said softly. "What's my reason, Giles?"

"Well, vanity really."

"*What?*"

Willie Garvin held his breath. Pennyfeather gave her a smile that was full of affection. "Perhaps I'm explaining badly," he said. "What I mean is, if Martel, or whatever his name was, had been murdered by a flame-thrower down in, say, the Gran Socco, you wouldn't decide to hunt down whoever did it. But Martel was a guest in your house and was murdered here, and that's an affront to you. So really you want to get El Mico because of what he did to *you*, not what he did to Martel."

She considered him, tight-lipped. Then: "Don't criticise me for defending the guest under my roof, Giles."

"Eh? Of course not, dopey. I'd help you do that, or at least I'd try to. But you're not defending Martel now. He's dead. What you're planning is to avenge him, and I think you're wrong. If you want to do something for the poor bloke, it would make much more sense if you tried to carry out his last wishes. Well, I suppose those were last wishes he was babbling when you were trapped after the earthquake. A bit incoherent, but you wrote it all down that night, I remember. And we've got the talisman, the strap with something in it, because it was burnt off his wrist, and I gathered it up with the rest of my gear after I'd finished bandaging Willie, and it's still in my case. I'm sure you could work out what Martel really wanted, you're marvellous at that sort of thing, and it seems a much better idea to me than knocking off El Mico." Pennyfeather paused, thought for a moment, then added. "That's all, really. I simply think you're wrong, Modesty, but there's no need to get in a temper about it."

She caught her breath, but her face was impassive as she said in a flat voice, "Temper? Who's in a temper?"

"You are. I can tell by your gluteal muscles."

"My what muscles?"

"Gluteal. What we in the medical profession call the bum. Yours goes all tight and clenched when you're angry. I could see it when you were prowling about just now, each side twitching in turn. You ask Willie."

"Oh, Jesus," said Willie, and stared fixedly in front of him, struggling against an explosion of laughter.

She leaned towards Pennyfeather. "Are you saying it *sags* when I'm not angry?"

He chuckled indulgently. "No, of course not, darling. It's jolly nice. But when you're angry it goes clenched, like it is now. Honestly it does. Willie, you're nearest. Give it a prod and you'll see what I mean."

Willie Garvin uttered a strangled refusal. Modesty's head snapped round. "And I suppose you're getting a good giggle out of this bum-watching doctor, Willie Garvin?" Lips pressed together and stretched in an attempted smile of denial, Willie shook his head mutely, feeling as if he were giving an impression of a ventriloquist's doll.

She turned from the two men and stalked away across the grass to the patio, then into the house, very conscious that her buttocks were indeed twitching but unable to prevent it. They watched her go, and when she had disappeared Pennyfeather said, "You see what I mean? Sort of clenched."

74

Willie exhaled a long breath. "Giles, you're a genius," he said. "I've seen the Princess keep 'er cool under all kinds of conditions, with friend and foe alike, but you're unique. You can actually make 'er hopping mad."

"Yes, I'm afraid we've upset her a bit."

"We?" Willie's voice rose indignantly, then he shrugged and gave a gloomy shake of his head. "I'm dying for a cup of coffee, but I'm not going into the 'ouse for a bit."

"I'll go and give Moulay a shout—"

"No, you won't. We'll just batten down the 'atches and sit 'ere nice and quiet for a while."

She was half-way up the stairs, going nowhere in particular, when the image of Willie's anguished face and mutely wagging head rose up before her, and she was seized by a totally unexpected snuffle of laughter. She stopped, and as she replayed the scene in her mind the laughter grew until she had to turn and sit down on the stairs, leaning against the banisters, almost silent now but with her body shaking.

After a little while the spasm passed, and she sat there with hands between her knees, absorbed in thought, unseeing. Moulay passed across the hall but ignored her after a single quick glance, and continued about his business. It was not the first time he had seen her thought-struck in the middle of going somewhere or doing something.

Two minutes later she went downstairs to the kitchen, and after another ten minutes carried a tray of coffee into the garden. Willie and Pennyfeather started to get up but she said, "Stay there." As they watched in uncertain silence she set the tray down on the low garden table, then moved to stand in front of them and turned round. "Note the condition of the behind, messieurs," she said.

They exchanged a glance, then Pennyfeather reached out and prodded a buttock with one long finger.

"Unclenched," he said.

"But not sagging," Willie added firmly.

"Good." She pulled a chair up to the table, sat down, and began to pour coffee. "You were right, Giles. It was vanity. Or perhaps injured pride, but let's not quibble. You pop upstairs and fetch that strap so we can have a look at the talisman. Oh, and will you bring the pad from my dressing table, please, where I jotted down those cryptic ramblings? Then we'll see if we can decipher Bernard Martel's last wishes."

five

From the window of the small flat, Sir Gerald Tarrant watched the first rays of the sun pick out the white dome of Sacré Coeur across the rooftops of Montmartre.

"There," said Modesty Blaise. She had emerged from the kitchen two or three minutes before, and stood with an arm linked through his, wearing a gingham pinafore, still carrying a wooden spoon.

"Thank you very much," said Tarrant. "Of course, the trendy thing these days is to wince if your attention is called to anything as common as a sunset, but I like them myself. I'm always awed by the thought that each one is unique." He drank from his glass of white wine.

"You get some jolly impressive ones in Chad," said Dr. Giles Pennyfeather. "A bit garish, like rainbow ice cream, but impressive."

From the kitchen Willie called, "Oscar Wilde said they're old-fashioned, and to admire 'em was a sign of provincialism of temperament."

"Silly bugger," Pennyfeather remarked.

"You're at least half right, Giles," Modesty said. "I don't know if Oscar was silly, but he always seems much too pleased with himself for my liking. Willie? How do you know clever things like what Oscar Wilde said?"

"Ah, that was Veronica. Remember the girl I brought along to the Newmarket races last year? She was at Cambridge, doing a thesis on Wilde, and most nights I 'ad to spend hours listening while she 'eld forth—" His voice changed, taking on a note of alarm. "Princess! Quick, it's *moving*!"

"He's only watching some soup," said Modesty, and went through into the kitchen.

Pennyfeather chuckled. "It's funny with Willie, you know. Modesty says he's marvellous on a Robinson Crusoe basis. Plonk him down in the middle of nowhere and he'll come up with a tasty meal, but he's hopeless in a kitchen. Mind you," Pennyfeather added handsomely, "I'm not all that great myself."

Tarrant lowered himself into an armchair and looked about him. He knew that between them Modesty and Willie had several *pied à terre* in various parts of the world. This one, off Place du Terte on the heights of Montmartre, was simple but remarkably pleasant. Tarrant was grateful to whatever winds of chance had brought Modesty to Paris at this particular time, for to be in her company was always a joy to him.

He had recently been persuaded to postpone his retirement, and had come to Paris only this morning for a meeting with his opposite number in French Intelligence, René Vaubois, head of Direction de la Surveillance du Territoire. Vaubois greeted him with the news that Modesty Blaise had telephoned an hour earlier with an invitation to dine at her flat that evening. When told that Tarrant would be in Paris she had at once extended the invitation to include him. Out of what he acknowledged to himself was an element of possessiveness, Tarrant had been careful to leave his hotel that evening in good time to ensure that he would arrive at least twenty minutes ahead of René Vaubois.

He glanced across at Pennyfeather, who was absently fingering a tarnished silver coin. They had met before, in England, and if Tarrant found it surprising that Modesty should choose this gauche and unworldly doctor as a companion, he did not let it show. It was clear that not only Modesty, but Willie also thought highly of their odd friend, which was more than good enough for Tarrant.

Willie came out of the kitchen with a look of relief. "Talk about intrepid," he said. "There's the Princess alone in there with pots and pans bubbling away all over the stove, and God-knows-what 'appening in the oven, and she's not showing a sign of panic." He poured himself a glass of wine. "Go on, Giles, show it to Sir Gerald."

"The talisman? Yes, of course."

Tarrant took the coin. It was silver, a little smaller than a 2p. piece, but heavier. On the obverse was a bust of Napoleon and the words *Napoleon Empereur*. The reverse bore the inscription *République Française* and the denomination, *1 franc*, enclosed in a laurel wreath. What appeared to be the date was given as *An.12*. After a little reflection Tarrant realised that this must stand for Année 12, the twelfth year of Napoleon's reign.

"This is a talisman?" he said.

"That's the word." Willie handed him a half sheet of paper with some lines of typing on it. "And 'ere's a few more words to go with it."

Pennyfeather said, "They're what this chap babbled who was—"

"Belt up, Giles," Willie broke in, and at the same moment came a protesting cry of "No, Giles!" from the kitchen. Willie went on patiently, "We decided we'd just let Sir G. *look* at the stuff to begin with, because telling 'im the circumstances might set up preconceived ideas. Remember?"

Pennyfeather frowned, thought for a while, then shook his head. "No. I must have been not listening, I expect. It's rather a failing of mine, I'm afraid. My mind sort of slips away and thinks about something else." He gave a sudden hoot of laughter. "I remember when I was a medical student old Frensham was smitten down by a sort of seizure right in the middle of one of his lectures. The other students said they owed it all to me because I'd enraged him so much by not listening, and they had a whip-round to buy me a new stethoscope as a mark of their esteem, because he wasn't very popular, you see, and I'd lost mine. I felt sorry for him myself, but it was quite funny to see the way everybody absolutely *sprang* forward when he hit the floor, jostling to get hold of a bit of the poor old sod and demonstrate their medical skill." He nodded approvingly at Tarrant. "But anyway, it's a jolly good idea, Sir Gerald."

Tarrant looked baffled. Willie said, "He means that it's a good idea for you to look at what you've got without being told anything. The rest was a digression."

"That's right," Pennyfeather agreed. "You carry on. I'll go and see if I can help Modesty."

Her voice from the kitchen said, "You set foot in here and I'll kill you, Giles."

He dropped back in his chair, unabashed. "Right-o, darling. As long as you can manage."

Tarrant collected himself and looked down at the piece of paper. On it had been typed some words and uncompleted sentences.

Le talisman.

Aladdin. Peacock. Shadow.

By June. By anything.

He is in Villefranche. Take the talisman to Georges Martel.

The oath. It must be honoured. Aladdin has it. *Pas la vie*(?) Peacock. Shadow. Enough for a thousand women. Shake, shake. Georges must bargain by June.

Tarrant read the words again, then yet again before opening his mind to whatever conscious or subconscious associations they might bring.

Talisman. Had the famous lamp been a *talisman* for Aladdin? A strained association, surely, but leave it without going too deep. Peacock . . . shadow. What was the Tennyson line? *Now sleeps the crimson petal* etcetera, then the next bit . . . *now droops the milk-white peacock like a shadow.* Yes? No, no, no, the word in the poem wasn't shadow, but ghost . . . *like a ghost.* No association there.

His mind roved on. Presumably something was to occur by June. 'By anything' held no meaning for him. The name Georges Martel, who was presumably in Villefranche, rang no bells. Then came the oath . . . *it* must be honoured . . . Aladdin has *it*. The pronoun here must surely refer to two different things, the first to the oath, the second to . . . what?

The sound of the door buzzer broke his train of thought. Willie said, "I'll go." Modesty came through from the kitchen, without her pinafore now, and shut the door. "All under control," she said. Willie returned from the hall with René Vaubois, a slender man, very well dressed with a baby smooth face and placid eyes.

"My dear Modesty," he said, "what a delight."

"It's good to see you again, René."

He took her hands, studied her carefully for a moment or two, then kissed her on both cheeks. "I hope I can be of help," he said, a little apologetically, "but you must first tell me what it is all about."

"After dinner, René. Now what will you drink? Willie can fix it while I introduce you to our very good friend, Dr. Giles Pennyfeather."

On a rooftop a hundred yards away, Dominic Silk and a dark stocky man stood by a tripod on which was mounted a piece of apparatus the size of a portable typewriter but of different proportions.

Dominic said, "Will it work at this distance?" He spoke in French, and looked like a Frenchman. His hair and stubble of beard had been darkened, and he wore a beret, a jacket, and denim dungarees.

The stocky man said, "It will work up to six hundred metres. The laser beam is directed on to the window, and some of the light is reflected back. Any sound within the room causes the glass of the window to oscillate, like an ear drum. We pick up these variations on the photo-multiplier and convert it back to speech." He held a headphone to one ear and made some adjustments to the controls.

Dominic said, "Will reception be clear?"

The stocky man shrugged. "With luck. Background noise can be a problem sometimes, especially if they are at table and there is the clatter of china and cutlery. If you wished for more certain results you should have asked for an electronic device to be planted."

"I would be surprised," said Dominic, "if you could enter that flat without discovery, and also surprised if they have not checked it for electronic bugs in the last hour."

"Like that? Then laser surveillance is the only way. Who are these people?"

Dominic's head came round sharply, and it seemed he smiled in the darkness, though perhaps it was not a smile. "The people I work for," he said, "have paid the people you work for twenty thousand dollars for this technical assistance, I do not think your employers will be pleased with you if they are informed by my employers that you became inquisitive."

The stocky man shook his head and waved a hand in negation. "Just an idle question," he said. "Let us forget that I spoke."

Sir Gerald Tarrant and René Vaubois stood on the small balcony with cigars. They had dined well, and were enjoying the night air while Modesty and Willie cleared the oval gate-leg table and let the leaves down to make more space in the room.

Pennyfeather was in the larger bedroom trying to make a telephone call to Moundou, in Chad, hoping to speak to somebody in the two-hut hospital there, where he had inadvertently left his best suit behind. His voice could be heard throughout the flat, full of surprise and indignation. It had been established that there were fewer than five thousand telephones in the whole of Chad, and this, together with the memory image of Pennyfeather's best suit and the sound of his astonishing French, had combined to induce an almost uncontrollable hilarity in Willie Garvin.

Vaubois drew on the excellent cigar and exhaled gently, looking out across the cluster of rooftops, remembering a time not long ago when he had been marked down for killing. It was little more than half a mile from this spot that the scene had been played out. There had been five men to do the job, all very expert, but the night chosen had by chance been a night when Modesty Blaise and Willie Garvin were with him. He remembered looking down on the eerie, chilling scene in the courtyard as moonlit figures of friend and foe wove patterns of deadly struggle amid the shadows.

"Strange," he said softly, "that neither you nor I would stand here tonight, my old friend, but for our young hostess."

Tarrant nodded. "I was remembering, too," he said. "It's like a colour film inside my head, René. I can see it whenever I wish."

"Yes." It had been worse for Tarrant, much worse, Vaubois reflected. He had suffered weeks of torture and deprivation before Modesty Blaise had found him when everyone else was sure he was dead. But to bring him out from captivity, half crippled and desperately weak as he had been then, she had first had to fight what must surely have been the hardest battle of her life, unarmed and naked against an opponent of matchless power. And Tarrant, lying exhausted and helpless on cold stone beside the black underground pool, had watched her win that impossible victory.

"When one has seen her like that," said Vaubois, "it is hard to recognise her as the same girl who sat with us at table tonight. One thinks of her as taller, bigger, more . . . more Amazonian. But she is not any of these things."

Tarrant laughed gently. "I know that curious feeling all too well. In fact I was once able to get a few brief words from Willie on the subject. He says she can take an Aspect upon her by an act of will, like the gods of legend, magnifying all her powers. He said it so earnestly that he was obviously having a joke at my expense, but I think there's an element of truth in it."

Modesty parted the curtains and came out on to the little balcony. Both men turned to her, studying her with new interest following their exchange. "Coffee and brandy when you're ready," she said. "Or port or a liqueur if you prefer it. Giles has decided to abandon his best suit, which I assure you only a man with nerves of steel would care to wear anyway, but he's had a nice chat with a girl on the International Exchange and recommended something for her catarrh. The great thing is that he was kept busy while we stacked all the washing up in the machine before he could volunteer. And why are you looking at me like that, you two?"

René Vaubois spread a hand. "For pleasure, *ma chère*."

She smiled and shook her head, a little puzzled. "Well . . . when you're ready."

She turned back into the room, and after a moment Vaubois murmured diffidently, "It is a little difficult to see what attraction the young doctor holds for her."

Tarrant nodded. "You're not the first to wonder. But I think among other things she admires his generosity."

"Generosity? But he is poor, Gerald. Well scrubbed, clean and fresh, but with no possessions, surely? He was even saying with great amusement at dinner how the Chad authorities had failed to pay him for five months."

"Generosity of spirit, René. You and I, yes, and Modesty too, had a little smile about the girl on the International Exchange with catarrh. But not Giles. Now listen, and doubt me if you wish, but I half believe that the girl's problem will be helped, not because Giles knows some wonderful cure-all, but because over the next few days he will spend some time thinking about the girl.

Just that. He will be *concerned* for her, will try to picture her as he would wish her to be."

Vaubois stared. "Do you speak of psychic healing?"

"I've no idea. I'm simply telling you what Modesty has told me. She says it works to a remarkable degree, and she seems quite unsurprised by this. The point is that Giles doesn't do it as deliberate practice, and he's no mystic. He thinks about his patients in this way because it's his nature to do so, I suppose. And it isn't only Modesty who likes him, you know. Willie has a great affection for him. He once described Pennyfeather to me as a man of infinite generosity."

Vaubois tipped the ash carefully from his cigar. "They continually surprise me, those two," he said. "And I find myself continually curious about them. Let us go in and see what it will be this time."

Fifteen minutes later, as Modesty took his glass and poured another brandy, Vaubois said, "That is the whole story?"

Willie said, "What more do you want, René? A plot by Liechtenstein to conquer the world?"

"It is just that I am puzzled. When Modesty telephoned this morning she said she would like all the information I could give her on Bernard Martel, alias Louis Gautier. We still have strong connections in North Africa, of course, but I did not know if we had any information at all on this man. In fact his French passport was genuine. His real name is Bernard Martel, and when I discovered how much information we had on him I was a little concerned, for in theory I have no authority to give out such information. However, I am a poor theorist. Now I learn that Martel was buried in an earthquake with Modesty and also with another man, who tried to kill him but who died in a later tremor. You tell me that Martel was a guest in Modesty's house, and that a criminal known as El Mico, on whom we have a file, succeeded in killing him there. At once I imagine that Modesty wishes to seek out El Mico and deal with him, but no. She wishes simply to elucidate, and then to carry out, what she thinks may have been Bernard Martel's last wishes." Vaubois shrugged and shook his head. "I am puzzled because it seems . . . small."

Modesty said, "We don't spend *all* our time fighting to save the world from Liechtenstein and suchlike."

"No. But I would have thought it might be your wish to go after El Mico."

"So would I, but Giles is bent on improving my character."

Tarrant laughed aloud. Vaubois made a helpless gesture and opened the document case he had brought with him. "Well, let me summarise," he said, "and since you also asked me about a Georges Martel, of Villefranche, I will deal with him at the same time. They were brothers, born in Corsica, in the town of Bonifacio, Bernard being two years older than Georges. Their father was and is a baker with his own shop. Their mother died when they were in their early teens. She was a Moroccan who emigrated to Corsica. Both boys grew up bilingual, speaking Arabic and French. Your friend Bernard was a serious boy, Georges was often in trouble. Bernard went into the army on leaving school, and did well. He became an officer in Military Intelligence and was later attached to S.D.E.C.E. for undercover work in Algeria and Morocco."

Modesty said, "Les barbouzes?"

"Later, I think. I did not put in a request for his full record at this stage. But let me turn to the brother, Georges. He served a prison term for attacking a man with a knife in the course of a robbery. He then left Corsica and disappeared for a time, later reappearing in Marseilles. He had been recruited by the Union Corse as an enforcer, and is now their senior executioner, so the police tell me. They do not have evidence to that effect, of course, but they are in no doubt on the matter."

Vaubois ran his eye down a foolscap page and turned it over. "Nothing of importance there," he murmured, "except general progress in the military career of Bernard Martel. But then, only three years ago, while on holiday in Corsica, Bernard encountered a young English woman, Tracy Chilton, also on holiday there. He appears to have been smitten by a thunderbolt of love, for within a few months they were married. He took his young bride to Morocco for the honeymoon, and three days later, in the medina in Fez, he lost her."

Tarrant said, "Lost?"

"They were together. He went to look at something. When he turned round he could not see her."

Modesty said, "You can get lost in the Fez medina easily

enough. It's a hell of a maze. But do you mean she was never found?"

"That is so, which suggests abduction, but official opinion was that she had wandered for a while and then been—how do you say it now? Mugged? By petty thieves. They usually work in pairs. Perhaps she screamed, and somebody was too quick with a knife. Then it was better for them that she should disappear rather than that her body should be found."

Willie said, "If there's no evidence, it's anybody's guess. There's still a few 'undred girls who disappear every year and end up in brothels anywhere from the Gulf to Buenos Aires. European girls, I mean. Or some of 'em get bought into harems still."

"So Bernard Martel well knew," said Vaubois. "It seems he was almost mad with grief, and kept insisting that his wife was not dead but a prisoner, sold into the vice trade. Six months later he resigned his commission and vanished. It now appears that he adopted a new identity as Louis Gautier, and then, a little later, entered a new profession as a lieutenant of the criminal El Mico. He would not have found that difficult, I imagine, since he may well have worked among criminals in that area when he was on intelligence assignments." Vaubois laid the foolscap sheet on the small table at his elbow. "I will leave this with you, but please destroy it as soon as you have studied it in detail."

Modesty said, "Of course." Willie added gravely, "We'll get Giles to eat it."

Pennyfeather woke from a reverie. "Eh? What's wrong with burning it?"

"Intelligence chiefs like you to eat it, Giles. It's more romantic. We could burn it first, if you like."

Pennyfeather chuckled. "Ah. You're pulling my leg."

Modesty said, "Could anyone have had a special reason for abducting the girl? Was she rich? Did she know something? Did she have enemies?"

Vaubois shrugged. "She came from the East End of London," he said, "and she was the daughter of a labourer."

After a little silence Modesty said, "Well, thank you, René. Perhaps you'd like to take another look at the talisman and my notes of Martel's ramblings. You didn't have much chance while I was telling the story."

Willie handed Vaubois the pad. He ran his eye down the type-written words and said, "It makes no immediate association of ideas in my mind. I find it a little surprising that he rambled in English."

"That was after I'd tried to encourage him by saying help was on the way and mentioning Willie Garvin. I'm sure he knew the name. It would be surprising if he didn't, seeing that he was working that area in *The Network* days. He would also have realised who I was. Perhaps that programmed him in some way, so that when he was half conscious he made an effort to speak English."

"It is possible," said Vaubois. "But why this odd fragment of French? You have written '*pas la vie*' but it could equally have been '*pas l'avis*' one imagines." He separated the two words distinctly.

Pennyfeather said, "I don't see the difference."

Modesty stood up. "They're both fairly meaningless, Giles. '*Pas la vie*'—not the life. '*Pas l'avis*'—not the advice, or opinion. You could juggle other possible versions, maybe, but all equally without meaning." She pushed a curtain aside, closed the French windows, and settled the curtain in place. "All right, let's go over it once more. I'd like to have some idea of what Martel wanted, but even if we come up with nothing I must still take that talisman to his brother and tell him all I can."

"Modesty Blaise seeking the Union Corse hit-man could be misunderstood," Tarrant said thoughtfully.

She sat down beside him and smiled. "I'll have to cross that bridge when I come to it. Now that Giles has brought out my angelic qualities, there's no turning back."

A hundred yards away, Dominic Silk lifted an earphone from one ear and whispered, "Ah! *Now* I can hear something at last."

The stocky man said, "That is because somebody has closed the window. Until now, there was no glass to oscillate."

Dominic swore softly, foully. "Until now I would have heard more sitting below the balcony with an ear trumpet."

The stocky man nodded. "It is always possible to be too clever," he said. "If you had asked for an ear trumpet, I would have provided one."

*   *   *

Little Krell came in very fast, pivoting on the ball of one foot and swinging the other in a reverse roundhouse kick to the chest, Jeremy Silk moved with equal speed, stepping inside the kick, blocking with forearm to calf, and sweeping with his right foot to kick Little Krell's standing leg from under him.

Little Krell allowed his leg to go freely with the sweep, dropped squarely on his hands and cartwheeled out of danger, coming easily to his feet with the great barrel of his body poised lightly as a butterfly. The almost spherical head gave a nod of approval. "Better," he said.

It was mid morning, and they had been at practice in the games room for over an hour now. Jeremy Silk wore plastic protection at heart, groin, and neck. Even with this, a blow from Little Krell could be devastating. Little Krell himself wore no protection except the layer of iron muscle that was part of him.

"We rest," he said, and sank down on his haunches. Jeremy moved to sit on a locker, reflecting that he had never yet seen Little Krell sit or lie. Perhaps he even slept in this poised squatting position.

Plucking his sweat-soaked gym vest away from his stomach Jeremy said, "Did you ever see Modesty Blaise when she was running *The Network* here?" The small eyes blinked and the cannonball head nodded.

"Tell me what you know about her."

A long silence, then the gruff bass voice speaking jerkily in French: "Little. I was with Rodelle. Bodyguard. And sometimes break in girls for him. Blaise don't like girl business. She come to Istanbul with Garvin for showdown. We know. Rodelle make trap. Six of us wait for them in warehouse, but they come under water. Aqualung. Kill main lights and catch us from behind. Big fight. Can see only little."

"Did you come up against Blaise? Or Garvin?"

"I go to take Miss Blaise with knife. She make very fast counter. Stop blade at one centimetre maybe. Kongo is new to me. Surprise. Hand, head—finish." He tapped a finger to his temple. "Later I wake up. All over. Rodelle with back broken after big fall."

"She took *you*?"

Little Krell nodded again, head rolling on the great shoulders.

"Surprise. And fast. I learn from that. Strong is not enough. Clever is not enough. Must also be surprise and fast. All this time I practice for that. All this time I teach you and brother that."

"Is Garvin good, too?"

"Yes."

"I've heard he's useless with a gun."

"Hand-gun he does not use. With other weapons, much expert."

"He's a knife specialist, isn't he?"

"Kiriacou, the best knifeman I know, he tell me Garvin is world best."

"And unarmed?"

"Very dangerous. Very, very." Little Krell tapped his great shaven skull. "Like Miss Blaise, he fight up here."

Jeremy Silk laughed. "And so do we, Little Krell, so do we. Let's make a bargain. One day, you kill Modesty Blaise and I'll kill Willie Garvin."

From the open door of the games room Nannie Prendergast said, "We don't decide things like that without giving them a lot of thought, Master Jeremy."

Both men stood up. Jeremy said, "No, I just meant it would be rather nice, Nannie."

"Well, we'll see." She looked at Little Krell, inclined her head graciously, and switched to French. "I was very pleased with the way you carried out your new duties the other night, Little Krell."

He shuffled with embarrassment. "Thank you, Miss Prendergast."

"You can go off for your swim now. I have business to discuss with Master Jeremy."

The round head ducked obediently, and he turned to run out of the games room, a squat figure moving with astonishing lightness on massive legs. Nannie Prendergast said, "Our French courier brought in a message from Dominic half an hour ago. Shall we go out for a nice trip in the punt while we discuss what he has to tell us? It's such a lovely day."

"Yes, of course, Nannie."

"Put your track suit on, dear. You musn't catch cold."

The boat house held several small boats, among them what was probably the only punt in the Mediterranean. A broad sandbank ran east from the point of the island, only seven or eight feet below the surface. With a calm sea there was no difficulty in using the punt, and Nannie Prendergast much enjoyed lying back on the cushions with a hand trailing in the water while one of the boys poled the long flat-bottomed craft back and forth in leisurely fashion. Her own countrymen might well have found the sight amusing, but the members of the Le Dauphin Yacht Club were rather proud of their English neighbour's dignified boating.

As he eased the punt out of the bay Jeremy said, "What does Dominic have to tell us?"

She took a long envelope from her handbag and slid two folded sheets of paper from it. "He contrived to overhear a substantial part of a conference between our friends and Sir Gerald Tarrant and M'sieu René Vaubois."

Jeremy whistled. "My God, if she called in big guns like that, she must know the whole thing!"

"Don't blaspheme please, Master Jeremy. And don't jump to conclusions. Both men are friends of hers. Dominic was unable to hear the whole discussion, but it's quite certain that she does *not* know about The Object. She is unaware that Gautier took it, or even that it features in this matter. For some reason Dominic could not discern, she is trying first to decipher and then to carry out a garbled wish expressed by Gautier when he was half delirious. Incidentally, Gautier's real name was Martel. He was a Corsican, and before he came to us he was with French Intelligence."

Jeremy's mouth tightened as he lifted the pole and slid it down into the water again. "He was *planted* on us?"

"No. Dominic had to make deductions from references back, but it appears that something happened to Martel's wife, and this affected him to such an extent that he gave up his career, changed his name, and took to crime. Gamekeeper turned poacher, we might say."

"So we're not blown?"

"That's quite certain, dear. Gautier or Martel did use words in his ramblings that offer a vague clue to The Object, but I don't think anybody would guess the answer, and certainly Miss Blaise and her friends haven't done so. He also used words that might offer a clue as to where he hid The Object."

"Ah! That's more like it."

"They're very cryptic, I'm afraid." She referred to one of the sheets of paper. "Here we are. *Le Talisman. Aladdin. By June. By anything. He is in Villefranche. Take the talisman to Georges Martel. The oath. It must be honoured. Aladdin has it. Georges must bargain by June.*" She looked up. "I've left out words which are to do with The Object, but you can study the whole message later."

They were nearing the end of the sand bar, and Jeremy turned the punt slowly round. "Georges Martel?" he said. "Isn't that . . . ?"

"Yes. He specialises in making an example of people for the Union Corse."

Jeremy grinned. "Dead examples. He specialises in making stiffs."

"We don't want any common talk thank you, dear."

"Sorry, Nannie. What's the connection between the two Martels?"

"The Georges Martel who works for the Union Corse is the brother of Bernard Martel, the man we knew as Louis Gautier."

"Good lord, what an odd business. It's rather like the Corsican Brothers, isn't it? Except that they were twins, I think. You know, one was good and one bad."

"Let's concentrate on the matter in hand please, Master Jeremy. The nub of what Dominic has to tell us is that nobody suspects the existence of The Object and therefore nobody is looking for it yet. But Modesty Blaise is going to see Georges Martel. She is going to tell him all that his brother said, and give him the talisman, which is a Napoleonic coin of some sort. You can read about that later. She hopes, of course, that this will have some meaning for Georges Martel."

"Then we'd better stop her getting to him, Nannie."

"That was my first thought too, Jeremy. But second thoughts are always best, aren't they? We simply want to discover where Gautier concealed The Object, and we must remember that he was Georges Martel's brother, so possibly Georges knows *something* already. Not everything, of course or he wouldn't be sitting in Villefranche at this moment."

"And is he?"

"Oh, yes. Dominic had the wit to check that with our man there. I feel it's really very likely that Gautier was in touch with his brother and told him part of the story. As much as suited him at the time. Then, when he was close to death in the earthquake, he wanted him to know the rest. What he said was very garbled, of course, but when Modesty Blaise tells it to Georges Martel it may fill in some gaps and make good sense. It may even be that he will then know *what* The Object is and *where* it it."

"If so, he won't blurt it out to Blaise."

She shaded her eyes from the sun, smiling up at him, and he felt sudden heat in his loins. Quickly he looked away, flushing with guilt. She would be very cross if she knew he was thinking about her in that way now. He was only supposed to do that when she came to him at night.

"Of course Martel won't tell Modesty Blaise what he knows," she said. "But I think if he were to be questioned immediately afterwards, then he could be persuaded to tell *us* all he knows, which could well prove to be sufficient for us to recover The Object."

Jeremy sent the punt sliding forward over the still sea. "Now that's a really super idea," he said. "After all, *we* know what we're looking for, and that's a big advantage. There's not much time to set Martel up for a snatch, though. Do you know when she plans to see him?"

"Not until next week, fortunately." Nannie Prendergast picked up the parasol beside her and opened it. "I think you should take a small team from here. It will be much more secure than having our French agent provide people for the job. Now, encouraging Martel to answer questions will probably be distasteful, certainly not a task for gentlemen, so you must take one of the Berber women with you. They have a gift for that sort of thing."

"Yes, fine. Would it be a good idea to deal with Blaise and Garvin at the same time?"

She tilted the parasol over her shoulder and looked up at him fondly. "It's nice to see my little monkeys wanting to put their shoulders to the wheel and do a really good job of work, but we must look before we leap, dear. If Martel can tell us all we need to know after his meeting with Modesty Blaise, then she and Garvin can go. But if not, she remains our best potential source of information. After all, she was with Gautier for the last three days of his life."

"Yes, that's true. And she must know a lot more than Dominic managed to overhear. Probably if *we* knew as much, we could make sense of it." He grinned down at her admiringly. "You're jolly clever, Nannie. If we're unlucky with Martel, we'll still have Blaise left to question."

Nannie Prendergast nodded. "It seems the sensible way, dear, but let's take things a step at a time. You know what they say. If you run after two hares you will catch neither."

six

Paul Casanova, head of the Union Corse, showed uneven brown teeth in a warm smile and waved a hand expansively. "Naturally you may speak with Georges," he said. "Any time you want. I trust you, mam'selle. I trust you." He placed his feet carefully, addressed the ball on the tee, then with a good swing drove it high over the stretch of rock and strip of private beach beyond, to drop into the sea. One of his two bodyguards moved forward with a box of balls and set another on the tee.

The house was on Cap Ferrat. The grounds reached down to the sea and were contained by mossy stone walls with concealed electronic devices. The morning was warm, but both bodyguards wore light jackets tailored to hide the bulge of shoulder-holsters. Casanova, a short man with a gnarled face and a sheen of grey in his thick black hair, wore a white shirt buttoned at the cuffs, and a spotted bow tie. Modesty Blaise and Willie Garvin sat together on the ample beach settee under a split cane awning. She wore a white skirt and a navy and white top with a round neck and short sleeves. Willie was without a jacket, to make it obvious that he carried no weapon, but wore a tie with a long-sleeved cotton shirt. They had dressed with care, knowing from their *Network* files that Casanova had something of a Mafia outlook in liking formality of dress and correctness of behaviour.

Waggling the driver as he prepared to address the new ball, he said, "We have had one or two small differences in the past, of course, but such things do not destroy the trust of good friends." Willie Garvin nodded solemnly, recalling that one 'small difference' had cost Casanova's organisation over a million dollars in heroin which went to the bottom of the sea instead of on to the streets.

"I'm very glad you feel that way, M'sieu Casanova," Modesty said with a quiet sincerity that would have seemed genuine to anyone but Willie Garvin. "Naturally I have approached you, and not Georges Martel direct. One must show courtesy to one's friends."

She fell silent as Casanova prepared to drive. He watched the ball until it fell into the sea, then turned to her again with his warm, ugly smile. "That is a courtesy I appreciate, mam'selle." He handed the club to one of his men and gestured towards the sea. "It is not so wasteful. Most of them come in again after an hour or two, and we find them on the beach."

He sat down on a bollard, his gaze resting politely on Modesty. Nothing in his manner revealed the sharpness of his suspicion. It was said she had retired from business some time ago, but that meant nothing. Certainly she had wound up *The Network*, but it seemed to Casanova that in the latter years her organisation had spent more time breaking up rival groups than making profits. She had hurt him severely on a major drug run, but she had also sent back his three men alive, when by dropping them into the sea she could have made sure he never discovered her part in the matter. One of the three happened to be Casanova's nephew.

He had long regarded the slate between them as being clean, and was inwardly uneasy about her sudden reappearance. She had telephoned soon after breakfast, asking if she might see him, and he had responded in the most friendly terms because he was immediately suspicious. Now she had explained that she wanted to talk privately with Georges Martel; that she had been trapped in the El Jadida earthquake with his brother, who had since died; and that the brother had asked her to find Georges and give him a message.

It was all quite possible, and even the strangeness of the story gave it a convincing ring of truth, but Casanova was a man of business, and as such he could not see what Modesty Blaise stood to gain. For him, this discredited her story. It occurred to him that she might be planning to kill Martel for some reason, perhaps because a friend had been the victim of one of his hits. It was difficult for him to guess what she was about because he was aware that he had no idea how her mind worked, or what was likely to motivate her. But he did not intend to risk a man as valuable as Martel.

She sat looking at him placidly, her hands in her lap. She carried no handbag, another courtesy he appreciated, for it saved his men the embarrassment of searching it. Willie Garvin was gazing out to sea, watching a sixty-foot motor sailer tack into Baie des Anges.

Casanova made up his mind. "When do you wish to talk with Georges, mam'selle?" he asked.

"As soon as convenient for you, M'sieu Casanova."

"And where?"

She made a little gesture. "Here, if you wish."

That was a strange offer, he thought, unless she knew it was bound to be rejected. He shook his head with an apologetic air. "Georges does not come to this house, you understand. We are business associates rather than social acquaintances."

"Ah, yes. Then would he receive me at his house, or apartment, or wherever he lives?"

"I think not. I think he would not wish Modesty Blaise to come to his apartment. It would perhaps cause speculation in various quarters. May I ask where you are staying, mam'selle?"

"I have a place in the old quarter of Cannes, but we have booked into the Martinez in Nice for tonight, or until I can arrange to see Martel."

Casanova nodded absently, his head turned a little to gaze out to sea. After a moment or two he said, "I believe M'sieu Garvin is a keen fisherman. My nephew once told me how he discussed the subject with you one night on a small ship, a year or two ago."

"I'm pretty keen," Willie said. "How's your nephew these days?"

"In good health, thank you." Casanova clapped his hands softly together as if struck by a sudden thought.

"I have an idea. Like M'sieu Garvin, I also find it a pleasure to go fishing, so now I will invite him to join me on my little yacht.

We will go fishing for a few hours and enjoy ourselves." He smiled benignly at Modesty. "Meanwhile, mam'selle, you may enjoy your talk with Georges, in the comfort and privacy of your hotel."

She crinkled her eyes at him in response to the smile, her mind suddenly racing. So Casanova was suspicious, and wanted a hostage. Wanted Willie Garvin for a hostage, as surety against her committing any inimical act. His suspicion was unfounded, and there could be no harm in letting him hold Willie, but her instinct rebelled against the idea. "Well, now—" she began, when Willie spoke almost at the same moment.

"I'd enjoy a day's fishing, Princess," he said amiably. When she hesitated he went on, "It's fine with me."

"You're sure?"

He grinned and shrugged. "No sweat."

"Thank you, Willie." Then, to Casanova: "When shall I expect Georges Martel?"

He glanced at the watch on his wrist. "I will telephone him now, and he will call at the Martinez to see you at noon, if that is satisfactory?"

"Yes, thank you. I don't think we shall need to talk more than half an hour. Will you ask him to telephone you after he leaves me?"

"Certainly. And if M'sieu Garvin is bored with fishing by then, we will bring him to the hotel by car." He stood up, and they rose with him. "So. It is arranged. Let us say au revoir for the moment, mam'selle. It has been a great pleasure to have you visit me."

Twenty minutes later, at the reception desk in the Martinez, she said, "I'm expecting a M'sieu Martel in about an hour. Send him up to my suite, please."

"Certainly, Mam'selle Blaise."

As she turned away, a man who had arrived at the desk a moment or two after her said to the reception clerk, "Have you a *Nice Matin*, please?" He was a young man, well-built, with sunbleached hair, a fresh complexion and freckles, who might have been English. She registered, subconsciously, that he spoke French like a Frenchman from North Africa, but otherwise took little note of him as she moved away to the lifts.

Jeremy Silk took the newspaper, thanked the clerk, and looked at his watch. He calculated that he had a minimum of an hour and half in which to make arrangements. Not a lot of time, but there was a good team at hand, and opportunity had knocked. As Nannie Prendergast would say, it was important to strike while the iron was hot.

When Modesty let herself into the suite Dr. Giles Pennyfeather was kneeling on the floor with his great medical bag beside him, empty, and an extraordinary collection of bottles, jars, syringes, ampoules, instruments, and medical impedimenta spread out around him.

His guileless face lit up at the sight of her, and he got to his feet. "Hallo, darling. I thought I'd do a thorough check on my gear, in case there's anything I need. Oh, I told you at breakfast, didn't I?" He grinned. "And Willie asked how my leeches were." He looked at her carefully, then reached out and smoothed a thumb over her brow where a small vertical crease showed in the middle of her forehead. "Are you worried about something?"

"No. Not really, Giles. But Willie's standing as surety against the possibility that I might do something nasty to Georges Martel."

"Oh." Pennyfeather considered this. "But you won't, so it's all right, isn't it?"

"Yes. I must be getting old and turning into a worrier. Look, I'm sorry to disturb your medical check, but Martel will be coming to see me at about twelve, and I'd like to talk with him alone. Could you get this stock-taking done and everything cleared away before then, if I give you a hand?"

"Oh lord, yes. I usually run out of enthusiasm after ten minutes and bung everything back in the bag, anyway. But I don't like the idea of leaving you alone with this chap, Modesty. I gather he's a very nasty gangster. A killer in fact."

"That's very sweet of you, Giles, but I spent a good few years being a gangster myself, and I'm sure I won't need protection. Now what about you? Would you like to go down to the beach for a swim and sunbathe? I could come and pick you up when I'm through with Martel."

"No, I think I'll sit around the marina and have chats with people, then I can practise my French. Anyway, I like watching people messing about with boats."

"All right. But let's not be defeatist about re-stocking your bag." She moved to the table and picked up a sheet of hotel writing paper. "You call out what you're short of, I'll write it down, and later we'll go shopping. After all, you want to make a good impression when you start your new job."

Georges Martel was dark, like his brother, but there the resemblance ended. He was big, with a puffy face and a slow manner, soberly dressed and with well manicured hands. In a film, he would not have been cast as a killer because he did not look like one, except perhaps in a close-up of the eyes. They were empty, two chilling vacuums.

Modesty had changed into dark slacks and a silk shirt with a tie. She sat at one end of the big settee, turned a little towards Martel at the far end. In front of them was a low table with a tray of drinks. Two glasses of chilled white white had been poured. Martel, when asked, had said politely that he would drink whatever Mam'selle Blaise was drinking, and he had waited for her to drink first before touching his own glass. He showed no hint of being nervous. The caution was entirely automatic.

Now he sat turning a Napoleonic silver franc in his fingers, unsmiling but with an element of jeering contempt in the empty eyes. "I knew he had died," he said in a throaty voice. "I heard two days ago. The embassy in Morocco informed Paris, and they informed my father, who wrote to me."

Modesty said formally, "Please accept my condolences, m'sieu."

Martel sketched a barely perceptible shrug. "It is several years since I saw him. I did not much like Bernard." He put the coin down on the table.

"Does that have meaning for you, m'sieu?" she asked.

"The coin? Yes."

She waited but he said no more. After a few moments she went on: "Your brother gave me the coin, calling it a talisman. He was in a fever and his mind was unclear, but there is no doubt that he urgently wished you to do some particular thing for him. He wanted me to bring you the talisman and ask you to carry out some task, some promise, perhaps. Because of his fever he spoke in a garbled manner, but I have shown you a transcript of all he

97

said. Does the fact that he spoke in English prevent you understanding it?"

Martel shook his head. "No. Our father taught us to speak English. He was with those taken off the beaches at Dunkerque, and he became a cook in an English ship."

"Then I should be glad if you would tell me what meaning you find in the coin and in the words, m'sieu."

Martel looked at her without expression but with his head tilted to one side. "I can tell you little, mam'selle, and I do not understand why you ask. You have brought the coin and the words to me, what more do you think to do?"

She drank some wine and put down her glass. "I wish to see your brother's last wishes carried out," she said slowly. "Call it a whim, if you wish. Perhaps you can decipher what he said, and are willing to do as he asks. If so, there is no more to be said. But if you are not willing, then I may try to attend to the matter myself." She allowed a pause before adding, "I am sure M'sieu Casanova would desire you to help me, or he would not have instructed you to meet me."

When he looked at her his gaze held the same contempt as when he had studied the coin. "Bernard was always a romantic fool," he said without emphasis. "When we were boys, we found two coins like this. Bernard had the idea that we should make an oath, of which these coins would be the token, the talisman. It was the kind of oath boys make in play, an oath giving each of us the right to use the talisman, once only, to call for a service from the other. Any service. And this was an obligation which could never be denied."

He looked at the coin on the table, and a corner of his mouth twisted down. "It does not surprise me that Bernard remained serious about such a stupid matter long after he became a man. Within himself, he did not grow up. He liked secrets, undercover work, a romantic cause. So he kept the coin, and this was a magic thing for him, because one day he could use it to summon me and call upon me for some great service." Martel shook his head and his lips stretched in what might have been a smile. "It is as well he did not live to hear the answer I would have given."

He reached for his glass of wine, and Modesty said, "What did you do with your own coin?"

His eyebrows lifted a fraction in surprise, "I have it still, naturally. It was always possible that a moment might arrive when I had urgent need of some advice I could neither buy nor command. Then I would have called upon Bernard to honour his oath."

"I see that you are a prudent man, m'sieu." She leant forward and picked up the piece of paper with the dead man's words typed on it. "I now understand about *le talisman*. Does anything else that your brother said to me hold any meaning for you?"

Martel shook his head. "I regret, mam'selle."

"Clearly he wished you to carry out some important service for him. Are you sure there is nothing here to indicate what he had in mind?" She reached out to give him the paper. With no outward sign of impatience he studied it again. She watched closely for any brief gleam of understanding in his face, but it was empty.

At last he said slowly. "There is nothing here. The name of my mother's brother was Alâeddin, but we have not seen him for thirty years. He lived in the mountains, beyond the Gorges du Todra. I would think he is dead now. He was much older than our mother."

"Alâeddin?" A spark of excitement touched her. Then her head swam and the excitement was swamped by quick terror, black and nameless, sprung from nowhere, yet so powerful that her body was damp with cold sweat. She held still, drawing in a deep breath, then another, and her vision cleared. Martel was looking at the paper as before, unaware of her sudden brief distress.

It was gone now, leaving her shaken and bewildered, wondering why she should have suffered a reaction so alien to her, so violent, and apparently so causeless. But even as she wondered, she felt herself draw back from seeking whatever reason might lie within her. When Martel lifted his head she had not moved but was still looking at him with polite inquiry.

"There is nothing else in these words," he said. "But I wish to ask a question. Do you know that Bernard married a girl who was carried off during the honeymoon?"

Modesty nodded. Martel laid down the piece of paper. "Then I will tell you one thing which is not here but which may be of interest," he said. "Whatever Bernard wanted, I am sure it concerned his wife. I have told you he was a romantic fool, and it is true. He was besotted with the girl. It is not I who say so, for he was not married when I last saw him, but my father told me this when I went to visit him in Bonifacio last year. He said that Bernard had been completely besotted with this English girl, and would not believe she was dead. So I think that what he wished me to do was concerned with this in some way, but I do not have any idea what it was."

He stood up, automatically touching a hand to the left face of his jacket, to prevent it swinging open and revealing anything of the shoulder holster he wore. "There is no more I can tell you, mam'selle," he said.

She had risen with him. "Thank you for coming to see me, m'sieu. Will you be so kind as to telephone M'sieu Casanova as soon as convenient, to let him know that our meeting has been concluded? I imagine that Willie Garvin's visit to him will also be concluded when he hears from you."

"Naturally."

Neither offered to shake hands. She saw him to the door, then went into her bedroom and sat down at the dressing table, remembering the moments of strange and nameless terror, looking at herself suspiciously in the mirror. "Now what the hell's got into you?" she said softly.

Georges Martel walked along the corridor to the lifts. One of the four had an Out of Order sign on it, but a workman removed the sign as he approached, gathered up a toolbox and said with a glance at Martel, "Vous descendez, m'sieu?"

Martel nodded, and preceded the man into the lift. They went down in silence. When the lift stopped and the doors slid back, Martel saw that instead of halting at the ground floor they had continued to the basement. The workman stood with a finger on the button which held the door open, making no attempt to get out. Martel began an irritable protest, but the words died in his throat, for now two men with stockings masking their faces were framed in the open doorway, one with a curious long-barrelled handgun which made a soft explosive noise as it was fired.

Martel felt a sharp pain in his neck, but did not let it deflect him from the movement already begun, of getting his gun out fast. The second man took a quick stride forward, pinning Martel's gun hand against his chest, and even as he made to bring up his knee he felt both strength and consciousness drain out of him. A small part of his mind told him as if from a great distance that he had been hit by an anaesthetic dart, then darkness engulfed him.

Jeremy Silk put the gun under his coat and said quietly, "Laundry basket."

"Here." A dark-visaged man pushed it forward.

Jeremy and Dominic lifted the unconscious figure into the basket, closed the lid, and peeled the stocking-masks from their faces. With the man who looked like a workman, they pulled the basket out of the lift and allowed the doors to close.

Jeremy said, "Get it into the van and down to the marina."

The workman opened the van doors, and all four lifted the basket in. Jeremy and Dominic climbed in with it. Both wore faded shirts and ancient slacks, like a hundred other of the boat people busy painting, scraping, cleaning, repairing and idling around the marina. They still looked like brothers, but not like themselves, for they wore superbly made wigs of Nordic fair hair, cheek pads, and a virtually undetectable make-up to cover their freckles. The team assigned by El Mico to this operation did not speculate on the nationality or identity of the two men in charge, at least not aloud. El Mico had said that these two would meet them at the airport and were to be obeyed. That was sufficient.

Dominic, sitting on the basket, grinned. "Not bad," he said. "Especially when you remember this is the great Georges Martel of the Union Corse we've got in here." He swung a heel against the side of the basket. "A pretty tough character by all accounts."

"Very," Jeremy murmured. "But he won't be so tough once we're a mile or so off-shore. I think Kermina's going to enjoy herself working on this one." He frowned an admonition at his younger brother." Do keep your voice down a bit, Dom. Security, you know."

Dominic folded his arms and studied his boots. He did not, he thought, need to be told off about things like that. He liked old Jeremy all right sometimes, but there were also occasions when he really hated him, especially when lying in bed knowing that Nannie had gone to Jeremy because it was his night. Most of the time it wasn't too bad, but there were some nights when he could really feel himself burning.

Jeremy said, "Are you going to watch?"

"Watch Kerima do her stuff on Martel?"

"Yes."

Dominic forgot his annoyance and gave a hesitant grin. "Well, I suppose so. It's one of those things you feel two ways about, isn't it? Like going to a horror film. It gives you the shivers but it's . . . sort of fascinating."

"Less than half an hour ago, Mam'selle Blaise," said the man at the reception desk. "Shortly after you left the hotel."

As soon as Martel had gone, she had walked down to the marina to collect Giles Pennyfeather and bring him back for lunch. With the heavy traffic it was less troublesome to walk, and in any event she could think better on her feet. The message had been awaiting her on her return.

She read it again. Pennyfeather stood beside her, looking rather less shabby than usual in a new shirt and slacks, both of which fitted him. The occasion of his birthday two days earlier had provided a heaven-sent opportunity for Modesty and Willie to take him out and set him up with a range of clothes.

"When you did not answer the telephone in your suite, M'sieu Vaubois asked to be put through to reception," the clerk continued. "I was able to tell him that I had seen you depart, and he then asked to leave an urgent message. I have written it down with care, mam'selle."

"Yes. Thank you."

Pennyfeather withdrew his gaze and his professional interest from a girl crossing the foyer whose figure defied all he had ever learnt of anatomy and said, "Is everything all right?"

Modesty took his arm, moved away from the desk, and showed him the slip of green hotel paper. The writing was in French, and he was slowly deciphering the first few words when she said, "It's from René Vaubois, and it says: *Have important news concerning B.M. cryptic and coin. Please meet my representative at Le Caribou, Tallard, between three and four this afternoon.*"

Pennyfeather ran a hand through his already tousled hair and looked about him furtively. "Is it really from him, though?" he whispered. "I mean, you're a girl who gets mixed up in all sorts of funny business, aren't you?"

She gave him a brief smile. "Good for you, Giles. You're learning a little caution. But, yes, it has to be from René. Apart from Tarrant there's nobody at all outside Willie and us who knows that Bernard Martel babbled crytic words and gave me the talisman, and that we talked to Vaubois about it."

"True." Giles tugged at his chin. "But it's a bit weird, asking you to meet some chap of his . . . well, wherever it is."

"Tallard's a small town on the Grenoble road, about ninety miles from here. Maybe there's something or somebody there we have to see. It's not really so weird, Giles, not for a girl who often gets mixed up in all sorts of funny business." She looked at her watch. "We haven't a lot of time, so we'd better go as we are."

"Righty-o," said Pennyfeather obligingly. "I'll just pop to the loo. We might get a bit peckish, so perhaps we could buy some bread and butter and cheese on the way out, then I could sort of feed you as we go along."

"I'm not going to drive ninety miles with you beside me smothered in grease and bread-crumbs, trying to poke bits in my mouth, Giles dear. We'll get some chocolate." She turned back to the desk. "And I'll leave a message for Willie."

They came to Tallard at a quarter past three and found the restaurant called Le Caribou just off the high street. Lunch was almost over, but the obliging patron provided omelettes and coffee. He regretted that no gentleman had inquired after Mam'selle Blaise, neither had there been a telephone call from anybody by the name of Vaubois.

When twenty minutes had gone by she began to feel uneasy, and was glad that Giles had the gift of knowing when not to chatter combined with the good sense to realise that empty reassurance was irritating rather than comforting. They sat over their coffee till four, when she left Giles in case the contact from Vaubois should appear, and went to the Post Office. Ten minutes later she was back, and in another three they were in the car. "I rang René's office," she said, "and he was there. He sent no message."

Pennyfeather sat frowning ahead. At last he said quietly, "I know it sounds silly, but do you think somebody could have managed to overhear what we said in your flat that evening with Tarrant and Vaubois?"

They passed a delimit sign and she eased the accelerator down. "It doesn't sound silly," she said. "It's what must have happened. There's no other answer."

"But who could it have been? And why? I don't mean why did they do it, because it's pretty obvious they must be interested in Martel's secret. I mean, why have they done *this*? Why send us chasing all the way up here?"

She shook her head. "I don't know, Giles. We seem to have got ourselves involved in a caper without realising it. Nobody's tried to jump us, so it looks as if they sent the fake message to get us out of the way. Maybe they wanted to search the suite, or Willie's room. I wish I'd rung the hotel before we left Tallard, to check if Willie's back safely, but I'm not going to stop now. There's nothing we can do until we get there."

The road ran with the Durance for the first forty miles, winding through the Préalpes de Digne before branching away from the river and striking south-east through the Alpes de Provence to the coast. It was not a fast road, but she drove hard and with total concentration to reach the Martinez by six.

As she gave the car keys to the doorman and ran up the steps with Pennyfeather beside her a man in a dark suite moved from near the swing doors to meet her. She had seen his face before. He had been with the man on duty at the gate-house of Casanova's villa when she and Willie arrived there that morning. He stopped in front of her and said without preamble, "Will you come with me, please, mam'selle?"

She eyed him impassively, and said, "Where is Willie Garvin?"

"Where is Georges Martel?"

After a little silence she said slowly, "Take me to Casanova. We must talk. There has been interference here."

"I have my instructions, mam'selle. I am to take you to Garvin."

She looked at Pennyfeather. "Wait in the suite please, Giles. I'll be back as soon as—"

The man broke in. "He is to accompany you."

Pennyfeather put a hand on her arm. "I was able to follow that," he said gently. "Don't worry. I won't get in your way."

The car was a big Mercedes, parked in the hotel forecourt. The driver wore a chauffeur's uniform, and was addressed by the man in the dark suit, somewhat surprisingly, as Ringo. A gesture invited Pennyfeather to take the passenger seat. The man in the dark suit sat beside Modesty in the back and picked up a telephone as the car pulled away.

"Laroque here," he said in French. "She is with us, and the other one also." A pause while something was said from the other end, then: "No. They came back to the hotel. She wishes to talk." He listened again. "Understood. We will be there in forty minutes." He secured the telephone in its niche and glanced at Modesty. "M'sieu Casanova also wishes that you talk," he said.

"Are we going to see him now?"

Laroque shook his head, and the man called Ringo laughed briefly. "No, mam'selle," said Laroque. "We are going to see your friend Garvin."

She sat back and closed her eyes. There was nothing to be done for the moment. When the car turned north on to a minor road leading up into wooded hills she opened her eyes again to take note of the route. Pennyfeather sat with folded arms, chin sunk on chest, seemingly asleep. She knew he had learned by now that this was her kind of business, and she felt thankful that he could be relied upon not to distract her or jog her elbow, no matter what happened.

Twenty minutes later the car pulled off the winding road into the cover of some trees. Laroque said, "I have to make sure you carry no weapons before we proceed further. You will descend, please."

Pennyfeather looked over his shoulder at her, and she nodded. They got out, and Ringo checked Pennyfeather carefully while Laroque stood back a little with one hand under his jacket. She knew he carried a gun in a shoulder holster, and had glimpsed the distinctive butt of a Harrington and Richardson 925 thirty-eight. She had also registered that Ringo's chauffeur jacket, buttoning across at the shoulder, allowed for no gun, neither was there any sign of a belt holster at the back of the hip; but the side pocket of the jacket showed a cigar-shaped bulge which might have been a flick-knife.

At a gesture from Laroque she stood with her hands on top of the car, legs spread, while Ringo patted her all over, not lingering, coldly professional. She had left her handbag on the seat, and now he took it out and opened it. The handbag was of the shoulder-strap type and held somewhat less than the usual amount of feminine essentials. Pennyfeather watched absently, wondering if the man would realise that the rather large black mushroom-shaped wooden clasp was in fact Modesty's favourite weapon, the kongo, which could strike so quickly from any angle. It meshed with a clip on the other side of the bag for closure, but could be detached by a sharp tug.

Ringo said, "No weapon," and tossed the bag back in the car. She had feared that Pennyfeather would give her a meaning glance or show relief, but he did not so much as look at her, and she loved him for it. At a word from Laroque they re-entered the car and drove on for another ten minutes, then turned off on a broad track which ran briefly through a grove of pine and chestnut before emerging on a promotory where some kind of construction work appeared to be in progress. The ground was torn and rutted by tracked vehicles. A number of huge iron pipes were laid out beyond a sturdy wooden hut with a padlocked door. To one side there was a trench-digging machine, a pile of steel reinforcing rods, and a great heap of sand.

Directly ahead of where the car had stopped was a mobile crane, its engine idling, its derrick pointing away, a man in a grey suit standing beside it. Laroque got out of the car quickly, and there was a gun in his hand now as he gestured to Modesty and said, "*Descendez.*"

When she slipped the strap of the handbag over her shoulder and obeyed, he made no protest. Pennyfeather alighted with a thoughtful air, followed by Ringo, who had slid across from the driving seat and now held an open flick knife in his hand. Laroque waved a hand towards the mobile crane and said, "*Marchez.*"

With Pennyfeather beside her and the two Casanova men fol-lowing she began to walk over the broken ground. There were still huge puddles from the storm two nights before, and planks had been laid here and there to bridge them. As the angle of her view changed she was able to see that the derrick of the crane jutted out over a great hole the size of a house, with rock walls, like a miniature quarry. The cable from the derrick hung down above the centre of the hole. As she moved nearer, more of the lower end of the cable came into her view, and suddenly her stomach tightened. At the same instant she heard a swift indrawn breath from Pennyfeather.

Willie Garvin hung by his bound hands from the hook at he end of the cable, suspended on a short length of thick rope. From a shackle at each ankle, a heavy chain ran down through a U-bolt set in a block of concrete which must have weighed a hundred and fifty pounds. He was soaked from head to foot, hair plastered to his brow, but fully conscious, and she saw the blue eyes narrow slightly as she came to the edge of the hole.

The water that almost filled it was yellow with mud, its surface three feet below the block of concrete. Willie said without inflexion. "About ten foot deep, Princess. The shackles are bolted on—" He broke off, sucking in his breath as the sound of the crane's engine changed and the cable dropped smoothly down. The yellow water engulfed him, leaving only his hands and wrists showing above the surface when the cable went slack.

Very careful not to move her hands, Modesty turned her head and saw that a man in workman's blues was at the controls of the crane. She looked down at the water, at the bound and swollen hands, and with a huge effort sent her mind reaching out through the sinews of her body, easing and loosening them against the freezing effect of fear.

Pennyfeather stood with hands clenched in front of him, staring down, biting his lip. She looked at the man in the grey suit, who had stepped a little away on her arrival, and said, "What is it you want?"

The man was burly, muscular, with a heavy face and wary eyes. He said, "Martel," and signalled to the crane driver. The engine roared and Willie Garvin rose from the tiny quarry, muscles stretched cruelly by the weight on his feet, water streaming from him, head back, mouth wide, sucking in air.

Modesty said, "I must speak to Casanova."

The burly man shook his head. "He is very angry. Martel was with you, and has vanished. M'sieu Casanova has instructed me to make you tell me what you have done with him. M'sieu Casanova is not interested in anything else you have to say." He signalled again, and with a clatter the crane lowered its burden into the water once more.

There was no room now for fear or alarm. Her mind held all the essentials of the situation in a small focus, as a lens focuses the rays of the sun. Martel had vanished, and no protest of hers would be believed. Casanova did not play games. If she did not talk, Willie Garvin would drown, and soon. This present immersion might even be the final one. Laroque stood behind her, the gun pointed at her back, keeping just out of distance. The man in the grey suit had not drawn a gun but stood with hands resting in his jacket pockets, thumbs outside. Pennyfeather stood beside her, staring down at the water, face pallid. Just beyond him was Ringo, with the knife. The driver in the cab of the crane was five or six paces away, head turned to watch the burly man's signals. She assessed the crane driver as a technical man rather than an enforcer. Probably not carrying a gun.

Letting her shoulders sag a little, she concentrated on what she must do with the pinpoint focus of a pole-vaulter preparing every nerve in the body for the immense task of co-ordination. "There is a telephone number," she said. "There you may speak to Martel. It is in my notebook. Now lift him out, quickly please."

The man in the grey suit said, "First, the number. You have perhaps two minutes, I think." He jerked his head towards the yellow waters. "His lungs are good, that one."

She brought the handbag round in front of her with a frantic movement and opened it, raking through the contents, then lifted her head and stared at Ringo. "The small red book, it was here," she said in a rising voice.

He shook his head. "I saw no book."

"Then it has fallen out in the car." She began to move, but behind her Laroque said sharply, "No. Ringo will go and look."

"Then tell him to *hurry*!" She had turned as she moved, and was a pace nearer to Laroque now. The clock ticking in her mind told her that fifteen seconds had passed since Willie had been submerged. When Ringo was ten paces away she looked at Penny-feather, reached out an open hand to him with the manner of one asking for a pen or pencil, and said angrily in English, as if asking a question, "Play up, Giles. Shape to thump me when I get ratty."

Only a colloquially bilingual Frenchman could have grasped her meaning. She allowed a second or two for Giles to absorb it, then shouted at him suddenly as if her control had snapped, and swung

108

the handbag to hit him on the side of the head. He gave a cry of wrath, glared, then took a step forward with one hand raised dramatically and declaimed, "You bitch!" It was a truly ham piece of acting, but she allowed the opposition no time to make judgments.

Swinging the bag at Giles again, she said furiously, "Back off now." The bag missed. Laroque had thrust the gun forward and was calling out sharply. The burly man had instinctively moved to intervene. She let the bag go, and it flew past Laroque's head, but the kongo was in her left hand now, and she was pivoting on the ball of one foot, leaning forward, seizing the split second in which Laroque was distracted to strike at the back of his hand. It seemed a light blow, but it was on the nerve centre below the middle finger, and the gun dropped, and she was still pivoting, poised on her left leg, the right lifting behind her to come round in a vicious reverse roundhouse kick that took Laroque on the hinge of the jaw and knocked him flat as if his feet had been scythed from under him.

For a brief moment she was on two feet, and then on none as her body rose and she took the burly man with a shattering drop-kick. She twisted, landing on hands and feet, scooping up the short-barrelled H. and R. Defender, saying, "Watch the man in the crane, Giles," and bringing the gun up to a two-handed aim at Ringo as he came running back. He slithered to a halt, and she said, "Throw the knife to one side, then get flat on your face, or you'll be using a crutch for the rest of your life."

For some fractions of a second he froze, holding his breath in shock, for this was another woman, a strange and terrible creature with huge black eyes set in features carved from pale brown stone, eyes that gripped, and held, and drained the strength from his limbs by the ferocious power of the will behind them. Fear wrenched at his stomach and dried his mouth. Quickly he tossed the knife aside and fell forward to lie flat on the muddy ground.

She swung round a little to cover the man in the cab of the crane. His hands were still on the controls and he was staring towards her. No more than five seconds had passed since she launched her attack, thirty since Willie had been submerged. Raising her voice above the sound of the engine she called, "Lift him out!"

The blue-overalled figure in the cab stared, then slapped a hand at the controls. The engine stopped dead, and in the same moment the driver jumped down on the far side of the cab and started to run, hidden by the bulk of the crane.

She heard Pennyfeather gasp, "Oh, Christ!" Then she was running forward at an angle to get sight of the man, and standing with legs astride, braced, taking careful aim at the running figure thirty paces away now. The gun was strange to her, and her first shot missed, but on the second he went down clutching his leg. She spun round to cover Ringo, but he had not so much as lifted his head, and the other two men still lay unmoving.

She pointed to them, saying, "Drag one on top of the other, knot their ties together as tight as you can, and get grey-suit's gun, Giles." She was already running for the crane. As she passed Ringo she said, "If you move, I'll kill you. I swear it." Once in the cab she steeled herself to shut out the mental picture of Willie under the water, and studied the controls. Slewing lever . . . hoist . . . lower. She had once watched Willie work a crane in the days of *The Network*, and the controls here seemed much the same.

There was the starter. She pressed it, and nothing happened. Twice more she thrust at the button, fighting to hold down panic. No result. Drawing in a long breath, she pressed the heels of her hands to her eyes and allowed the whole picture to form in her mind. Willie Garvin was shackled to a concrete block under water. If he had managed to fill his lungs, he would be able to hold out for perhaps three minutes before he began to drown. One and a half of those minutes had already gone. There was no way he could help himself, no way she could lift him by her own strength, and the crane would not start. By the time she had dragged the wounded driver here and made him operate it, Willie Garvin would be long dead.

She had seen an adjustable spanner in the open toolbox on the floor of the cab. With that, she could dive and unbolt the shackles at his ankles. But to make the necessary number of dives in that opaque water would take at least ten minutes, and probably longer.

Pennyfeather was calling, his voice cracking with anxiety. "I've done what you said, Modesty! Can't you get that bloody thing started?"

seven

She caught up the spanner and a roll of insulating tape from the toolbox, then dropped from the cab and ran towards Pennyfeather. He had taken an automatic from the man in the grey suit, and stood holding it gingerly. Laroque's head now rested on the other's chest and their ties were knotted hard together. Ringo still lay sprawled in the mud, head twisted a little to watch her with a wary eye.

She put a shot from the Defender six inches from his head and snapped, "Up, Ringo. Up, you bastard, *quick*, or I'll ruin you. Over here. *Move*! Lie face down across those two. Hands behind you. Right. Giles, go and bring me his knife." She put a knee in Ringo's back, pushed the gun into her waist-band, and wound insulating tape three times round his crossed thumbs. He made no attempt to resist.

A hundred and ten seconds.

She rose, and took the knife from Giles. The revolver would be more reliable than the automatic he held, she decided, and drew him to a position behind Ringo, clear of his feet. "Put the automatic in your pocket, Giles. Now hold this revolver in two hands, so." She put the gun in his hands. "That's right. Finger on trigger, and aim it. The other man's got a bullet in his leg, so he won't worry you." She was stripping a length of insulating tape from the reel, securing one end to the spanner, the other round her wrist. The flick-knife, closed, was in her pocket now.

Two minutes, plus.

"Giles dear, I have to rely on you. If they move, shoot. Don't hesitate, or we're all dead."

He nodded, white-faced, mouth set in a straight line. "Trust me. Tell this Ringo chap in French, so he knows. Then for God's sake help Willie." His voice cracked with fury.

She rattled out the warning in French, kicking off her shoes. Then: "Don't look round, Giles, don't take your eyes from them, and don't worry if I'm a long time."

From the corner of his eye he saw her run to the pit and dive from the edge. He could not begin to imagine how she hoped to save Willie now. A long time? But there *was* no time. Another minute and Willie would surely drown, if he hadn't done so already. Sweat beaded Pennyfeather's brow, and he caught at his thoughts. If Modesty hadn't given up, then there had to be some kind of hope. Leave it at that. He looked along the barrel of the gun and steeled himself to wait.

Willie Garvin hung upright in the water, the buoyancy of his body tugging gently at the chain holding his feet. His head hung on his chest and every muscle was relaxed, save those holding the air his lungs were now struggling to expel, stale air, its oxygen content diminishing every second. He had pulled a black velvet hood over his mind to keep it blank, to shut out hope and fear, for both would consume precious energy.

His body was not yet desperate. If he had allowed his mind to be aware, he could have calculated that in another minute he would no longer be able to control his diaphragm. It would relax, emptying his lungs; then it would contract, seeking to draw in air. But there was no air, only water.

Somewhere in the depths of his darkened mind lay the knowledge that enabled him to do all that he had been doing to keep himself alive till the last possible second, the knowledge that she was at hand and that her resource was incomparable.

Unnatural swirling of water triggered a signal to arouse him, and a moment later he felt her hand on his leg, just above the knee. She had dived deep, to make contact low and come up. Quicker and less exhausting than swimming down from the surface. Her hands were at his waist . . . now his shoulders. She was pressing close, wrapping her legs round his thighs to hold herself in position, sliding her arms round his neck.

Relief surged through him as he allowed his diaphragm to relax, exhaling steadily through his nose. Her lips were on his mouth, pursed a little, nudging. Carefully he let his own mouth open until it encompassed hers. Her head was tilted sideways, and she maintained pressure to keep their joined mouths sealed against the water. Then she exhaled into his lungs, and new relief spread like balm through his body as hungry blood devoured the oxygen it craved.

The air she was breathing into him had served her for less than fifteen seconds, and to Willie Garvin seemed fresh as mountain air. He drank deep of it, feeling his heart-beat slow to a more normal pace and the throbbing in his head fade to quietness. She was reaching up to grasp his arms above his head, allowing herself to rise. A hand patted his cheek reassuringly, then she was still, her knees resting weightlessly on his shoulders.

Her head broke the surface close to Willie's bound wrists and the hook from which he hung. Ringo's flick-knife was in her hand now, and as she eased the sharp blade under the rope she called: "It's all right, Giles, but I'll need ten minutes. Don't relax.

She could not see him, but his voice, harsh with relief, came to her from beyond the edge of the pit. "Marvellous! Don't worry about my bit."

The rope parted, and she pulled it away from Willie's wrists. His hands were bloodless. He probably could not feel that they were free now. She inhaled a deep breath and went down again. It was important to give him a steady supply of almost-fresh air at this stage, to get his body fully re-oxygenated.

Beneath the water Willie felt her take his shoulders and drawn herself down. His brain could register no sensation in his hands, but he found his arms drifting down and realised that she must have cut him free. Her legs and arms were wrapping round him again, her mouth seeking his, finding it . . . then the long, slow, glorious flow of air into his lungs.

Again . . . and again.

When she came down for the sixth exhalation, he felt her take his arms and put them around her waist. His hands were hurting badly now, but this did not prevent him being able to hold her close for their mouths to meet, and now she had no need to wrap her legs and arms about him. He could feel her wriggling as she exhaled into his lungs, and knew she was wrestling her slacks off. She completed the exhalation, then pressed his still clumsy hands to her waist in a signal to hold her. He obeyed. Her toe touched his leg and scraped upwards in another signal. He lifted her. Ten seconds passed. Her toe touched his chest and scraped downwards. He drew her down, and as he did so his head came smoothly out of the water into something dark and bell shaped, forking into two smaller bell-shapes.

He exhaled and inhaled quickly, panting like a dog as he eased the muscle tension that had built up with the repeated holding of breath. As the air grew stale, he lifted her again. Water closed over his head. He waited for her signal, drew her down, and once more his head was enclosed in a mishapen balloon of air, a crude diving bell improvised from her slacks, with the legs knotted at the knee and the zip fasted. As he breathed, and breathed again, a little air leaked slowly away through the fabric in micro-bubbles, and a little more through the zip, but the inverted slacks retained air for long enough to allow him twenty seconds of blissful breathing. She wrapped her legs about him. He read the signal and lifted his hands to take over the slacks from her, then she was gone.

Treading water, she watched as Willie's hands emerged with the knotted slacks, waved them about to scoop in fresh air, then drew them down again over his submerged head. She saw them balloon out, knew that he could manage his own air supply now, and lay back on the water, resting for a moment, breathing deeply, and feeling for the spanner tied to her wrist.

In took five minutes and three dives to free his right ankle from its shackle, with the whole of the first dive taken up in getting the spanner adjusted to the hexagonal head of the securing bolt. Once this foot was free, the chain between the shackles slid through the U-bolt set in the concrete to give an extra eighteen inches of slack on the remaining shackle. This allowed Willie to rise just far enough to bring his head out of the water. With the spanner already adjusted, the second shackle needed only two dives and three minutes. She surfaced, pointed to a part of the pit wall where the seaming gave good holds for climbing out, then swam over to it with Willie following.

The first thing she saw as her head cleared the brink of the pit was the frozen tableau of Giles Pennyfeather and the three men. He was standing just as she had left him, staring down with the gun held at the aim in two hands. She looked to her left. The man in blue overalls was still curled up on the ground thirty yards away, clutching his leg and groaning.

She called, panting, "All safe, Giles. Stay with it just a minute longer."

"Will do!" He did not turn his head, but the words were like a cry of relief. Then, as she dragged herself out, he called earnestly, "I'd like to have a look at that wounded chap as soon as you're ready, Modesty. Hello, Willie."

She rested on hands and knees, head hanging, chest heaving, weak with reaction, hearing Willie croak, " 'Allo, Giles." Slowly she sat back on her haunches and pushed wet hair from her eyes. Willie lay face down, brow pillowed on a forearm. He had brought her knotted slacks out with him. She saw that his wrists were raw and his ankles bleeding, knew that in every muscle he must feel as if he had been on the rack.

"Willie?"

He began to kneel up, and managed a feeble grin of reassurance. His lower lip was bleeding, and she realised her own lips felt swollen from the pressure of the mouth-to-mouth breathing. She made a little gesture and said, "I'm sorry, Willie . . . somebody took Martel, and . . ."

"I know." He coughed and wiped mud from his mouth. "Casanova thought it was you. First I knew, there was a gun stuck in each ear and one under me nose."

He looked beyond her, remembering the scene as it had been etched on his mind as he was lowered into the water for the last time, little more than two minutes before she had come to him down in the darkness. Then she had been unarmed, outnumbered, and at gunpoint. Now, three of the Casanova men lay disarmed, helpless to make any sudden move, with Pennyfeather guarding them. Beyond the crane, the driver lay huddled on the ground, apparently with a gunshot wound in the leg.

Willie turned his head slowly to look up at the jib of the crane, following the cable down to the hook and the yellow water which hid the block of concrete. Softly, fervently he said, "Blimey, Princess . . . I'm glad it was no one else but you."

Lussac put down the phone and turned to Casanova. "That was the gate," he said sombrely. "Ringo and the others are back."

The second bodyguard, Jaffe, moved to look out of the window, and saw the grey car coming up the long drive. He could just make out the head and shoulders of Modesty Blaise, in the passenger seat beside the uniformed figure of Ringo. With a wary glance at Casanova he said, "It is an unfortunate business."

Casanova looked at him from stony eyes. "Most unfortunate. One does not say to Modesty Blaise, '*I am sorry, mam'selle, but we have made a small mistake in killing Willie Garvin.*' " He shrugged and turned away. "Now she must go also. It is regrettable, but if we leave her alive she will make it her business to kill me."

There was silence. Casanova stood by the open patio doors, hands behind his back, looking out towards the sea. Lussac was still by the telephone, Jaffe on the far side of the room by the big fireplace. All were listening. There came distant sounds from the hall. Ten seconds later the door of the room opened and Modesty Blaise was pushed roughly in, her hands behind her back. Her hair was tangled, her clothes stained and damp.

As Casanova turned his head she surveyed the room and said, "Nine o'clock." With the words she brought a .38 Defender from behind her back and turned slightly right to cover Casanova and Jaffe. In the same breath she said in French, "Don't even think about moving."

Willie Garvin, no less wet, and begrimed, followed her in. Lussac, not covered on her left, snatched for the gun under his armpit. Willie's eyes were on the nine o'clock position as he entered, and the thrown flick-knife took Lussac hard in the bicep. He gave a startled cry, then sank to his knees, blood draining from his face with shock.

Modesty said, "The next one dies. You're advised to believe me."

Willie Garvin closed the door behind him, put a chair under the handle, walked across to Lussac, took his gun from the holster, put a hand on his face for purchase while he jerked the knife free, then moved to a position from which he could look obliquely out to the patio.

Casanova had not clawed his way to leadership of the Union Corse without sustaining many severe tests of his nerve. During that climb to the top he had fought in three periods of gang warfare and had rarely been afraid. But he was afraid now, not so much because a gun was pointing at him as because of something quite intangible. There was an aura of menace about the dishevelled, dark haired girl, an emanation so powerful that it seemed to strike him like a physical blow to the heart, sapping his confidence and will. It was there in Garvin, too, and no less powerful. Something big, cold, crushing.

She said, "Yes, Casanova?"

He reached down into his reserves of courage, met her gaze steadily, and said dry-mouthed, "Before you shoot, mam'selle, may I show you something to explain what has occurred?"

She studied him for a moment, then gave a curt nod. Hands spread, he moved very slowly to one side and said, "If Willie will disarm Jaffe, then assist him to carry in something which is at present on the patio . . .?"

Willie moved across, took Jaffe's gun, tossed it on to an armchair with the gun he had taken from Lussac, then jerked a thumb towards the patio doors. As they went out, Modesty said to Casanova, "If he tries any tricks, he's dead. Willie's in a bad mood. And so am I."

Casanova made a regretful shrug, but said nothing. Twenty seconds later Jaffe reappeared carrying one end of a stretcher. Willie was carrying the back end. A blanket had been draped over the figure lying on it. They put the stretcher down. Willie waved Jaffe away, then bent and pulled the blanket off. As he straightened, he said softly, "Oh, Christ . . ."

Modesty moved forward. Shock and horror pumped ice into her blood as she looked down at the naked body of Georges Martel. From head to foot it had been worked on with a delicate savagery that made her stomach twist in revolt and brought a pallor to her cheeks. Willie spread the blanket over the dreadful thing on the stretcher, and stepped back. She looked at Casanova and said incredulously, "You thought I did *that*?"

"No, mam'selle, no,' he said urgently. "It was this which told me that Modesty Blaise was not responsible for the disappearance of Georges Martel, and that I had been mistaken to believe so. Yet I ask you to acknowledge that it was a most natural mistake." He glanced down at the stretcher. "It was only half an hour ago that we found Georges. Too late to prevent . . ." he hesitated, and gestured apologetically towards Willie, "to prevent what my men were to have done up at the construction site."

Modesty said, "Where did you find Martel?"

"That was a matter of strange chance, mam'selle. The sea

brought his body into the bay here. From this I can tell you that whoever put his body into the sea must have done so from a boat not more than one kilometre off-shore, and only a little south of east. I think also that they did not know these waters well, or they would have realised that the body would be carried almost directly into the bay." He looked at the blanket-covered thing on the stretcher again, and his voice sank lower. "I think also that the torture was Arab work. It had the style of an Arab woman."

She exchanged a glance with Willie, and nodded agreement. "Is there any group you suspect?"

"No. At present this is a mystery to us." Casanova looked across to where Lussac was still on his knees, a hand gripping his wounded arm, hunched forward and breathing through his teeth with a hissing sound. "Will you permit Jaffe to take him away and attend to his arm, mam'selle? There is no quarrel between us now, I hope." A smile without humour. "And you have me at your disposal."

She looked at Jaffe, lowered the gun and stood away from the door. "All right, take him out."

Casanova said, "With your permission . . .?"

"Yes?"

"My men who were . . . who were with you at the construction site. They are dead?"

"Ringo's outside with his hands tied to the wheel. The crane driver has a bullet in his leg, just above the knee. The other two have sore heads. They're tied up in the gatehouse, with the man on duty there, who also has a sore head. The crane-driver is in your other car, a hundred yards down the road, with a doctor. You can give orders for your people to start sorting things out now. They must bring my doctor friend here at once, treating him with the greatest deference. The rest is up to you."

Casanova said soberly, "I am grateful for your restraint, mam'selle, and I should be glad to prove my gratitude if at any time I can be of service to you." He turned to Jaffe, who stood supporting his fellow bodyguard, and rattled out curt orders. When the two men had left the room he moved to a cocktail bar in the corner. "Mam'selle?"

"Not now, thank you."

"Willie?"

"Some other time."

Casanova poured a small whisky for himself, and said, "Is there any person you suspect of having done this to Martel?"

She moved to sit on the arm of a big settee, but did not put down the gun. "I can offer only one possibility. You have heard of El Mico?"

"Yes." Casanova shrugged. "One hears, naturally, but I have no business with him, and no interest in his organisation."

"He killed Georges Martel's brother a few days ago, at my home in Tangier."

Casanova's eyes widened. "There is a connection, then? And that it why you wished to see Georges?"

"In a way." She hesitated, then went on, "I hardly knew the brother. As I told you, we were trapped in the El Jadida earthquake together. He had a last wish, a dying request that I couldn't understand because it was garbled. But it involved seeing his brother, Georges, so I did that, hoping he might throw some light on the matter."

Casanova looked a query at her. She shook her head. "Nothing. And he wasn't even interested."

Casanova sat down and took a sip of his drink, eyes thoughtful in the gnarled face. Several minutes passed in silence. In was a silence which seemed not to trouble any of the three in the room. Modesty leaned against the wall, eyes on the patio, and obviously watchful, but never looking away. At last Casanova gestured towards the form on the stretcher and said, "Somebody believed Georges knew something, and tried to make him talk. But I think he did not know what they wanted. He would have talked long before they had done so much."

There was a knock on the door, and Pennyfeather's voice called, "Modesty, it's me. They said I was to call out before opening the door. Is it all right to come in?"

"Yes, Giles."

He came in, looking about him with a vaguely puzzled air, then his gaze settled on Casanova and he glared pugnaciously. "Ah! Is this the bugger who tried to have Willie drowned?"

"Shut up, Giles," she said mildly, and stood up, looking at Casanova. "You can lend us a car, I'm sure."

He moved to the telephone, spoke into it briefly, put it down and said, "My Cadillac, with my personal chauffeur will be in the drive in one minute, mam'selle."

"Good."

"Again let me say I regret what has occurred. May I assume that the matter is now closed?"

"We won't be pursuing it."

"Thank you. Your mention of El Mico confirms my view that poor Georges suffered persuasion by an Arab woman. I intend to investigate this El Mico. Would you care to be kept informed of whatever I may learn about him?"

"Very much so. Anything cabled to Blaise, London, will reach me. You'll see us to the car, of course?"

He smiled, a little ruefully. "It will be my pleasure. It is not, in fact, necessary, but I cannot blame you for the precaution."

Two minutes later, as the car glided out on to the road, Penny-feather said, "I'm still jolly steamed up about it, you know. I'm not a violent chap at all, but if you hadn't shut me up, Modesty, I was going to punch that fellow right on the nose."

She patted his hand absently. In the front seat, Willie said, "That'd teach 'im to go around drowning people. But try an' keep your temper if you run into 'im again, Giles. He's top man in the Union Corse."

Pennyfeather gave a snort. "Personally," he said, with austere contempt, "I've no time for these unions."

Half an hour after midnight, the blonde Swiss air hostess sprawled on Willie Garvin's bed said, "What in heaven's name have you done to your ankles?"

"Oh . . . I was a prisoner in a chain gang." He drew a finger down her spine, and she rolled over to look up at him.

"But those are new hurts," she said. "I think you are telling lies again, Weelie."

All foreign girls called him Weelie, he reflected. None of them could manage the short 'i'. He summoned up a look of indignation and said, "What d'you mean, *again*?"

"That is what the other girls say, too. That you tell beeg lies."

Suddenly alert, but hiding it well, he said, "Other girls?"

"Air hostesses. We often meet the same girls on the same run, and we talk together. I know that you know Julie, with British

Airways, and Monique, with Air France—oooh, that's nice, Weelie."

"And you're a beautiful girl, Adrienne."

"And you still tell lies, especially about what you are. You told Julie that you were an unfrocked priest, and Monique that you trained seals for a circus, and you say to me that you have been in a chain gang."

"Well, I've 'ad quite a varied life, really. The bit about the chain gang was just a joke, though. I got these sore ankles when I was out scuba diving. There was this big octopus got 'old of me by the ankles. They've got suckers on their tentacles, see, and—"

"Weelie, stop doing that, just for a moment. It's lovely, but I can't think. What about your wrists? They are bad too."

"Well, I doubled over to pull me feet free, and this octopus caught me by the wrists with two of its other tentacles."

She shivered. "Ugh! I would be so frightened."

"So was I. But it's all over now."

"No, wait, Weelie. How did you get away?"

"That's a big difficult to describe. I sort of wrestled with it so it got tangled up. Look, suppose you're the octopus. Roll over a bit. That's right. Now, you 'old my ankles. Not the sore bit, just above. You'll 'ave to use your legs for the other two tentacles, and you can't grip with your feet, so I'll grip you, same as if you were holding my wrists. Right?"

"I think so. What happened next?"

"Well, let's see if I can remember. I sort of twisted like this, then I got a leg round 'ere . . . no, wait a minute, let me 'ave a think about it."

"I am in a very funny tangle. Ooh! Weelie, that is not thinking about it! That is . . . that is . . . very nice. Please, never mind about the octopus now, Weelie."

Later she said sleepily into his shoulder, "I think you are very good to make love so nicely when you have had such a bad time with the octopus today."

"It's better after a bad time. You appreciate it more."

"Will you still be here next Thursday, Weelie? Or in Cannes?"

"Sorry, love. I'll be gone by then."

"Perhaps I will change to a London flight, and see you there."

"Fine. But leave it for a bit because I'm not going 'ome yet."

"Where are you going, then? To meet some other girl, I bet."

"No, it's business. I'm going to Corsica to 'ave a word with a baker."

She gave a drowsy chuckle. "Always you tell such beeg lies, Weelie."

eight

The small bakery lay in a side-street which ran across half the width of the narrow mile-long peninsular carrying the town of Bonifacio. It was very hot in the living-room, because this backed on to the ovens, and the morning air was warm with both sun and bakery heat in the tiny courtyard where Henri Martel sat with Modesty Blaise. The baker wore a thick cardigan, for fifty years with the ovens had thinned his blood.

They sat in two folding chairs, both facing a white-washed wall with a sad-looking vine straggling across it. A low rickety table with two glasses of pernod stood between them. Henri Martel was a quiet, soft, pear-shaped man with a moon face and sad eyes, bearing little resemblance to either of his sons. Like most of the inhabitants of Bonifacio, he usually spoke the Genoese dialect. It was only two hundred years since the Genoese had been driven from the island, and the good people of Bonifacio were not going to be hurried into adopting Corsican ways.

At this moment Martel was speaking very reasonable English with a mixture of foreign accent and a Devonshire intonation picked up from the mess-mates he had served with in the British Navy. His use of English expressions from that era gave added quaintness to his conversation. "I got the wire from M'sieu Casanova two days ago, mam'selle," he was saying with a weary shrug. "Poor Georges. But I always know that this can happen any time. As a kid he was a right little bastard, and then he grew up to be a spiv."

During the flight from Nice, Willie had suggested that it might be better for her to talk with the old man alone. She had been doubtful at the time, but was glad now. Martel was talking freely to her, but she sensed that two people would have been too much for him, making him nervous and reticent.

"Georges was lost to me long ago," he said reminiscently. "He did not come home even for his mother's funeral. But Bernard . . . he was a good boy. A fine soldier with a good career." He shook his head. "Then he made a cock-up of it, and all because of that silly cow."

She sipped pernod, and said, "His wife?"

"Of course. Tracy June. He always called her June, you know. He liked it better than Tracy. She was very beautiful, I got to admit that." He tapped a finger to his forehead. "But no intelligence. A real scrubber, as we used to say." He picked up a thin, grubby album he had brought out into the courtyard with him, opened it, and sorted through some loose photographs which lay at the back. "Ah, here she is, mam'selle."

The girl was standing on a rock with her back to the sea, wearing a green bikini and holding up a beach-ball, a very fair girl with a splendid figure. Her oval face was of remarkable beauty, but as enigmatic as the Mona Lisa. The old man said, "She went missing in Morocco. Everyone knows she had it, but Bernard don't believe. No, no, she is alive, he says, and some sheik got her. That's what he says all the time." The sad eyes turned to look at Modesty. "You know what he did? There is a gang called El Mico, and he went and got himself into this gang, because he thinks that through them he can find her."

Modesty said, "He told you this? Told you he penetrated El Mico's organisation simply to find his wife?"

"That's right, mam'selle. How daft can he get, eh? For him, there was nothing in the whole world but this girl. So he got to find her, even if it takes for ever, and he is sure that through El Mico is the best way to get the gen." Henri Martel's pallid baker's face twisted in a curious smile, and he nodded his head ponderously. "And after all, he was right."

Very slowly Modesty put down her glass on the wobbly table. "You mean he found her?" she said gently.

"He found where she was taken." Martel fumbled under his cardigan, took a watch from his waistcoat pocket, examined it carefully, and put it away again. "He told me last time he was here, just a few weeks ago. It was the El Mico gang, like he said. They had a customer for a beautiful fair girl, like Tracy Jane. Perhaps she was picked out at the airport, see? They would put a small team on the job, he said. They grab her, and she goes through the El Mico . . . uhh, what do you say? The pipe thing. I forget."

"Pipeline?"

"Ah, yes. She goes through the El Mico pipeline to the man who buys her."

She looked up at the sky, marvelling. It was like finding gold. After trying to make sense from Bernard Martel's cryptic ramblings, and almost getting Willie killed while learning nothing from Georges Martel, she now sat with a man who had the answer to many questions and was quite willing to tell what he knew.

She said, "Did Bernard discover who bought her?"

"Oh yes," he said simply. "It was a man in Morocco. A sheik. A prince, I think. Wait a tick, mam'selle." He turned over the loose photographs and some odd scraps of paper, then picked out a used envelope. "I wrote it down. Bernard liked me to take an interest, because there was nobody else he could talk to, you understand. The man was Rahim Mohajeri Azhari. I think that's how to say it."

"I know of him," she said, and watched some pigeons circle across the rooftops to soar in the thermal above the bakery. "He spends half his time as a jet-set playboy and the rest in a palace he's built in the High Atlas."

"Perhaps," Martel said vaguely. Jet-set and playboy were words he only half understood. "Certainly the girl is at this man's palace in the mountains. Bernard told me she must be there. He was planning to get together a small group of ex-legionnaires, commandoes, to make a rescue." A shrug of the heavy shoulders, powerful from years of kneading. "Crazy about her, mam'selle. Poor Bernard."

He picked another photograph from the album and passed it to her. Here in black and white was a young Arab woman with a strong jaw and steady eyes. The likeness to Bernard Martel was marked. "That was my wife, Fauzia. Many years ago, of course. She was from Morocco, in the south. I never been there, but twice she took the boys when they were young. I could not leave the bakery, see? There is still an older brother of hers there, Alâeddin. I think Bernard visited him once or twice in these last years. He is—ah, what is the word? *Un ermite?*"

"A hermit."

"Ah, much the same word. A strange person, by all accounts."

"Your son Georges mentioned him—" She broke off with a little gasp as icy terror sprang from nowhere to catch her by the throat. For an endless second her vision blurred and her body was rigid with locked muscle as she fought the wild compulsion to scream and run . . . blindly, anywhere. Then the moment passed, and Henri Martel was saying politely, "Mam'selle?"

"I'm sorry. I was . . . I was just recalling that Georges spoke of his uncle. Alâeddin." She touched her brow and felt cold sweat. "I would like to make contact with him, if possible."

Martel shook his head slowly. "I cannot help you, mam'selle. He is just a name to me. I never visited him, never even been to Morocco." Again the watch was extracted from under the cardigan and studied carefully. "He lives somewhere in the mountains, I think. Stupid old twerp, from what Bernard told me. He spent his life collecting the biggest heap of rubbish you could imagine. Are you feeling lousy, mam'selle?"

Her face felt pinched and pallid. She managed a smile and said, "Perhaps I was in the sun for too long yesterday. It's nothing."

"You want to rest." The watch was still in his hand. "And I got to say cheerio now. Always at the time of déjeuner I play bezique with my friend Dufay for an hour. He'll be here soon."

"You've been very kind to give me so much of your time." She gathered up her handbag, and he rose with her as she stood up.

"It seems a bit funny to me," he said, "that you want to carry out Bernard's last wish."

She thought of Giles Pennyfeather, who had nudged her into this and was now in Cairo on the way to his new job. "It's a little strange to me also, m'sieu," she said wryly, "and I have yet to discover what Bernard's last wish was. Perhaps I could come to see you again when I've thought over what you have told me today."

Slowly he shook his head. "Excuse me, mam'selle, but now is enough. I am tired of it all. Bernard and Georges, they could stay with me to become bakers, as my father was and his father was. But no. They go away, and one is bad and one is good, but now they are both dead and I am alone. And also I am bloody cheesed off with it all, I can tell you."

When she parked outside the small hotel in Porto Vecchio, eighteen miles north, Willie Garvin appeared and opened the car door for her. With an amiable smile he said. "You could've been tailed, Princess. Bloke in a green Renault went by when you pulled in. Sort of face you don't notice, but I'm sure I saw 'im on the plane when we were coming off at Campo dell'Oro."

She locked the car and took his arm. "I followed a green Renault most of the way to Bonifacio. He could have been doing a front tail. There's nowhere much else to go once you're heading south."

"Did you spot 'im on the way back?"

"No. I was a bit distracted on the way back."

One of his eyebrows lifted slightly. "Where d'you want to talk, Princess?"

"Somewhere safe, if there might be an ear around. You go and hire a sailing dinghy, Willie. I'll slip up and change. Be with you in ten minutes."

"Did you 'ave any lunch?"

"No. What about you?"

"I thought I'd wait till you got back. But you ought to 'ave a bite now. You look peaky."

"That's something else. But anyway, I'll get some bread, goat's-milk cheese, olives and smoked ham on my way to the boat. We'll picnic at sea."

"Great. I'll pick up a bottle of wine."

Twenty minutes later, with the dinghy running before a gentle wind, she said, "According to Henri Martel, the girl was very down-market and dumb. A scrubber, in the words of his old navy mess-mates. But to my earthquake friend she was obviously the sun, moon and stars combined."

"Not so easy to put a label on someone foreign."

"I expect that was it. Bernard certainly had Tracy Jane labelled as fabulous plus. He was sure she was alive, and was ready to do anything to find her, even if it meant going bent and joining El

Mico's mob. Eventually he found out that she'd been sold by the El Mico organisation to Prince Rahim Mohajeri Azhari."

Willie gave a soft whistle of surprise, but said nothing. She spread a thick mash of cheese and black olives between pieces of crusty French bread and handed the sandwich to him. "We'll come back to Prince Rahim later," she said. "I don't know how Martel located his wife. Probably he worked his way into a position of trust, and finally got access to El Mico's records. Certainly he was convinced, and when he last saw his father he was planning to hire a task force and make a surprise smash-and-grab rescue. But I think something happened to make him change his mind."

She stretched her long legs across the boat, bare feet resting on a coil of rope, and bit into her own chunky sandwich, frowning a little as she stared out across a sea of dappled blue and gold. At the tiller, Willie watched her without appearing to do so. He was a little anxious. Something had happened to her some time during the morning, and it had shaken her. As he had ample reason to know, she was not easily shaken.

"Look, Willie," she said, coming out of her reverie, "bearing in mind what we've learned today, have a fresh think about the things Bernard Martel babbled to me when we were trapped under the Hotel Ayachi."

He brought the dinghy round on to a northerly heading, then half closed his eyes and conjured up a mental image of the type-written phrases he had shown Sir Gerald Tarrant and René Vaubois in Paris.

Le talisman. All right, that was solved now. *Alladin.* Could be a reference to Fauzia Martel's brother, Alâeddin. *Peacock. Shadow.* Nothing Modesty had told him threw any new light there.

He finished his sandwich and she passed him another, with butter and a thick slice of strong-flavoured smoked ham. *By June. By anything.* Nothing there. A little warning light flickered somewhere in his mind. Something trying to surface? All right, come back to that. The bit about the oath, and taking the talisman to Georges Martel, that was all solved and done with. *Aladdin has it.* Yes, the mysterious IT. But still as much a mystery as before. *Pas la vie? Pas l'avis?* He thought about that for a while, but it remained meaningless. *Enough for a thousand women.* A sort of Arabian Nights connection there, surely. But what was enough for a thousand women? IT, perhaps? Keep going. *Shake, shake* . . . ah, now! Sheik . . . sheik. That made more sense. Prince or Sheik Rahim was the lucky purchaser, presumably for his harem, of Tracy June Martel, née Chilton. What was the last bit? *Georges must bargain by June.*

Well . . . yes. In obedience to his oath, Georges was to rescue Tracy June by bargaining with the sheik. What did he have to offer? IT, presumably which was enough for a thousand women. Must be something pretty special, then. But why must Georges bargain by June, which was now ended? And what was the meaning of *By anything*?

The little light flickered again in his mind, and with it the billion or so brain cells which associated one idea with another flickered out the word he had used mentally only seconds ago.

Purchaser. Buyer. And Modesty had been careful to tell him that Martel called his wife by her second name, June, not Tracy.

Switch the ramblings around a little. *Georges must bargain. Buy June. Enough for a thousand women.* Enough to *buy June.* To *buy anything.*

He allowed himself a small grin and looked up at the sail. "I reckon Bernard Martel wanted 'is brother to bargain with the sheik and buy Tracy June from 'im—offering something Bernard reckoned could buy a thousand women. Could buy anything."

She poured red wine into a cheap glass and passed it to him. "That's a rotten thing to do to an old friend. It took me an hour to work that out."

"You cued me there was something to look for, Princess. Can I 'ave another cheese and olive?"

"I'll think about it. What did Bernard Martel have that you can buy a thousand women with, Willie? What is IT?"

"No idea."

She broke off a piece of bread and split it. "Well, whatever it is, our best bet is to assume that Uncle Alâeddin has it."

"But we don't know where to find 'im."

"No . . ." Her voice wavered, and he looked at her quickly. She had paused in putting the filling into the sandwich, and sat as if frozen, eyes almost closed, face drawn. Then she shook her head quickly, drew in a breath, and went on spreading the cheese and olive mash.

Willie said quietly, "Please tell me, Princess. I mean . . . this is me. Willie."

"Sorry." She wiped her brow with the back of a hand. "That's three times now. Mention of Alâeddin makes me jump with sheer yellow funk and break out in a sweat. Must be something I bottled up way back, and it never quite dissolved."

He leaned forward, troubled. "Alâeddin triggers it, but not Aladdin? Just that difference of pronunciation? I wonder if . . .? Well, Georges Martel spoke about the Todra Gorge, didn't he? Said Alâeddin lived thereabouts. And you were down around that area a couple of times when you were a kid—"

"Leave it, Willie," she broke in quickly. "Probing only drives it deeper. I've found that out for myself. Now I'm just trying to relax and let it out, that's why I didn't tell you before."

He nodded slowly, and drank some wine. "Did you tell Giles before we saw 'im off to Cairo? He's good at that sort of thing."

"No. I didn't want him worrying about me. Here you are."

She held out the freshly made sandwich, and Willie Garvin smiled. "You spoil me, Princess. All right, suppose we talk about Prince Rahim Mohajeri Azhari."

"Yes. What have you got in your memory banks about him?"

He sat gazing absently into space for perhaps half a minute, then: "He's one of the army of Saudi princelings. Educated Eton and Oxford. Very sophisticated. Blotted 'is copybook with the king, and was told never to darken the Arabian doorstep again. So he moved to Morocco with 'is retinue and set up a sort of private estate in the mountains, somewhere east of that river . . . what's its name now? Not the Draa. It runs with the road between Marrakesh and Ksar es Souk. Ah, the River Dades. That's it. I suppose you could call 'im a sort of latter-day remittance man, except his remittance is about thirty million dollars a year."

Willie glanced up at the sail and brought the boat round on a south-easterly tack. Modesty said, "I know he drove a road into the mountains and built a palace. That was back in the early *Network* days, and I toyed with the idea of raiding it. He's supposed to have a pretty good collection of jewellery there."

"Must 'ave been before my time. What stopped you, Princess?"

She shook wind-blown hair from her face and gave him one of her rare warm smiles, the kind that made him feel rich, the smile he wanted to have in his mind's eye the day he died. "If you'd been with me then, Willie love, we might have done it. But as it was, I couldn't figure a way that wouldn't involve a shooting match, and that wasn't our style."

Willie nodded. "Pity, though. He's a nasty man, Prince Rahim."

"The gossip columns certainly aren't kind to him."

"Even they can be right sometimes. He spends 'alf his time jet-setting around doing a playboy of the western world act, mixing with all the beautiful people. No fool, though. Gambles in moderation, doesn't drink too much. Great womaniser. The rest of the time he spends on 'is estate in the High Atlas."

"Wait a minute . . . the gossip columnists gave it a name. From the first lines of *Kubla Khan*, wasn't it? Xanadu?"

"That's right. *In Xanadu did Kubla Khan a stately pleasure-dome decree* . . . nobody knows a lot about the place because it's pretty much cut off from the world, and Rahim won't allow visitors. I think there's just 'is retinue, staff, and a few dozen guards."

"Staff consisting of?"

"Anyone's guess, Princess. I suppose whatever it takes to run a place like Xanadu, from technicians and maintainance men down to road-sweepers. Plus a sizeable harem, I reckon."

"Yes. Including Tracy June Martel, if he hasn't sold her off down the line."

She picked up the bottle and poured wine for them both, thinking how little the western world realised the intensity of feudalism in the Arabian peninsular even today. And in recent times it had been stimulated by the great god Oil, who had showered the few hundred princelings of the area with riches almost too vast for the imagination to encompass.

Once, as a child, she had lived for a time with a Bedouin tribe, herding goats. Years later their leader, Sheik Abu-Tahir, had become oil-rich from the patch of desert his people owned. By then he owed his life to Modesty Blaise and Willie Garvin, for she had long since paid the childhood debt. It was now only two years ago that Willie had accompanied him on a visit to a minor prince in neighbouring Saudi Arabia, an English educated young man in the outer reaches of the sprawling royal family, who had expressed an interest in marrying one of Abu-Tahir's many daughters. The old man wanted to have Willie's view of the suitor, since he found it difficult to assess one so anglicised.

It was out of the question for Modesty, a woman, to be included in the visit, but Willie had described it to her in detail later, and rather dazedly. The palace of this minor prince, standing in the desert miles from anywhere, was air-conditioned and contained more than eighty sumptuous apartments, excluding the private wing. Willie's suite had been furnished by an expert in Venetian style, and he understood that a dozen other period styles had been adopted for other suites.

Artesian wells had been sunk to an enormous depth. These supplied abundant water for the bathroom suites with their solid gold fittings, also for the six swimming pools and the extensive gardens which had been planted in soil imported from France. A small army of slave-servants were so attentive that it was barely possible to lift a finger without being anticipated. This was somewhat claustrophobic, and brought a sense of being constantly spied upon—which was probably the case.

There were three cinemas and an enormous stock of films. The finest food and most toothsome delicacies were flown in from all over the world. The prince had a harem of between forty and fifty concubines, five of them from Europe. This, however, was for status rather than for use, since His Highness preferred the pale honey-coloured boys from Baluchistan with their long oiled hair. Abu-Tahir had been able to deduce this preference without Willie's help, and the engagement had not taken place. In revolt against such ostentation, the old man presented Willie with a box of cigars for his trouble, which pleased him greatly.

Fluent in Arabic and knowing the Middle East well, Willie Garvin had still been stunned by the unbelievable opulence he had seen. To him, now, and to Modesty, who knew the Arab world even better, there was little surprising in the idea of Prince Rahim Mohajeri Azhari building Xanadu in the High Atlas and sustaining a small feudal enclave there.

She said, "So he's both a western style playboy and a traditional sheik, but that doesn't necessarily make him a nasty man."

"No," Willie acknowledged, "that was just an impression. But it was Janet's impression, so it's reliable."

Her eyes widened a little. Lady Janet Gillam, daughter of a Scottish earl, worked a farm in Berkshire not far from Willie's pub, *The Treadmill*, and was his steady girlfriend. Modesty said, "How did she come to meet him?"

"It was before I knew 'er, back in the days before the car smash, when she was running around with the swinging set. She met 'im at two or three parties one summer when he was over, and he tried to get 'er into bed." Willie pitched his voice a little higher to produce a remarkably good imitation of Lady Janet's mellow accent. "Och, he came on with the charm like Omar Sharif, but there was something a wee bit frightening behind his eyes, Willie. A kind of cat-and-mouse heat. I think there's an awful thick streak of nastiness in that man."

Modesty wiped her hands on a paper tissue and nodded. "If Janet says so, that's good enough."

There was silence for a while, then Willie said, "Ready to go about." The dinghy came round on a south-westerly tack and she ducked under the boom as it swung over. When the little boat had settled on its new course he said, "So what's the plot, Princess? Suppose we find IT. Do we go to Rahim and offer to swap it for the girl?"

She hunched her shoulders for a moment, then relaxed. "Lord knows, Willie. Here I am trying to do something virtuous for once because Dr. Giles Pennyfeather says I should . . . and the whole thing's a mess, isn't it?"

He grinned. "Enough to drive anyone back to sin, I reckon."

"Try to fulfil a dying man's last wish, and look where it gets you. Oh, damn Giles." She stared down into her glass and was silent for a few moments. Then, thoughtfully, "Still, if we *could* get the girl out . . . I mean, that's what he wanted."

"She might've been sold down the line, Princess, like you said just now."

That was true. Some girls lasted for only a few weeks in a harem. Then, the novelty exhausted, they would be sold to the highest bidder. There were plenty of slave-traders to handle such matters. The price would drop with every sale, naturally. It was much like the used car market. Tracy June might have ended up as junk in a small brothel by now, if she had been unlucky.

Modesty drained her glass and said, "I think I'll give it a whirl, anyway." She lifted an eyebrow at Willie. It was her practice never to take him for granted, no matter that his help would be given as surely as the sun would rise.

"Count me in, Princess," he said, and leaned sideways to survey the distant shore. "We'll be going back to Morocco, then." It was more a statement than a question, and he was careful not to speak the trigger word 'Alâeddin'.

She registered the omission, and he saw her blink and hold her breath for a moment. Then she nodded. "That's where we have to start. Somewhere there."

"What about the bloke in the green Renault?"

"Probably one of Casanova's people keeping an eye on us. Or it could be a tail put on us by whoever had Georges Martel tortured. Whoever they are, they want something pretty badly."

"IT?"

"I expect so, Willie. And I'd be certain there's an El Mico connection if we hadn't seen El Mico kill Bernard Martel. That makes no sense. If he was after IT, he'd want Martel alive."

"Want me to deport this green Renault bloke? Dump 'im up in the mountains for a long walk?"

She thought for a moment, then shook her head. "No need. When we're ready to fly out we can easily shake him off so he won't know we've gone until it's too late."

"Book tickets with our other passports, and come into Ajaccio by boat after dark for the airport, maybe?"

"Something like that."

"When d'you want to go, Princess?"

Her shoulders moved and she gave him a ruefully contrite smile. "I'm not sure yet. Haven't quite got myself sorted out. But I'll sleep on it."

He reached out and touched her knee briefly in a rare gesture of reassurance. "You do that," he said gently.

She walked ahead of the tall, bony, dirty man on the mule, her eyes on the ground.

Below the ragged hem of her single garment she saw the skinny legs and bare brown feet. Unshod, those feet had brought her here from the great city in three hundred days.

Fear, sickness, hatred writhed within her. There was a rope halter about her neck. Flesh chafed raw now. He had caught her as she bathed the dust from her body in the mountain spring that wound with the trail. No chance to run. No chance to reach the crude little weapon that had been left with her garment.

She feared for Lob, the little old man whose protector she had been for three winters now. Without her, he would be helpless.

She was sick with repugnance at what the bony man had done to her these past two nights. Knew it would be the same this night.

The hatred was something new. The same bad thing had happened to her before, long ago, far away. Frightening, but not understood. Now she was . . . fourteen, perhaps? Lob thought so. Lob knew everything in the world. Had taught her much.

There were unremembered hours, and then there was night and the bony man was upon her, dragging up the short ragged garment.

But he had grown careless. The weapon, the long nail bound with a wire to a wooden handle . . . it was no longer in the tattered pannier beside the mule, but under her thigh.

She had often drawn it to deter trouble in time past. Had sometimes been compelled to wound with it. Neither would serve her now. She felt for the ribs of the dreadful, stinking, panting body upon her, angled the point upwards, and thrust with all her strength.

And heaved him aside as he died, and rolled away herself, shuddering, curling into a ball, knuckles thrust in mouth, screaming inwardly, silently, the horror beyond all bearing . . . the ground moving now, and different . . . awareness blurring . . .

And Willie Garvin was holding her, saying, "Easy, Princess, easy now. I've got you. It's Willie. Come on, wake up."

The rigidity went out of her and she slumped against him with a sob of relief, her body quivering with reaction. The door between their two bedrooms was open, and there was light from the bedside lamp in Willie's room. He was sitting on her bed, wearing shorts. She was huddled against him, half turned away, her head resting against his shoulder. His arms were wrapped tightly round her naked and sweat-soaked body from behind, hands gripping her wrists.

"Gently now, Princess." His voice was low and soothing. "You're okay, Willie's got you. Just a rotten dream. Try and wake up now."

She said limply, without moving, "All right, Willie, I'm awake. I won't lash out." He released his hold on her wrists and she said quickly, "Hang on to me for a bit, though. Please."

"Sure. Just take your time." He pushed wet hair away from her brow. "Blimey, that was a bad one. I thought someone was throttling you by the sound of it."

She said in a whisper, "Sorry. I'll tell you in a minute."

"No rush."

She lay quiescent in his arms, breathing deeply, letting her conscious mind review every detail of the hidden memory which had now been uncovered by the nightmare. At last with a long sigh she patted his chest and sat up. "What a performance. Let me get a robe, then we'll talk."

She stood up, ruffled his hair, took a short robe from the chair by the dressing table, and belted it about her. As she came back to the bed she saw her smile in the semi darkness. "There's one thing, Willie. We don't have to search for Alâeddin. I know exactly where to find him."

He looked at her curiously as she lay down with her hands behind her head. "The nightmare, Princess?"

"Yes. It opened a little box that's been locked for years. Might as well stretch out and make yourself comfortable, Willie. Nobody gets back to sleep till I've got this off my chest."

He grinned and put his feet up. "You don't 'ave to twist my arm. I'm agog."

"It was a rape, when I was about fourteen. I dreamt it again, pretty much the way it was."

He stared up into the gloom. "But . . . that 'appened earlier, didn't it? I remember you telling me."

"That was another time, in Syria, when I was a year or two younger and hardly knew what it was about. This was out beyond Marrakesh. A trail by one of the springs that run down into the Dades. It was after I'd taken Lob under my wing. We'd wandered south to Cairo, then right across North Africa and down almost to the Sahara. Don't ask me why. We just never stayed long in one place."

Willie nodded. "You came back east and then did it all again a couple of years later, didn't you? That was when Lob died."

"Yes." Tears pricked her eyes.

Lob. She could never quite remember why he had told her to call him by that name, but suspected some obscure literary reference. She had found him in a D.P. camp. He was Jewish, and had once been a professor in Budapest, a small, gentle old man, quite unable to look after himself in the jungle of the camp. The child she had then been had become his protector, and later they had quietly left the camp together, eventually to wander like nomads for several years and thousands of miles around the Middle East and North Africa.

It was Lob, chuckling, who had given her the name Modesty. Before that she had known no name, had only misty memories of walking endlessly towards the sun from very far away, through mountain and valley, field and forest, desert and plain. Blaise was a name she had chosen for herself, later, when Lob told her the legend of Arthur, king of Britain, and his magician, Merlin, whose tutor had been called Blaise.

She lived mainly by stealing, sometimes by working, rarely by begging. It was not difficult to make enough to eat, and she was already skilled in the art of living off the land. During their first weeks together she stole a donkey to carry their few belongings. Soon these belongings included three books and some packets of coarse paper. Lob spoke five languages, and taught them all to her. Each day of every five days they used a different tongue. There were many hours of the twenty-four when they were idle, and once Lob found how she devoured his lessons he made good use of those hours, giving her a basic education on which she could build for herself.

But always they moved on.

Lying on the bed in the hotel in Porto Vecchio she said, "This was the first time we'd come to Morocco. There was no special reason for where we went. Thinking about it now, I suppose we must have come over the Tizi n'Tichka pass and along the road past the Dades Gorge. It wasn't much more than a track then, with a chain of those little fortified villages dotted along it. The *ksour*."

Willie Garvin lay back and closed his eyes, conjuring up a

picture of this strange pair in the stony desert valley of the High Atlas, a fierce young girl and a gentle-mannered professor from Budapest. The quiet voice beside him went on to tell how she had managed to steal a spare wheel from an old jeep-like vehicle in Tinerhir one night a week earlier, and wanted to sell it not less than fifty miles away. But Lob hurt his ankle, so she had to leave him in one of the small villages while she went on to find a buyer for her loot.

The wheel, wrapped in a blanket, was strapped on their donkey and proved difficult to sell in this stretch of country. Then, in another village, she heard of Alâeddin, who was quite mad and would buy anything at all, simply because it was there. He had no thought of selling anything he bought, they said. A hermit, he lived alone in a great cave where the desert met the mountains, well off the road and four days travel by mule from Ksar es Souk.

In that town he had a shop which for twenty years now had been run by his wife and children. From it Alâeddin drew whatever money they allowed him, enough to live, and to buy whatever the nomads might bring. This included every imaginable item of junk that could no longer find a buyer even in the poorest *souk*, together with whatever the years of war had left scattered across the desert.

She said, "You've never seen such a place, Willie. A big cave with smaller ones running off it, and lined with makeshift shelves. He must have spent a lot of time sorting stuff, putting it in boxes, and generally keeping the place tidy, but it was still stacked from floor to roof with junk. I suppose he was an obsessive hoarder. Still is, apparently, though God knows where he'd put another fifteen years of stuff since I last saw the place. I wasn't much interested at the time. All I wanted was to sell my wheel and get back to Lob. I knew Alâeddin wouldn't pay much, but the way we lived, I hoped it would see us through for a couple of months."

She had concluded the bargain, left with the money and her donkey, and decided to take the northern trail through the mountains back to where she had left Lob, rather than the main track. Even before Lob had civilised her somewhat, she had discovered for herself the pleasure of feeling clean and fresh, and so it was that two days later, towards dusk, she was stripped and bathing herself in an icy mountain spring when the tall, bony, dirty man on the mule came upon her. He called to her, and when she would not come out of the water he took her donkey and began to move away. Then she ran after him. When he turned and caught her she fought with her teeth and her nails, but he threw her down and hit her on the side of the head with the thick staff he carried. When she emerged from the grey fog, retching with nausea, her hands were tied behind her.

Willie Garvin muttered, "Oh, Jesus." He got off the bed and began to prowl aimlessly about the room.

She lay with a forearm resting across her brow and said, "Don't fret, Willie. I'm fine now." A little pause, and she went on, "After he'd had me, he hobbled my feet. When it was time to sleep, he tied one end of his staff to my neck and the other end to my wrist, so if I moved he'd know. Next day we moved on, heading back the way I'd come from Alâeddin. He untied my hands and lengthened the hobble on my ankles, so I could walk. I think I might have been able to run away, and maybe to climb up the rock face beside the trail quicker than he could follow, but I couldn't afford to lose the money and the donkey. That was all we had."

Willie Garvin returned and sat on the edge of the bed, looking down at her, chewing his lip. She grinned at him suddenly and said, "Cheer up, this isn't a sob story. I'm just telling you what happened."

"I'd like to find that bastard and kill him."

"You're too late. He had me again the next night, but by the night after that I'd managed to get hold of my homemade chiv."

"The big nail bound to the bit of wood?"

"Yes. I'd acted cowed and harmless the night before, so he didn't tie me up this time, and when he was on top of me, groping to get into me, I killed the bastard."

He nodded slowly. "That must've been a bit . . . traumatic."

"Lord, yes. I think I was in the foetal position for half an hour. When I could stand, I hauled his body up a one-in-eight slope of rock and rolled it down into a crevice. I don't suppose it was ever found. Then I took his mule and my donkey, and went on in the darkness for a few miles till I came to another spring I remembered. More like a river, with rock banks. It comes out from underground and it's freezing, but I kept going right under and scrubbing myself with a bit of torn blanket, and just sitting there in the water till I was nearly blue. Then I'd come out for a while. It was a hot night, the rock was still warm from the sun, and I'd lie there for a time, then go back into the water and scrub myself again. It was like trying to scrub him out of my memory. In the end I fell asleep on the rock . . ."

She had lain there, pushing the memory down and down into black velvet darkness, covering it with layer upon layer until her senses blurred and she was neither asleep nor awake. But from this limbo she finally drifted into sleep, until the later coldness of the night woke her. Then she put on the short ragged djellaba, still damp from furious washing, and went on with the laden mule and the donkey, on down the trail to the cave of Alâeddin.

At noon she arrived there and asked him to name a price for the mule and all it carried, telling him that she had found it on the trail, and that whoever owned it must have met with some mishap. Perhaps by now she believed this herself. He was a stooped, greying man, placid, slow of speech and movement, with a courteous manner that reminded her somewhat of Lob. They haggled amiably for several hours. She sensed that he was keen to have the mule, and when she thought about his own ancient mule, lying outside the cave, she could understand why. It would certainly not carry him on his occasional trips into Ksar es Souk much longer. She insisted that he must take everything else with the mule, and in the end he yielded, paying her twenty-five dirhams, then worth about three English pounds.

Four days later, when at last she returned to the *ksar* where she had left Lob, she told him that she had been compelled to travel right on to Ksar es Souk before being able to sell the wheel, but that she had got a fine price for it there. Perhaps she now believed this herself. Certainly the tall, bony, dirty man was wiped from her memory, together with Alâeddin and his cave.

"So that's why I got the sweats when Georges Martel spoke of somebody called Alâeddin living around the Todra Gorge," she said, and got off the bed to pour herself some water from the flask on her dressing table. "It happened again in Corsica, when Henri Martel spoke the name. Big old grown-up me wanted to remember what I knew, and skinny fourteen-year-old me didn't want to remember the moment when I rammed a nail into the heart of that stinking creature lying on top of me.

She drank, then looked at Willie with a small grimace. "But I've certainly got it off my chest now in a big way. Thanks for staying awake through the great outpouring."

He ran a hand through his hair, noting that she was relaxed now, her eyes quiet and serene. With a little gesture of reassurance he said cheerfully, "That's all right, princess. Anyway, it wasn't the sort of story to induce pandiculation."

Her response came without a flicker of hesitation. "No, I suppose it wasn't. As for the next step, I think we'll spend tomorrow making arrangements to throw off any tail before we leave the day after."

"Right."

"Goodnight, Willie, and thanks again. I hope you get back to sleep okay."

"About thirty seconds. You know me." He went through to his own room, closing the door behind him.

She said softly to herself, "Pandiculation?" Slipping out of the robe, she got into bed, pulled the sheet up to her waist, then turned face down and lay with her head pillowed on a forearm. Pandiculation. One of Willie's obscure words. But he hadn't quite caught her out with it, even though she had been off guard. It was deliberate, of course. A neat distraction to haul her out of the past and into the present.

Pandiculation. She wondered if it might be possible to find a good English dictionary in Porto Vecchio. It would have to be done without Willie's knowledge, of course, so she could win the round by using the word casually to him in its correct context.

Turning on her back she yawned and stretched, then began the rhythmic breathing and mind-focus that would put her to sleep.

Nannie Prendergast said, "Lost them? Piraud *lost* them?"

"I'm afraid so, Nannie. They must have twigged that they were being watched." Jeremy Silk reached for another cucumber sandwich, and Nannie said sharply, "Finish what's on your plate first, if you please, Master Jeremy."

"I beg your pardon, Nannie." They were having tea on the terrace. Jeremy had flown in from Ajaccio an hour ago, and had showered and changed.

"I hope you admonished Piraud," she said.

"Yes, I had him brought aboard and spoke to him as El Mico. Said he'd be heavily fined for incompetence. I'm not sure that we shouldn't remit it though, Nannie, because he'd dug out something rather good."

"I'm glad to hear it." She was very controlled, but he noted dark smudges under her eyes and lines of strain at the corners. The loss of The Object had hit her more severely than he had imagined. He hoped it didn't mean that she might not come to him tonight. There was a burning in his loins, and with an effort he prevented himself staring at her slim legs as she sat neatly in the swing-seat, ankles crossed.

"They'd got on to Gautier's father," he said. "Martel's father, Henri Martel. The baker in Bonifacio. Modesty Blaise went to see him, and Piraud said he felt she'd learned something important there. So I sent Dominic in to lean on him."

With proper caution, I hope."

"Yes, of course, Nannie. Dom looked like a *mafioso*. As it happened, he didn't have to do much leaning. He presented himself as a friend of Georges, whose employers wanted to know all that Henri had told the young English lady who had visited him the day before. Mr. Bun the Baker went a bit pale round the gills, and sang like a bird."

"Ah, that's very satisfactory. What did he say?"

When Jeremy had told her she sat looking out towards the sea, occasionally taking a sip of her tea. After a while she said, "From Martel's ramblings when he was buried alive with Modesty Blaise, it seems The Object must have been left in the custody of this man Alâeddin, who may be ignorant as to what it is. He probably lives in the part of Morocco from which his sister, the baker's wife, came. The baker doesn't know where that is. Our friend Gautier, or Bernard Martel knew where it is, but he's dead. The same applies to his brother, Georges." She looked inquiringly at Jeremy. "Did Georges speak of it while Kermina was questioning him?"

"No, I'm afraid not. I'm sure he'd have been glad to tell us anything, but I suppose it didn't emerge from our questions. As a matter of fact, Nannie, he lost his grip rather quickly and was pouring out a chaotic mass of secrets about his work in the Union Corse. We thought at the time that he was doing it to avoid telling us anything he knew about The Object, but I'm afraid his break-down was genuine."

She put down her tea-cup. "Modesty Blaise will be looking for Alâeddin. Do you have any reason to think she knows where to find him?"

"No, I don't, so we've every chance of finding him first, Nannie. I left Dom in Corsica to check official records of the baker's wedding. That ought to give some clue as to the wife's maiden name and place of birth. With any luck Dom will fly in tomorrow, and then we can start."

"Yes." Her mouth twitched uncontrollably as if with pain. "El Mico must put all his resources behind this search. Everything depends upon it." Her voice began to shake. "All the years of work . . . we must succeed, Master Jeremy, we *must*. Then we can leave this sordid continent . . . turn out backs for ever on these dirty foreign creatures. You and Dominic will be English gentry, true English gentry. Oh, I can't tell you how wonderful it will be."

Tears filled her eyes. Jeremy leaned forward and held her hand. "I'm sure it's going to be absolutely super, Nannie." He hesitated, then went on, "Look, I wish you'd have a word with Dominic. There was quite an argument when I told him to stay behind and check the marriage records. In fact he was jolly sullen about it, and wanted to know why *he* couldn't come on home and report while *I* did the checking. After all, I'm the oldest, and he ought to do what I say."

"The older, Jeremy. Not oldest."

"Sorry, Nannie. But will you have a word with him? He'll listen to you."

"Yes," she said slowly, "but I don't like my little monkeys to quarrel, so *you* must be careful too, dear. After all, it takes two to make a quarrel, and it's usually six of one and half a dozen of the other. I know you're a little older, but you do sometimes tend to be rather a bossy-boots with Master Dominic, you know."

He looked down to hide his indignation. She would be angry if she saw that. The white linen skirt had moulded itself to the shape of her thighs, forming a V-shaped valley between her legs. From the top of the valley, running away at an angle to her flank, he could see the faint raised line made by . . . by what Nannie wore under the skirt.

Desire leapt in him. Still holding her hand, he mumbled urgently, "Nannie, I know it's not bedtime, but . . . well, I mean, I've been a bit busy, and . . . I wouldn't mind, you know, a bit of a lie-down. But if I did, if I went to bed now, would you . . . I mean, you know. Would you come and tuck me in and . . . pop in with me for a little while?"

His voice faded with the last words, and he knew he had made a dreadful mistake. Nannie Prendergast drew her hand away and stood up. He rose with her, hands behind his back, head hanging low, cold with apprehension.

"I'm ashamed of you, Master Jeremy!" she said in a voice pitched high with shock. "Yes, ashamed! What on earth's got into you? Don't you realise this is *teatime*?"

"I'm sorry, Nannie." A low mutter.

"I think you'd better go straight to your room, young man. And you can be quite sure that it will be some time before Nannie comes to tuck *you* in again."

nine

Modesty touched his arm and said, "We turn off soon, Willie. About another mile, I think."

He nodded, and took a hand from the wheel of the Range Rover to wipe a sweating palm on his trousers. If she said about a mile, he reflected, it would be just that, even though it was perhaps fifteen years since she had been here. Her gift for orientation was magical, and was equalled by her memory of terrain.

It was ten days since they had left Corsica, for they had come the long way round to throw off any surveillance. If you travelled by air you posed few problems for anyone with an organisation who wanted to keep tabs on you, for you moved along fixed lines and emerged at fixed points. They had driven across Spain to Lisbon and then been picked up by boat one night from a beach east of Cascais. Four days later they had landed at Essaouria, where the Range Rover awaited them, fully equipped for the task ahead. Painted on the side in neat lettering was the inscription *Pascale et Cie (Arpenteurs)*. A theodolite and other surveying equipment could be seen in the back of the truck. Moulay was a skilled and experienced organiser.

They had passed through Marrakesh by night, crossing the High Atlas by the Tizi n'Tichka pass and dropping down to the Dades valley to follow the long east-west road between the two great ranges. To the north, the mountains were riven by gorges, dry now, but scoured by ferocious torrents in the season of rains. Between the occasional tiny walled villages lay an emptiness of stony desert relieved only by camel-thorn, Barbary fig cactus, and the strongly multicoloured rock, full of reds and blacks, yellow, purple, brown and sombre green.

Modesty said, "Here it is," and Willie took the broad rough trail which forked slightly north off the main Ksar es Souk road. It rose slowly for half a mile, then began to drop again. Here another track branched off directly north. Modesty said, "That's new. I mean, new since I was here."

Willie braked to a halt. It looked like a track which had once been heavily used, for where it emerged from the cutting the rock wall on both sides was scored and chipped as if by heavy vehicles. Incongruously, there was an international sign indicating No Through Road.

Modesty said, "Xanadu."

Willie nodded. When Prince Rahim Mohajeri Azhari built Xanadu, a service road had been cut through the mountains for delivery of materials. Modesty knew a French journalist who had researched the subject and written a piece about it for *Paris Match*. She had rung him from Marseilles to learn that Xanadu lay eight miles into the mountains from the main Ksar es Souk road, east of the Todra Gorge. It had taken six months to cut a road for access, even though the road followed an ancient mule track for a good part of the way. At a point two miles from the palace, this road left the track to cross a ravine. After completion of the work, the sixty foot long temporary bridge had been dismantled and replaced by a drawbridge, a single leaf bascule on the Xanadu side of the ravine. This ensured that nobody entered Xanadu without the sanction of the prince. Or left it, either, the French journalist had added dryly.

Willie let in the clutch and drove on past the access road. He said, "So we're pretty close to the cave now?"

"About twenty minutes on this track." She studied the mountains to her left. "That's where he caught me, somewhere along that mule trail."

Willie glanced at her. "Is it worrying you, Princess?"

She shook her head, and smiled. "Not a scrap, now. That was somebody else who got raped. Somebody I used to know a long time ago."

"Well, good. But it's a wonder it didn't put you off Arabs from 'ere to Baghdad."

She gave a little shrug. "Not after knowing Abu-Tahir, and Big Hassan, and Ahmet, and—oh, so many of them when I was with the Bedouins. And later I spent a while with a Touareg tribe down in the desert south of here. They were lovely people. But you get all kinds wherever you go."

Willie eased the truck over some deep ruts in the track. There was no road here now, except what nature had provided. "I'm glad we were very careful coming 'ere, Princess," he said pensively. "Not sure why."

"Ears prickling?"

"Not exactly. I've just got a feeling that somebody somewhere might be looking very 'ard for us."

"Or for whatever we're looking for."

"Could be. Could be both."

The walls of rock fell away and the Range Rover emerged on to a small rocky plain, perhaps a quarter of a mile wide. To the right it extended out of sight, presumably narrowing to rejoin the main road eventually. Ahead and to the left it was bounded by the mountain wall, rising sheer for a hundred feet or more, then sloping back in a series of crests. Modesty said, "Bear left now."

The Range Rover came round towards the southern face of the mountains. Ahead lay two small outcrops of rock jutting from the plain to almost the height of a man. To Willie, as he headed to pass between them, they brought to mind the backsight of a rifle, for in the mountain wall a hundred yards beyond, like the blade of a foresight, was the dark aperture of a cave.

Modesty said, "Go round the outside of those outcrops, Willie. The ground drops for a foot or more between them, like a deep curb. I remember now."

He grinned. "Who wouldn't?"

They swung clear of the outcrops, then came back in line with the cave, for the ground was heavily scattered with big stones and small rocks except where a slight gulley, a shallow depression in the dark, sandy basalt, ran directly up the little gradient to the cave. She said. "Not too close, Willie." He nodded his understanding of the courtesy, and lifted the truck out of the broad crease, weaving across the rock-strewn ground to the shadow of the mountain wall fifty paces to one side of the cave.

Braking to a halt, he switched off the engine and they climbed out. It was very hot, and suddeny very quiet now. Modesty plucked the shirt away from her damp body and ran thumbs round the waistband of her slacks. Watching her as she picked up the small draw-string canvas bag she was using as a handbag, Willie could see a mixture of amusement and exasperation in her expression.

She gave a shake of her head as if to clear it, and said, "All of a sudden everything feels unreal."

Before Willie could answer a man came slowly into view from within the cave. He wore a white homespun djellaba with the hood thrown back, and sandals made from chunks of tyre. A small man, probably frail beneath the djellaba, he had wispy grey hair, an inch of beard, and blue Berber eyes behind a pair of wire-rimmed spectacles. One of the lenses had evidently come loose, for it had been refastened by half an inch of black insulating tape over the top of the frame.

When Modesty put her hands together and greeted him in the dialect of the area, his head tilted to one side in surprise. She moved towards him unhurriedly, still speaking, and Willie followed. "We are friends of the son of your sister, Fauzia."

The old man blinked and looked bewildered. She waited for her words to sink in, then went on, "I speak of Bernard Martel, who came to visit you not long ago."

The bewilderment cleared slowly. "Bernard? Ah, yes. And you are friends of his?"

"Yes. May we talk with you for a little while?"

His eyes went past her to the truck. He bent forward to peer at it, and the loose lens hung down vertically from the spectacle frame, hinged on the insulating tape. When he straightened, it moved back into place. He said, "You have things to sell?"

"Many things, if you wish to buy."

"We will have tea, and talk."

He started to turn towards the cave, then swung back, squinting up at her with furrowed brow. Suddenly he gave a chuckle, beckoned, and turned towards the cave again. "Come, woman. The man also."

It was cool inside. Willie took off the peaked khaki cap he wore and looked about him. The roof was high and domed. Four minor caves led from the main one, and each was high enough for a tall man to walk upright. To the right of the central area was a large annexe with a lower roof, and this was evidently Alâeddin's living quarters, for there was a low bed, some rugs, cushions, a cupboard, and a little stove.

Light came from a number of small bulbs strung throughout the cave and fed from a bank of four big twelve-volt batteries of the kind used by a mobile signal detachments during the war. The walls of the central cave, and the whole of the branch caves apart from a narrow access path down the middle of each, were stacked with boxes, parcels, bundles, and unwrapped junk of every kind, but all was neatly arranged. Wire had been strung between long nails driven into crevices in the roof, and from these wires hung another collection of junk. A crude ladder was propped against one wall. To the right of the entrance, a mule stood dozing, its ancient saddle hanging above it.

Alâeddin, with a polite request to them to wait, vanished down one of the branch caves They could hear him grunting as he wrestled with some task. Willie said, "What's he up to?"

"I can't imagine. He seemed amused about something. You know, he looks exactly the same as when I last saw him, Willie, except for the glasses. So does the cave. Either he's cleared some stuff out or these branches run deeper than I thought."

There came a little cry of triumph, and seconds later Alâeddin reappeared, rolling a wire-spoke car wheel with a well-worn tyre. "See!" he cried proudly. "Here is something I bought from you many years ago when you were a young girl."

Willie said, "Blimey," and ran a hand slowly through his hair, staring. Modesty looked at the wheel for a long time, then lifted her eyes to Alâeddin's grinning face. "You recognised me?"

"I remember the eyes. I remember how you looked when you brought me the mule of Mahjoub, and his belongings."

"You . . . knew they were his?"

"I knew. I knew Mahjoub. A man without honour. Once in every two moons he passed this way. I think he did a bad thing to you that day. After you came back with the mule I did not expect him to pass again, and it was so." He shrugged and made a gesture as if brushing away a fly. Rolling the wheel to one side he said, "Come. I will make tea and we will talk. How are you called? And the man?"

"I am Modesty. This is my friend, Willie."

"Mod-es-tee. Willee." He gestured for them to enter the annexe, produced plump faded cushions for them to sit on, then bustled about making tea, repeating their names at intervals as he brought water to the boil three times to make a strong brew, evidently judging from their facility with the language that they were well accustomed to Arab ways and Arab tea.

For ten minutes there was polite talk in general terms. Alâeddin was of the old school, asking no question which might be considered inquisitive. Modesty congratulated him on his tea; Willie on his collection of so many interesting objects. Both felt admiration for the way this eccentric old man was conducting himself. In his world, a woman rated only just above a mule and was often used for the same kind of work, yet here in his hermit's cave, because Modesty was a guest, he was contriving to put aside a lifetime's prejudice by treating her as an equal.

When they had finished tea, she edged nearer to the point of the visit by telling him, with proper commiseration, that Bernard Martel was dead. She felt it was simpler and less disturbing to give the impression that he had died during the earthquake, and that in dying he had made a last request to her that she should visit his mother's brother, Alâeddin.

The old man nodded slowly when she spoke of his nephew's death, and muttered the inevitable *Insh' Allah*. After she had completed the story he sat in silence for a while with eyes closed, then opened them and said, "Do you bring some message for me, Modestee?"

Sitting cross-legged, her hands in her lap, she held his gaze as she said, "He was in a fever, and the message was not clear. I have since spoken with his father, the husband of your sister, and I believe that Bernard's great wish was to recover the wife who was stolen from him. Did he speak of this to you?"

Alâeddin shook his head. "No. He said there were matters it was better not to speak of. He left a possession of his with me, and said he would return for it when he had made certain difficult arrangements."

After a brief silence she said, "I believe he thought it would be possible to regain his wife by using the possession he left with you. Do you feel able to tell me what it is?"

"I do not know what it is. The boy gave me a steel box. It had been broken open, but was held by a strap. He asked me to hide it, and to speak of it to nobody until he returned."

"And now he will not return."

"So it is written. Are you saying to me that you wish to take what is in the box and use it to help his wife?"

She looked at Willie, then back at the old man. "I do not know how to answer that question, Alâeddin. In the beginning, a friend I much respect told me that I should try to do what Bernard wished to be done." Her shoulders lifted slightly. "But there are many mysteries, and the whole matter is far from simple. Will you open the steel box now, so that we may see what it contains. Then perhaps we can more easily judge what may be done."

He sat for a long time with eyes closed, rocking very slightly. The loose lens of his spectacles swung back and forth in time with his movements. At last he said with a sigh, "I think it is some precious thing. I have been unhappy that he brought it to me. I do not wish to have precious things. They are dangerous." He uncrossed his legs and got slowly to his feet. "Come, then."

They followed him out of the annexe. Behind the mule, an ancient charging engine stood on a board fitted with trolley wheels, presumably so that it could be easily moved out of the cave when running to recharge the batteries. Above the engine, on a hook, was a Tilley lamp. As the old man began to go through the business of lighting it, Willie looked slowly round the central area of the cave again. Although much of the junk was boxed, some could be seen, and there was a sense of order and grouping about the way it was arranged. A polystyrene box heaped with rusty bolts; a crate with odd lengths of lead and copper piping; cogwheels from a gearbox, strung on wire; a steering wheel . . . all mechanical junk.

On a shelf above, a box of false teeth, another of broken spectacles, a skull, an iron leg-brace, half a stethoscope . . . all medical junk. Modesty touched his arm and murmured, "The sports section." She lifted her chin slightly, and he looked up. Above him hung an ancient cricket bat.

He held back a sound of astonishment and said, "I'd love to know the story be'ind that."

"I saw it here before, but I didn't know what it was then."

"Wonder what old Ali Baba makes of it."

Beside the cricket bat hung a squash racket without strings, a walking stick, an assegai, a wooden ski, and a pelota *cesta* in remarkably good condition as far as Willie could tell. None matched the surprise of the cricket bat. There might well have been a Basque pelota enthusiast in Rio de Oro, a Spanish province until 1976, and only five hundred miles away to the south-west; that could account for the *cesta*. The ski undoubtedly came from even closer to home, for there was ski-ing as late as June up among the cedars of the Middle Atlas. The assegai would have found its way from much further south, in Black Africa, and even this was not particularly surprising, for the nomads still travelled the ancient caravan routes across the monstrous wastes of the Sahara to the Niger and beyond. But the cricket bat . . .

Alâeddin said, "Come." The hissing lamp gave off a strong white light as he led the way along one of the four branch caves. They had to move in single file between the junk-lined walls, but after fifteen paces the cave ended in another annexe, almost circular, and smaller than the living quarters, but clear except for a work-bench and an array of tools which appeared to have seen much use.

Alâeddin hung the lamp on a hook which was set in the roof to one side of the work-bench, then moved round behind the bench and pushed aside some rough pieces of timber which lay on the ground there. Beneath the timber was a hole. He knelt, reached into the hole, and with an effort lifted out a dull steel box, a fifteen inch cube secured by a broad leather strap. Willie moved quickly to help him, taking the box and waiting for the old man to get creakingly to his feet before setting it down on the bench. Modesty made a gesture of invitation, but Alâeddin wagged his head, lifting his hands in refusal. "You," he said.

She moved forward, unbuckled the strap, then looked at Willie. "It wouldn't be booby-trapped?"

"Not with the lid loose like that. It's been broken open."

She lifted the lid away. The box was made of three millimetre sheet steel. The lid was hinged, and had a deep flange all round which fitted perfectly except at the point where some kind of lock had been. Here the metal of both box and lid had been roughly cut away as if by hacksaw and cold chisel.

Willie lifted out a wad of cotton-waste packing. The light of the lamp was reflected in scintillations of green and red and white from within. He glanced at Modesty, saw her barely perceptible nod, and reached down.

Fiery colour blazed all about his hands as he lifted out the great crown. It was tall, with a high arch and two wings. From the arch, a magnificent gold filial set with diamonds rose above an emerald as big as a man's eye. Against the inner padding of red velvet, the silver and gold framework was almost entirely hidden by the diamonds, pearls and emeralds encrusting it. Two rings of huge pearls encircled the base, widely separated by blazing gem-set curlicues. The wings and arch continued the theme of pearls and diamonds, and in the centre was a tremendous sunburst of gems set about a diamond that dwarfed the great emerald of the filial.

The old man whimpered and lifted an arm, clamping his teeth on the sleeve of his djellaba as if to stifle any further sound. Willie set the crown gently down on the work-bench under the light.

Modesty said in a whisper, "I was a bit slow, wasn't I?"

"Me, too."

"Bernard Martel pronounced it the way it's spelt . . . Pahlavi. Not peh-levi, the way you and I would recognise. But even so . . ."

Willie moved his head slightly to watch the shift of light in the hearts of a thousand gems. "It fits the titles," he said softly. "King of Kings, Shadow of the Almighty, Vice-Regent of God, Centre of the Universe . . . and Tenant of the Peacock Throne. I suppose that's what was running through Martel's mind when he said Peacock and Shadow." With an effort he took his eyes from the Pahlavi Crown. "I always reckoned the Shah must've whipped this and the rest of the Crown Jewels out of Teheran before the Ayatollah came in to spread peace and joy. Stashed it away in a Swiss bank."

She gave a shake of her head. "If he had, it wouldn't be here. But somebody saw the chaos coming in Iran well before it happened, and they set up a caper to take advantage of it at just the right moment, when the collapse of authority came and the police and army melted away. I know it was in a high security vault in the National Bank of Teheran, we made a feasibility study of the idea ourselves back in *The Network* days, and it wasn't possible then. But if you were ready when the balloon went up, if you'd spread your bribes and had your replicas made, and laid on a really skilled task force . . ."

"Like El Mico did, maybe?"

"It seems likely, now. And Bernard Martel pulled a double-cross."

Modesty moved slowly round the bench, studying the crown from every angle. She was a skilled lapidary, with a small workshop in her London penthouse, and she knew her gemstones.

Willie said, "More than three thousand three 'undred diamonds, if I remember right. That's apart from everything else. What's it worth, Princess?"

Again she shook her head. "You can't price it. Together with the lesser Crown Jewels, this thing was the backing of seventy-five per cent of the Iranian currency."

There was a silence in the cave, a silence dominated by the coruscating, almost awe-inspiring creation that held their eyes. Both knew that the crown itself had been made little more than fifty years ago, but it had been fashioned from booty seized centuries before, when the Persian conqueror, Nadir Shah, had sacked Delhi and brought home chests of emeralds, diamonds and pearls from the treasury of the Great Mogul.

Alâeddin lowered his arm from his mouth and said in a shaking voice, "I do not want this thing in my home. Please take it away."

Modesty said, "Is that truly your wish?"

"Yes. And again, yes," he said with frail urgency. "It was never in my thought that the boy had brought me such a thing as this to keep for him. A dangerous thing, Modestee. Dangerous. I will be happy if you take it quickly."

"Very well. But please don't be afraid."

Willie lowered the Pahlavi Crown into the box, replaced the packing, and closed the lid. "What d'you reckon to do with it, Princess?" he murmured wonderingly. "I suppose Martel reckoned to offer this to Rahim in exchange for Tracy June. *Enough to buy a thousand women . . .*"

She stood holding her elbows, frowning a little, lower lip caught in her teeth. "I don't know," she said at last. "We set out to meet Martel's dying wish, which means getting Tracy June out of Xanadu—if she's still there. But everything seems to have got rather out of hand."

Willie fastened the strap. "Can't say I fancy the idea of the Pahlavi Crown going back to that bloodthirsty old maniac who took over in Teheran," he said. "I'd rather you sent it to Oxfam."

She gave a short laugh. "So would I. But for the time being we'll just get it away from here and hidden safely away somewhere else, then we can think what to do about it. And let's keep remembering the main issue. Tracy June is why we're here."

Ten minutes later Willie eased the Range Rover down the middle of the broad valley, round the rocky outcrops, and then on to the rough spur which led to the main road. The steel box, wrapped in a sack, lay in the back beneath their luggage and surveying impedimenta.

"Which way, Princess?"

"Let's take the quickest way home to Tangier, Willie. Ksar es Souk, then north through the mountains to Fez."

"Right. 'Allo, what's that?"

They were turning out of the spur on to the main road, and only fifty yards to their left stood an off-road vehicle similar to their own, an International Scout. A man in a blue shirt and brown slacks knelt beside it in the meagre patch of shade it offered. He was bending over another man and holding a water bottle to his lips. As Willie brought the Range Rover to a halt alongside, the kneeling man looked up. He had sunbleached fair hair, a fresh complexion, and freckles, and looked so English that it was mildly surprising when he spoke in French, his voice rough with anxiety. "My brother, he collapsed. I almost ran off the road when he fell against me. Do you think it is heatstroke? He has never done this before."

Willie switched off and glanced at Modesty. For a moment she hesitated, then gave a little grimace of self-mockery and opened the door. Willie followed suit, knowing that her reactions had paralleled his own: a moment of suspicion, followed by the quick realisation that this sprang solely from knowing what lay under their luggage in the back of the truck.

The man lay supine, his bush shirt open and spread away from his chest. She knelt and took the water bottle from his brother, saying, "You might choke him like that, while he's unconscious."

"I am sorry, madame. I did not realise."

She sprinkled water liberally over the man's chest, neck and face. "Do you carry ice?"

"I regret, madame."

She bent low to study the man's lips, pushed back one of his eyelids, and said over her shoulder in English, "Bring the ice-box please, Willie. It doesn't look like heart. Doesn't look much like heatstroke either, but it can't hurt to cool him down." Then, in French: "Is your brother diabetic?"

"Ah, no, madame." The man shuffled awkwardly aside on his knees, then got to his feet as Willie approached with a plastic thermos bag. Modesty was checking the pulse rate as he bent to put it down beside her. She heard a sound, a small soft thud, and Willie Garvin crumpled forward across the legs of the man on the ground. Her head came round and her arm swung up in an instinctive guard, even before the shock had registered of seeing the standing man in the follow-through of a blow with the kongo that jutted from each side of his fist.

She had started to roll back, to free her legs from beneath her, when the man who lay on the ground brought his clenched hand from beneath the concealment of the open bush shirt, and swung his arm up and over to strike with the kongo to the nerve centre behind her ear.

Slumped on the sandy road, senses blurring, fighting to hold back the darkness, she heard English voices, excited, exultant. Then powerful hands were holding her, something pricked her arm, and with a dying spark of angry contempt for herself she sank down into the black depths of nothingness.

The view from the great arched window was startling. Immediately below lay the gardens, expertly landscaped, a blaze of flowers and small blossoming trees, separated from the glittering blue and white pool by a line of young cyprus. Beyond lay nothing but the ancient rock of the High Atlas reaching on and on between a series of overlapping spurs to the white peaks on the horizon.

Nannie Prendergast said, "One lump, please."

Prince Rahim Mohajeri Azhari gestured to the veiled girl by the silver trolley and spoke a word. The girl picked up a lump of sugar in her tongs and slid it carefully into Nannie Prendergast's cup. Another word and she withdrew, moving without a sound across the tiled, rug-strewn floor.

Rahim surveyed the woman sitting on the couch facing him, hiding his wonderment behind an expression of polite solicitude. "I trust it was not inconvenient for you to visit me without delay," he said in perfect, slightly drawling upper class English. "But as soon as my agent in Fez telephoned to say that The Object had been secured, I did not wish to lose a moment in completing our transaction."

"Not at all inconvenient, Your Highness." Nannie Prendergast sipped her tea. "On our side we are also most anxious to complete." When she looked at the prince she was careful to keep her eyes on his face, for with his white slacks he wore a red shirt unbuttoned to the waist, exposing his chest in a manner she found ostentatious. It was the kind of disgustingly overt sexuality that went with his good looks and his way of life, she decided, and it had proved a very satisfactory trait from a business point of view. But she did not intend to show any awareness of it on a personal basis.

Three hours ago, towards noon, she had been in Fez, waiting

with Little Krell at the airport for Prince Rahim's personal helicopter to come and pick them up. Little Krell was now in the cool, picture-hung corridor outside the big room overlooking the gardens. The prince was not in the least offended by the fact that his visitor had brought a personal bodyguard. He would have been astonished if she had not. But he was finding it quite difficult to adjust to the identity of El Mico's representative.

She was in many ways a typical nannie, he thought. His judgment here was from experience, for he had himself had a Scottish nannie. He put Miss Prendergast's age at thirty-eight or thirty-nine. She had a good figure and good legs, to judge by what he could see of them. She was not beautiful, either by European or Arab standards, but there was something intriguing about her face with its curiously unmatched features.

He said, "As you can imagine, it is something of a surprise to discover that El Mico's agent is an English lady."

"I am half Welsh, Your Highness." There was a tiny hint of admonition in her tone. "And I am a principal in this matter, rather than an agent."

He smiled. "Forgive me. When the notion of securing The Object was first conveyed to me through my own agent, I understood that he had talked face to face with El Mico. We were not told that El Mico had a female colleague of equal standing."

"That is something which has been known to less than a handful of men for years past, Your Highness. And they have all passed on now."

"Recent employees?"

"Yes."

"Ah, I understand. El Mico is to retire after this coup, and wishes to leave no loose ends?"

"That is so. Perhaps I should explain that El Mico is in fact a composite person. I hope you will shortly be meeting the two young men who have played the part from time to time."

"They are at present in possession of The Object?"

"Yes." She gave him a warm smile. "But they will not bring it here until I speak with them personally by means of the radio that Little Krell was carrying when we arrived."

He nodded, dark eyes sparkling with humour. "And you will

be happy to speak with them as soon as your Swiss banker telephones confirmation of receipt of twenty million dollars?"

"I shall indeed be happy to do so, Your Highness." She indicated the low table at her elbow. "Is this a radio telephone you have here?"

"No, Miss Prendergast. A line was laid by helicopter from Midelt, when Xanadu was first built. So when your banker calls, you need have no fear that your conversation will be broadcast."

He turned his head to gaze absently out of the tall window, thinking how fascinating it would be to bed this remarkable Miss Prendergast. A very different experience. Perhaps highly enjoyable. But out of the question. The Object was a great deal more important than a hundred interesting experiences.

He said, "When my agent made inquiries recently, at my instigation, as to the cause of delay in completing our transaction, some mention was made of Modesty Blaise. I know of her, of course. And I once sat at a baccarat table in Beirut with her tame dog, Willie Garvin. That was some years ago, however, and I was not there under my own name. Perhaps while we wait for the call from Switzerland you could put me more fully into the picture as to what has occurred?"

"Certainly, Your Highness. As you know, your agents have had dealings with El Mico in the past. We have always given you first offer of the most interesting girls. Then I had the notion of obtaining The Object, and El Mico put this to your agent. Through him, you agreed a price."

"Subject to certain conditions, Miss Prendergast."

"Which have been complied with, Your Highness. Knowledge of this affair is now confined to myself, the two young men who are El Mico, and yourself."

"Excellent. Please continue."

"The operation was very difficult and very complex, as you may imagine, but in the event it was carried out successfully."

"To be truthful, I did not dream that it would succeed. I am filled with delight and admiration."

"Thank you. I regret to say that an act of treachery then occurred. It has been thoroughly dealt with, but it resulted in The Object being lost for a time, and almost falling into the hands of

Modesty Blaise." She put down her empty cup and lifted a hand in polite refusal at Rahim's inquiring gesture. "No more, thank you. I will not conceal from you, Your Highness, that Modesty Blaise and her friend Garvin located the missing Object before El Mico was able to do so. Fortunately it was very marginal . . . in fact less than an hour before. El Mico observed their vehicle outside the dwelling of a person called Alâeddin—"

"The cave? The cave of that old lunatic?"

"I understand it was a cave of some kind."

Rahim threw himself back on the couch and laughed with a flash of white teeth. "Good God! He must be removed, of course."

"That would be prudent."

"Your two-man El Mico didn't attend to him?"

"No. They set a trap, overcame Miss Blaise and Mr. Garvin, and drove off with their vehicle. With both vehicles, in fact."

"Having checked that The Object was aboard the Blaise vehicle, I take it?"

Nannie Prendergast smiled. "Oh yes, Your Highness. Then they drove up into one of the gorges some way from here, and called me by radio. I had moved to Fez as soon as we located the whereabouts of The Object. They reported to me, in code of course, and I made immediate contact with your agent there."

"Revealing your identity to him?"

"No. My bodyguard made the telephone call and gave him the code phrase which had been agreed with you as a means of authenticating any message from El Mico. I must thank you for responding to the message so promptly."

"My dear Miss Prendergast, when Hassan came through to tell me El Mico had secured The Object and now wished me to have two persons flown in from Fez as soon as possible, I was unable to finish my breakfast with excitement. Daoud found you at the airport without difficulty I presume?"

"Daoud? Oh, the pilot. Yes, he located Little Krell with the agreed recognition signal, and I was standing by."

"I must confess to you that I am somewhat disappointed to find that The Object did not arrive with you. I am longing to see it."

Hands folded in her lap, she said rather primly, "An ounce of wisdom is worth a pound of wit, Your Highness."

"I beg your pardon?"

"We are about to exchange a precious object for twenty million dollars. It would not be wise of either of us to do so without proper precautions."

He laughed again. "You are a business lady, Miss Prendergast."

A man entered soundlessly, a servant in lustrous gold trousers, bolero, and babouche, like a character from some Hollywood version of the Arabian Nights. He bowed to the prince, touched a hand to mouth and ear, then withdrew, Rahim indicated the telephone resting on an onyx base beside the couch where Nannie Prendergast sat.

She picked it up and said, "Miss Prendergast speaking."

An accented voice said, "This is Herr Keller, speaking from Geneva."

"Good morning, Herr Keller. Do you have the Prendergast/Silk joint account before you?" A pause. "Will you please state my middle name, so that I may be sure of your identity? Thank you. What do you have to tell me?"

Herr Keller said, "Within the last thirty minutes we have received from the Swiss branch of Morgan Guaranty a draft for twenty million American dollars to be credited to your account. We also received a request to telephone you immediately at this Moroccan number to confirm that the transfer had taken place."

"Thank you, Herr Keller."

"Do you have any further instructions, Miss Prendergast?"

"Not at the moment, thank you, but I shall be paying you a visit shortly."

"I shall look forward to it."

"Good-bye, Herr Keller."

She put the telephone down. "That was most satisfactory, Your Highness, I'll call El Mico and tell him to come in with The Object now."

"Splendid. I gave orders for your little radio to be taken up to the roof, for better communication. It's quite high up, but there's a very comfortable lift. I should be glad to escort you there myself."

"Most kind of you."

As they stood up he said, "I don't think you made clear precisely

159

what had happened to Modesty Blaise and Willie Garvin. Did your two young men dispose of them somewhere in the mountains?"

"No, they put them under sedation, just in case any information was required of them. But the matter is concluded now, so I shall give instructions for El Mico to cause the two of them to pass on at once."

The prince looked out of the window again, hands on hips. So this extraordinary woman, who had introduced herself as Nannie Prendergast, could give instructions to El Mico. She was evidently behind the whole El Mico organisation, and now she had capped it all by stealing the fabulous Pahlavi Crown. This was incredible, and he found himself feeling mildly annoyed that a woman should have achieved such a coup. It seemed vaguely insulting to him, as if in some measure there was an intent to unman him.

The transaction itself was quite splendid, of course. At twenty million dollars it was costing perhaps eighteen months' expenditure. A trifle. And the Pahlavi Crown would last longer than oil, which would last longer than the oil sheiks. In a few years their time would run out, and then, after a little while, the oil would run out. But Xanadu would still be secure, and by that time the Pahlavi Crown would be worth . . . half a billion dollars? Certainly not less.

Yes, the transaction was magnificent, and Nannie Prendergast was rightly feeling a huge sense of achievement at having brought it off. But she was, after all, only a woman, and as such should be reminded that her writ did not run in Xanadu.

"Be so kind," said Rahim firmly, "as to give instructions for Miss Blaise and Mr. Garvin to be brought in alive, Miss Prendergast. I should like to meet them, and I feel confident that they can provide Xanadu with some excellent entertainment before, as you put it, we cause them to pass on."

ten

The room was small, the floor and walls of a synthetic material with a surface like hard rubber. There were no windows, no furniture. The door had no handle and could be opened only from outside. There was a small flap in the bottom of the door, about three inches deep and nine wide. Light came from behind a translucent panel in the ceiling. Off one corner of the room was a small closet with a tap, a hole in the floor, and two small concrete platforms for the feet. A primitive lavatory.

Willie Garvin was sprawled on the floor, half sitting. Modesty knelt beside him, supporting his head and shoulders with one arm, gently slapping his face. Their clothes lay scattered about the floor. She said, "Come on, Willie. Wake up." A more severe slap. "Come on now, try harder."

Her own head was almost clear, but her mouth was parched and she felt sick. There were dreamlike memories of lying huddled in the back of a truck, either the Range Rover or the Scout, wrists bound with cord; of sleeping, half waking, struggling to drag herself out of the heavy torpor. Then . . . voices. Another prick of a needle, and nothingness again. There had been the sound of the engine starting up. Two sounds. Another engine. Laboriously her wavering mind had fitted a few fragments of awareness together. Two men. Willie drugged in the back of the other vehicle. Swaying, bumping. The rough track up through the mountains. A bridge . . .? She could not remember. She remembered the English accents of the two men, the excitement in their voices, the quick laughter, and the self-congratulation that even to her clouded mind had seemed oddly schoolboyish.

She slapped Willie again, and pinched his ear hard. He stirred fretfully. "Good. That's right, Willie love. Come on now, come on . . ."

He opened an eye, gazed owlishly up at her for some seconds, then muttered, "Awri' Princess . . . jus' minute." The other eye opened with an effort.

She said, "That's better. Come on, Willie, start getting it all together. You must have had a heavier shot of valium or whatever it was when they gave us the last injection. Are you listening? I think we're in Xanadu, and I'm damn sure we're in bad trouble. Try to sit up now."

He came slowly up, helped by her arm, and lifted his head from her bare shoulder to stare blankly at the scattered clothes. Then he leaned forward, resting elbows on knees, and rubbed his eyes hard with the heels of his hands. "Xanadu?" he said thickly.

"I think it must be. This room looks like a *bait-at-ta'ah.*"

He lifted his head and looked about him, then nodded. She had put on a pair of pants now, and was fastening her bra. He crawled round gathering his clothes, then began to check the pockets, the seams and cuffs, the belt. At last he sighed and stood up to pull on shorts and trousers. "They made a tooth-comb search then, Princess."

"Yes." She was buttoning her shirt. "I've nothing much left. No kongo, no gas-pen, no wire, no lock-picks."

Willie grimaced. He was beginning to be able to think now, but it brought little comfort. When in potential danger they carried a number of useful items, apart from weapons. His harness with the twin throwing knives had gone, so had the little phial of anaesthetic nose-plugs, the razor blade in the book of matches, the selection of probes in the belt, and the boots with the special heels which could be detached and primed to make tiny grenades. Modesty's boots, with their small hidden armoury, were also missing. Spare shoes from their luggage had been thrown on to the floor with the rest of their clothes.

On Willie's middle finger was a plain silver ring. If he took it off and squeezed the sides hard, it would separate into two thinner rings, partly hollow and with a few inches of fine wire between them. Tungsten wire, coated with silicon carbide paste. A very efficient tool for cutting through metal—the bar of a grille, for example. Unfortunately there was nothing on which to use it. He slid a thumb and finger round the waist-band of his slacks, and could just feel within it the strands of thin nylon cord that the searches had missed. They were of no more use at the moment than the flexible cutter.

He ran his tongue round his teeth, shuddered, then went into the closet and drank from the tap, gargling, splashing water over his face and neck. When he came out she was sitting with her back to the wall facing the door, arms resting on her drawn-up knees. He sat beside her, and she said softly, "When somebody comes, I'll be having pains in the stomach. Don't try to jump any guards, even if there's a chance. We've no hope until we know the lie of the land a bit better. But it might be worth establishing a touch of the gripes for later."

"Right, Princess."

They sat in silence. For the moment there was nothing to be discussed, no point in self-reproach over their capture, and none in speculation. For some reason they had been kept alive so far. Presumably something would follow from this, but the next move was not theirs to make. They sat relaxed, breathing slowly, seeking mental balance. After a while, Willie allowed his attention to focus on the door, the area of the external lock in particular, contemplating it with affection, and holding the concept in his mind with gentle regard. There could well come a time when he would be greatly concerned with that Door and that Lock, and to cultivate a warm relationship with the inanimate was often highly rewarding when there was to be interaction between it and himself. Perhaps the apparent response of the inanimate was entirely from within himself, and subjective. Perhaps not. It was something he had learned long ago, and sceptically, from Modesty. But it worked.

Half an hour later they heard sounds from beyond the door. When it swung open she was kneeling hunched over with hands pressed to her stomach Willie crouching anxiously beside her. An Arab in a white robe, submachine gun held at the port, filled the doorway. He looked at the two prisoners, then stepped back and beckoned to somebody behind him. Modesty lifted her head. Both she and Willie were looking towards the door, taking in details of the lock; a mortice lock, with a pierced steel plate screwed to the jamb to receive the tenon.

A man came from behind the Arab and entered the room carrying a worn leather bag. For a moment Modesty looked at him with blank eyes, then her head snapped round and she cried out in an agitated voice as if to Willie, "Don't speak a word, Giles, not a bloody *word*." She ended on a sudden wincing groan, doubling up to fall sideways to the floor.

Giles Pennyfeather's mouth hung open, his eyebrows almost touching his hairline, startled eyes huge in a drawn white face.

But the Arab guard could not see his expression. Willie looked past Giles to the guard, glimpsing another armed man beyond. No chances were being taken. He said in Arabic, "The woman has strong pains in her stomach. Ask your master if she may have medical help."

The Arab pointed with his chin at Giles. "This one is an English doctor. He is to examine the prisoners and report to Prince Rahim, who will have you brought before him later. He wishes you to be recovered for this."

Modesty groaned. Willie said, "The doctor must find what is wrong, and make the pains go away."

The guard shrugged. "He has time. It will be evening before Prince Rahim sends for you." He took a pace back and closed the door. There was the snick of the tenon clicking into place.

Modesty knelt up and whispered incredulously, "*Giles?*"

He had dropped to his knees beside her, and now blinked in new surprise. "I say, are you all right really? Just pretending?"

"Yes." She took his face between her hands and studied him anxiously. "Listen, Giles dear, I've probably won us a little extra time together with the stomach cramps, but we mustn't waste any. Keep your voice down and talk. Tell us everything you can, everything, whether you think it's important or not."

"Yes. Right." He drew a hand down his face and shook his head as if to clear it. "Well, this was the new job, you see. I met the agent in Cairo, and we flew to somewhere, I'm not sure where, and then we were picked up in a helicopter. This place is called Xanadu, and honestly, Modesty, it's absolutely weird. I haven't been here long, of course, but the head is Prince Rahim something-or-other, and sometimes he's terribly English and Oxbridge, you know, but at other times he's an absolute sod. I wouldn't say he's schizo, technically speaking, because I think he switches from one personality to the other at will, as it were—ooh!"

They had moved to sit in a corner, and as Pennyfeather leaned back against the wall he winced.

She said, "What's wrong?"

"Oh, nothing much." He managed an effortful smile. "I had a bit of a row with my employer the other day. Got stroppy about a patient, one of his guards, and told him a few home truths."

"Told Rahim?"

Pennyfeather blinked. "Yes. Do try to listen, darling. Anyway, he got angry and very Arab-princey and said he'd have me flogged if I spoke to him like that, so I got angry and told him not to talk bloody rubbish, and next minute he had me hauled out and strung up and whacked with a whip. I was jolly surprised, I can tell you."

Willie said, "Let's 'ave a look. Turn round, Giles."

He pulled Pennyfeather's shirt out and lifted it. There were half a dozen long weals, and bruising had spread across the whole of his back. Modesty said, "It could have been a lot worse. I suppose he didn't want you crippled."

"I suppose not." Giles knelt up to tuck his shirt in. "But it was a bit worrying, because it meant he was never going to let me out of Xanadu again. I mean, you can't flog a member of the British Medical Association and then let him go around telling people, can you?" He touched Modesty's hand and smiled his ingenuous smile. "Come to think of it, I'm jolly glad you've turned up, darling. I don't know how I'd have got away from here otherwise."

She gave Willie a wry glance and said, "It's nice to have your confidence, Giles. But go on about Xanadu. Where are we now, and what else is here, and what's the general layout?"

"You're in the palace now, below ground. This is where the prince puts a girl if she gets a bit sulky or something. He doesn't want them damaged, you see. So they have a bit of solitary confinement, with just bread and water. They call it a bate something."

"*Bait-at-ta'ah*. A room of correction. Is it guarded?"

"Oh, yes. There's a couple of chaps with machine guns." He opened his bag and took out a note pad. "I can't draw very well, but as a general idea of the layout you've got the palace here . . ." He began to sketch with a stub of pencil, the tip of his tongue protruding as he concentrated. "Then the gardens here, and a kind of natural wall with steps cut into it. That leads up to the hangar where they keep the helicopter. They have lights on at night, and guards with dogs. Over here there's what I call the barracks, where the troops are. I think Rahim told me they were Berbers that first day when he showed me round. Fierce looking chaps in robes, and carrying guns. He couldn't have been nicer that day. Made me very welcome. Then there's a sort of flat bit here, stables one side, transport the other. And storerooms behind the barracks. There's only one road out, and after a while that goes over a sort of drawbridge, I believe. At least, so Tracy told me."

She said, "Tracy? An English girl in the harem?"

He blinked. "How on earth did you know?"

"It doesn't matter now, Giles. But don't say a word to her about us knowing each other. We haven't much going for us, but at least let's hang on to what we've got. You've done marvellously well so far in painting a picture for us, so keep it up while I ask some quick questions, and keep it brief. First, how many people here?"

"Oh lord, that's difficult. About two hundred servants, I suppose. The palace is huge, you know. Then maybe a hundred chaps in the barracks, and forty-eight women in the harem. Tracy's the only one who's English."

"What's your particular job?"

"Medical care of the Berbers and the women. There's an Arab doctor looking after the servants, but he was trained in Italy and only speaks Italian, so we haven't talked much. I've got a little hospital here with twenty beds. Marvellously equipped. God, I wish I'd had it in Chad."

"What happened to your predecessor?"

"Took to drink. He was a Czech. Died of an overdose according to Tracy. Nobody knew if it was an accident or suicide."

"Is the drawbridge guarded?"

"Don't know, darling. Sorry. I expect I could find out."

"Can you do it without being obvious, Giles?"

He gave a rueful smile. "Yes, I think so. I've acquired a bit more low cunning than I used to have."

"That's from keeping bad company. What transport is there?"

"Two or three big lorries for supplies, and about half a dozen things like Land Rovers, except I think they're French. Oh, there are some Cadillacs for running around Xanadu, and there's a Rolls for outings. Tracy says they drive it down to the main road in the back of one of the big lorries if ever the prince wants to use it."

"And just the one helicopter?"

"No, a big one and a little one."

"What sort are they?"

He stared indignantly. "Sort? Oh, don't be bloody silly, darling."

"Sorry. Where are your quarters?"

"Just off the hospital building. That's on the other side of the gardens." He pointed to his incomprehensible sketch. "Here."

"Where's the power house?"

"Power house?"

She glanced up at the light in the ceiling. "There's electricity here, Giles. They couldn't run the place on batteries, so there must be a pretty substantial generator. Probably two. Do you know where they're housed?"

He thought deeply. Then: "Sorry. I suppose they could be down in the basement."

"*Is* there a basement?"

"I don't know."

"Try not to confuse me, Giles dear, I'm just a simple girl. We'll forget the generators. What are the troops for?"

"Eh? Well, I suppose they're sort of personal bodyguard. He said he recruited them from the Berber tribes because they're traditional warriors. Ah, wait a minute. He also said something about the Moroccan government being quite happy to let him settle here because his troops would be handy if ever the poly-something guerrillas got as far north as this."

"The Polisario Front."

"Yes, I expect that's it. Anyway, the troops don't do any fighting, except between themselves. They go in for all sorts of pretty hairy contests, you know. I'd hardly call it sport. One of them got disembowelled trying to kill a panther two days after I got here. There used to be lions in the mountains, Rahim told me, but they've been wiped out for some years now. There are still some panthers, though."

"And this man went hunting panther?"

"No, it was one they captured. They've got several here. It wasn't a hunt, it was a fight. They held it in The Pit."

"The Pit?"

"Oh, that's here, beyond the barracks." He pointed to his sketch again. "It's a sort of natural arena, like a bull ring, but oval. This chap reckoned he was going to kill a panther with his bare hands. They have a legend about it, you see. One of their sheiks did it about two hundred years ago, and anyone who managed it again would be a big man for the rest of his life, so Rahim said. This chap didn't manage it and died two hours later, and everyone seemed highly amused. They're a very hard lot, you know."

She said, "I know. I lived with them. They're not impressed by losers. Can you move around freely, Giles?"

He looked annoyed. "Not since I fell out with His Nibs."

"Could you get out of your quarters by night, and come here?"

Pennyfeather considered. "I'd have a chap with me as escort. I mean, I've got an orderly who speaks not bad English, and I could say I'd forgotten to give one of the women an injection, or something. Then he'd get the duty guard to take me across to the harem. That's only a couple of minutes from here, at the other end of the corridor."

"Would he go in with you?"

"God, no. One of the eunuchs would take me in and let me out. The escort chap would have to wait in the annexe."

"Could you slip him in a mickey finn before you went across, so he'd be asleep when you came out?"

Pennyfeather scratched his head. "I might manage it with Yusuf. He usually has a cup of coffee with me in the little guard room between the hospital and my flat. But he's not on duty tonight. He'll be on tomorrow, I think."

"All right. Try and find some way of getting to see us tomorrow evening, Giles. We'll concentrate on staying alive till then, and try to get a better idea of the whole problem. I imagine Rahim has something in mind for us, so we shouldn't be cooped up here for long."

She stopped, head cocked, listening. There was no sound from beyond the door. Pennyfeather said, "Those buggers on guard could leave me here for hours, if they haven't been told otherwise."

"Good. Let me have a look at what you've got in your case."

"All right, but what for, darling?"

"Anything useful. A blade, a plastic jar, a tin of ointment, a bottle of ether . . . you talk to Willie."

"What about?"

Willie said, "What goes on 'ere, Giles? What's the routine? How does Rahim keep 'imself amused all day?"

"Oh, well, it's all pretty feudal. He's got a bunch of cronies, the senior blokes among the Berbers, I suppose, and they go hunting and hawking and suchlike. Harun, that's my orderly, he says they go down to the desert hunting gazelle, and sometimes bring in a couple of boars for a hunt in the mountains." He grimaced. "Manhunting, too. Then there are squash courts and swimming and shooting with rifles—not much swimming but lots of shooting. They have mock fights in The Pit, and sometimes a real grudge fight, so Harun says. Oh, and the ball game. Then there are four cinemas here in the palace, and loads of films, right up to date. One cinema is just for the women, and they like old romances best, Tracy told me. The men are potty about Westerns. Bang-bang, you're dead. I think Rahim goes in for porn and horror stuff."

Willie said, "Hang on a minute, Giles, I want to go back to two things. First, did you say something about manhunting?"

"That's what got me into trouble. Some guard did something wrong, I think he laid one of the servant girls, anyway he was hauled up before Rahim, and next day they gave him two hours start and then went hunting him in the mountains. He ended up with three bullets in him, but they brought him back alive because at one stage, even with a bullet in him, he managed to jump one of the hunters and knock him off, and they like that sort of thing. 'Very brave man,' Harun kept saying to me. I couldn't save him, though. I got the bullets out and patched him up, but one of them had wrecked his liver, and he died an hour after the operation. I was pretty upset, and that's when I had a go at Prince Rahim, and ended up getting flogged."

Willie said, "Now the other thing. You spoke about a ball game."

"Ah, that's some sort of five-a-side game. They strip off to breech cloths and play it in The Pit. Rahim invented it himself. He told me the Aztecs used to have some sort of ball game they played, and this was his idea of what it might have been. I've only seen it once, but it was a real rough-house. He said the Aztecs used to sacrifice the losing team, or the winning team, nobody's quite sure which, but you'd think they were playing for their lives here in Xanadu, the way they go at it. Am I telling you the things you want to know?"

Modesty looked up from his open bag and said, "You've been lovely, Giles."

"Succinct, would you say?"

"Never known anyone succincter. Can I keep this?"

"It's just an old scalpel I use for sharpening a pencil and that sort of thing."

"It might help us to get that door unlocked when we need to."

"Oh, good. But surely there's other stuff there you can use? I mean, as well."

The blade of the scalpel was wrapped in a grubby piece of plaster, stiff with age. She said, "We can just about hide this behind the pipe that feeds the tap in that closet. There's nowhere to hide anything bigger, and if we tried it we might compromise our biggest advantage. You." She passed the scalpel to Willie, who got up and vanished into the closet with it.

Pennyfeather said, "You know, I realise now that I was asked a lot of questions by that agent in Cairo, and some of them were just to make sure I had no ties or connections. Nobody to ask questions if I sort of faded into the blue." He frowned. "I'll be a bit more careful when it comes to the next job, I can tell you."

She touched his hand, loving this gawky, guileless, simple-hearted man. Giles Pennyfeather had a quite unconquerable spirit, a virtue of which he was completely unaware. "Yes, you be more careful next time, Giles dear," she said gently.

Willie returned from the closet. Giles said, "Now then, what are our other advantages, Modesty? I mean, you said about the biggest one just now. What about the smaller ones?"

She managed not to blink as she said, "We'll come back to that. Have you seen anything of the two men who brought us in? Maybe French, but more likely English. Fair, and about Willie's size—"

"Yes, I caught a glimpse of them. Rahim's sent them on a guided tour of Xanadu in a couple of his Cadillacs, with that woman and that chunky chap with enormous shoulders. They flew in earlier, you know."

"Who did?"

"The woman and the chunky chap. Really, darling, you're a bit woolly today."

"We can't all be incisive, Giles. What woman?"

"Sorry. Don't know. The two English chaps called her Nannie."

"*Nannie?*"

"Yes, I know it seems a bit odd, but I heard it myself. They were calling from one car to the other as they came past my flat. Mind you, I thought for a moment she might be a nurse Rahim had hired. White dress, hair in a bun, efficient sort of look. A bit under forty. Anyway, she could easily have been a nannie, except there aren't any children here. Harun said the two chaps were El Mico, but of course he was talking balls. I mean, there were *two* of them, and they were nothing like that chap with the flame-thrower."

Modesty and Willie looked at each other. He said, "A wig and a moustache. What was it Inspector Birot told you about 'im? No base, no residence, no location . . . almost as if he didn't really exist."

"And sometimes it was claimed he'd been seen in two places at the same time." She looked at Giles. "You've no idea where the woman fits in?"

He shook his head. "Sorry. I just know that Rahim's making a great fuss of them all, really switching on the old-school-tie charm. I got the weird idea that this chunky chap was a sort of bodyguard for the nannie woman. He wears a leather thing without sleeves, a jerkin I suppose you'd call it, and I think he was wearing a gun in a holster underneath. I've become a bit sharp at spotting guns under armpits since that business in Nice."

There was a silence. She looked a query at Willie. He said, "I can't figure 'er, Princess."

She nodded, and turned to Pennyfeather again. "All right, let's use what time we have left in going over the layout of Xanadu."

Pennyfeather looked indignant. "I already drew it for you."

"I know, Giles. But pretend you're the world's worse drawer, and go over it all again."

Pennyfeather sighed, raked out his note pad, and took the stub of pencil from his shirt pocket. "All right," he said patiently. "But do try to pay a bit more attention this time."

Two open Cadillacs hurtled down the avenue of fountains and came to a swaying halt at the foot of the curving marble steps fronting the palace of Xanadu. Prince Rahim descended from the first, and turned to offer a hand to Nannie Prendergast.

Jeremy and Dominic Silk emerged bouncily from the other Cadillac. They were in a state of high stimulation, filled with excitement and euphoria. Little Krell got out from beside the driver.

"Quite fabulous, Your Highness," Jeremy said with huge enthusiasm.

Dominic spread his hands with a gesture of being overwhelmed. "Absolutely fascinating."

The prince waved a hand. "I am glad you find Xanadu fabulous and fascinating. It is equally fascinating for me to meet the fabulous El Mico."

The Silk brothers looked smugly deprecating. "It's El Mico's last appearance, of course," said Jeremy.

"A great finale, on which I congratulate you all." Rahim made a little bow in Nannie Prendergast's direction. "I hope you will honour me by remaining as my guests for a few days." He smiled at the two men. "There is much sport to be had here, I assure you, and I fancy you chaps are good sportsmen."

"Delighted," said Jeremy, and his brother nodded. Adrenalin from the day's excitement had given added sparkle to their eyes.

Nannie Prendergast said, "It's most kind of Your Highness, but I feel we should return to Fez this evening. There's much tidying up to be done, and we've not come prepared to stay overnight, I'm afraid."

"My dear lady," the prince said with smiling protest, "I assure you Xanadu can provide whatever you and these gentlemen may need in the way of clothes or toiletries. Have no concern on that score. And of course you will be most handsomely accommodated. I thought we might dine together this evening, when you have bathed and rested after the day's labours. We might well find it amusing to have Blaise and Garvin up at the coffee stage, and we could also enjoy a leisurely study of the Pahlavi Crown." He looked at Nannie Prendergast with warm eyes. "You would probably wish to retire then, Miss Prendergast, but I think the executive side of El Mico has earned a little celebration." He glanced at the Silk brothers with a roguish wink. "We can cater for all tastes here in Xanadu."

Nannie Prendergast stiffened. "There'll be no debauchery for Master Jeremy and Master Dominic, thank you, Your Highness."

Prince Rahim looked amazed. "Heaven forbid, dear lady. I was thinking of some uplifting music, or a classic film, perhaps."

"Most kind of you, but I think we should leave shortly, as planned."

The prince sighed. "But I have a man flying in from Amsterdam, to confirm that the Pahlavi Crown is genuine."

There was a brief, heavy silence, then Jeremy said sharply, "Of course it's genuine."

Prince Rahim put a hand on his shoulder. "I don't doubt your good faith, old chap, and I've no more than a grain of doubt about the crown, but you didn't bring the thing all the way from Teheran with your own fair hands, did you? And as we all know, only an expert with a refractometer can tell the genuine from the fake gemstone today. If you'll bear in mind that I've actually paid over to you twenty million dollars, I'm sure you'll see that it's reasonable for me to ask you to hang on here for another day, until we're absolutely certain about the crown." His face was turned away from Nannie Prendergast now, and he flickered an eyelid. "I promise you won't be bored. We'll have a lot of good clean fun."

Nannie Prendergast's face was blank. Inwardly she was fighting against minor shock. With all the detailed planning, this was a point she had missed—that the crown must be authenticated. Jeremy and Dominic had missed it, too. In the long run it was not an important omission, but the fact of having made it was alarming to her.

Dominic was saying slowly, "He's right, you know . . ."

Nannie Prendergast smiled, and Prince Rahim was startled by the sudden beauty it brought to her oddly assorted features. "Indeed he's right," she said briskly. "And we owe His Highness an apology for missing the point. A fault confessed is half redressed, so I hope he will forgive us."

"I shall do so," he said, placing his hand on his chest, "if you will permit me the familiarity of calling you Nannie, and if you will all refrain from calling me Your Highness. It's necessary for my people here, of course, but I never use it when I'm on the party circuit in Europe or the States."

Jeremy grinned. "Super. You must come and visit when we've settled in England."

"Love to, old boy."

The prince raised a finger. Two young veiled women came from within the portico and hurried down the steps, making an obeisance as they reached the group. Rahim said, "These are your personal servants, Nannie, and they'll take you to your suite now. That's Hassiba on the left and Nadia on the right. You speak the lingo, so just ask for whatever you want. Anything at all. If you have a problem, simply pick up the phone and ask for me."

When the three women had disappeared into the palace Dominic laughed and said, "It's a pleasure to do business with you, Rahim."

"My dear chap. Can't tell you what a delight it is to find that El Mico is a couple of truly civilised fellows. Your pater was up at Oxford, so Nannie tells me. I had quite a chat with her while we were waiting for you. Damn shame you weren't able to get to Oxford yourselves, we might well have run into one another. Mind you, you wouldn't have been as well educated as you were under Nannie Prendergast. Isn't she a simply marvellous woman?"

Jeremy said, "Absolutely top of the milk."

Dominic nodded agreement, but with a wry look. "Still a bit strict, though."

The prince chuckled. "My dear fellow, you simply mustn't allow that, not even from Nannie. Now I expect you're anxious to get cleaned up and into fresh clothes, so let's go along. I'm sure you'll be very comfortable. Just phone for anything you want." A knowing grin. "And I do mean anything at all you fancy. Nobody's going to split to Nannie. What about this splendid chap of yours here? Little Krell, did I hear you call him? Would you like him quartered with you, or near you, or what?"

Jeremy said, "That's very good of you, but not in the palace, I think. He's a solitary creature, so it's best if he sleeps in the

Scout and uses what's left of the food we brought along. What do you think, Dom?"

"Fine. As long as he can come and go for Nannie, if she wants him."

"What the hell would she want Little Krell for?"

Dominic held down his irritation. "Maybe to lay on a training session for us. She hates us to miss a day, and we've missed several lately."

Rahim said, "There's no problem at all. Little Krell has the freedom to come and go as Nannie pleases. But I'm intrigued by your mention of training, Dom. What kind of training?"

Jeremy answered quickly, asserting himself as the elder brother. "Martial arts, Rahim. Little Krell is a complete master, and he's a weapons-master too."

Rahim's eyes were alight with interest. "He's training you two?"

"He's been training us for several years now."

"Ah! That would account for El Mico's reputation. My God, you must be pretty damn good."

"Well . . . we're not too bad, actually."

Rahim laughed. "You English. My chaps beat their chests and tell the world how great they are. Look, I'd like to come back to this, because it's really very exciting and it's given me one or two interesting ideas, but I mustn't keep you gabbing when all you want just now is to get under a shower. Come on, I'll show you blokes to your suites."

eleven

It was soon after nine o'clock that Modesty Blaise and Willie Garvin were brought out of the *bait-at-ta'ah*, one at a time and under the muzzles of two submachine guns. When their arms had been strapped to their sides to inhibit any ideas of a surprise assault, they were taken along an arched passage ornamented in stucco relief. A curving flight of steps entered the passage from the right. At the top, a very long corridor ran through a number of tall scalloped arches to an annexe from which a great arch opened into the dining-room of Prince Rahim.

It was a lofty room of Islamic design and furnishing, the walls lined with richly polychromed tiles in geometrical patterns. Clearly it had been furnished for dining in Arab style, but the low couches and the mounds of cushions had been pushed back to make way for a great U-shaped table and chairs of carved mahogany, partly gilded.

When the two prisoners had been prodded forward to within a few paces of the foot of the table they were halted there. Modesty glanced over her shoulder, and saw that the two guards had stepped back and moved apart, one to each so, so that they could fire on the diagonal if need be, without endangering the prince and his guests. She looked back at the table. Dinner had apparently been served and eaten in western style. Now the coffee and brandy stage had been reached. There were evidently no Muslim rules of abstinence for the master of Xanadu.

The man at the head of the table, wearing a white silk tunic and nursing a glass of brandy, was clearly Prince Rahim. On his right was a woman, perhaps in her late thirties, not beautiful but with a curiously impressive presence. This was surely the mysterious Nannie spoken of by Giles Pennyfeather. On her right was one of the two men who had faked the breakdown on the K'sar es Souk road and shown such skill in the use of the kongo. The other man was on the prince's left. They were casually dressed, but in fresh clothes now. Standing in the shadow of a tapering pillar, a few paces behind the woman, was a freakishly proportioned man in a leather jerkin, very short, with immense shoulders and a large shaven head. This would be Pennyfeather's 'chunky chap' who had flown in by helicopter with Nannie. To judge from the present situation, one of his functions was that of personal bodyguard to her. The sight of him struck a vague chord in Modesty's memory, but she could not identify it.

The great arched table still bore dishes of fruit, a silver bowl of nuts, several cheese boards, decanters and side plates, but less than half of it was occupied by those who had dined. In the centre of the lower part, resting on a pad of black velvet, stood the Pahlavi Crown.

Prince Rahim flashed a well practised smile down the table and said, "Ah, Miss Blaise and Mr. Garvin. I don't think you've met Nannie Prendergast, have you? She is, as it were, the creator of the renowned El Mico. May I also introduce El Mico himself, in the persons of Jeremy and Dominic Silk. I believe you met them very briefly earlier today."

Dominic laughed. Nannie Prendergast looked at the prisoners for a moment with little interest and a shade of distaste, then resumed gazing absently at the Pahlavi Crown. Modesty said, "That's a fine replica you have there, Your Highness. It must have cost a lot of money."

There was a moment of highly charged silence, then Rahim chuckled softly. "I think you are trying to promote a little trouble, Miss Blaise."

She gave a dismissive shrug. "It's your affair."

Willie allowed himself a knowledgeable smirk. On principle she was trying to sow a seed of mistrust between the prince and his guests, but to labour at it would invite disbelief. A shrug and a smirk were the most likely rooting compound for the seed.

Prince Rahmin said, "An expert will be here tomorrow. The crown will be masked to reveal only one gem at a time, of course. If he certifies the four largest, I shall deem the crown to be genuine." He leaned forward, arms folded on the table, studying Modesty with interest. "I do hope you'll believe that your presence here is simply an unfortunate occurrence, Miss Blaise. I bear you no malice, but I'm sure you appreciate my position. I simply can't allow you to go home and tell everybody that I've acquired this bauble." He nodded to the crown.

She said, "We might come to an arrangement."

Nannie Prendergast sniffed audibly. Jeremy Silk grinned and said, "My God, she's stupid, Rahim. Where on earth did she get her reputation?"

"A sound question, Jeremy, dear boy. Nevertheless it's quite a substantial reputation. Or was so." He looked down the table and lifted a dark eyebrow. "I do wish I could invite you to stay on here permanently with my other ladies, but I really can't offer you harem status." He smiled. "Rather too dangerous, I fancy.

But since you have to depart, I'm sure that both you and the good Mr. Garvin would rather go down with flags flying and boots on, as they say, than be squalidly dispatched with a quick bullet or a cord round the neck. Wouldn't you?"

She said dryly, "Let's talk about that when your expert has had a look at this bauble. You might see the whole situation differently then."

"Perhaps." The prince's smile was not quite unforced, and for a moment his heavy-lidded glance hung speculatively on Nannie Prendergast, who was looking away from him towards the crown.

Jeremy saw the glance, and said angrily, "Look, Rahim, that bloody woman's trying to—"

"*Master* Jeremy!" Nannie's head snapped round. "Language if you please!"

He said resentfully, "I beg your pardon, Nannie."

"Prince Rahim is perfectly well aware that the woman is lying."

"Yes, Nannie."

Across the table, Dominic was enjoying his brother's discomfiture. The prince noted this, and was privately amused. "I shall assume," he said, "that you would rather go out with a bang than a whimper, Miss Blaise. In any event, we Arabs have a great taste for strong entertainment, and it would be a pity to waste the talents of two such renowned persons as yourselves, so I shall concoct a Happening for you to take part in tomorrow."

A sudden decisive sparkle lit Dominic's eyes. Seeing it, Jeremy knew what was coming even as his brother began to speak. "I'd very much like to take part in the Happening myself," Dominic said, his voice a little loud with excitement. "How about myself versus Modesty Blaise, tomorrow, in the Pit? Would that be strong enough entertainment for you and your boys, Rahim?"

Before the prince could answer, Jeremy said indignantly, "That's *my* idea you've pinched, Dom! I spoke about wanting to have a go at her hours ago, in the Cadillac."

"There are two of them, aren't there? You can take Garvin."

"Don't tell me what I can take, please."

Nannie Prendergast had drawn breath to speak sharply when the prince laughed and lifted an admonitory hand. "Steady, the Buffs. I rather gather that the chance of writing off the notorious

Modesty Blaise and Willie Garvin is something that meets a long-nourished ambition in your chaps. Single combat in a death duel will be splendid entertainment for my Berbers, thanks very much, but shall we let Nannie decide who does what?"

She said politely, "Thank you, Prince Rahim. May I have a little more coffee, please?"

"Of course." He gestured, and a servant hurried forward. Nannie Prendergast watched the man refill her cup. Her expression gave no hint of her feelings. She detested Prince Rahim Mohajeri Azhari, with his stupid aping of English ways. In some subtle fashion he was encouraging the boys to get out of hand. Also, she was certain that he had secretly offered them women for the night. She wished they could all have left Xanadu as soon as the Pahlavi Crown had been delivered, but at least another day as guests here would have to be endured.

The trouble was, of course, that Jeremy and Dominic were over-excited after this final triumph of El Mico's. They needed some way to discharge the tension, and what better way than the dispatch of Blaise and Garvin? The prospect of such a task to-morrow would ensure against their being tempted to the experiment of taking women to their beds tonight; Little Krell's ascetic training was too ingrained in them for that. Possible danger? No. There was surely less risk in it than El Mico had faced on many occasions before. Jeremy and Dominic had developed bodies of steel and acquired immense skills in weaponry and all the martial arts. More, they had already defeated Blaise and Garvin once, on the road, and done so with ridiculous ease.

There was another advantage to the notion. This Arab at the head of the table was becoming too patronising. It would be good psychology to let him see the power of El Mico. But which of her little monkeys should fight Blaise, and which Garvin? Better to let Jeremy deal with the woman. Dominic was impulsive, and might be inclined to take the task too lightly. He would not do so against Garvin.

The servant finishing pouring coffee for her, and Nannie Prendergast looked up with a smile. "I'm sorry, Dominic dear," she said sympathetically, "but I have to remember that Jeremy is the elder. He shall have Miss Blaise, and you may have Mr. Garvin."

Dominic grimaced, then looked again at the two captives and gave a rather thoughtful nod. "All right, Nannie. Might be a bit more interesting for me, really."

The prince said, "This is really splendid. Which weapon will you choose, Jeremy? If any, of course."

Jeremy thought briefly, then said, "Knives."

Nannie gave a little nod of approval. That was a sensible choice. Garvin was the knife expert. She had never heard of Blaise using one. The prince turned inquiringly to Dominic, who grinned, pushed back his chair and said, "Can you spare a cheese board?"

Prince Rahim looked amused and puzzled. "Feel free, old chap."

Dominic picked up one of the boards and tilted the cheese on to the table. He stood up, holding the thick teak in one hand, turned, and with sudden tremendous speed brought the edge of his other hand flashing down. The board split from end to end, and half of it fell to the floor. He tossed the other piece on the table and glanced with a smile at the squat figure by the pillar. "I even get commended by Little Krell on my *shuto* work." He held up his hands. "I'll use these."

Prince Rahim laughed and said, "Most impressive." Nannie Prendergast looked smugly proud. The prince lit a cigarette and exhaled through his nose. For a moment a glint of provocative glee shone in his eyes, then he said blandly, "Now, what procedure would you recommend, Jeremy, in the event that by the worst of ill-fortune Miss Blaise survives her encounter with you?"

Nannie Prendergast stiffened. Jeremy stared at the prince from narrowed eyes for a second, then relaxed with a laugh. "Who's trying to pull whose leg?" he said.

Prince Rahim inclined his head in smiling acknowledgement, then looked down the table towards Modesty Blaise and Willie Garvin. "There," he said cheerfully, "it's all arranged. A bang, not a whimper. We shall be out hawking in the morning, so the entertainment will be held after siesta. Nice to have made your acquaintance, Miss Blaise. Yours also, Mr. Garvin, though in fact I've seen you before."

Willie nodded. "I've been trying to place you," he said. "Now I remember. It was in Kentucky."

"Beirut, in fact."

Willie smiled patronisingly and shook his head. "Come off it," he said. "You're the bloke I saw in Kentucky when you won the tobacco-spitting contest. The accuracy event."

There was a silence. The prince stopped smiling. Modesty took a slow pace back and to one side, as if disassociating herself from Willie. The move brought her nearer to the guard on her side. If Willie's ploy worked, she would have to disable the man with a kick. Rahim started to stand up, then sank back in his chair and waved a hand. "Take them away," he said abruptly, in Arabic.

Four minutes later, when their arms had been unstrapped and the door of the *bait-at-ta'ah* closed behind them, Willie said, "I just reckoned it was worth a try, Princess. I could have bust the strap all right."

She nodded. The tobacco-spitting insult had been intended to provoke Rahim into coming close enough for the personal satisfaction of hitting Willie in the face. If Willie could then have got his hands on Rahim's neck, shielded by him from one guard while Modesty dropped the other, they would have been in a strong position. It had not worked.

The narrow flap at the foot of the door opened. A tray with bread and goat's milk cheese was pushed through. They took it across the room and sat down side by side, backs against the wall. "Princey wants us in reasonable nick for tomorrow," said Willie. "He reckons we'll still be 'ere, of course."

She chewed slowly. After a while she said, "Do you think we can get that door open tonight?"

"Not too sure, Princess. We've only got the scalpel, and it looked like a pretty long latch on that lock. Might not be able to work it back unless we can get the point between the solid bit and the barrel at the tip."

"And we daren't use too much pressure on the blade. We'll see how it goes, but anyway I'm not too sure about making a break tonight, even if we could. We've made no arrangements with Giles, and his more obliging escort won't be on duty till tomorrow night, so we couldn't get hold of the girl anyway."

Willie paused in the act of putting a piece of cheese in his mouth, momentarily puzzled. Then: "Tracy June?"

"That's who we came for. Remember?"

"Sure." He put the cheese in, telling himself he was an idiot to be surprised. They ate in silence, went to drink from the tap in the closet, then lay down on their backs by the wall opposite the door. Willie said softly, "What about general policy for tomorrow's entertainment?"

Lying with her hands behind her head, eyes closed, she said, "I'd say they're both highly skilled and trained to a hair. But they've never grown up. That squabble was a give-away, together with the Nannie bit. So their big disadvantage hasn't dawned on them yet."

"No. I don't reckon it will until too late."

"So all right. We take them. But then Rahim's going to set up another Happening for us, and another, and so on until we go down."

"He might like to spread it out a bit."

"That's our best hope. I read him as a would-be swashbuckler. There's no way he can rule these Berbers with an iron hand, because they're not his own people and they're very independent. So he likes to keep them happy, and he's right when he says they like strong entertainment. We'll have to improvise because we don't know what's coming, but . . ." She was silent for a while, trying to give shape to an amorphous concept in her mind.

"It could pay us to play to the gallery," she went on at last, slowly. "A bit of heroics, a bit of defiance, and some *very* classy handling of whatever we're up against . . . that's what to aim for, Willie. If we get it right, the Berbers will love us and won't want us killed off. That feeling isn't likely to last more than a day, then they'll be eager to see another performance. But it gives us a bit of grace to find a way out of here."

He lay reviewing her summing up, found his own instincts were in agreement, and said, "Right, Princess."

She opened her eyes. "Gile's chunky chap, the one somebody called Little Krell . . . does he ring any bells with you?"

"No. Should he?"

"I've a vague recollection I can't pin down. Something to do with a fork-lift truck, which seems pretty weird. But it's not important. We'll sleep till about two, Willie, then try that lock."

"Right."

They had both acquired the ability to sleep at will and to wake up by an internal clock. Their watches had been taken, but when Willie opened his eyes he knew that the time was within five minutes of two o'clock either way. Modesty was coming from the closet with the scalpel in her hand, drawing the blade carefully from its makeshift sheath of plaster. He got up, stretched and yawned. She whispered, "Nice bit of pandiculation, Willie."

He nodded, and followed her to the door. Where the hell had she managed to look it up? Surely not in Corsica . . . and the chance of access to a good English dictionary had been even smaller since then.

She knelt and began to work with the scalpel, probing carefully while he sat with an ear pressed to the door, listening for any sound of approach by the guard. At last she shook her head and sank back on her heels, then handed him the scalpel and shuffled round to take his place. For ten minutes he tried to work the latch of the lock out of its mortice. It moved against the spring, but he could not hold it to take a fresh purchase with the point of the blade.

When he sat back she handed him the plaster sheath and said, "We'll need to be better equipped next time we try, so let's keep our eyes open."

He started to slide the sheath over the blade, then paused. "Worth hiding this on one of us somewhere tomorrow?"

She thought, then shook her head. "We couldn't use it without compromising Giles. Hide it again, then we'll go back to sleep. There's a long day ahead."

Nannie Prendergast sat in a comfortable chair in what she thought of as the Royal Box, a large recess cut in the rock above a natural arena. Prince Rahim sat on her left, wearing a djellaba now. On his other side was Dominic Silk. Behind them a few of Rahim's intimates among the Berbers lounged and talked among themselves. Little Krell stood apart, at one end of the recess, hands resting on the wrought-iron balustrade enclosing its open side.

The Pit, as Pennyfeather had called it, was roughly oval in shape, and floored with a layer of hard-packed earth. Its walls varied in height between fifteen and thirty feet, and had been trimmed sheer, though there were one or two places where an agile man might have climbed out. Where the ground fell back above the wall on the side opposite the Royal Box, there were scores of robed figures, some perched on vantage points, some moving along the narrow paths seaming the slope, others gathered in little groups. These were Berbers, and every man carried a rifle at all times, not from need but by tradition.

The arena was rather more than half the size of a football pitch. At one end a narrow section of the wall had been cut away and replaced by a tall grille. Beyond this, a passage sloped up beween rock walls to reach ground level. There were steps up the middle of the ramp, running between rails.

Set high on each long side of the arena was a vertical hoop of stone jutting at right angles from the wall, reminiscent of the great Mayan ball court at Chichen Itza. Set in the centre of the arena was a very thick wooden pole, twelve feet high surmounted by a carved wooden hoop matching the stone ones.

It was late afternoon, and still hot. For the last half hour two five-man teams, naked but for breech cloths, wearing hard leather gloves studded with metal like the Roman gladiatorial cestus, had played the Xanadu ball game devised by the prince. Nannie Prendergast had not enjoyed the event. It was brutal, warlike, and in her opinion, highly unsporting.

Prince Rahim said to Dominic, "I think my chaps are very much looking forward to the next item. We've never had a knife duel in The Pit before."

Little Krell slid a knife from one of the twin sheaths of the light leather harness that hung from his shoulder, the Garvin harness, designed to carry two knives in echelon on the left side of the chest. The second sheath was empty. Jeremy Silk had taken the weapon from it when he left the Royal Box five minutes ago. Little Krell handled the knife delicately, reverently, feeling its perfection. They said Garvin made his own knives, and Little Krell believed it now. This was no mass-manufactured thing.

"I understand those knives of Garvin's are for throwing," the prince was saying, "but do you think your brother or the unfortunate Miss Blaise will in fact use them in this way?"

Dominic shook his head. He had loved the hawking that morning, and the wild ball game. Now he was aglow with eagerness for what was to come. "I doubt it," he said, his eyes on the grille entrance to The Pit. "It's not impossible to dodge a thrown knife if you're ready for it and watching the thrower."

"Ah, and in that event the thrower is left disarmed, of course. So it is a gamble."

"Right." Dominic sat up straight with excitement as there was movement beyond the end of The Pit and a buzz of raised voices from the Berbers. A few seconds later the grille swung open and Modesty Blaise walked into the arena. She wore flat lace-up shoes, the same lightweight brown denim trousers she had been wearing in the Range Rover and the same dark green shirt, rumpled and grubby now. Her hair had been drawn back and plaited into a short club at the nape of her neck, fastened with a piece of green material torn from the hem of her shirt.

She looked round The Pit, lifted her gaze to the spectators, turned slowly to take in the whole scene, then strolled unhurriedly, almost arrogantly, to the western side where the Berbers were spread out on the slope above the wall of the arena. At two points along this wall there were places where it was just possible for a man or an animal to climb out, and here two men had been posted at the top, each with a stout ten-foot pole.

Dominic watched as she sauntered along on the far side, straining his ears, for her head was turned away and she was saying something to the Arabs above, not loudly, but conversationally. There came a guffaw from the men.

"That must have been a remarkably dirty crack," the prince said in amused surprise. "Nothing else would get a laugh from my licentious soldiery."

It happened again, and then again, little waves of laughter rippling along the slope. She stopped below one of the men who stood holding a pole in readiness to prevent any escape from The Pit. Hands on hips she looked up, surveying him for several seconds, then called out a question. There was a widespread burst of amusement from above, and the man with the pole grinned and bestrode it suggestively.

"Yes, we can guess what that was about," said Rahim tersely. "She knows how to entertain those idiots all right. Of course she lived with them for some time, I understand."

Dominic said, "Where the devil's Jeremy? Still busy with his solemn limbering up, I suppose." Again there was movement beyond the end of the arena, and they glimpsed the figure of Jeremy flanked by two Arabs as he made his way to the head of the ramp.

The prince called, "Miss Blaise! Your attention, please."

She completed whatever she was saying to the Berbers, raised another laugh, then turned and looked across the area. "What is it, Your Highness?" Her very politeness was in some way cavalier.

With an effort he managed to hide his annoyance as he called down to her across The Pit, "We are moving on to the serious business of the afternoon now, Miss Blaise. Here is your weapon."

Dominic said quietly, "Little Krell."

Little Krell took the knife by the blade, lifted it reluctantly, then threw. It flashed across the arena to drive into the central wooden post at shoulder height from the ground. "You will be duelling with Mr. Garvin's knives," called the Prince.

She walked towards the post, unbuttoning her shirt and pulling it out of her trousers. Shrugging it off, she draped the shirt over her left arm, then took the hilt of the knife and worked it up and down until the blade came free of the post. There was a clang of metal as the grille closed behind Jeremy Silk. He walked forward, Willie Garvin's second knife held point-down in his right hand, his thumb on the blade. He wore desert boots, giving him a sure footing. His shirt and slacks were newly laundered and pressed.

Dominic Silk drew in a long breath and leaned forward, nerves taut with excitement. Old Jeremy was a bit of a sober-sides, but it looked as if he was really going to enjoy this. You could see he was bursting with confidence and really bouncy at the idea of knocking off somebody with a rep like Modesty Blaise. Dominic's awareness narrowed to the two protagonists in The Pit, and his long-trained fighting brain keyed itself to miss nothing of what was to come.

She moved round and leaned back casually against the post, arms half folded, the knife hidden under the shirt, which was now wrapped two or three times round her left forearm. Jeremy walked towards her. When he was within five paces he halted and dropped into a crouch. She turned her head and called to the Berbers in their own tongue, "I think he's going to have a crap now."

Laughter broke from the robed figures spread across the slope.

Ribs were nudged, shoulders slapped. Jeremy came forward very quickly with a spread-leg shuffle to maintain his posture. She moved round the post so that it was between them, and he halted. Dominic thought: *You'll have to get her away from there to nail her. Lost your advantage of reach and muscle while she's got that post between you.* Then he gave an inward gasp, for she had simply turned and walked away.

Jeremy came in quickly. She was still moving away from the post, head half turned to watch him over her shoulder. When she broke into a little trot he came after her at a run, flicking the knife over in his hand to hold it by the blade for a throw. On that instant she stopped and was suddenly facing him again, arms still crossed low in front of her and half hidden by the shirt, poised on her toes, leaning forward, ready to evade the thrown knife.

Jeremy slid to a halt and held his throw at the last moment. To Dominic there was something odd about him now, something very puzzling. In only a few seconds he seemed to have become tense, wary, and uncertain. Dominic thought with mounting irritation: *She nearly disarmed you then! Get the initiative, you silly bugger, you've let her dictate the whole fight so far.*

Jeremy came in again, fast, with perfect footwork, perfect posture, perfect balance. She seemed to drift back unhurriedly, and yet her speed was greater than his, and Dominic heard Little Krell suck in his breath as if in disbelief. Then the shirt was hanging loose, and her right hand was pressed against the back of her thigh, hiding the knife from her opponent, hiding it from everybody, for it was out of sight, presumably held flat against her inner forearm.

Still he came in, and still she remained out of distance. The shirt whirled in her left hand. One sleeve came free, swinging in a swift obliquely upward arc. Jeremy reacted frantically, breaking his posture to leap awkwardly back. For a fraction of a second Dominic could not see why, then he saw the sun glint on the moving blade and realised that her right hand, pressed to her thigh, was empty. The blade of the knife had been thrust through a double or triple thickness of shirt cuff, perhaps even knotted there, so that it jutted out like an extension of the sleeve. This was what she had been doing during the early moves, and Jeremy's wild backward leap had only just saved him from a long body gash at best, or a killing upward slash between neck and chin at worst.

He was still off balance when the shirt whirled on a different plane to bring the blade slashing towards the side of his neck. It was coming from his right, and his knife arm went up instinctively to block the swing just behind the cuff. In that moment he was wide open, and in that moment she was perfectly poised for the high leap that brought her into distance, one long leg flashing out to transfer all the combined energy of her weight and muscle to the point of her toe as it took Jeremy Silk precisely on the solar plexus.

He was armoured by the iron muscle developed over years of training, but no human tissue could have protected the nerve-centre against such a blow. Instant paralysis froze him. He was still on his feet when her own feet touched the ground, his body leaning forward a little, arms spread, mouth gaping, head tilting slowly back. She was holding his knife wrist before his arm fell, catching the knife by the hilt as it dropped, then turning to move unhurriedly away as his muscles went suddenly slack and he fell limply to the ground.

There was a moment of total silence, then a rising roar of satisfaction and approval from the scores of watching Berbers. Prince Rahim said thoughtfully, "It appears she isn't going to kill him."

Nannie Prendergast was hunched forward, staring wild-eyed, and saying in a cracked voice, "No! It was a trick! That woman . . . she—she—"

"My dear Nannie," said the prince politely, "trickery is the name of this particular game." He lifted his voice and called out an order. The gate opened and two men came into The Pit with a stretcher, making for Jeremy Silk. He stirred feebly and rolled on his side, knees drawn up.

Modesty Blaise had strolled to the far side of the arena and was talking with the Berbers again, detaching the knife from the shirt cuff, her voice pitched to carry now. "Was that one truly El Mico? I would employ him to wipe the arse of my camel—with his right hand." She was grinning up at them, insolent, eyes alight with gamine mischief. "Hey, are any of you up there from the Sorgu tribe? You there, the handsome one! Do you know if old Abdul

One-Eye is still alive? I knew him years ago. If ever you meet again, take him greetings from Modesty Blaise."

She held up the two knives. "Now, who would like a truly beautiful knife, the best you have ever seen in your wicked lives, you goat-screwing bastards." The insult brought guffaws, and eager hands seized the knives as she tossed them up one at a time.

Across the arena, Dominic was on his feet. A huge excitement possessed him. Old Jeremy had blown it! Bossy big brother had been hit for six by a tricky lady, and now was the moment to show Nannie that just because Jeremy was *older* it didn't mean he was *better* at everything and therefore had the right to give orders.

He said quietly, "All right, Nannie, I'll see to it." Then, to the prince, a little brusquely, "This won't take long, Rahim. I'll kill Garvin as an encore."

The prince nodded gravely, with an air of sympathy, and waved an elegant hand. "Feel free, dear boy."

Jeremy was being carried through the iron gate on the stretcher now. Dominic pulled off his shirt, swung a leg over the wrought iron balustrade, and hung by his hands from the base of it to give himself a twelve-foot drop to the ground. Across the arena the crowd-sound changed in note as Dominic landed springily and walked forward.

He saw Modesty Blaise turn, look at him, then move at a leisurely walk towards the centre post, her hands behind her, busy with the shirt. He moved quickly to get beyond the post so that it would not be between them, then dropped into a karate stance, stiffened hands held forward with palms down, elbows out slightly. Without taking her eyes from him she stopped and half turned her head to say over her shoulder, "This one is the other half of El Mico, they tell me. I think he is the bottom half."

Laughter. She had established a pattern now, and they would laugh at anything she said.

Dominic held down his anger at her mockery. He was going to be very careful. He was going to take no chances. He was going to watching out for tricks. If he kept to that strategy, she was as good as dead, for he had only to land one good blow with hand or foot. If it did not kill, it would disable. The next would kill.

She had stopped five paces away, her hands still behind her, simply looking at him, and abruptly he felt a prickle of cold sweat across his brow. Her eyes were very dark, midnight blue, and it came to him with the suddenness of a knife-thrust that those eyes had looked upon death before, many times perhaps. They held an age of experience that made him feel like a child, for with the impact of her cold destroying gaze there dawned a dreadful realisation . . . that *he* had never been in such a situation before. Never.

As El Mico he had killed eighteen times. For years he had trained in all the arts of killing, and was a master in the trade. But El Mico had always struck from the cloak of anonymity, in his own time and his own way. El Mico had never truly fought for his life, never fought against odds, or at a disadvantage, or even on equal terms; never confronted an enemy of lethal capacity, never faced an opponent in the fearful context of kill or be killed. Unlike the girl with the dreadful black flame in her eyes who stood before him, and who had done all these things, he was facing a totally new experience.

Now he understood what had happened to his brother. Now he knew that Jeremy, too, had looked into her eyes and realised that this latest victim was not like all the others, the men and women who had simply provided material for El Mico to practise the art of slaughter. This one was entirely different. Confidence draining from him, Dominic knew that he was at last facing mortal danger as a reality. A horrible reality. For him, it was the first time. But not for her.

He fought for control, for balance and concentration. *Steady . . . steady now. You're stronger, heavier, just as quick. All the advantages. One strike finishes it. Don't let her take the initiative. Go in and keep attacking. But cool. What's she doing with that shirt behind her? Remember it, but don't be distracted. Now . . . fast but careful . . . GO.*

He was remarkably light on his feet, and closed very fast, but she was gone, straight back and with greater speed than his own. His stomach clenched. Nobody could retreat that fast—! *Don't think about it, fool. Keep going with your guard up. Trap her against the wall, then . . .*

He moved forward. Again she used that curious melting-away retreat, but this time stopping abruptly, bringing the shirt out from behind her. It had been knotted again and again into a crude tight ball. Her eyes gripped his as she held it forward and dropping it in front of her. He would not be tricked into following it down with his gaze, but came on with surging hope. She had tried misdirection and failed. *One strike now, one bone-cracking strike, that was all* . . .

Something flew up and struck him softly in the face. In the half second that he was without vision he knew that she had kicked the wadded shirt up as it hit the ground. As a blow it was harmless, but he had lost her visually, and pain exploded in his leg as she came slithering in low, feet first, hooking a foot behind his right ankle, her other heel slamming against the inside of the same knee, all in one movement.

He went down sideways, and as he fell she was on her feet. A sharp kick to the elbow numbed his left arm. He rolled, seeking purchase with the right. She came down on that arm with both knees, paralysing the muscles that could so easily have broken her bones. Then she had the wrist in both hands, rising with it, a foot on his chest, leaning across him and falling back, hauling on his arm, hoisting him on a long steely leg so that he arched across her in a flying somersault.

He tried for a breakfall, but she jerked the arm to destroy his posture, and he landed heavily on his back, breath exploding from his lungs. She back-rolled, still with his wrist secured, and came up into the same position as before. Again he was hoisted in a great arc and slammed down on his back, then again and yet again, gasping, grunting, head spinning, sick and terrified as darkness closed in and the world went away amid a thousand tiny flashing lights.

She left him lying sprawled limply on the ground, and walked away to pick up her shirt. The Berbers were laughing, calling out to her, and from one group an ululating cheer went up. She acknowledged with a wave of her hand, and began unknotting the balled shirt.

Across the arena Nannie Prendergast sat white-faced, hands clenched in her lap, saying with bemused fury, "A pantomime . . . it's nothing more than a pantomime! I shall have something to say to you about this, Little Krell . . . you have *failed* them!"

The big shaven head did not turn. Little Krell stood gazing down at the figure of Modesty Blaise as she slowly pulled on her shirt. The prince leaned over to rest a hand on Nannie's arm. "I think it would be a good idea if you went to give comfort to El Mico," he said with a bland smile. "Miss Blaise has been considerate enough to avoid doing him any serious damage, but it hasn't been much of an occasion for the poor chap."

She closed her eyes to hide the hatred in them and said, tight-lipped, "Very well, Your Highness. And what is to be done about . . . *her*?"

"Miss Blaise?" He leaned back and lit a cigarette, looking across The Pit. She was tucking in her shirt, talking to the Berbers again, but not joking now. He saw her spread a hand palm up, and just caught some of her words " . . . had your fun for today . . . at least earned a night's sleep?"

The prince frowned. "I fancy Miss Blaise is trying to curtail the entertainment," he said. "That won't do at all, Nannie."

"I want her dead, Your Highness." She was fighting for composure.

"It shall be so. But would you care to run along now? The two halves of El Mico are being taken to their respective suites. Hassim will drive you in the Cadillac. Do you wish Little Krell to accompany you?"

"No. I wish to be alone with Master Jeremy and Master Dominic for a while."

"As you please, Nannie. Do tell them not to feel badly about this. Nobody thinks any the less of them, I assure you."

This time he caught the gleam of pure hatred in her eyes before she turned away, and he chuckled inwardly. She went quickly up the steps from the Royal Box, and the Cadillac driver followed. Little Krell had not moved. He was still gazing down at the figure of Modesty Blaise. She stood leaning with her back to the post, one sleeve flapping open where it had been slit, fingers tucked in her waistband, looking meditatively down at her feet. Dominic Silk had been carried away.

The prince turned to the Berber cronies behind him and lifted an eyebrow. "That film a week or two ago," he said. "Quo Vadis?"

Heads were shaken. The Berbers took no interest in titles. Prince Rahim said patiently, "It was in the time of the Romans. There were scenes in an arena, like The Pit. They tied a girl to a post and turned a bull loose. A big slave had to kill the bull to save her. That would make interesting entertainment for us?"

One or two shrugs. No enthusiasm. Rahim hid his contempt. For the moment they were glutted with sensation and felt sympathy for the girl. Tomorrow they would cheerfully watch her die an unpleasant death. One of them said at last, "We have no bull."

"But we have a panther. A hungry panther," said the prince. "And we have a girl, and the man called Garvin to play the slave."

An exchange of glances. A rekindling of interest. Heads nodded.

The prince looked down into the arena. "We'll do that now," he said.

twelve

Seven minutes had gone by. She stood with her back to the post, facing the grille at the end of the arena. Her arms were stretched above her head, her wrists bound to the post with leather thongs. Her ankles were secured to the base in the same way. The four men sent to do this had approached her warily, but she had offered no resistance, and her only protest had been a biting taunt.

If she turned her head to the right she could see Rahim and his entourage. To the left, and she could see the Berbers massed along the slope above The Pit. She had tested the bonds securing her wrists, and knew it would take half an hour or more to stretch the thongs enough for any hope of escape. Whatever was to happen would be over long before then. The outcome lay in Willie Garvin's hands, and for that she was thankful.

The grille swung open, then closed behind him as he came into The Pit. She watched impassively, inwardly approving as he strolled forward, thumbs hooked in his belt, looking about him with an interest completely unshadowed by disquiet. Perhaps his guards had told him what had happened in The Pit so far, perhaps not, but in his manner there was no hint that he had been troubled by anxiety.

There came a buzz of talk among the Berbers at his appearance, and he gave them a casual wave of greeting, then moved on towards the post where she was bound, showing no haste, no puzzlement, no concern, only perhaps a touch of amusement. When he had almost reached her the prince called, "Mr. Garvin!"

He halted, looking up towards the Royal Box, and said politely, "Your 'ighness?"

"I will speak in Arabic so that all may know what is to happen now." The prince lifted his voice, "My Berber friends still sing the praises of a mighty sheik of their tribe who, two hundred years ago, was attacked in the hills by a panther, and slew it with his bare hands."

Willie glanced at the Berbers. "A great man," he said respectfully in Arabic, and looked at the prince again.

"A few have tried to match this deed," Rahim went on sonorously, "but in all the long years there is no word of one who succeeded. Today brings an opportunity for *you* to do so, Englishman." He showed beautifully capped teeth in a flashing smile. "And in order to give spirit to your struggle, we have placed the woman called Modesty Blaise as you now see her, so that you and the panther may dispute possession of her."

Willie nodded briefly. He had turned away from the prince before the last words were spoken, and was looking slowly round the arena. The blue eyes came to Modesty, rested on her without recognition, then moved on. She knew he was making an urgent appreciation of the situation, noting every element of it that might be of use.

There came a clanking of metal and an angry, hissing snarl. The grille was open again, so was the door of the cage which had been run down against it on the two rails. Next moment, under goading through the bars of the cage, a black thunderbolt flew into The Pit and went racing like a shadow along the eastern wall.

Willie Garvin stood quite still. Modesty fixed her attention on him, then withdrew from herself, making her mind a void, becoming one with the unliving post to which she was bound, ceasing to be there, in the way of the ancient art of *ninjutsu*. It was the only help she could give Willie now, to make it as difficult as possible for the panther to become aware of her.

Willie Garvin turned slowly, breathing deeply from the pit of the stomach to control tension, seeking a balance of adrenalin, enough for added strength and speed, not so much as to burn up energy uselessly. Carefully he held his mind open to every circumstance, knowing that to let it narrow to a small focus on the panther alone would be to lose flexibility.

His experience with the circus that he partly owned had given him no liking for cats, but he had learned a little about them. What he knew about the panther was not reassuring. It was more malevolent and more intelligent than a lion or tiger, and not much inferior to either in fighting ability. Because it was smaller, it would not normally attack an adult human unless provoked, but occasionally could become a man-killer. Hungry, frightened, and recently uncaged, this one would be likely to attack anything it could reach.

He had known three tamers who worked with big cats, and two South African game wardens, but had never heard of any man killing a panther with bare hands. It might just be possible, with a very old creature, and if you could get a throat-grip from behind. In any other body-contact a man would have little chance. The jaws might not kill instantly, as a lion's would, but those rear paws with their great talons could rip your guts open in seconds.

This one was big for a panther; or leopard. They were the same animal. About eight feet long with the tail, it would weigh well over a hundred pounds. At the moment it was looking for a way out, and Modesty was probably in little danger as yet, particularly since she would be using her skills to make minimal impact on the panther. His own danger would be greater to the extent that he made himself obtrusive by movement. For a while the creature would be busy with its own concerns, but once it had accepted The Pit as the limit of its freedom, once it began to explore and to give suspicious attention to the humans, then aggression would mount swiftly and attack would soon follow.

The panther had found one of the two possible ways to climb from The Pit and was half-way up the wall now. The Berber waiting above with the long pole suddenly yelled and swung the pole to hit the cat on the side of the head. With a snarl it dropped soundlessly to the ground and continued to lope on round the wall.

Willie Garvin began to move stealthily towards the point where the second man stood guard with a pole above a narrow section of wall offering hand and foot holds. Someone hurled a stone across the arena. It missed the panther but was close enough to make it veer and spit. There was laughter from the Berbers and shouts of encouragement aimed at stirring up the cat's anger. It padded on at a steady run, still hugging the wall. Willie stopped moving as it passed in front of him, fifteen paces away. The yellow eyes touched him, but showed no interest for the moment.

As soon as the creature had passed, Willie ran for the wall and began to scramble frantically up. A burst of jeering and howling came from the Berbers. The man with the pole bent forward and jabbed downwards. Willie's hand clamped on the pole and he dropped back to the ground. The guard, his balance lost, gave a yell of dismay and fell sideways, just managing to catch a projecting stub of rock. He hung there for a moment, then Willie Garvin lifted the pole, rammed one end under the man's buttock's, and boosted him back to safety.

A great roar of approving laughter went up as the assembled Berbers realised that Willie's attempt to escape had been a pretence. Modesty watched remotely, as if through a mental telescope reversed. The panther was within the angle of her vision now. Its initial alarm had abated and it was standing still, the head moving slightly as it stared from the figure of the man by the wall to the only other feature in the otherwise empty arena. Its nostrils flared as it took a scent, then it began to pad slowly, curiously, towards the post.

All sound vanished. Every eye watched. The cat moved closer. From somewhere nearby came the thin bleating of a goat. The black head snapped round, and the panther stood still, eyes searching. There was a stir of puzzlement around The Pit. Modesty watched without emotion. None of the spectators had yet located the source of the sound, but she knew Willie Garvin's gift for mimicry. He made the bleating noise again, and now there were chuckles as the Berbers realised what had happened. The panther moved towards Willie, who backed slowly away, trailing the pole after him.

Modesty noted that his hands were busy. He must have transferred the hidden nylon cord from his waistband to his pocket before coming to the arena, on the principle that even if you had only one asset left, probably useless, you might as well make it quickly available. There were ten feet of the cord. It was woven of six denier nylon filaments and had a breaking strain of over eight hundred pounds. He seemed to be knotting it to the pole, a little way from the end, so that it hung down in three loops.

The panther was suspicious of the pole, but kept following the trailing end warily. Willie Garvin retreated in a wide circle, then stopped with his back to Modesty. The cat stopped, too. After a moment it batted at the end of the pole with a paw. Willie jumped forward a pace, pushing the pole along the ground, and the panther sprang back, spitting menace. As the animal crouched, snarling, Willie lifted the pole, drew it back and swung it quickly round, so that the end with the dangling loops was presented to the panther.

Modesty noted passively that his shirt was black with sweat. She did not allow herself the mental activity of trying to anticipate his purpose or of imaging the huge stresses that must weigh upon him. The nylon loops lay on the ground. The cat eyed them for long seconds, then stalked round them. Willie moved the pole to keep it between himself and the panther. In the almost audible silence that pressed down upon The Pit now, she could hear Willie's breathing. She noted that it was deep and slow.

The panther moved. The pole moved. The cat swatted petulantly with a paw, and splinters flew from the end. Willie edged back obliquely, lowered the loops to the ground again, nudged them open with the tip of the pole, and waited. The panther moved. The pole moved, lifting slightly to point at the yellow eyes above the snarling mouth. A pause, and the whole sequence began anew.

Modesty noted the repetition, noted that it was no longer important for her to remain withdrawn. Willie and the big cat were fully engaged now. She drew a long breath and brought the scene into close focus. As she did so, the panther took a pace forward, eyes on Willie, ignoring the pole now. Its paw came down in one of the spread loops. Willie said briskly, "Princess."

She folded her tongue between her teeth and gave a piercing whistle. The black head snapped round. In that moment of distraction Willie Garvin twitched the end of the pole up so that a noose looped over the panther's head. Its reaction was quick as a bullet, a backward bound to free itself. But both nooses were drawn tight by the movement, one round the neck and one round a leg, high up by the shoulder.

Willie almost lost his balance, but recovered. Then he was bracing himself as the panther, screaming with rage, tried to thrust forward and reach him. A great roar of excitement rose from the Berbers. Fully alert now, Modesty knew that soon a lashing paw would find the thin nylon and rip it apart. Willie's only hope lay in destroying the panther within the next thirty seconds or so. But he had no weapon, no means of destruction.

She saw that he was turning, bending, swinging round suddenly so that his back was to the panther and the pole lay over his shoulder. Then he was braced again, lifting on the fulcrum of his shoulder, leaning forward, rear leg extended behind him, like a runner frozen in action, eyes closed, lips drawn back, teeth clenched in a fury of total effort . . .

And the panther came clear of the ground, swinging from the pole, unable to reach the suspending cords with claws or teeth now. As it rose high, the black body swung forward. One scrabbling hind paw flicked Willie's back, low down to one side, ripping away shirt and skin. Blood gleamed in the sunlight, spreading over his haunch. He showed no reaction. Already he had begun to turn on the spot, so that the panther swung out and away from him. The movement was slow at first but gathered speed smoothly. After the fourth turn, with sufficient momentum gained, he suddenly twisted away from beneath the pole, turning and leaning back, arms extended so that now he was swinging the panther round in a huge circle at the end of the long pole.

There was continuous uproar from the Berbers, with every man to his feet. Modesty was looking to her right, watching as Willie rotated, his feet moved in a tremendously fast shuffle, his body leaning back at an angle to maintain the balance of forces, the panther screaming its anger. Beyond him she was vaguely aware of the prince and his entourage.

Then with a final heave and a great wordless cry he released his hold, falling back on to blood-sprayed ground, watching as the panther with the pole trailing after it went soaring through the air towards the iron balustrade of the Royal Box.

A wild shout of alarm. Upheaval as Rahim flung himself back

amid his cronies. Then the bellow of a heavy calibre handgun, and Little Krell was holding an automatic in his fist, blasting the animal as it came towards him. The gun was a Colt Commander .45, a weapon of impressive stopping power, and Little Krell put three shots into the panther in less than a second, two in the area of the heart, one in the head.

The creature was dead when it fell across the balustrade, an arm's length from where he stood. Little Krell looked at the body, put the gun away in its holster under his jerkin, then rested his hands on the wrought iron railing again and resumed his steady gazing down into The Pit.

Prince Rahim picked himself up slowly from where he had fallen in a tangle with several of his entourage. He was breathing like a man who had just sprinted a hundred yards, and his face was mottled with shock. The Berbers were silent now, but with wonderment rather than shock. Down on the floor of the arena Willie Garvin was getting slowly to his feet, one hand pressed to his back just below the left side of the rib cage. He stood looking up at the Royal Box for a moment, then turned towards the post.

A sound began to grow among the Berbers, a crowd sound that rippled along the rocky slope above The Pit, a rumbling murmur that held several clearly defined notes, of satisfaction, respect, and acclaim. From among the robed figures something soared through the air, glittering. A curved knife struck into the ground point-first, a few paces from Willie Garvin. He lifted an open hand in acknowledgement, pulled the knife out of the ground, then moved to the post and reached up to cut the thongs binding Modesty's wrists.

His face was impassive, but she could read his mind as if the thoughts had been her own. Willie Garvin was thinking he had blown it. In his battle with the panther he had seen a chance to bring the day's entertainment in Xanadu to an end, and he had made an instant judgment. Use the maddened panther to kill or injure Prince Rahim, and there would be no more duels today. In all probability they would be locked up again until decisions could be taken. But now . . .

She whispered without moving her lips, "I still think you've made it, Willie. Listen to the Berbers."

Dry lips twitched in an effortful grin. "Let's 'ope so."

She took the knife, bent to cut her ankles free, then drew him to lean forward with his shoulder against the post while she pulled up his blood-soaked shirt and looked at the great nine-inch furrow torn by a raking claw. It was a flesh wound only, but it would be full of filth from the panther's claw. She moved away towards the watching Berbers and spread her arms, hands red with blood. "Will the men of Xanadu refuse so small a thing as a chagal of water to such a fighter?" she demanded coldly.

The rumbling crowd-noise grew louder. A man moved to the edge of the slope and tossed a half full goatskin bottle down to her. She caught it, and walked back to Willie. He had sunk to one knee now, and muttered, "I'm okay, Princess, just laying it on."

"Good." She cut a piece of his shirt away and began to use it as a swab to wash the wound, never for a moment looking towards the Royal Box.

Prince Rahim Mohajeri Azhari stood gripping the top of the iron balustrade, muscles locked, trying to stop his legs trembling beneath him. The panther's body was still draped over the balustrade, very close to him. Its jaws hung open, and Rahim kept imagining what those terrible teeth might have done to him. He wanted to have Garvin killed *now*, without a second's delay. And Blaise, too. But he could not summon the will to over-rule the manifest feeling of the Berbers. After such a display, they had no wish to see Blaise and Garvin slaughtered like goats.

With a great effort the prince drew back his lips so that what he hoped was a devil-may-care smile could be seen by the men on the far side of the arena. "Let us respect a brave enemy," he cried, and screwed up his courage to lean forward with a hand on the panther's body. "Our enemies must die, but these two shall live to fight another day."

A roar of approval went up from the Berbers. The prince flourished a regal hand. "Let their hurts be attended to by a physician," he called, and turned away, trying to keep the black anger from his face so that his entourage would not see it. The iron gate swung open and men came into the arena. Rahim had started to move up the steps, but now he looked back and said in

French, "That was very well done, Little Krell. An excellent piece of shooting."

The shaven head on the immense shoulders dipped forward in acknowledgment, and the deep throaty voice said, "At your service, Highness." But Little Krell did not turn as he spoke, and not for a moment did he take his small brown eyes from the figures of the man and the woman in The Pit below.

Dr Giles Pennyfeather tied another stitch, then eyed his handiwork with head cocked to one side. "That ought to be all right," he said, "but don't do anything energetic for a few days."

Willie Garvin, lying prone on the examination table in the hospital surgery, a towel wrapped round his loins, rolled his eyes at Modesty and said, "No tennis or anything like that?"

Pennyfeather said absently, "Oh, they don't play tennis here, you know." He pressed a dressing over the long wound and added, "I found out about the helicopters. The big one's called Sikorsky, but that flew out today for some special stores, and it won't be back till tomorrow. The other's called a Gazelle, and it seats five."

Modesty, sitting wrapped in a blanket, answered casually without glancing at the guard who stood in the open doorway. "That's good. We've both flown a Gazelle. Pretend to make a general examination of Willie, then start on me, Giles. We need time to talk. But pretend you're giving medical instructions."

"Right."

She had wrung the most out of Rahim's orders that the prisoners' hurts should be attended to. Veiled threats of the prince's wrath in the event of unsatisfactory treatment had brought good results. She and Willie had both been permitted to take a shower in the hospital bathroom, and their luggage had been brought so that they could select fresh clothes. But the two guards had allowed them no chance to acquire any additional equipment. Every stitch of clothing had been examined, and this time the nylon cord had been discovered in the waistbands.

Willie's wound had been cleaned under local anaesthetic, and treated with antibiotics. His tetanus shots were up to date, but Pennyfeather had given him a booster. Now he rolled on his back while Pennyfeather began to go through a pantomime of sounding his chest, peering into his eyes, taking his blood pressure.

Modesty said, "Can you get hold of the Tracy June girl tonight and bring her to us between three and three-fifteen?"

He nodded judiciously. "Yes. As a matter of fact I've got her here in the hospital. Thought it best. Said I wasn't happy about her recent check-up and wanted her in for observation."

"Check-up?"

"My predecessor's notes. The Czech chap."

"You haven't told her anything?"

Pennyfeather peered into one of Willie's ears with an aurioscope. "No. You said not to."

"Is she the sort to keep her head, or could she get hysterical?"

"Can't say." Pennyfeather straightened up and spoke brisky. "I've been thinking. If it's going to get a bit tense tonight, you can't take chances on her getting the heebie-jeebies."

Willie said, "Right, doctor. Can you dope her so she can just about do as she's told but won't realise what's 'appening?"

"No. Impossible to judge the dose. That's what I've been thinking about. I could use narco-hypnosis. Had quite a success with that in Chad, when I ran out of anaesthetics. All right, you're done, Willie. Get dressed.

Willie rolled off the table and moved to where his permitted clothes had been laid on a chair after examination. Modesty dropped the blanket and took his place, wearing a towel like a sarong. Pennyfeather, about to slip the stethoscope in his ears, looked down at her soberly, his back to the guard in the doorway. "It's got to be tonight, darling," he said. "The word is that His Nibs is dreaming up something very nasty for you tomorrow."

"I'm sure he is. Have you any seriously ill patients in here at the moment?"

He smiled down at her, and began to sound her chest. "Worried that I might not feel I could leave them?"

"Yes. It happened once before."

"Willie's the most serious case I've got at the moment, so you needn't worry. Deep breath, please. I'll see that all the patients get sleeping pills tonight. There are only nine of them, anyway. And I'll give Yusef and my orderly enough knockout drops to keep them asleep till morning."

"Can you get across to the palace?"

"Yes. The central area isn't guarded, only the helicopter hangar."

The guard in the doorway spoke suddenly, suspiciously. "What is it that you and the English doctor say?"

She turned her head to look at him and spoke coldly in Arabic. "He is a fool. I tell him I have a pain in my back, and he says it is not so."

The guard grinned. "With all doctors it is the same."

She scowled up at Pennyfeather and snapped, "We're quarrelling, so look annoyed. Can you manage to get a wad of cottonwool in my mouth without him seeing you?"

Willie said idly, "I'll distract."

Giles glared down at her. "All right, when?"

"Is there anything else important to say?"

He bent to look in her eye and said irritably, "Yes, I almost forgot. You asked about the drawbridge yesterday. I'm told there are two chaps guarding it day and night."

"All right. Anything else?"

"No. Except please try to get some sleep. I think you're very tired. Dangerously tired."

"I'll get some sleep, and I'll be all right."

"Was it bad for you in The Pit?"

"No. Just demanding. I had to make it look easy, and it wasn't, so I used up a lot of juice. But Willie had it really bad. Better relapse into angry silence now, Giles. And don't forget the cottonwool."

Nannie Prendergast sat in the drawing-room of her suite, to one side of the great arched window which looked out upon distant, purple-shadowed peaks. Jeremy and Dominic sat in brooding silence, one at each end of the long couch facing the window. Earlier the prince had sent a message to their respective suites saying that he would understand if they were tired and would prefer to dine on their own this evening.

A choice of splendid meals from three silver trolleys had been offered in Nannie's suite, but they had only toyed with the food. Now the table was cleared and the servants had withdrawn. In the hour since they had assembled here, conversation had been sparse, forced, and had not touched upon the debacle of the afternoon.

Dominic lifted his coffee cup and drank, furtively and disconsolately eyeing Nannie's slim legs. It was impossible, but he wished to God she would come to him tonight. And stay with him, holding him in her arms. He felt more miserable than he could ever remember, and hated the thought of being alone. He was sure that Jeremy, beside him, was feeling the same. Well, serve him right. Perhaps he wouldn't come the high and mighty big brother so much in future.

Nannie turned her head to look at them. For a time she had been very strange, quite unlike herself, and this was frightening, but her eyes were quiet again now. She said, "I want you boys to know that Nannie is very proud of you. Today you were tricked and cheated and victimised by a thoroughly hateful and unscrupulous woman, in front of a crowd of disgusting foreign scum. Yet you fought honourably and without flinching. It's an ill wind that blows nobody any good, so perhaps today will help you realise that young women are *not* to be trusted. Remember this when we settle down in England, for you'll find plenty of them making sheep's eyes at you there."

Jeremy said, "Yes, Nannie."

Dominic eased his bruised back into a more comfortable position and said, "Is Rahim going to have her killed tomorrow?"

"So he has assured me, Master Dominic. He's extremely angry, especially with Garvin."

"I'd like to watch whatever he's cooking up for them."

Nannie Prendergast shook her head. "We shall leave tomorrow morning," she said firmly. "Xanadu is a perfectly horrible place, and I'm thankful that our business here is completed. The sooner we put this whole wretched visit out of our minds, the better."

Jeremy said slowly, "It hasn't all been wretched, Nannie. Just think."

Her eyes softened, then glowed. "You're right of course, dear. After all these years of hard work, we've finally achieved the ambition Nannie always had for her little monkeys. Soon we shall be home at last, home in England, and looking for a lovely estate where we can live like gentry. No more dealing with common felons and foreign filth. No more danger for El Mico. He's vanished now for ever, leaving no trace of his identity."

"Little Krell's the only connection left," said Jeremy.

"I hadn't forgotten, dear, but we can leave that till we're back on Le Dauphin. It would seem very natural if Little Krell failed to return from one of his long swims, I think. All you'd need would be your speargun and some heavy chain."

Jeremy nodded. "I'll see to it, Nannie."

Dominic thought, "Bossy bastard."

It was ten o'clock. Modesty drank from the tap in the closet and came back to sit on the floor beside Willie. Since leaving the hospital they had slept, roused to eat some bread, cheese and olives pushed under the door, and were now preparing to sleep for another four and a half hours.

On entering the *bait-at-ta'ah*, shepherded by two watchful guards, Willie had screened Modesty for two or three seconds as she was in the doorway. Halting, he had turned to shout at the surprised guard immediately behind him. The accusation of having jabbed his gun against Willie's wounded back was indignantly denied by the man. In that time Modesty rammed a wad of wet cottonwool solidly into the mortice socket of the door-post. This allowed the tenon of the latch to spring only half-way home when the door was closed. The *bait-at-ta'ah* appeared to be securely locked, but the latch could now be levered back with the scalpel. They had tested this ten minutes later.

Willie turned to lie down on his front, head pillowed on his arms, looking at Modesty as she lay down on her back beside him again. "I reckon old Giles is doing great," he said in a whisper. "I mean, he's usually a bit woolly, but not this time. No waffling. Right on the ball."

"We're his patients," she said softly. "That's how he sees us, and he can always do whatever's needed for a patient. If it means he has to concentrate on being efficient for a bit, that's what he'll do. How's the back, Willie?"

"Not too bad. It won't slow me down. I'll get Giles to shoot another local into it when he gets 'ere."

"Yes."

They planned to begin the break-out at a little before three by dealing with the guards in the hall outside the *bait-at-ta'ah*. It was a time when any relief of shifts would normally be long completed. If Pennyfeather had not appeared with the girl after fifteen minutes, they would make for the hospital to pick them up. After that, the options were open. Giles had said it would be impossible to seize the helicopter. If a quick reconnaissance proved him right, they would take a vehicle from the transport lines and push it to where the long mountain road to the drawbridge began its downward slope from the edge of Xanadu.

Since they had been escorted from this rear part of the palace to The Pit, then to the hospital and back to the palace, they now had a fairly full picture of the Xanadu layout to add to what Giles had told them. Immediately outside their door was a square hall with another *bait-at-ta'ah* opening off it. From this hall their way led past several stairways, up a single flight to the annexe of the harem quarters, which was no more than a small guard room, and through this to a side entrance of the palace. Two mattresses lay in the hall, presumably for the benefit of two night guards. These men would probably be at least half asleep by the early hours, and would therefore give little trouble provided the *bait-at-ta'ah* door could be opened without noise.

Modesty reviewed the situation once more, then reached out a hand to ruffle Willie's hair. "Let's get back to sleep now," she said. "And I'm glad it was no one else but you there this afternoon, Willie love."

thirteen

The latch slid back into the lock. Crouched by the door, she listened for a few moments then slipped her fingers under the slit at the bottom and eased the door open an inch. The light in the hall was dim, as it was in the room. She stood up and passed the scalpel to Willie. It was not much of a weapon, but would have more potential in his hands than in hers.

They had saved two or three olives and crushed them to rub oil into the hinges of the door. There was no sound as she opened it wide. Across the hall, one guard lay huddled on his mattress, the other was sprawled awkwardly with a leg flung wide. She stepped silently into the hall, Willie at her shoulder, then stood listening, nerves tightening as she realised something was amiss.

She signalled with a finger, and in three strides they were across the hall, each crouched above a guard, a hand poised in the *nukite* form for a silencing lunge to the throat. Neither guard stirred. Modesty saw that hers lay with his head at an impossible angle, the neck broken. She looked to one side. Willie was going slowly down on one knee beside the second man, staring at the hilt of a knife that jutted from his throat.

There had been no sound of breathing, that was what had been amiss with the scene. Willie was looking at her, baffled, questioning. There came the faintest of sounds, and she whirled to face the corridor. Little Krell stood there, the Colt in his hand, poised on stumpy legs, eyes narrowed to slits.

She took a half pace back and sideways, back to avoid any threat in the movement, sideways to cover Willie's hand as it stole towards the hilt of the knife in the dead guard's neck. Then, incredibly, Little Krell's gun vanished under the jerkin and he was holding up both hands palm out, saying in soft, gutteral French, "No need to throw the knife. I come to help."

A silence, then: "You?" She kept her voice flat, but the disbelief came through.

"Please, mam'selle. I speak truly." He nodded towards the guards. "Is my knife. I kill these men, four-five minutes ago. I go to kill other man, guarding harem. I come back to take you out. Truck is ready."

Willie came slowly to his feet. The knife was in his hand but he made no move to throw it, for Little Krell's eyes had opened wide as he spoke, and in them was a desperate plea for trust that struck a deep chord in Willie. There was a time, years ago now, when he too had stood before Modesty Blaise, longing with his very soul for her to believe in him. He had no idea what might be driving Little Krell now, but murmured in recognition, "He means it, Princess."

She stood still, watching the squat powerful man carefully.

Willie's instinct was good, but . . . this was Little Krell, body-guard and strongarm man to El Mico. Her mind raced as she tried to fit his astonishing behaviour into some deep and subtle trap.

He said, "Better we go, mam'selle. Not lose time."

She shook her head. "We're waiting for the doctor." No harm in saying that now, for Willie held a knife and Little Krell was empty handed. He looked blankly at her and said, "The doctor comes?"

"With an English girl from the harem."

He let out a hissing breath between his teeth. "Not easy, mam'selle."

"That's my business."

"Please believe I am friend."

"Why?"

The ugly mouth moved in the beginnings of a wry smile, and the big shoulders hunched in a shrug. "If we must wait, there is time today, mam'selle. When there was *The Network*, one day you and Willie Garvin go up against Rodelle . . ."

The name opened her memory, and it all came back to her now, the fork lift, the warehouse, the face of Little Krell, the night in Istanbul when she and Willie had smashed the Rodelle gang of flesh peddlers. That battle had been fought out in a warehouse. She remembered Rodelle on a catwalk in the half-light, firing down, falling as a knife from Willie flashed up from behind a stack of crates to bury its blade between his ribs. There had been half a dozen of Rodelle's men to begin with, and the battle had been a dogfight of stalking and pouncing, climbing and ambush amid the crates, machinery, and miscellany of stores that filled the dimly lit warehouse. When Rodelle fell, only two were left.

She remembered the short massive figure bounding from the shadows of a forklift with astonishing lightness, the knife lunging, her instinctive defensive tap with the kongo to numb the hand as she twisted aside, and the follow-through counter that found precisely the right place behind the ear. He had gone down, and now she could even recall knowing that she had been very lucky in the encounter, had won it by perhaps a fifth of a second. Few thugs had much skill in combat, but this one had moved like a master.

It was as he fell stunned that there came a choking cry out of the darkness, a cry cut suddenly short as a last wild shot triggered by a dead man's finger ricocheted from the engine of a hoist to hum past her legs and hit the man at her feet, ripping open his arm below the bicep. Blood spurted. Willie Garvin appeared and said, "That was the last of 'em, Princess, and I can 'ear a police siren."

They were both wearing wet-suits and had come in from the Bosporus. Their scuba gear was at the foot of wooden steps leading from a trap door down into the water. She picked up a piece of galvanised wire cut from a crate and said, "On your way." As she knelt beside the great squat figure Willie said, "Right," and moved off quickly. In *The Network* nobody questioned her orders. She slipped the wire round the arm above the gushing wound, drew it very tight, and twisted the ends together. There was more than one siren now, and they were very close. The pulsing blood dwindled to a trickle. She was vaguely conscious of small eyes in the big ugly face, watching her dazedly. Then she rose and moved quickly after Willie Garvin.

In the hall outside the *bait-at-ta'ah*, Little Krell had been speaking for no more than five seconds. " . . . I was one of Rodelle's men, with him in the warehouse that night, and—"

She gestured to cut him short, relaxing a little, and said, "I remember now."

"Remember all, mam'selle?"

"All that matters. I didn't leave you to bleed to death, is that it?"

"Doctor tell me wire has saved me." He tapped a finger to his brow. "Always after, I see your face, mam'selle. Here in head. When arm better I try for place in *The Network*." He laid a hand on his chest. "I have much respect for you. Want to serve you, like they tell of Willie Garvin. But is no good. Your man who does hiring, Garcia, he send back word to say no. He knows Little Krell work for Rodelle. He knows Mam'selle not want bad man like that."

She looked round at Willie with a wondering gaze. He grinned crookedly and said, "Cast your bread on the waters . . ."

"It's certainly come back at a very good time." She turned to Little Krell again and spoke in French. "Can we get to the helicopter?"

He shook his head. "Not possible. The dogs make noise and many men come. But one thing is good. The pilot sleep in hut near workshop place. Alone."

"Why is that good?"

"Because now he is dead, mam'selle. I kill him before I come here, so he cannot follow by air when we take truck."

She exhaled, and pushed back a lock of hair from her brow. "You have a very direct approach, Little Krell."

"Mam'selle?"

"It doesn't matter. Can you move freely around Xanadu?"

"Yes, mam'selle."

"Then, I'd like you to go across to the hospital now and—"

She stopped, listening. There came a soft scuffle of footsteps. Little Krell bounded forward and turned, gun in hand again. Giles Pennyfeather appeared from the corridor, carrying his great shabby case in one hand and holding the arm of a girl with magnificent natural blonde hair, expertly cut in mushroom style. She was of medium height, with a generous figure, and wore dark slacks with a grey sweater. The beauty of her face began with the bone structure and was quite remarkable, but at this moment the lovely grey eyes were empty, the symmetric features without animation. She simply stood there, gazing without interest.

Pennyfeather said in a hoarse, indignant whisper, "There's a dead chap outside the harem. Why did you kill him?"

Modesty said, "We didn't, but let's not complain, Giles. If you'd blundered into him we'd be in trouble. This is Little Krell, and he's with us now. Did you have any problem getting here?"

"No, it's all quiet outside, nobody about."

"And Tracy June is under hypnosis and biddable?"

"Gosh, yes. She's a very good subject. I only had to use a spot of pentathol to get started." He stared across the hall at the two dead men, frowned at Little Krell, then looked at Modesty again. "If you have any more chaps to deal with, just knock them out, will you? I've brought enough chloral hydrate to put an army to sleep."

"We'll play it the way it comes, Giles." She turned to Little Krell and switched to French. "You lead the way. Once we're in the open, we'll keep fifty paces behind you." To Pennyfeather,

"Let me have your aurioscope, Giles." He fumbled in his bag. She took the lamp from him, tested its pinpoint of light, then passed it to Little Krell and went on, "Carry that behind you, and switch it on if you see anybody and want us to stop. Understood?"

"Understood, mam'selle." The little brown eyes were eager, the uncomely face a glow of pleasure. Little Krell reached behind him, unclipped a sheath from his belt, and tossed it to Willie. "For the knife, Willie," he said.

"Thanks." Willie slid the knife into the sheath, then pushed it into his waistband.

Pennyfeather said to the blank-eyed girl, "We're going for another little walk now, Tracy, and we have to be very quiet. You won't talk, and you won't make a sound. Everything's fine, and you won't be at all worried, you'll feel nice and safe and happy. Nod your head if you've understood me."

Tracy June Martel nodded dreamily.

The Scout coasted steadily along the track that wound down through the mountains. Modesty drove with a foot on the brake, easing it on and off to keep down the build-up of heat. Willie sat beside her, leaning forward to keep his back from the seat. A submachine gun, a 9mm Uzi with a folding metal stock, rested across his knees. In the back, Little Krell cradled a similar weapon, both taken from the dead guards. Beside him sat Pennyfeather, an arm round Tracy June, her head resting on his shoulder. A half moon and a mass of stars in a cloudless sky gave fair visibility.

There had been no problem in getting clear of Xanadu. Little Krell had positioned the Scout near the road that led out. He and Willie had pushed it for no more than a hundred yards before they came to where the road began its long down-slope. The gradient varied, but was nowhere particularly steep, and Modesty had been able to keep the speed down to a safe ten miles an hour without difficulty. For just under ten minutes they had been coasting in silence except for the crunch of the tyres. Now Willie touched her arm. She had been watching the road, but he had seen ahead the sixty-foot tower of steel from which the bascule of the drawbridge operated.

She brought the Scout to a gentle halt at the point where the road widened into the bridge approach. Moonlight glinted on the girders of the tower and on the steel plates of the bascule, which was drawn up vertically now. Here the ground was flat. Two thick cables of stranded wire ran through guide wheels at the top of the tower, angling down away from the ravine and vanishing into a small power house built of local stone. To one side of this was a prefabricated hut. It had no window looking out towards the road. Twenty paces west of the tower a simple rope bridge with a footway of planks strung together spanned the ravine. Modesty turned her head and spoke in a whisper to Little Krell. "Go with Willie. Do whatever he tells you."

Little Krell nodded, put his gun down carefully on the seat, and moved off at Willie's side. Pennyfeather whispered, "He's not going to kill any more people, is he?"

"Only if Willie says so. Now shut up, Giles. We're not here on a conservation project."

Willie and Little Krell disappeared behind the hut. A minute passed, then reflected light showed from a door on the hidden side. Willie came into view and beckoned. Modesty released the brake and let the Scout run forward on to the flat ground. It drifted to a halt by the power house.

Willie spoke in his normal voice. "Two guards in the hut, Giles. Go and squirt some of your knockout juice into 'em."

Pennyfeather said to the beautiful girl beside him, "Wait here and rest, Tracy. You're quite safe and happy. Nothing to worry about." He climbed out of the Scout and went towards the hut, hugging his bag.

Modesty said, "Let's have a look at the lifting mechanism, Willie." The door of the power house was unlocked. Inside, Willie found a switch and clicked it on. A bank of batteries supplied current to two lamps, giving a good light. Part of the area was occupied by a diesel engine connected through massive gearwheels to a long shaft bearing two drums on which the 2-inch diameter wire cables were wound. The starter of the diesel was fed from the same batteries as the lights.

Willie ran his hands over the simple controls, and looked up to where the cables entered the power house through steel sleeves piercing the wall. "Start the engine, engage the shaft, and the cables unwind from the drums, lowering the bascule," he said. "But it's going to make a bit of a noise, Princess."

She thought for a moment. "Not likely we'll be heard in Xanadu. There are three massive ridges of rock between the palace and here. Anyway we'll have to start the engine of the Scout soon. There are bound to be ups as well as downs on the six-mile run to the Ksar-es-Souk road. Can you sabotage the bridge once we're across?"

Little Krell entered quietly. He did not speak but stood by the door, watching Modesty. Willie switched to French so that Little Krell would understand, and said, "We can wreck the motor and the gears, and jam the cables. They can always cut through the cables outside and hope the bascule won't destroy itself when it drops, but they'll need two or three hours for that." He looked across at the wall where some maintenance tools stood, a sledgehammer, a crowbar, a three-foot fishplate spanner, and welding equipment. "Especially if we dump those tools down the ravine," he added.

Modesty said, "Two or three hours start is all we need. Go ahead."

He pressed the starter on the control panel, saying doubtfully, "I don't suppose the maintenance is all that special, so we might 'ave a bit of trouble getting this started—" The motor coughed once, then began to idle smoothly.

Modesty laughed. "It heard you. Will you be needing a hand, Willie?"

"It'll be quicker."

"All right. Little Krell, stay with Willie please."

"Mam'selle." The door had swung to, and he jumped to hold it open for her. She thanked him and went out to the Scout. Tracy June sat gazing absently into space. Pennyfeather stood beside her. The note of the diesel changed. The top of the bascule separated from the tower and began to move slowly down in a great arc towards the recess on the far side, which was floored with massive balks of oak to receive it.

Two minutes later Modesty started the engine of the Scout and drove across the heavy steel plates of the drawbridge. Little Krell stood just outside the power house door, watching. When she switched off he went inside and said, "Okay, Willie."

Willie Garvin put the engine into reverse and allowed the motor to take up the drive again. The bascule rose. When it was vertical, and with the engine idling, he beckoned to Little Krell and said, "I want to stand on your shoulders so I can reach that guide." He pointed up to one of the sleeves through which the cables ran.

"*Bien*, Willie."

Little Krell stood like a rock, great arms reaching up to grip Willie's legs securely. Willie slid the fishplate spanner into the sleeve beside the cable. It was a tight fit. Little Krell passed up the sledge-hammer. Willie drove the four-foot steel spanner home with three ponderous blows, jamming the cable solidly. The crow-bar served to jam the second cable in its guide.

Willie dropped to the ground, handed the sledge-hammer to Little Krell, and gestured with a flourish towards the motor. Little Krell drew in a deep breath, nodded his satisfaction, and braced enormous shoulders. The first blow smashed the block completely, the second hurled shattered gearwheels from their shafts, the third broke the handle of the hammer.

Willie Garvin laughed and said, "*Ça va, mon vieux*." He looked at the jammed sleeves. Nobody was going to free those cables in a hurry. Little Krell had gathered up the broken bits of the hammer and was picking up the oxyacetylene torch. He had remembered that no tools were to be left. Willie registered approval. Little Krell straightened up and said, "Will she help me, Willie? Go to England, away from all the bad things. Do work?"

"She'll help," Willie said, and jerked his head towards the door. "Let's go."

As they came out of the power house Little Krell said softly, "In The Pit yesterday . . . she was more than perfect, Willie. Like miracle, I swear. For different opponent, she use different style, different plan. New ideas. Brain and body work together. Movement exact to millimetre. Timing exact to . . . to zero second. But only Little Krell comprehends we are seeing magic. You also would comprehend, Willie. But those fools, they make noise and cheer. Better to be silent." He bent his head and touched fingers to his brow. "Show respect for lady who makes miracle."

Willie Garvin sighed. "Wish I'd seen it."

"I try to tell you later. But is not the same."

They went one at a time across the rope bridge. Half-way over,

Little Krell dropped the broken hammer and the oxyacetylene torch into the depths. On the far side he went to the Scout, rummaged amid a jumble of equipment on the floor, produced a hand axe, and went back to chop through the ropes.

Willie settled himself beside Modesty and said quietly, "Were you a bit special in The Pit yesterday?"

She looked at him curiously. "Did Little Krell say so?"

"In large capitals. And he knows what he's talking about."

She gave a nod. "Yes. I did get into overdrive yesterday, anyway for long enough to make the Silk brothers look silly. It was just as well. They're very good." She turned in her seat. "All right, Giles?"

"Yes thank you, darling."

"And Tracy June?"

"Fine. Not really with us, of course. What are you going to do about her when we get home?"

"Could we think about that when we get there? We've had a couple of busy days, and we're only just out of the wood."

Little Krell chopped through the last of the ropes. The end of the bridge fell. He turned and came running towards the Scout, astonishingly light and fast for his bulk. Willie Garvin rubbed an ear thoughtfully as Modesty started the engine. "I 'ope you're right about us being out of the wood, Princess," he said. "But my ears are prickling."

Her mouth tightened. "Let's not relax, then." She switched on the lights and let in the clutch.

Behind her, Little Krell leaned forward and said, "Mam'selle, just now I think of two things maybe you want to know."

"What are they?"

"Yesterday I hear the prince talking with Miss Prendergast. She say that the old man in cave, he know about the big crown with all the jewels, so better he die. Prince say yes. He will arrange."

After a moment Modesty said, "Thanks, Little Krell. I'm glad to know that. We'll pick up Alâeddin as we go. What was the second thing?"

"The big crown. They keep it in small room with guard of two men." Little Krell reached down by his feet and lifted a canvas sack with something half filling it, something cube-shaped. "Before I come to *bait-at-ta'ah*, I kill the guards and bring crown here to truck. For you, mam'selle," he said.

Prince Rahim Mohajeri Azhari hurled a chair against the wall of the reception hall and whirled to glare slowly from face to face, eyes murderous, a fleck of spittle at one corner of his mouth. There were half a dozen Berbers in the hall, with Jeremy and Dominic Silk. The two brothers had pulled on some clothes. The prince still wore karate style pyjamas.

"Gone?" said Jeremy.

"That is the word I have now used twice," Rahim said with passion. "I hardly know how to put it more simply, old bean. Gone. Blaise and Garvin have gone. By courtesy of your tame gorilla, it appears. *So has the Pahlavi Crown*. Gone. They have taken your Scout for transport, and that idiot English doctor. Oh, and possibly a woman from my harem, though this isn't yet clear."

"When?" said Dominic.

"The best estimate is an hour ago. One of the hospital patients found an orderly drugged and the doctor gone." Prince Rahim drew in a long breath through flared nostrils. "The drawbridge guards do not answer the telephone, so we can safely assume that our friends have crossed. We can hardly doubt their ability to have sabotaged it behind them."

Jeremy said, "Have you sent men to check?"

"Of course." The words were spat out.

"Where's Nannie Prendergast?"

The prince said through his teeth, "In her room, dear boy. I've rung her to give her the fascinating news, but told her to stay there. This isn't the Hilton, and my chaps would think me a fool to have a woman in nightwear drifting around at a moment like this."

Dominic said, "If they've only been gone an hour, you can cut them off with the helicopter before they reach the main road." His voice was jerky, his eyes feverish.

"A nice thought," said the prince savagely, "but uninformed. The Sikorsky, with pilot, is in Fez. The small machine is here, but our friends had the forethought to kill the pilot before departing."

Jeremy said, "Dominic and I can both pilot the Gazelle."

Rahim stood very still, chin lifted, looking sideways at the brothers, a new light in his eyes. "You'll have room for three more men," he said softly, and snapped orders to his bodyguard before turning back to the brothers. "I want the Pahlavi Crown. I want Blaise and Garvin and Little Krell dead. Plain *dead*, no fancy stuff. If Pennyfeather and the harem girl have to be included, so be it. You understand?"

Dominic said, "You'll get what you want."

He started to turn away, but the prince said sharply, "Wait." When the brothers halted he went on deliberately, "Let there be no mistake this time. If you are able to make a quick kill, so much the better. But our friends will be armed with at least two submachine guns, so I am told. If for any reason you are *not* able to make a quick kill, then your task will be to pin them down."

Jeremy said, "But—"

"No!" The word was an angry shout accompanied by a slashing gesture to silence protest. "Will you never learn? They must have no opportunity to destroy you, so be careful of the machine and of yourselves. Failing a quick kill, pin them down and report by the helicopter radio. I have telephoned Fez and ordered the Sikorsky back immediately. In less than two hours it will be here, to bring you thirty men if need be. Then, and only then, you can complete the job."

Jeremy nodded agreement. "It makes good sense. Will you tell Nannie what's happening?"

"Of course." The prince smiled, and there was only a small trace of venom in his eyes now. "I'll tell Nannie right away. Good luck, you chaps."

Five minutes later, as the Gazelle was lifting from the pad, Rahim gave a peremptory knock on the door of the suite and entered at her call. She stood by the window, wearing an ankle-length dark blue dressing gown buttoned to the neck, her hair loose and tied back, small mules on her feet. Her face relaxed, almost slack, and as he moved towards her he realised that she was in shock.

"You said they have gone, Your Highness?" Her voice had an oddly mechanical sound. "Actually gone? With the Pahlavi Crown?"

"Yes, Nannie." He studied her absently. Large eyes, smooth

neck, fine complexion, the faint hint of delicately perfumed soap. Part of his anger was converted suddenly to desire. "Yes, they've gone, with Little Krell and the Pahlavi Crown. But it will soon be first light, and El Mico has gone after them in the helicopter with my three best men."

"Ah!" It was a small gasp of relief, and he saw her face begin to grow firm. "Then I'm sure everything will be all right, Your Highness. All's well that ends well."

"A perceptive thought, Nannie." He lifted a hand and took her chin in the fork of it, thumb and fingers pressing hard into her cheeks as he drew her face nearer to his. "And we must hope for the best, mustn't we? Because if old Jeremy and old Dom make another balls-up, you can unpack your bags, Nannie. You won't be leaving."

fourteen

For the fourth time in two minutes Alâeddin said, "It is a great kindness in you to be troubled for me, but I cannot leave my home."

Modesty held down her irritation. "If you do not come with us, you will die," she said patiently.

"If I go, robbers will come and steal all that I have saved in my life-time." His gesture encompassed the complex of caves and the junk-lined walls.

"If you are dead, robbers will steal it."

"I do not think the prince will wish to kill an old man such as I."

"He has said so. You must not stay here, Alâeddin."

"It is a great kindness in you—"

Willie entered the cave, looking puzzled, and said, "I just came to see if there was anything wrong, Princess."

"Only that I can't get through to him. He doesn't want to leave his home."

Willie glared at the old man and said in Arabic, "Now hear me, old one. Are your brains made of goat droppings? Every moment we delay here, our danger grows—"

The noise came as suddenly as a clap of thunder, a clattering roar of rotor blades that echoed down the broad valley and bounced back from the walls. As they reached the cave mouth they heard Little Krell shouting, then a quick burst of fire followed by the sharp crack of single shots.

Modesty came out of the cave with Willie at her elbow. The helicopter's approach from the road had been muffled until the moment when it swept round the angle of the mountain wall into the valley. It was now only two hundred feet up, heeling over as it turned, with a figure on a safety strap braced in the open doorway, Dominic Silk holding an automatic rifle but no longer firing.

The Scout stood thirty paces from the cave, close to the rock wall. Alâeddin's mule lay dead beside it. Pennyfeather was walking towards them, holding Tracy June by the arm and speaking with his mouth close to her ear. His medical bag was in his free hand. Little Krell bounced along just beside them, keeping them screened from the helicopter as far as his height allowed. In one great hand he carried his Uzi and a pouch of spare magazines. Balanced on the other was the steel box containing the Pahlavi Crown, held up and out towards the helicopter as if to offer a target, but in fact providing a shield much larger than its physical bulk.

As the helicopter hung still, Dominic put a burst of automatic fire through the Scout, seeking the petrol tank. With a muted explosion the vehicle became engulfed in flame. Willie dropped to one knee and brought his Uzi up to the aim, but as he fired the helicopter shot up fifty feet and swung away. The quick burst of fire passed beneath the machine, then it was hidden by the rising pall of smoke from the Scout. They heard it change direction, and glimpsed it moving away at a good height down the valley in direct line with the cave. A moment later it had swung round a spur and was out of sight again.

Pennyfeather paused as he reached the cave mouth and said to Modesty with an air of complaint, "I thought you told me they couldn't chase us with the helicopter."

"I got it wrong, Giles. Is Tracy June all right?"

"Yes, she thinks she's at the pictures. She likes the pictures."

"Good. Get in the cave." As Giles moved in with the girl she touched Little Krell's shoulder and said, "You handled that well."

He wagged his head sadly. "When Master Dominic fire single shot I know they don't want to hurt crown. I push doctor and girl out, hold box up to make him afraid to hit." He looked down the valley. "But I am stupid. I know Miss Prendergast make them learn to fly aeroplane. I don't think how maybe they learn helicopter, too. Sorry, mam'selle."

"No need to be."

As they moved into the cave Willie said thoughtfully, in English, "He's been wasted all 'is life."

"Yes. There's a brain there." Just inside the cave they stood against the wall so that they could look down the valley. Modesty glanced at Alâeddin, in the doorway of his living quarters, his face drawn with shock, the loose lens of his spectacles swinging gently on its hinge of insulating tape. She said, "I want a mirror, please." He nodded and moved away. She turned her head to gaze down the valley again and said, "Giles, can you put Tracy June to sleep on the bed in there?"

"Yes, darling. What are we going to do?"

"Quiet a minute." Her head and Willie's were cocked, listening. The muted sound of the helicopter had been constant over the last few seconds. Now it stopped, and silence came upon the valley. Pennyfeather saw Modesty, Willie and Little Krell exchange a glance of bleak comprehension. He took Tracy June into the living annexe of the cave, told her to lie on the bed and sleep, waited for her to obey, then went back into the main cave. Willie was lying on the ground to one side, looking towards Modesty, who was farther back in the cave and propping a cracked make-up mirror on top of a low crate.

Willie said, "Left a fraction. Stop. Now tilt it back just a touch. Whoa! That's fine."

Pennyfeather said, "You three seem to know what's going on. How about telling *me*, Modesty?"

"In a moment. But first take Willie's place and look in the mirror, Giles. That's right. Now settle yourself so you can see right down the valley."

"Ah! I've got the idea. I can keep watch like this, but I'm not in the line of fire if they shoot into the cave."

"As they will. They've landed the helicopter farther down, round the spur, and they'll be coming up the slope on foot to that ridge with the two outcrops of rock. You see them?"

"Yes, of course I can see them."

"Right. Well, they'll be on dead ground till they get to that point. Any farther, and they'll be in the open. There can't be more than six of them, probably only five, and if they try to make an attack we can drop them with the sub-machine guns. That's what we're hoping for."

"You *want* them to attack?"

"The alternative is that they lie there in cover and keep us penned in here while the chopper goes back for more men, and then more."

Little Krell said, "No, mam'selle. Between Master Jeremy and Master Dominic is big jealousy. One brother will not fly helicopter and leave other here. That would be to do chauffeur job. He would be afraid that while he is gone the other will find way to kill us, and win good favour from Miss Prendergast."

She looked at him quickly. "You're sure?"

"I know them, mam'selle. It is sure."

Pennyfeather had been unable to follow the conversation, but he sensed relief in her as she said, "Listen, Giles," and translated what Little Krell had told her.

"Oh, well, that sounds jolly good, Modesty. It means you've only got this lot out there to deal with."

"Not quite. It buys us a little time, but Rahim will still send reinforcements."

Willie, carrying a sack of grain towards the back wall, said, "Both ways."

Pennyfeather blinked, and almost took his eyes from the mirror. "What the hell does he mean, both ways? You wrecked the draw-bridge, and Little Krell just said we needn't worry about the helicopter."

"Yes. But it won't be long before they manage to get a rope with a grapnel on the end hooked across the ravine. Then a man can cross. Then he can haul up the end of the rope bridge and do a makeshift repair. In a couple of hours they'll have a whole bunch of Berbers heading down that mountain road. Alternatively or as well, Rahim can get the big helicopter back from Fez and use that."

Pennyfeather said with feeling, "Christ, the sooner we get out of here the better."

"If we step outside we'll be dead. They have automatic rifles, and probably submachine guns as well. Better fire power than ours."

"So what are you going to do?"

"Ask me later." She was still gazing down the valley. Behind her, Willie and Little Krell were moving soft material into position against the cave wall directly in line with the mouth, old rugs, skins, wooden crates, bolts of cloth, a table, anything to reduce the likelihood of ricochets. She saw a hint of movement by the rock outcrop and stepped quickly to one side. "Leave it, Willie. They'll be trying a shot any moment."

Willie and Little Krell moved out of direct line. Ten seconds later there came the crack of a bullet passing though the cave and vanishing into a bundle of skins. Four more shots followed, then there was silence. After a while Willie said, "Looks like they're just going to make sure we stay 'ere till they can bring in the 'eavy mob. That gives us maybe a couple of hours, if we're lucky."

She nodded. "Let's see what Alâeddin has to offer. Giles, keep watching that valley and shout if you see anyone coming."

"You bet I'll shout. It'll be bloody deafening."

Five minutes later they stood by the workbench at the end of the branch cave, looking at three cardboard boxes Alâeddin had produced. One contained a First World War revolver, a French Lebel of 8mm calibre. Another was full of pistol parts—springs and catches, rods and cones, hammers and pivot pins. The third and largest held an assortment of ammunition.

Modesty spoke in Arabic. "You have no other weapons here?"

The old man shrugged. "Two bayonets, some knives, a sword from a ship, with a curved blade."

"No grenades? No other firearms?"

A shake of the head. Willie Garvin blew out his cheeks, rested his hands on the bench and closed his eyes. Modesty watched him. Little Krell watched them both, a Uzi hanging from one hand, ready to dash to the cave mouth if Pennyfeather called.

Modesty said, "Think out loud, Willie. And in French, for Little Krell."

Eyes still closed, he said, "The revolver's useless. We've got two submachine guns and Little Krell's automatic, but they won't get us out of here. Even if Alâeddin came up with a box of grenades it wouldn't be any good. The range is about a hundred and twenty metres. Much too far. All right, forget the problem of delivery for a minute. We could make one or two grenades. Half this ammunition is for the Lebel, which means they're the old black powder cartridges. Gunpowder, Charcoal, sulphur and saltpetre. Fill a can with that, and a handful of nuts and bolts for shrapnel, and you've got a bomb. Need a fuse for it." A pause. "Not a big problem." He opened his eyes. "But there's still no way to throw it that distance.

Modesty stood with arms crossed, holding her elbows, staring into space. After a few moments she said, "You could make a fuse?"

"Black powder's seventy-five per cent saltpetre. Put some in a little water, and the saltpetre dissolves. Soak some twine in the solution and dry it off on a pan over Alâeddin's stove. You've got a fuse. You'd need to test it to get the rate of burning. So many seconds to the inch. It wouldn't be all that accurate, but you could get it to plus or minus two seconds, I reckon. So you've got a working bomb." Willie shook his head. "There's still no way to reach that outcrop with it."

Modesty said, "There's a way *you* could throw it that far, Willie. If it was round, like a ball. Like a pelota ball."

His eyes widenened slowly. "Could be, Princess," he said after a moment or two. "Let's see."

Half a minute later Little Krell lifted her by the knees to bring down the *cesta* from where it hung with the cricket bat among Alâeddin's collection of sporting implements. The curved basket had seen much use but was in good condition. Willie wriggled his hand into the glove and swung his arm tentatively. Little Krell, who had looked baffled, nodded his head in sudden gleeful understanding.

Modesty said, "You start breaking out the black powder and making the fuse, Willie. We'll hunt around for a bomb casing." She turned to Alâeddin and cupped her hands as if holding a ball. "Something round, like this. In metal if possible. If not, we shall need wire for binding."

He put a hand to his head. "I . . . I do not know, lady. It is hard to remember."

In the next ten minutes, as they moved through the complex of caves, he produced a box of ancient copper ballcocks, a set of chipped and battered snooker balls, and a curious metal sphere the size of a football, hollow, and with spikes jutting from it, which had presumably once been a decorative finial.

She called, "All quiet, Giles?"

"Nothing moving, darling."

"Good. Willie, we haven't found anything yet."

"Mam'selle." Little Krell was beckoning. She moved along one of the branch caves and found him standing beside a brass bed-head, a hand resting on one of the two big knobs. "Maybe this, mam'selle."

Her eyes sparkled, "You think well." She began to unscrew one of the knobs. Little Krell unscrewed the other. When they took them through to Willie at the workbench he gazed at them for several seconds, turning them over in his hands, then a contented grin spread slowly across his face.

"Just about perfect, Princess," he murmured. "Look, they're the female part of the connection. Hollow with an internal thread on the hole, so they screw on to the male lug which is part of the post. That means we can use the lugs as stoppers."

She smiled. "It sounds a bit pornographic, Willie. What do you want done?"

"Grab that drill from Alâeddin's tool rack, and use a one-eighth bit. Drill down through the lugs on the bed-head, right through the middle. Then use a hacksaw to cut them off so they'll be flush when we screw them into the brass knobs. I'll come and give you a hand when I've got this fuse drying out."

Thirty minutes later Willie Garvin carefully filled two bed-knobs with black powder and a good selection of steel nuts. The two lugs, each with a narrow hole through it, stood ready to be screwed in. "Can't do any more till I've run some tests on the fuse," he said thoughtfully. "I've made a couple of feet of it, so there's plenty for testing."

Little Krell said, "What time you aim for, Willie?"

"I reckon seven seconds." He mimed tossing up a ball, catching it in the *cesta*, and throwing; then waited, counting silently as he visualised the trajectory of the missile. "Six to seven seconds. I'll borrow Giles's watch for testing. It's a good job you bought him a new one, Princess."

She eyed Willie Garvin with her lower lip caught in her teeth. He was being a shade too casual, and she knew why. "Look," she said, "to make that throw you have to run clear of the cave and then go through all the movements. But there are five or six rifles and guns out there, waiting for any of us to show. They've already signalled that, with those early shots."

They were still speaking in French. Willie measured an inch of the now dry twine lying on the bench, and cut it off. "I'm expecting them to miss," he said.

"While you throw two bombs?"

"I might get the first one just right. The second you can bet on."

"If you're still alive."

"I don't suppose their sights are all that accurate."

Little Krell said, "I don't like, Willie. Master Jeremy and Master Dominic, they shoot good."

Willie Garvin picked up the small piece of fuse, the long piece, and the matches Alâeddin had provided. "I'll need to run several tests," he said easily, "but I'll do it somewhere away from where we've been messing about with gunpowder." He lifted his voice as he moved off, and called in English. "Giles, I want your watch."

Little Krell's eyes were on Modesty. She was staring at the workbench. On it lay a little heap of the 8mm cartridges, a tin plate with some black powder on it, a box of hexagonal nuts, and some of the tools Willie had been using. In the light of the Tilley lamp, now moved well away from the bench, her eyes were pools of black, and there was an aura of concentration about her so intense that Little Krell felt he could almost see it.

For a full minute she stood without moving, scarcely seeming to breathe, then she said, slowly, very quietly, "Break open the rest of the cartridges, Little Krell. We're going to do some bomb-making of our own."

A hundred and thirty yards away, Jeremy Silk peered along the barrel of the FN light automatic rifle. He lay prone, with the rifle slid forward along the edge of the rock outcrop. A Berber with a submachine gun squatted with his back to the rock. To Jeremy's right, across a small gap, his brother Dominic and two more Berbers lay in the cover of the other outcrop. Between the two humps of rock, the ground dropped in a low step to a shallow gulley which ran straight up the valley to the cave.

Dominic said, "No movement?"

Jeremy wiped a trickle of sweat from above his eyebrows. "Nothing. Do you think there's another way out of that cave?"

"These chaps say there isn't. They ought to know."

After a moment Jeremy said, "Why the hell haven't they tried to make a break for it?"

"Because you insisted on slamming a few shots into the cave, big brother. If you hadn't, we might have lured them out by doing nothing. As it is, they're trying to lure *us* out from cover."

Jeremy glanced at his watch, and said, "That's my fifteen minutes. Your turn again."

Dominic extended himself in the prone position and slid his automatic rifle forward so that it was lined up on the cave mouth. When he was set, Jeremy rolled over and sat up behind the rock. "Keep watching," he said.

Through clenched teeth, and without turning his head, Dominic said, "For Christ's sake stop giving me orders!"

Jeremy stared, eyes narrowed. "I'm going to tell Nannie about you, blaspheming," he threatened.

Willie picked up the *cesta* and ran his hands gently over the long wickerwork scoop, eyeing it with affection, encompassing it with friendly warmth. He set it down on the bench and picked up the two brass spheres, cradling one in each hand, giving them the same flow of regard that he had given the *cesta*. In that time he was also absorbing into the fibres of his being a sense of their weight and ballistic characteristics. He had just spent five minutes lying well back from the cave mouth, chin on forearms, looking down the little slope of the gulley to the two outcrops of rock where the enemy lay hidden, gauging the distance, soaking the concept of it into his subconscious.

The lugs had been screwed home, flush. One fuse barely protruded from the hole in the centre of the lug. The other protruded by perhaps half an inch. He took the two bombs in one hand, holding them as a tennis player holds two balls for service, then tucked the *cesta* under his arm and walked along the main cave. Modesty met him half-way along, and said, "What's the rate of burning for that fuse you made, Willie?"

"Half an inch in eight seconds. I made ten tests, and they came out pretty standard."

"Good." She turned back, and he followed her, puzzled. For the last half hour he had been totally absorbed in his preparations and unaware of anything else. Now, as he reached the main area of the cave, he saw Little Krell crouched beside a wheel with a worn tyre. This was the wheel Alâeddin had produced two days ago, the wheel Modesty Blaise had sold to the old man fourteen years before. Two one-pint paint tins had been securely fixed to the wheel by galvanised wire, one on each side, just above the hub. Both tins had been heavily bound with wire to lock the lids tightly in place. A small hole had been punched in the side of each tin, and from the hole a short length of Willie's home-made fuse protruded.

Modesty knelt beside Little Krell, a few inches of broken flexible rule in her hands. "We'll time one for sixteen seconds and the other for twenty," she said. Little Krell nodded, waited for her to mark the spot with her nail, then cut off the surplus fuse with a pair of nippers. As they repeated the performance for the other tin, Little Krell kept glancing up at Willie, his great ugly face agleam with sheer delight.

"I help mam'selle make this," he said. "We light fuses, roll it from cave. It go on down straight, always straight, because of gulley. Hit step between the rocks. Then *boom*! You like, Willie?"

Willie Garvin sighed a slow, happy sigh. "I love it," he said.

Modesty was still squatting by the wheel, holding it upright, both hands resting gently upon it, studying it with the same quiet warm regard as Willie had given to the *cesta* and the bed-knob grenades. After a while she nodded to Little Krell to take the wheel, and stood up. "We can only guess at the speed it will roll," she said, "and it's going to explode on the wrong side of that outcrop. On this side. But it ought to keep their heads down long enough for you to drop your bombs on them, Willie."

He stood gazing down at the wheel, smiling a little, shaking his head in wonder. At last he said, "Your old wheel. Talk about cast your bread on the waters. It's lovely, Princess. Thanks a million." In a gesture that had long ago become his way of greeting her, he took her hand and lifted it to touch the knuckles to his cheek. Little Krell watched.

She said, "Ready to go, Willie?"

"All set."

"We'll light the fuses of the bombs on the wheel simultaneously, and send it off. Then what?"

"Soon as it blows, you light these two. I'll get them off one after the other, short fuse first. Then all we can do is follow up fast with guns."

"Right. Let's tell Giles. All clear, Little Krell?"

"All clear, mam'selle."

"One thing. They'll probably shoot at the wheel. They're not likely to hit the bombs, but can you keep their heads down while it's rolling?"

He nodded and patted the Uzi. "I shoot good, mam'selle." His hand moved, and the Colt .45 appeared in it. "You must have gun also, mam'selle. This very good."

"Thanks. I'll leave the other Uzi for Willie."

Thirty seconds later, with Pennyfeather and Alâeddin standing back and watching wide-eyed, she touched two smouldering pieces of spare fuse to the two fuses of the wheel bombs. Little Krell was ready, and sent the wheel rolling from the cave with a swing of his huge shoulders. As he dropped flat and brought his gun round to the aim, a bullet split the air at waist-height above him.

Modesty and Willie were pressed back against the cave wall a few paces from the entrance, watching the wheel as it rolled with gathering speed down the middle of the shallow gulley. It bounced as it hit small rocks and ridges, but kept its momentum, sometimes swerving when it bounced but always being brought back on course by the lie of the gulley. It was impossible to see the glow of the fuses in the dawn sunlight. Little Krell, in the prone position, had his Uzi at the aim and was firing skilfully controlled bursts of four shots at a time, to send chips of stone flying from low down between the outcrops. Spare magazines lay at his elbow. Two rifles were firing at the wheel from the outcrop now, but erratically under Little Krell's accurate covering fire, and if there had been a hit it had failed to deflect the wheel in any way.

Modesty was counting silently. Nine . . . ten . . . eleven . . . she bit her lip. The wheel was going to reach the outcrop too soon. On the count of fourteen she saw it strike the low step between the outcrops hiding the Silk brothers and the Berbers, but such was its impetus that instead of bouncing back it shot high in the air, jumping the ledge and twisting as it flew forward. The explosion came as it fell, a single blast, surprisingly loud. Presumably the first bomb had set off the other.

Willie's hand was in front of her, holding the two brass spheres. She touched the improvised slow-matches to the fuses, and reached for the automatic in her waistband. Willie was gone. So was Little Krell. As she came out of the cave at a run she saw a golden sphere drop into the upraised *cesta*, then Willie's arm came swinging down and up in a hissing arc, and the brass bomb went soaring high in the air.

She glimpsed him poised, watching the fuse of the second bomb, waiting for it to reach the marked spot, but she was gone before he tossed it up for the throw, running hard but still twenty yards behind Little Krell, hearing a chatter of fire from the outcrop, knowing it must be wild and wide because there was no sound of bullets splitting the air nearby. She expected to overhaul Little Krell, but his massive stumpy legs were moving him at surprising speed. The first of Willie's bombs landed on top of the right-hand outcrop, exploding as it touched. The second fell beyond, when Little Krell was perhaps thirty paces from the rocks. For a moment nothing happened, then came the bellow of its bursting, immediately followed by a long, fading scream.

She changed direction slightly, angling up the side of the gulley to come behind the outcrop from the flank. Little Krell was still ten paces ahead of her, the Uzi held in one huge fist, like a handgun. He took the step in his stride as he passed between the outcrops, and she heard the chatter of his gun, joined an instant later by the sound of another submachine gun. Then she was beyond the outcrop, seeing Little Krell fall back with what looked like giant stitching across his chest, seeing bodies sprawled about the area where the rocks gave cover, snapping a shot from the .45

into the head of a Berber lying on his side with gun half raised, the gun which had brought down Little Krell.

Silence, strange and abrupt. Only the slight sound of pounding feet as Willie Garvin came sprinting down from the cave. The air was heavy with smoke, the ground spattered with a sooty substance from the bombs. She moved to Little Krell, running an eye over the still figures of the Berbers and the Silk brothers as she did so. It was hard to tell which had died by the bombs and which had been finished off by Little Krell. Certainly the shrapnel of steel nuts had done ferocious damage.

She dropped to her knees beside Little Krell, eased his head on to her lap, and gripped his massive hand. Four bullets had torn his chest open, and she was kneeling in a pool of his blood now. He opened his eyes, and the thick lips twisted in a painful smile. "Two . . . could still shoot," he croaked. "Arab . . . and Master Dominic. I take him first. Always he talk like Little Krell is dirt." The eyes closed. She heard Willie moving from body to body, checking. Then he was crouched beside her. Little Krell spoke again. "Was bad combat move," he whispered. "Better I take Arab first . . . he have submachine gun."

The voice trailed away. She did not offer reassurance, or pretend to believe he would live. This was a man well schooled in the grim art of killing, and he knew he was dead. She said, "Thank you for helping us, Little Krell. Is there anything I can do for you?"

After a few moments he said, "Leave me . . . on top of mountain, please, mam'selle . . . away from the world."

Giles Pennyfeather came through the gap in the outcrop at a lumbering run, panting, leaning sideways with the weight of his bag. He stared about him, then moved to kneel on Little Krell's other side, facing Modesty. After one look at the dreadful wreckage of the chest he opened his bag and took out a box of morphia ampoules. As he pierced the ampoule with a hypodermic, Little Krell sighed and spoke again in a slurred whisper. "I . . . happy to be with you . . . little time, mam'selle." Eyes still closed he drew her hand up slowly, effortfully, until her knuckles rested against his cheek, in the gesture he had seen Willie Garvin make. Then his head lolled sideways, and they heard the life go out of him.

Pennyfeather emptied the hypodermic and began to put it away.

Modesty laid Little Krell's head down gently, and got to her feet. "God damn," she said tiredly, "Oh, God damn it all."

Prince Rahim snatched up the phone at his elbow and said, "Yes?" He was taking breakfast in one of the smaller rooms of the palace. Nannie Prendergast sat at table with him, neatly groomed and dressed now, but making no attempt to eat.

The voice on the phone said, "This is the communications room, Your Highness. We have reports that men have now repaired the rope bridge and are crossing the ravine—wait, please." A pause, then: "We have a radio call for you from the small helicopter, Your Highness."

"Connect me."

There were some clicks, a faint buzzing sound, then a background of mush. The prince said eagerly, "Jeremy? Dominic? Are you there?"

The voice of Modesty Blaise said, "They're both dead. So are your three men. We're now airborne in the Gazelle. The only reason I've called you is to tell you that I'll be putting out a contract for you with the Union Corse. If you ever stick your nose outside Xanadu again, you're dead. Acknowledge."

There was a click as her vox-operated radio switched to receive. Rahim was gripping the phone as if trying to crush it. He could feel the blood beating in his temples. Black despair and red fury surged and merged within him. *The bitch had won! No Pahlavi Crown now. She could crucify him if she told her story. And there were witnesses. Pennyfeather. The English girl they had taken from his harem. And to cap it all the bitch was going to imprison him here in Xanadu . . .*

He lifted his eyes and looked at Nannie Prendergast. The phone clicked and the voice of Modesty Blaise said again, "Acknowledge."

With an immense effort Prince Rahim Mohajeri Azhari spoke calmly into the mouthpiece. "Your message understood, Miss Blaise," he said, and put the phone down.

Nannie Prendergast was looking at him from huge eyes in a bone-white face. "Miss Blaise?" She said in a cracked voice.

"Yes, Nannie." The prince poured himself more coffee. There would be considerable interest in training Nannie to be a useful bed-fellow . . . and he would have plenty of time for it now, he thought bleakly. "The fact is," he said, "that old Jeremy and old Dom are dead. So are my three chaps."

"No!" She spoke in a low voice, her hands clenched on the table. "It's not true! You're lying to me, you dirty foreign pig! How dare you say my boys are dead?" Her voice was rising, growing shrill. "How dare you? How dare you? How—"

The prince swung his arm to hit her casually across the face with the back of his hand, and she slumped in her chair, clawed fingers thrusting into her hair, eyes closed, moaning with grief.

"Cheer up, Nannie," the prince said grimly. "There's a whole new life about to begin for you."

Ten miles away to the north, Modesty Blaise clipped the microphone back in place and turned to look behind her. Tracy June was asleep again, head resting on Giles Pennyfeather's shoulder. Beyond them, huddled in the small deck space, lay the blanket-wrapped form of Little Krell. Below, the peaks and valleys of the High Atlas lay all about them. At the controls, Willie Garvin was holding the Gazelle on a steady forward climb.

She touched his arm and leaned towards him, lifting her voice above the noise of the engine. "All right, Willie. Let's find a mountain top for Little Krell."

fifteen

A small table with a white cloth had been set for breakfast on the terrace. Willie Garvin sat at one end eating croissants and drinking coffee, straddling a chair turned the wrong way round. He wore only shorts and sandals, and a fresh dressing covered the panther-claw wound on the lower part of his back. Every few moments a quiver of suppressed laughter shook him as he savoured the richness of a lunatic situation.

Modesty Blaise, in a towelling robe, and Dr. Giles Penny-feather, in shirt and slacks, stood facing Tracy June Martel. Dr.

Pennyfeather was scratching his head. Modesty's face was blank with bewilderment. True to the Hollywood cliché, Tracy June looked beautiful when she was angry. The blue eyes were wide and sparkling with fire, the fine shoulders were braced back, lifting the splendid breasts. The bare legs protruding from one of Willie's shirts were of memorable elegance.

Twenty-four hours had gone by since the helicopter lifted from the high peak where Little Krell now lay. Only ten minutes ago, Tracy June had awakened from the sound natural sleep into which she had fallen after the hours of narco-hypnosis. She had found herself in a handsome bedroom of a house which stood on a hill and looked down over a wooded slope to the sea. She was very hungry, and wearing a man's shirt in place of a nightdress. On the bedside table was a reassuring note inviting her to ring the bell or make her way downstairs when she woke.

It had just been explained to her that she was quite safe, in a house on the outskirts of Tangier, and that she had been brought out of Xanadu by a girl called Modesty Blaise, a man called Willie Garvin, and Dr. Giles Pennyfeather. The last named was the only one known to her.

Tracy June's great beauty did not extend to her voice. "Oo the bloody 'ell d'you think you are?" She was demanding in a shrill Cockney whine. "Kidnappers, that's what! I'll 'ave the bleedin' law on you, see if I don't. Oo said you could come barging in an' dragging me off without a by-your-leave, eh?"

From a memory fogged by astonishment, Modesty recalled René Vaubois quoting from the Bernard Martel dossier. Asked about the wife, he said, '*She came from the East End of London, and she was the daughter of a labourer.*'

Pennyfeather said placatingly, "Please, Tracy June, you really mustn't go on like this. I'm afraid we have some bad news for you—"

"*You're* the bad news, I reckon!"

"Tracy, come and sit down," said Pennyfeather firmly. "There's something very sad I have to tell you, about Bernard."

"Oo?"

"Bernard. Your husband. I'm afraid he died a little while ago."

"Oh." She looked taken aback for a moment, then the belligerence surged up again. "Well it's not *my* fault, is it?"

Modesty stood with fingertips pressed to her temple and said wonderingly, "Don't you care?"

"Eh? Well, 'course I care, in a way. But I never knew 'im that long, did I? Anyway, what's that got to do with it?"

"He . . . wanted to rescue you from Xanadu."

"Oh, 'e did, did 'e? So where do *I* come in, eh? Oo said I wanted rescuing?" She shrugged and gave a toss of her head. "I know it was a bit funny there at first, till I got over 'aving the wind up, but I never been so well off in me life." She glared at Pennyfeather. "You ought to know bleedin' better, you did, if you're supposed to be a doctor. I never said nothing about wanting to sod off 'ome, did I? 'Ome? That's a laugh. I never 'ad anything but aggravation most of me life till I got to Xanadu. It's all right there, though. Us girls in the harem 'ave a smashing time. Anything you want, you just say. Know what I do all day? I sleep till I want to get up. I watch lovely films any time I want, any film I want. Eat like a pig if I want. Rahim don't mind if a girl gets fat, 'e likes a few fat ones, being an Arab. I can lie around, play music, 'ave a chat with the other girls, swim, sunbathe, lie by the pool, give Rahin a bunk-up when 'e fancies me, and just let 'im know if there's anything I want. It's a good time all the way, and I never 'ave to lift a finger."

There was silence on the terrace except for a slight choking sound from Willie Garvin. At last Pennyfeather said feebly. "You mean . . . you wish we'd left you there?"

" 'Course I do, silly bugger!"

Modesty said slowly, "All right, Tracy June. Go back to the bedroom, and I'll send you some breakfast. Your clothes are being sponged and pressed now. In an hour I'll have Rahim's agent from Tangier here. You can go with him, and he'll get you back to Xanadu."

Tracy June drew breath for further complaint, then caught the chilly look in the midnight blue eyes, and changed her mind. With a flounce that lifted the shirt to offer a brief display of shapely buttocks, she turned and stalked back into the house.

Giles Pennyfeather said, "That's interesting. You could tell she was jolly angry, but did you notice her gluteal muscles weren't clenched?"

Modesty said in a taut voice, "Mine are though." She moved

to the table and sat down. Willie Garvin was resting an elbow on the table, a hand covering his eyes. She said, "You laugh out loud and I'll kill you, Willie."

He wagged his head protestingly, gained tenuous control of his features, and said in a shaky voice: *"For while I 'eld my tongue, my b-bones consumed away . . . Psalm 32, Verse 3."*

Pennyfeather said, "What's up, Modesty?"

"Up? What's *up*? I'll tell you, doctor. When El Mico roasted that poor devil Martel on the grass there, I just wanted to do the simple, primitive, Blaise thing of going after the bastard and signing him off. But oh no, I don't do that. On doctor's orders I forgo my duty to a guest. Instead I go to enormous trouble and nearly get all of us killed trying to carry out Bernard Martel's last wishes. Still, we managed it somehow. We got little Tracy June back safe and sound didn't we? And now look what's bloody happened!"

Pennyfeather nodded sagely. "I can see it might be thought a bit irritating," he agreed. "But if you hadn't done it, darling, then I'd have been stuck in Xanadu for ever, you know. And after all, you did knock off El Mico in the end."

She gazed at him speculatively for a while. Then: "Do you know what I'm going to do with you, Giles? I'm going to stop you being so virtuous for a bit. I'm going to get you a job as a doctor on a luxury cruise ship in the Caribbean. You'll live high off the hog, you'll be surrounded by the rich, and you simply won't have a chance to do anything good or decent for anybody. Are you listening?"

Pennyfeather laughed indulgently. "Of course I am. But I was just thinking, it really is a bit comical about Tracy June, isn't it? I mean, you almost break your neck to save the damsel in distress, and then she gives you a bollocking for it."

Modesty sighed and looked at Willie. "All right, laugh out loud if you want to."

"Thanks, but I'll save it for later, Princess. One good thing, though. This solves a problem. We don't 'ave to work out what to do with Tracy June now."

"I had in mind a shot-gun marriage for her with Giles. It might have stopped him continually getting me into trouble."

Pennyfeather chuckled. "I'll take the luxury cruise."

Willie said, "We still 'aven't thought what to do about you-know-what, though."

An urchin grin lit her face and she gave him a slow wink. "There's no hurry. That little trinket is a weapon, Willie love. We'll find a use for it.

"With a great deal of luck," said Sir Gerald Tarrant, "I shall now get you a taxi."

"No, please don't bother, I'd rather walk. I've arranged for Weng to be waiting for me with the car in Hyde Park, and he'll take me straight on to Heathrow."

She looked, Tarrant thought, like the proverbial million dollars. They had just strolled back to his office from the club in Pall Mall where he had given her lunch, and were now standing in White-hall. She wore a black jersey top with a camel skirt, and her only jewellery was a pearl necklace, a gift from Willie Garvin who, secretly over several years, had bought up every one of thirty-seven magnificently matched pearls from different pearl beds all over the world.

"It was good of you to come," said Tarrant.

"I've enjoyed it. But I've been wondering why you took Willie to lunch yesterday and me today, instead of both together. We get on quite well, you know."

He laughed. "I know. But I'm a cunning old gentleman and I wanted to get as much of the Xanadu story as I could. You're most unforthcoming in these matters, both of you, but when I'm with you singly I can at least keep up a steady probing. When you're together you keep contriving digressions."

"It's not deliberate. We don't go in much for reminiscing about a caper, even between ourselves. Well, except for the occasional funny bits, perhaps. But we don't relish the grim bits, and there are always a lot more of those. Anyway, I think you've got more out of us than usual this time."

"I have indeed. May I tell Fraser the story?"

Fraser was Tarrant's assistant. In his days as an agent in the field he had been the best in the history of the department, so Tarrant held. Outwardly he was a small meek man with an ingra-tiating manner. There were some who had realised Fraser's true nature only in the instant of dying. Behind the insignificant persona was a ruthless cynic, and behind the cynic was a man dedicated to confounding and destroying the enemies of his country.

Modesty said, "Yes, by all means tell Jack Fraser about the Xanadu business. He'll find it enlightening."

Tarrant lifted an eyebrow. "I don't quite follow you."

"That's good. I'm trying to be more enigmatic these days."

"I'm suitably puzzled, then." He glanced up at the block of offices, took off his bowler hat, and sighed. "I'm reluctant to leave you. Later this afternoon I have to endure an acrimonious meeting with Boulter, presided over by our Minister."

"Yes. Willie said you mentioned it yesterday."

"I'm sure I did. It's been much on my mind. Boulter is basically a nasty man, and he compounds this by being quite unable to accept that his department and mine should complement each other. He can only regard me as an arch rival."

She watched a mounted policeman ride by at an easy walk and said absently, "It happens a lot in your line of business. I made a fortune out of inter-departmental rivalry in several countries back in the days when I was wicked. But I know Boulter, and he's worse than most. The only way to deal with him is to hit him hard below the belt."

"I shall seek an opportunity. If you're flying out from Heathrow this afternoon I take it that you and Willie are having a holiday after your labours?"

"Yes, but not together. Willie's off to Jamaica with Lady Janet for what he claims is going to be three weeks of lotus-eating and unbridled debauchery."

Tarrant smiled. "And you?"

"Well, first I'm going to indulge myself shamelessly. Go on a great shopping spree, buy some lovely clothes, spend hours being beautified, spend every night at the theatre or ballet, fly Concorde just to have lunch with a couple of friends in New York, all that sort of thing. Then—" She hesitated. "Will you promise not to look surprised? People look surprised when I do the most ordinary things."

"I promise."

"Did you know Willie owns half a tenting circus?"

"Oh, yes. I met his Hungarian partner, Georgi, down at *The Treadmill* last year."

"I'm joining it next month at Marseilles and touring for six weeks until they go into winter quarters, that's all."

Tarrant gave a perfunctory nod. "Performing?"

"No. Driving one of the trucks and helping to look after the horses. They're a groom short."

He contrived to look as if he were trying not to look bored. "A lot of people are doing that sort of thing this year."

She gave him a sparkling smile. "You did that very nicely."

"Thank you. I've been hoping you would enlighten me concerning one particular detail of the Xanadu affair, but since you haven't mentioned it I'm now driven to ask . . . what on earth have you done with the Pahlavi Crown?"

She laughed, "Well, our first idea was to send it anonymously to the Queen, but then we realised it would only be a huge embarrassment, and we couldn't have that."

"You're royalists, you and Willie?"

"Of course we are. Then we thought of the Salvation Army, that was Giles's idea, but it wouldn't have done them a bit of good. When you start thinking about it, you realise dumping that thing on anybody honest isn't at all friendly. They can't explain it, so it makes them look either an idiot or a crook. How would you like to find it on your desk?"

Tarrant blinked, and felt a feather of apprehension touch his spine as he glimpsed tiny devils in her innocently wide eyes. "Modesty," he said a little throatily, "you haven't . . .?"

"No, of course not. But you see what I mean."

He exhaled a long breath of relief. "I do indeed. So what did you decide to do with the thing?"

"This is where I go into my enigmatic bit again. A hint of a smile, and slightly narrowed eyes. Does that look fairly enigmatic?"

"Not bad."

"Faint praise." She looked at her watch. "I must dash now, or Weng will tell me off. Try to think what *you* would do with the Pahlavi Crown, and we'll compare notes one day. Thank you again for the lunch."

She pressed his arm, leaned forward to kiss his cheek, then turned away with a little wave and a warm smile. He stood with hat in hand, rueful, watching the lovely swing of the long legs as she walked away towards Parliament Square, and he wondered how it was that she could at the same time be the most exciting and the most restful woman he had ever known.

When Tarrant entered the office adjoining his own, Fraser rose from the desk where he sat and said humbly, "Good afternoon, Sir Gerald."

"Afternoon, Fraser. Any messages?"

"Only two, sir, neither of them important. Might I have a word with you?" Tarrant felt mild surprise. Nothing important, yet Fraser must be anxious to talk, for his request had been unusually hurried.

"All right, come in." Tarrant led the way into his own office, hung up his hat and umbrella, and sat down behind his desk. "What is it?"

Fraser fidgeted with his tie and produced a servile smile. "I wonder if I need to describe to you the nature and provenance of something called the Pahlavi Crown, sir?"

Tarrant leaned back in his chair. "Isn't it the great crown of Persia?" he said slowly. "Of Iran, as they prefer to call it now? A bauble made for the Shah from thousands of diamonds and gemstones originally seized from the treasury of the Great Mogul? Worth a few tens of millions, I believe."

Only the complete immobility of Fraser's face betrayed his surprise. "Why yes, sir," he said after a moment or two. "That is correct."

"What about it?"

Fraser leaned forward. "Mr. Boulter has it, sir," he said in a voice that shook slightly. "I'm told he's very distressed about it."

After a long silence Tarrant said reverently, "That's beautiful. Where did it come from, Jack?"

The use of the Christian name told Fraser to drop the mask he wore for all but a very few. He gave a cackle of laughter and his thin sour face lit up with malicious joy. "Parcel left at the door this morning, addressed to him. Checked by security for explosives, of course, then they dump this bloody great crown on Boulter. Nobody knew exactly what the hell it was for about an hour, till they got a bloke round from Garrards who identified it.

Tarrant sat with closed eyes, a feeling of blissful affection expanding within him. Willie had reported the Boulter thing to her yesterday, of course. Now this. The Pahlavi Crown was probably the most potent source of embarrassment in the Western world, the hottest of all hot potatoes, and it was sitting in Boulter's lap. When you had Modesty Blaise for a friend, small miracles became possible.

"The Minister's going to crucify Boulter," Fraser was saying with gleeful satisfaction. "Nobody's going to believe someone just left fifty million quid's worth of loot at the door for him." He shook his head. "Christ, I don't believe it myself. Boulter's *got* to be mixed up in it somewhere. But that doesn't figure either, because I'm told he's been having near heart attacks all morning. So who the hell could lay hands on the Pahlavi Crown in the first place, and then who the hell would dump it on Boulter?"

Tarrant opened a drawer and took out a box of cigars. It was an indulgence for him to smoke one at this time of day, but he was too full of pleasure to feel guilty about it. "Who indeed?" he echoed lazily. "Sit down and prepare to be enlightened, Jack. I have permission from Modesty Blaise to tell you a little story."